THE BOOKSHOP AT
WATER'S END

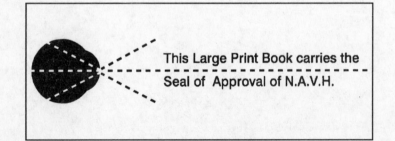

THE BOOKSHOP AT WATER'S END

PATTI CALLAHAN HENRY

WHEELER PUBLISHING
A part of Gale, a Cengage Company

Farmington Hills, Mich • San Francisco • New York • Waterville, Maine
Meriden, Conn • Mason, Ohio • Chicago

LIBRARY OF CONGRESS CATALOGING-IN-PUBLICATION DATA

Names: Henry, Patti Callahan, author.
Title: The bookshop at water's end / by Patti Callahan Henry.
Description: Large print edition. | Waterville, Maine : Wheeler Publishing, a part of Gale, a Cengage Company, 2017. | Series: Wheeler Publishing large print hardcover
Identifiers: LCCN 2017028693| ISBN 9781432842352 (hardcover) | ISBN 1432842358 (hardcover)
Subjects: LCSH: Family life—Fiction. | Domestic fiction. | Large type books. | BISAC: FICTION / Family Life. | FICTION / Contemporary Women.
Classification: LCC PS3608.E578 B66 2017b | DDC 813/.6—dc23
LC record available at https://lccn.loc.gov/2017028693

Published in 2017 by arrangement with The Berkley Publishing Group, an imprint of Penguin Publishing, a division of Penguin Random House LLC

Printed in the United States of America
1 2 3 4 5 6 7 21 20 19 18 17

In honor of Pat Conroy
October 26, 1945–March 4, 2016
Your life and work taught me both the
power of story and of truth,
and your death the same.
You are and will be achingly missed
for all time.

I had that familiar conviction that life was beginning over again with the summer.

THE GREAT GATSBY,
F. SCOTT FITZGERALD

I've been biding all my time for you . . .

"WHAT I'D GIVE,"
ALISSA MORENO AND J. P. JONES

PROLOGUE:
MIMI THE BOOKSELLER

We are defined by the moods and whims of a wild tidal river surrounding our small town, cradling us in its curved basin. We don't shape it; it shapes us. The gray-blue water brings us what it will and only when it desires. One sweltering, languid afternoon as I shelved dusty paperbacks, I looked up to see a ghost. The girl was the spitting image of a woman I knew years ago — too many summers ago to count. It could have been another whim of the river.

Just when it seemed things were settled and placid in Watersend, South Carolina, in breezed the daughter of a Summer Sister. I should have been expecting her because of course I'd heard that Bonny Blankenship had returned to the old Moreland family house. It's that kind of town; I hear everything. But that doesn't mean it wasn't a bit of a shock seeing her walk through my door.

A young girl, I guessed on the brink of

her twenties, stood in my bookshop, a daughter of the past who walked in all wide-eyed and exhaling like she'd finally found what she was looking for. It was a look I knew well. So glad to be in a cozy book-shop, in air-conditioned comfort, sur-rounded by stories, and to find that in the chaos of the world there was still a place like this. A place where books were piled to the ceiling and tables were crowded with the paraphernalia of reading: bookmarks, reading lights, stationery, pens and framed quotes to inspire. I'm no dummy. I keep the air conditioner set to frigid. I know I'm lur-ing customers and some might call it brib-ery, but whatever works, works. I lost my store once, and now that I have it again, I'll do pretty much anything to keep it alive.

Her blond ponytail pulled at the skin around her heart-shaped face, moist at the hairline and cheeks flushed pink. Her round eyes, almost disproportionate to her other tiny features, were wide open to wonder as she looked around the store. She possessed an ephemeral quality one can't buy with plastic surgery or proper training. Her mother had been the same, almost floating through childhood with her best friend, Lainey. They came in here for the same reasons — cold air and escape. Two little girls who were so close it seemed that they'd been sewn together by the seams of their flowered sundresses. History, they say, repeats itself. I surely hoped not.

Was she like her mother, Bonny, all fire and no ice? Older than her years and too young to know better is how I once described her to a customer. The years blended together, but those three summers in the late 1970s stood out like a beacon in the fog of my memory.

I welcomed this ghost into the store but then walked away, and allowed her to roam at her leisure. Thirty minutes later, she chose a poetry book and set it on the counter. I approached her with a smile. "Did you find what you were looking for?"

She held a cell phone in her hand, and it appeared permanently attached, just as it did to all the young ones who came in here. Cells are an appendage now, I'd told my book club.

"I did find exactly what I was looking for. This is a great bookshop." The girl sounded like her mother, too. A certain lilt to her voice like she was about to break into song and then changed her mind. How do I remember all these small details from so long ago when I can't remember where I put my car keys or glasses? I know why, of course — for reasons I've never told a soul.

"Thank you. I'm Mimi. The owner of this messy store. Welcome. Are you visiting Watersend?" I kept my voice light, but I wasn't much good at pretending.

"Yes," the girl said. "I'm here on vacation." She caught my gaze. It took my breath away; so familiar and yet completely foreign. "My name's Piper," she said and brushed at a wayward hair falling into her eyes.

"Well, Piper. I'm glad to meet you. I hope you'll come back while you're in town."

"Oh, I will," she said. "I'm glad I found this on my first day."

"Me, too. And if you're here for the summer, there are plenty of summer book clubs that you can join." I handed her a sheet of paper that listed the clubs and dates and times. "There's even a poetry one."

"Thanks," Piper said. "I might stop by. But I'm going to be . . . busy."

"Well, busy is something for sure," I said.

Piper laughed, but it sounded rusty with disuse. "What do you mean?" she asked.

"I mean, busy is something to be but maybe not the best thing to be?" I took off my glasses and they dangled from the purple string that held them there so I wouldn't lose them. I smiled to let her know that my advice was harmless, just an old woman rambling along. I didn't want to scare her off. I rang up the book and placed it in a brown paper bag with our book logo stamped onto it with my favorite quote, "Books may well be the only true magic. Alice Hoffman." And then handed it to Piper.

She smiled in a sad way. I wanted to tell her how much she looked like her mother, but she didn't seem to be the kind of young woman who would want to hear such a thing. There she was trying to carve out her own place in the world with her little nose stud, like a sparkling freckle, and black eyeliner smudged around her blue eyes like dark curtains.

"Well. Anyhow, Watersend is a great place to be for the summer. I think you'll like it. What brings you?" I already knew the answer: the river. But she would believe it was her mother, or the house.

Piper exhaled and rolled her eyes in that perfect way all teenagers do. "I'm here to help my mom and babysit her best friend's kids. They used to spend their summers here and my mom fixed the old house and . . ." She trailed off like she'd forgotten why she'd arrived at all.

"That sounds like a better job than most

get in the summer," I said, straightening some papers on the counter that didn't need straightening.

"You're probably right," Piper said, "but I just didn't imagine spending my first college summer with my mom and her friend and little kids."

"You say they've been here before. Do I know them?" I looked away with my false questions, feeling slightly ashamed for prodding into what I already knew.

"I don't know. Maybe. My mom is Bonny. Her maiden name was Moreland. Her friend is Lainey."

"The Summer Sisters." I smiled. "For gravy's sake, who could forget them?"

"You *know* them?" Piper leaned forward conspiratorially. "And isn't that the stupidest name? Summer Sisters."

"Not such a bad name if you knew them then."

"It sounds ridiculous to me."

"Ah. I'm sure it does."

She nodded, this young girl, and she looked at me the way the young can and do when the aged baffle them, when they don't believe that they will ever be the older ones.

"Well, least tell your mother I said hello."

"I will." Piper held up her book, now

wrapped in a paper bag. "And thanks for this."

"You're welcome. Come anytime and make your escape."

I sidled out from around the counter and walked Piper to the front of the store, struggling for something to say, anything. But nothing seemed right. She hesitated at the entrance and then asked, "Did they have other friends or was it just the two of them?"

"I forget, dear. It was so, so long ago."

Piper pushed open the door and let herself out without another word.

Now, everyone knows I believe in stories being told. Why else would I own a bookshop? I also know that some stories should stay crouched in the dusty corners of the past. It had been a record-breaking hot summer the last time those Summer Sisters were here with their boozy, somnolent parents who paid the children no mind, almost forty years ago now. The town had loved those girls: silly and full of sass, buzzing around town pretending to be Nancy Drew, solving mysteries that should have never been solved.

That night, at our monthly poker game over bourbon and pound cake with Loretta and Ella and my beau, Harrington, I would say, "You will not believe who walked into

15

the store today." And they would guess until they couldn't anymore and I would say, "A Summer Sister's daughter."

I walked outside and watched Piper as she headed toward the market, her poetry book in a paper bag and dragging one of those wagons that announces, "I'm a vacationer": rolling carts that people tug around full of towels and toys, groceries and kids.

Heat wavered off the brick sidewalk like Watersend was one large coffee mug. Posters hung in store windows to announce the summer concert series on the square, and the new market awning was bright yellow and garish against a sky where gray clouds gathered into thunderheads. But instead of a young girl with a cell phone and a nose stud, I saw her mother, Bonny, a wildflower of a child, walking along the same street sure as punch that nothing could ever go wrong.

Overhead, clouds gathered into an afternoon congregation — a reminder that once the past begins to nudge itself into the present, the future changes. Soon the thunder would begin and yes, indeed, a summer storm was coming.

CHAPTER 1
BONNY BLANKENSHIP

It wouldn't be a secret much longer.

Behind the locked exam room door I held the phone to my ear with the particular thrill and sense of finishing a job well done. All the planning, all the night shifts and research papers and grueling interviews had finally led to this job offer as the new emergency room director at Emory Hospital in Atlanta. It wasn't that I didn't love my job as an ER doc in Charleston; I actually did. It was that I needed to leave Charleston. If I was going to leave my husband, then I needed to leave the city where his family was as entrenched as Fort Sumter.

No one knew about this change or move, except of course the administrator on the other end of the line.

"Let me ask you something," she said. "I'm just curious. When did you know you wanted to be a doctor? Your path has been as straightforward and unwavering as I've

17

ever seen."

"I knew when I was eight years old." I fiddled with the oxygen gauge on the wall, straightened the tissue paper covering the exam table. How very many times I'd been here saving a life, or calming a woman who believed her husband was having a heart attack when he was experiencing a panic attack. I'd inserted IVs, administered CPR, stitched and set and soothed. I'd diagnosed correctly and incorrectly, and spent my hours untangling confusing symptoms in this room — the same room where I was accepting my new job.

"Well, your dedication has paid off. Congratulations, Dr. Blankenship."

"Thank you so much," I said. "I'm thrilled for this new chapter in my life." I spoke in a low voice, almost a whisper. "Will you please allow me a couple days to inform my hospital before you announce it there?"

"Of course. You just let us know when you're ready and we'll get things rolling on our end. We look forward to seeing you in thirty days."

"Absolutely," I said, this time louder. "I will see you then, and I'll be in touch."

I hung up with an irresistible need to let out a joyful "yes!" but instead I returned to the emergency room to do my job. I would quietly fulfill my duties while inside I celebrated the last accomplishment before I left my husband and this city.

Make sure Piper was off to college. Done.

Fix the old family river house in South Carolina to sell. Almost done.

Get a new job out of town. Check.

The ER at Medical University of South Carolina, affectionately called MUSC, was as familiar to me as my own home, maybe even more so. There was the squeak of shoes on the linoleum, the beeping of machines and the harsh ringing of phones. The soft swish-hush of the doorways opening and closing, the antiseptic aroma sometimes mixed with the metallic smell of blood and sweat. The nurses and doctors here were like family. I'd spent long hours with them in the intimate confines of small rooms and cramped hallways, but soon I would give them up as I would so many other things — the cost of being free to start a new life without Lucas.

When had I known I wanted to be a doctor? The administrator's question echoed in my mind. There were insights I've known slowly, like the need to leave Lucas. And there were others that happened in a flash, like wanting to become a doctor.

When I was eight years old I saw a toddler drown. The lifeguard pulled a lifeless three-year-old body from the deep end's faraway bottom under the high dive and then screamed for a doctor. A woman, another child's mother in a pink and green Lilly bathing suit cover-up, appeared and kneeled before the body. She then breathed and pumped life back into the little girl. When the child sputtered and coughed and cried for her mama, the dead risen to life, a true-world Lazarus from Sunday school lessons in a little girl's body, I knew what and who I would become. I never learned that mom's name, but I think of her often — a doctor and a mom. In that moment, all the world flowered open with possibility. There was no either/or. There was anything and everything.

From that point on, while others had photos of John Travolta and Stevie Nicks on their walls, I'd had anatomy posters labeling the muscles and veins and organs. A full-size plastic skeleton I'd begged my dad to buy me from a flea market in downtown Atlanta stood sentinel on a metal pole in the corner of my childhood room.

I became a doctor for the same reasons I imagined others became astronauts — to explore an unknown that spreads into infinity. The body is something that can never be fully discovered, its intricacies astounding and its mysteries boundless. Just when science understands what one organ or cell does — a liver or a stem cell — we are wrong, or partly wrong, and there's more, always more.

I'd never wavered or turned back from the desire.

That particular unseasonably warm May afternoon, the air crackled with lightning and the emergency room felt overcharged and electric. I'd filled in an extra shift for another doctor, not only for the padding in my paycheck, but also for the itchy need to be away from home as much as possible. The house felt empty and lifeless without Piper in it. Loneliness echoed along the hallways and through the rooms of my immaculate house. But I tasted a new life waiting for me. It was time. I'd been patient and I'd been meticulous.

I went from exam room to exam room, writing orders on charts, listening to patients and writing prescriptions with both skill and intuition. Just before sunset, I sat in a cubicle stitching the forefinger of a young mother who had cut herself in the most mundane of ways — slicing carrots. Just one more patient. Just one more shift.

Exhaustion held tight to me, even as I

poured another cup of bitter coffee from the break station and splashed cold water on my face in the doctors' locker room. The months of double shifts, the many sleepless nights and the low thrum of constant worry had taken their toll. My sympathetic nervous system was on high alert, the fight-or-flight adrenaline pushing me forward against my will. Secret keeping depleted me, as if each withheld word and admission rotted the life out of me. Fatigue and blurry-mindedness were the prices I paid for finding my way out of my marriage.

But in a breath, the evening shifted. A multicar wreck and a kite-boarding accident blew through the double doors within minutes of one another. Screams, slamming doors and sirens arrived as the accouterments of emergency.

Time bends and slows for me in emergency situations; I don't feel the fear until it's over. I see with acute vision and can tell everyone what to do and when and how. I know the reasons for this are chemical — adrenaline from the adrenals, serotonin from my neurotransmitters — but I also know it's what I'm *meant* to do.

The first stretcher came through: a man with dark, windswept hair and an arm twisted at such an odd angle that for a moment there was an illusion of two people on the same gurney because that would be the only way that arm would make sense. He was silent, his jaw clenched as he bit down, teeth on teeth — a controlled pain until it wrenched free in a groan.

I ran to his side and I felt the world tilting beneath my feet. My heart pulsed high into my throat and my arms tingled. I couldn't make sense of his face here in my ER — so familiar and in pain — but the electric shock under my ribs told me what I knew before my mind could piece things together. Time warped and stood still, moved backward and then forward.

Owen McKay. This was the man who held both my childhood and my heart in his wild hands. My best friend Lainey's brother.

Until he rolled in on a stretcher, I hadn't seen Owen McKay in over twenty years, since the night before my wedding to Lucas. Why was he here? Wasn't he somewhere with wilderness and cliffs and silence?

"Owen?"

"Bee." He opened his eyes. They were the same deep brown, but filmed with pain.

"What are you doing here?" I asked as if I'd run into him in a bar or on the street, a casual old friend.

"Kite boarding." A low groan escaped as

23

he tried to speak. "The wind took me. I . . ."

"Doc," the paramedic shouted at me. "What room?"

"I got this." I grabbed the stretcher's cold metal edge, rolling it into the cubicle with two other nurses. The paramedic rattled off the facts of his injuries: broken collarbone, possible internal bleeding, water in his lungs, dislocated shoulder and probably more.

I went into automatic mode and activated trauma protocol: I ordered the ultrasounds, the IV line, the vital signs and the fluids. Owen faded in and out, and the paramedics professed another fact: he'd almost drowned. A surfer on the beach had administered CPR. I hollered orders, desperate to keep him alive. It was this way with every patient, but I was not in love with every patient.

Past and present blended. He was flat on the stretcher with his eyes closed; he was flat on a warm splintered dock in South Carolina, holding my hand and stargazing. He was calling my name in pain; he was whispering my name to jump into the river. He was holding his arm above his head with a broken bone; he was waving at me across the beach. He was old and he was young and we had all our life ahead of us and then

24

none at all.

I would have to tell Lainey, call her. She'd be devastated and worried, because that's what she did — worried about Owen. But first, very first, I would have to save him.

Later, maybe ten minutes, another doctor, Marie, called for me. Owen had been wheeled into surgery, and I rushed off to the next urgent need: in cubicle C was one of the victims of the multicar crash. Others were being treated in separate rooms, doctors and nurses on call from all parts of the hospital to pick up the load. This patient was older, his hair gone gray but wavy and thick, like a young man's. His heart rate was high and erratic; his blood pressure was dropping and pupils were dilated. Same course of action: trauma protocol, and immediately he had two large-bore IV needles in his veins and Lactated Ringer's coursing through the tubes to his body. I ordered a fast exam ultrasound that showed abdominal bleeding. He needed to go straight to the OR. No CAT scans, no X-rays. "Oxygen sat low. Restless. Blood pressure dropping. We have stage three shock and he needs to get to the OR stat," I called out.

This man screamed, blind in his pain, his gaze searching for help. I didn't check his chart, but drew a dosage of Dilaudid, the same dosage I'd just given Owen, and pushed it into his IV, relief only moments away as it coursed through his blood and dulled the agony.

Then his eyes flew open, and his gaze fixed on mine. He reached his hand out, bloody and mangled from the car where he'd been trapped; they'd released him with the Jaws of Life. Fear surrounded him like wavering fog.

"If I'm dying," he said in a voice strangled with pain, "tell my wife and kids I have never loved anyone as I love them. Tell them."

I'd been here before with patients who've said the same thing. It's a natural instinct — don't let me leave this world and let those I love have any doubt that I love them. *Love* — it's the final word of so many and ultimately all that remains.

Not very often do humans get to see all that truly matters, but I often do. Those fearful of death don't say, "Tell my wife to check my bank account." Or "Do I look okay?" They talk of love and making sure those around them know of their love. Mostly.

"Stay with me," I said to him, motioning to the nurse to grab the end of the stretcher. "You can tell them."

He winced as the nurse and orderly prepared to move toward the OR, but he didn't release my hand. Sometimes patients don't realize they're holding on to me as they hold on to life.

He closed his eyes and spoke on an exhale. "God, please let me live. I haven't done the one thing I meant to do."

"What?" I asked as we ran down the hallway. The surgical suite doors swished open and we pushed his gurney inside. I bent over and he focused directly on my eyes, steady.

I've seen people die before, many times. I've seen the light fade slowly or sometimes in an instant, how the body becomes only that — a body, a vessel, which once held animation or spirit. And he was fading.

"Tell me about your one thing. What is it?" I needed to keep him talking, let him find a reason to live. "Tell me."

But this was not a slow fade; it was instant, immediate and final. He was gone. Completely. His pupils dilated, filling the blueness of his eyes with darkness. He exhaled without inhale. His mouth slackened and his limbs fell free to dangle from the sides of the stretcher.

"Code blue," I screamed.

They arrived quickly — the nurses and

the other doctor, Marie, with the paddles and the intubation tubes, but I knew it was no use. You come to know these things. This would be one of those times when I would grope my way through the darkness and into the waiting room to gather the family. I wasn't up for it. I wasn't ever up for it. I needed to save, not lose.

His wife ran into the emergency room; she'd come after she received a call from the police. In the consulting room with her, I was so detached and alert it was as if I'd left my body with the gray-haired man on the stretcher. Her name was Tory, and she wore cropped white pants and a pale blue button-down; her long white hair was pulled back in a tortoiseshell barrette.

"His wounds were too traumatic. He didn't make it," I said. "We'll know more after an examination, but we did everything we could. Everything. He was on his way to the OR when he died."

Already, even as I spoke to her in the robotic words I'd had to say before to others, I felt the hum of something amiss. What med had I ordered? Had I done it for Owen or for the gray-haired man or both? It was a vertiginous feeling, as if I were jumping from the cliffs of the Grand Tetons with Owen, where I'd last known him to be, but without the wings or the parachute. Nausea rose and I clenched down on my throat to talk to Tory.

"No," she said quietly. "No."

I was silent and untethered. Owen was still in surgery; the night, elongating and spreading out like an oil stain, already changing my life.

"Did he say anything? Was he in pain? Did he . . ." She dropped her head into her hands and the wracking sobs began. "He's my world."

"He did," I managed. "He did say something."

"What?" She lifted her gaze as if this might change everything, maybe whatever he said would bring him back to life.

"He said to make sure that you and your kids knew how much he loved you. That he had never loved anyone as he did all of you. Those were his last words." It was a partial truth.

The next sob seemed to tear her into two, and she fell to her knees. She shook her head so violently that her barrette fell loose, clattering to the floor.

I dropped my hand onto the back of her head, felt the warmth of life and the living. "I'm sorry."

The overhead speaker bellowed my name

over and over. *Dr. Blankenship. Dr. Blankenship.*

"Someone will be in shortly to help you." This was where the nurses and social workers and chaplains took over; this was where I exited.

For all my training, despite all I knew, all I could know, I couldn't save a gray-haired man who bled and suffered. It seemed the simplest thing in fact — car wreck; internal injuries; broken bones — but it wasn't ever simple. I hobbled back to the exam room where he'd been and flipped his chart open: he'd been given the same dose of pain medicine in the ambulance. I hadn't checked and they hadn't told me. A slow tingle of panic began in my fingertips and worked its way to my lungs, where it stole the air. Had I given him an overdose of pain med?

Later that night, almost into morning, I stood in the parking lot of the hospital, the sky folding over me, and I bent over to be sick. The wracking heaves felt like food poisoning or flu, but I knew it was neither — this was fear and its minions of shame and desperation. Maybe, for the first time, I'd contributed to death instead of life. But I knew that if I'd been given a choice in that moment, if someone had said, "You can save only one of these men," I would have chosen Owen. There wasn't a heartbeat's hesitation.

But no one had asked. A choice hadn't been offered. In fact, there'd never been a choice; I'd done my best for both. Yet still a dark cloak of fear fell over me: *Oh, dear God, did I make a mistake?*

Chapter 2
Bonny Blankenship

"Don't let anyone know about this fuckup." Lucas rested both his hands on my shoulders. I still wore the pale green scrubs I'd gone to work in the evening before. Dots of blood freckled the left sleeve. "This is *not* good," he said.

What was I thinking? Why had I told him? I'd stumbled in from work, shot a glass of whiskey and paced the kitchen until he'd come downstairs. I had to tell him; I had to tell someone. But the conversation wasn't even over and I regretted opening my mouth.

"I know it's not good." Tears and mourning were still trapped inside me like a hurricane that hadn't appeared in the sky but instead had shown on the radar screen a few miles offshore. What if I'd stopped the patient from doing or living his one thing? What if . . . My glazed eyes stared out the window and I muttered. "His one thing," I said to Lucas. "Did you hear me? The man said he didn't do his *one thing*. That. One. Thing. Don't you want to know what that is? What mine is? What yours is?"

"No," he said. "There's no such thing."

Morning spilled through the windows and into our family kitchen, a light too bright and cheerful for this conversation. Lucas was dressed for work, his khakis pressed with a thin, fine line so crisp down the middle it seemed I could cut my finger on the crease. His white button-down was ironed flat as paper and a bright blue tie hung down, its Windsor knot pressed into the base of his throat. His face was a mask of disappointment. He glanced at his watch — this beleaguered conversation might make him late to court for his "big" case. (It was always a "big" case.)

I'd disappointed him again. I'd done it for years — and Lucas's way of telling me I'd disappointed him? Divorce threats. Like any threat, it usually worked and I usually changed: cooked more; worked less; entertained his clients; joined the PTA. It wasn't Lucas's fault that he wanted me to be someone else. I'd pretended to be that someone else for a very long time.

"Let's just wait and see what happens," he said. "Wait until they call with the results of the autopsy. Lie low until then."

I couldn't tell him what else was at stake: the new job. But it wouldn't matter anyway. As a lawyer he tasted malpractice in every word. As a husband he was annoyed at the inconvenience.

"Okay," I said. "Right now I just need sleep."

"Don't call anyone or do anything," he said. "When I get home tonight we'll figure something out."

"Got it." The fatigue felt like concrete in my veins and sand scraping across my retinas with every blink. I had nothing left in me but agreement.

He walked out the back door without another word.

There hadn't been a life-saved-at-the-pool moment when Lucas had become this man I needed to leave. I had loved him. I know I had. The change happened incrementally — like growing old or gaining weight — and it had come with his burgeoning success. Maybe it started the night he told me to quit my job because his was more important, because he was the head of the house and the breadwinner. I'd spent a few years analyzing our descent the same as I would a diseased cell under a microscope, trying to find ways to diagnose our marriage's demise as I would a set of complicated symptoms in the ER. But in the end it didn't matter *why* he'd changed; it only mattered that his alteration had destroyed our marriage. Or, in better terms, it had destroyed our love and partnership. I'd gone from living with my best friend to living with a boss. And it had become untenable and exhausting.

This time I didn't do as Lucas asked — I didn't lie low. After a long, hot shower, and a few restless hours of tossing around in the bed, I returned to the hospital and marched into the office of Frank Preston, my administrator.

The man's name, I learned, was Nicholas Rohr. Yes, it appeared that the dosage of pain med had contributed to death, dropping his blood pressure, but more facts needed to be gathered. I was asked to take a sabbatical; after all, I was one of their best doctors, and they didn't want to take action until they knew what had really happened. This was just a precaution. A rest. I'd been working too much and too long. My hours had been obscene.

With Preston's condemnation and my exile, I stood outside his office. The familiar post-op hallway of ward 2D wavered. The world that was mine — of doctors' rounds and medical jargon mixed with the low hum of machines and softly padded shoes hurrying along the halls — now felt precarious and dreamlike.

This was one of the many times in my life I wished again for Lainey's physical presence. She was my best friend. I'd call her the minute I arrived home, but California was as far away as another world when I needed her as I did right then.

Marie, the doctor who had been there with me in the ER, stood a few feet away talking to a resident I didn't recognize. I shifted my feet, heavy with dread, to speak to her. Maybe she would remember something, anything, about last night, a moment that would free my fear. But I heard her before I arrived at her side. "I don't know what happened to her," Marie said. "She just fell apart."

I didn't need to hear my name or be told that she spoke of me. I froze in place; a paralysis of shame.

Marie continued, her voice low but not quiet enough. "She had it all."

I came behind Marie and spoke the truth. "No one," I said, "has it all."

CHAPTER 3
BONNY MORELAND
THIRTEEN YEARS OLD

Summer 1978
Watersend, South Carolina

We believed in magic and in rivers, and that quite possibly they were one and the same. Our tidal river, pulsing behind the river house, called that night in a haunting whisper that beckoned us outside. Lainey and I lay flat on the splintered wooden dock peering at the swirl of stars, the full moon bloated and resting on its invisible bed.

We were forbidden to enter the river's blue-gray waters. But our moms and dads were inside playing poker on the back screened porch, half-drunk and full drunk, their voices falling into the backyard, punctuated by laughter and the distinctive deep reverberation of my father's voice. The world orbited around us, doing whatever it is the world does, while Lainey and I existed as a nucleus, bound tight. Thirteen years old and best friends. *Summer Sisters,* we called each other.

The tide was so high that it licked the very edges of the dock. I stared into the sky, believing that if we just found the perfect crack in the world, we could have anything we wanted. The little metal johnboat slapped against the pillars in a tinny, one-two beat. We held hands, our fingers knitted together.

The cloudless sky domed over us, small holes pricked through the fabric of the universe so we could see diamond glimpses of heaven. "I bet that if we dive into the river at high tide, naked, under a full moon, any wish we make will come true," I said in a voice full of something I hoped was older, grown-up.

I stood first and stripped off my shorts and T-shirt, my white training bra glowing in the moonlight.

"Really naked?" Lainey asked.

"Yes," I whispered. "I think it's the only way."

Lainey jumped to her feet and stripped. Warm air and whispers surrounded our bare skin.

"Hold hands," I demanded. "We have to hold hands."

Together, we jumped into that water. The river appeared peaceful, but once inside, it was a powerful force that could whisk us away. But that night, under that full moon, the river felt asleep. The sluggish water was warm while our legs thrashed below, keeping us afloat in the ebb tide — a stillness that came twice a day for a slice of eternal time.

"Go underwater and make your wish," I said.

Together we sank into that murky darkness, perhaps not knowing the magic that can be wrought while wishing underwater with the unseen inhabitants of that saltwater vein. The dolphin and the otter, the fish, the baby sharks swam invisibly around us. The oysters clung to the sides of the banks, and the crabs scuttled below. We floated alone and yet completely surrounded by life. A baby dolphin, about the same size as us, swam past. I reached out and stroked its silky skin, felt my fingers trail along its back until it was gone as if it had never been there at all.

Salt and particles of pluff mud stung my eyes as I opened them to the brackish water. I believed that the longer I held my breath, the longer I stayed under, the more likely it would be that my wish came true. I remained until my lungs burned as much as my eyes, until I believed that I could breathe water as I did air.

I finally surfaced with a gasp to find Lainey clinging to the edge of the dock, wide-eyed with fear. "You scared me," she said. "How did you stay under so long?"

The river flowed stronger then, the muscle of the earth pulling as a slow draw. I grabbed the side of the dock so the tide wouldn't carry me out to sea, and yet there was an instinctual part of me that wanted to ride that river, allow it to take me. I closed my eyes to the feeling and when I finally peeked at Lainey, I loved her as fiercely as I'd ever loved anyone.

I kicked my legs, holding tight to the warm wood of the dock, and I whispered, "I love you." I spoke to Lainey, but also to the core-burning ember of myself, to the river, to the world.

"I love you, too," Lainey said from a few feet away, both her hands clinging to the dock and her face bobbing above the water, a silhouette and a moon in eclipse. "What did you wish for?" she asked.

"We can't ever tell," I said in the most solemn voice. "It won't come true if we tell." I took in a cleansing breath. "Right here we promise to never leave each other. To always be there for each other. To be best friends for all time."

"For all time," Lainey said.

We moved our hands along the splintered wooden dock, scooting closer until our legs found each other, winding and unwinding, our skin stroked by the silken water. The tide pulsed through us, moving away, taking our wishes with it.

But tides return; they always do.

Bonny Moreland's
River Wish

■ ■ ■ ■

I wish for two things: to be a doctor and to love and be loved by Owen McKay for all of my life.

CHAPTER 4
BONNY BLANKENSHIP

Late afternoon in Charleston, South Carolina, can be the most beautiful sight on earth. The soft light feathers through the Spanish moss, the water reaches and pulses to absorb the sun, reflecting it back to the sky, and the breeze carries an earthy elemental mix of sea and fecund earth. I stood on my back porch, noticing each of those details and holding the cell to my ear until Lainey answered.

"Hello, love," she said, her voice reaching me all the way from California.

In the background, soft music composed of flutes and chimes played on. I calculated that I'd caught her in her art studio before her two kids arrived home from school.

"You busy?" I asked, my hint that this wasn't a quick call.

"Not for you."

I imagined her sitting in her large floral chaise lounge, her legs curled into lotus and her back straight. She'd close her eyes and focus only on me. She knew how. I bet incense burned slowly and everything around her smelled like sage. I desperately ached to be there with her.

"Something terrible happened," I said.

"Not Piper."

It was an incantation, a statement of fact that she would not form into a question. Piper was her goddaughter and although they rarely saw each other, Lainey loved her deeply.

In my life and in our conversations, Piper was always the low-grade and constant worry: my daughter who couldn't seem to stay out of trouble, who couldn't color inside any line, or stand still, who ran instead of strolled, who slept in a wildflower field, who talked too loud and too fast, who memorized entire paragraphs from her favorite books before first grade, who found meaning in every small sign offered her. Wildness and vulnerability were her curses in a world that wanted her to sit straight and take notes. Now she was off at college in Vermont, and still I'd had a call from the campus security about public intoxication and another call from administration about academic probation. But this wasn't the reason for my call — not this time.

"Nothing more than her usual," I said. "This is about me."

"I'm listening," she said.

I poured out my story to Lainey, telling her of the job offer in Atlanta and then the terrible mistake in the ER. All my plans shattered. Fear coursed through my body in a river of adrenaline.

"Are you sure, Bonny? Are you *positive* you made a mistake?"

"No. And that's the hell of it. There was so much chaos that I don't know. I've tried so hard but it's like trying to bring back a dream: the more I try to remember the less I do."

"What was it that made the night different from any other?" she asked.

"The chaos. Too many of the same kinds of injuries all at once. Exhaustion. Long hours. Preoccupation. Incompetence on my part. And, Lainey . . ." I took a breath and paused to watch a cardinal light upon an oak branch, flicker its head left and right before swooping to my bird feeder. Smart, I thought, check for danger *before,* not after. "Your brother. He was here in town for a kite-boarding competition, and he had a terrible accident. He's okay now; please don't worry. But when he showed up without warning, I was thrown off balance."

"Oh, God, Bonny. I haven't heard from him in six months and he was there with you?"

"No. He wasn't *with* me. I didn't even know he was in town until he was rolled into the ER on a stretcher. I had no idea . . ."

The silence that momentarily rested between us vibrated with the barbed resentment we rarely acknowledged — how Owen contacted me more often than he did his own sister. This hurt her, and I knew it. Mostly I avoided the subject of Owen with her and, honestly, with myself. I tried not to think about him or what we'd lost or what could have been. I'd never even told Lucas about my first love. I'd wanted it to be over and needed it to be over, and talking about it didn't seem to help to that end.

But it was the truth — I'd been in love with Owen since I was thirteen years old. Our first kiss was the night before his mom left. He found me on the dock, spread like a starfish and gazing at the sky, memorizing the constellations, ones even now I can name: the Big Dipper, Cassiopeia, Taurus, the Seven Sisters. His presence carried warmth, and I spoke before he knew I'd seen him. "Isn't the sky a mystery?" I asked quietly. "It's a thing without being anything.

It's air and emptiness and nothing and everything."

"You're crazy," he said and sat next to me.

At thirteen years old I wanted to be a lot of things but crazy wasn't one of them. "I am not."

"It's okay to be," he said. "Some of the best are."

What I really wanted was for him to love me. Even then, I knew that he must love me or something fragile inside me would fracture. I sat, gazed at him, brought my knees to my chest and rested my chin there. He peered back at me as if *I*, not the sky, was the mystery, a star just found, something unknowable that he wanted to know.

The first kiss landed on my hairline, and maybe that was all he'd ever meant to do. I've never asked. But I lifted my face, at thirteen years old, to the fifteen-year-old boy I loved, to the wish I'd made inside a river, to all I thought I wanted, and he kissed me again.

I was too young to date or even understand much about the stirrings inside that began that night, a low-grade fever that loosened my limbs and distracted me from my schoolwork. I couldn't have said what it was that uncurled, but from that moment on, whatever awoke inside me longed for

Owen McKay.

Lainey's voice startled me from the past. "But he's okay?" Her voice shifted with a tinge of annoyance.

"Owen?"

"Yes, Owen."

"I think so, yes. When I left the hospital he was already in recovery and doing fine. All they had to do was set his bone and . . ."

"I'll call him when we hang up," she said. "Did you go check on him?"

"No, Lainey. I didn't. I only went to meet with my administrator to find out what happened with the patient who died." I sounded angry and maybe I was. I didn't want it to be about Owen.

"Whatever happened, the hospital knows and you know that your mistake wasn't on purpose or even negligence. Right?"

"I *don't* know."

"What can I do?" Her voice softened, sounding like my best friend again.

"I don't know what you can do or what I can do. I have to take some time off, I'm told."

Crickets, and one lone bellowing frog, joined our conversation and I almost couldn't tell which sounds came from Lainey's background music and which were from my backyard.

"What did Lucas say?" she asked quietly.

"He's angry. He hopes it isn't true and wants me to hide until we know all is well. I hadn't even told him about Atlanta yet. He didn't know . . ."

"Does he now?"

"No. Because I'm going to have to tell Atlanta about this . . . and I will tell them tomorrow. But that's not the worst part. It's the thought that I might have killed a man. I'm scared to death."

"You didn't kill anyone, Bonny. Even if you made a mistake, it was the car wreck that killed him. Words have power. Don't say that."

"I don't know what to do next. Everything was . . . ready to go."

"Go home," she said, so simply.

Those two words shimmered in the evening, and I knew what she meant. She spoke of Watersend, South Carolina. Until last year, I hadn't returned since our summer together at thirteen years old. And neither had she. But whenever I talked of that town and that river house I used the word "home." After Mama had died last year, I'd gone to see the house but only to make plans to fix it and sell it. I hadn't dipped my toes into the water or even ventured into the quaint town to satisfy my internal thirteen-year-old's curiosity.

In our family, the river house held no sentimental value for anyone but me. Only I still held a candle for the sand-crusted memories of childhood summers. Mama and Daddy had owned numerous rental homes in various coastal towns — Dad's retirement job (hobby) and source of income. When they'd passed, they'd left it up to my brother, Percy, and me to sell off the houses, one by one. The river house in Watersend, South Carolina, was the last to go. I'd hired a fix-it crew and had modernized the house, opening the kitchen to the family room, and repainted. I'd ordered stainless steel appliances and planned on staking a For Sale sign in the front yard in three weeks. I'd been dragging my feet through the Lowcountry mud and muck of memories, hesitant to give it up.

"It's still a mess," I said. "I've had the management company working on it. I haven't checked on it in months. They send photos, but I was going to go before . . . before the new job. The last I heard, a vagrant had made herself at home."

"I think you should be the vagrant." Her laughter was as comforting as it had always been. "It can't be that bad. It's been rented until only a year ago. If you really are being forced to take some time off, for God's sake, use it."

The sun sank lower and faded into the horizon as Lainey's advice melted through my panic and I wondered why *I* hadn't thought of it. "I'm supposed to start at Emory in thirty days, if I still have that job," I said. "Maybe I could go for a couple weeks while the storm dies down here. But, Lainey, I won't go without you."

She was silent, and the flutes and chimes were louder, as if she'd set the phone down. She had vowed, long ago, to never return to the place where she and Owen had lost their mother. I was testing her vow. I tried again. "We'll both go," I said. "Together. Bring the kids. I'll bring Piper. I'll finish fixing it and we can go for one last visit before I sell it."

"I can't," she said. "I can't go back there. You know that."

"It's been over thirty years. Maybe it's time."

"I only meant for *you* to go. You need to clear your head. You need to have some time alone in your favorite place in the world. Your mother never let y'all go back. You can go now . . ."

"Not without you," I repeated, and I knew I was pushing hard.

"Let me think about it, Bonny."

"I can get it cleaned and ready. When your kids get out of school, you can meet me there."

"I love you, but I don't know if I can do this."

"It was your idea," I said. "And now it makes sense as if that's what we were meant to do all along."

"For you, not for me."

"We promised each other — for all time." I threw out my last desperate rope.

"Oh, Bonny. I'll think about it."

We hung up and I closed my eyes as the sun disappeared and ended the day I was exiled from my hospital and decided to return to Watersend.

CHAPTER 5
BONNY MORELAND
EIGHTEEN YEARS OLD

Prom 1983

I melted the eyeliner pencil to make it goopy and dark. My eye shadow was sparkly blue and my neon pink blush was definitely too much. Baby's breath flowers were clipped into my French-braided hair. I wore a white eyelet dress and later that night I changed into a flowered sundress I'd made in sewing class. I was naïve, and my date, Eglan Davis, was both popular and arrogant — a terrible combination, which I was drawn to until I married the same. He was a prototype of my charming father, who ruled the world with the surety that only a privileged male, who has been granted an all-access pass to authority, could get away with.

We stood outside the gymnasium, streamers bleeding in the rain, swamping on the pavement. Eglan puffed a cigarette and I waited, holding the umbrella over both of us so he could finish smoking before we left to meet a party on the Chattahoochee River, where all our friends were lighting a camp-fire and setting up for the *real* party. Then I saw a car just like Owen's: an electric blue Camaro. But there were so many of them at that time and I didn't want to get my hopes up — not at all. This was the stuff of my dreams — a fairy tale as romantic as a white horse and prince.

All I knew about Owen at that time was that he'd quit college to work in ski resorts or wherever he could find a job out west. Of course it wasn't Owen in the parking lot of my high school. First, he probably didn't own that car anymore, and second, Colo-rado was too far away for him to make it there for my prom. But the thrill of the *maybe* was always by my side.

I shivered and watched Eglan smoke the last of his cigarette and crush it under the shiny toe of his rented shoes, the ones that came half price with the tuxedo with the baby blue ruffles on the shirt. His tux was supposed to match my dress, but at the last minute I'd switched to an all-white dress, which "pissed" him off, thus the pouting since the pictures taken at my house with a group of friends that afternoon.

Eglan grabbed me for a kiss, and I pulled away, which only made him draw me closer, his tongue shooting into my mouth like a lizard. "Stop," I shouted and pushed at him. "Seriously, you taste disgusting — part ashtray, part whiskey. Not my favorite flavors."

"Why do you always have to be such a cold bitch?" he asked and pulled the umbrella away so I stood alone in the rain while he was covered. His lips curled in a nasty scowl. I didn't want to be anywhere near this guy, and the night had just begun. There was only one way out of this — to get sick and go home — but in doing so I would miss the event of a lifetime: prom.

The baby's breath was sopping wet, drooping into my eyes. I yanked the flowers from my hair and threw them on the ground. "I don't know, Eglan. Why do I have to be such a bitch? Probably because you are such a dick."

Owen's voice sounded so close that I knew it had to be coming from my imagination. "Go ahead," he said. "Call her a bitch one more time."

But it wasn't my imagination. His voice came from his mouth, which was next to me along with his body and his clenched fists and his brown leather jacket splattered with rain.

"Who the hell are you?" Eglan asked and

dropped the umbrella, his fists raised and ready. The umbrella wobbled on the ground, a bowl of black nylon catching the rain in the opposite way it was designed for, swaying back and forth in the wind, skittering like an empty boat.

"Stop," I said and stepped between them. My back was to Eglan, and my face to Owen. "What are you doing here?"

My heart beat wildly against my chest; it was a wonder they couldn't hear it.

"It's your prom. I didn't want to miss it." Owen grinned at me, and I couldn't help but smile back.

"Well, it might have been nice if you'd told me that. You can't just show up like this whenever you want. I have a date, you see."

"Well, he's quite the charmer."

Eglan stepped from behind me and swung his fist in a sudden and unannounced movement. Owen, although he stared at me, ducked and bobbed, coming to kiss me just as Eglan punched through air, lost his balance and landed on the umbrella. The flimsy spikes collapsed under his weight and a stream of curses exploded through the high school parking lot. Owen grabbed my hand and we ran through the puddles to his electric blue Camaro and I stopped pretending that I didn't want him there or wasn't waiting for him or didn't need him.

Through the five years since his mother had disappeared, we'd flirted and we'd kept in touch, but this was the night he came to me. "I've been waiting," he said. "All these years I've been waiting until you graduated." And he kissed me the same way I'd always dreamed about.

And we didn't stop kissing even as he drove to the motel an hour away in the North Georgia Mountains where he'd paid for a room. We didn't stop kissing as he carried me into that room and laid me on the bed with the red-and-blue-checkered bedspread that smelled like pine. "I have loved you for so long, Bee. For so long. Since the day I found you on the dock staring at the sky and mumbling the names of the stars, and maybe even before then. Maybe I loved you the moment I arrived in Watersend and saw you standing in front of the river house in that silly sundress covered in daisies."

And I told him what I'd always kept hidden in the secret corners of my soul. "I've loved you since that afternoon when you climbed out of the back of that car all rumpled and bleary-eyed to stare at only me."

"You were meant to be mine," he said as he covered me in kisses, as his lips found the parts of me that had expected him.

"I waited for you," I told him. "All this time, I waited for you."

That was the first night we made love, but it wasn't the last. I loved him completely and unalterably, and for years afterward he consumed my thoughts and my bed. I was as desperate for him as I was for air or water. And he for me. There wasn't anything we didn't talk about, and even when he was away from me we spent those free hours on the phone. Letters on stationery and on legal-lined paper, on napkins and on any scraps of paper we could find flew between us. We quoted our favorite lines from books or poetry. We clipped and sent articles. We were consumed with each other to the exception of all others.

Yet throughout college and my early twenties, this was a scene that repeated itself too many times to count: Owen would come to me when I needed him most, and then he'd leave for some adventure with promises to be back soon. He loved me; I never doubted it. When we were together, nothing else seemed to exist. We'd lose days, and sometimes weeks, until he left again.

Lainey knew only that we saw each other every so often. I confessed to her my love for him, but never told her the extent of our affair. It had seemed so private, so simply ours, that to share it would diminish it.

But what if I'd stopped him at the *first* leaving? Did the form of our love repeat itself because I was too weak to stand and say, "Stop"? Or did the pattern repeat because I wanted him so desperately that each time he came to me, I convinced myself he would stay.

When he'd leave, I would tell him it was *over*. It was over when I graduated from high school and left for Vanderbilt. It was over when I was a sophomore in college and he found me on a date at a fraternity party. It was over when he left for Colorado to train for wilderness rescues. It was over when I begged him to stop leaving and he said he couldn't. It was over when I went to medical school. But it was *never* over. He always showed up when I was done crying. He always appeared when I'd convinced myself that I didn't need him anymore. He ran and ran and returned and returned.

Finally, at twenty-seven years old, I desperately needed to move on. My heart was bloodied and exhausted. I met the charming and quick-talking Lucas and found safe love. The laughter and the parties and the Charleston society life caught me in their sweet net. I believed I was free of Owen's heartbreak, until the night before my wedding to Lucas, when Owen arrived and asked me to wait a bit longer. "Please be a little more patient."

"Don't come back," I told him. "Let me get over you. Let me have a good life. My heart can't take any more and I've found a safe place to land with a good man." Which was exactly what I believed was true.

Owen did as I pleaded — he physically stayed away, even when there were times I wished he didn't. But he didn't leave me alone. No, not that. There were phone calls, texts and e-mails with long letters. Over the next twenty-two years, we never stopped communicating for more than a month or two. We confided in each other and shared our lives with merely words. I didn't see him; I didn't touch him; but my heart never listened to the edict to stay away — it didn't abstain from loving him at all.

CHAPTER 6
PIPER BLANKENSHIP

There I was, exiled to Nowhere, South Carolina, to spend the summer with my mom and her childhood best friend, Lainey, my godmother. Oh, yes, and as an added bonus I would babysit Lainey's bratty kids. Well, okay, it might not have been fair to call them bratty. I hadn't even met them. And "exile" might be too strong a word, but it was exactly how I felt.

Mom had dropped me off the day before and then she'd gone home to finish packing. She'd be back the next day and Lainey would come with her kids the day after. Meanwhile, I needed to get the house perfectly ready: make the beds, wash the sheets in Mom's Laundress #22 detergent and fill the refrigerator with groceries. I'm surprised she didn't ask me to drop little chocolates on their pillows.

It'd been only a couple weeks since Mom screwed up at work. It was like a bomb had been lit that day — she blew up everything in our lives. I think she left Dad, which I don't blame her for, but it sucked because it only made him a bigger jerk than he was before. Then she began spending all her time going back and forth between Charleston and here to fix up her parents' old house in this crap town. "I'm saving it to sell it," she kept saying, as if she still had a job in the ER but the ER was for houses. Meanwhile, our *real* house, the one we lived in in Charleston, the one I grew up in, had just Dad and Gus, our sweet blond terrier, in it like a ghost house. Mom packed so much stuff it was like she never planned on going back.

If asked, I could tell anyone why I'd been sent here to work for my mom and Lainey — failing my freshman year of college and a tiny little arrest (public intoxication, which shouldn't even be a real thing) would do that. But it sounded worse than it really was. If it mattered, I could explain what happened. But it didn't seem to matter and this was my punishment: Keep the house clean. Stock the refrigerator, make the beds, do the dishes and cook the meals. And let's not forget — watch two little kids. But children were like aliens to me. I was Cinderella, but worse, because a prince did not exist. And there would be no ball at the end of this summer, only a "trial semester" at a junior college if I was lucky.

Yes, it would be ideal if I was a better daughter, if I was still a virgin at nineteen, if I hadn't "marred" my body with a little tattoo of my favorite flower, a sunflower, if I'd gone to class, if I didn't drink too much. But *ideal* was never my thing. Even though I wished, at least once, for it to be my thing.

Anyway, there I was and I had to admit to myself (definitely not to Mom if asked) that the house was super cute — white shingled with the brightest blue shutters and doors. Mom had painted our bedroom doors at home this very color. Now I understood why — some frosting-covered kid's memory of the river house where she spent her childhood summers. I'd heard her and Grandma and Granddad (before they died) talk about it for years. Should we sell it? Keep renting it? Should we go back? But they never did anything with it. Until now.

I'd nosed my way through the entire house already, kind of freaked out that Mom wanted to be here all summer while she waited to see if she could still be a "real" doctor. It was a creaky house, like its joints needed exercise. The floorboards seemed to be held together by sand. The doors didn't close all the way, warped like they'd been underwater for years. There were four bedrooms spread out in the back of the house.

Outside, behind the house, was the river — a tributary from the sea. It wasn't the kind of water you swam in, or at least the kind of water I would swim in, what with so many crabs and shrimp and otters and fish and all manner of disgusting, squishy things that I did not want touching my skin. I was more of a beach girl, so thankfully that was exactly what was across the street — sand and ocean. It was a house between river and sea.

Since the house rested on the banks of the tidal river, the view was beautiful. A dock stretched across the water like it was waking, its wooden sun-warmed arms spread apart in a stretch. A boat, only big enough to fit two or three people, bobbed on the water like a little kid wanting attention. One minute I glanced outside and there was nothing but a blue-gray basin parallel with the earth, a flat landscape separated only by the colors of earth and then water. And the next minute the dock's plankway dropped ten feet, baring the crushed oyster shells, discarded like sea trash, on the banks of the marsh.

But there wasn't much enjoying any of it until I finished the to-do list from hell. So I walked along the sidewalks of Watersend on my way to the market. The air felt like it was being pumped through a furnace. Not that I didn't know what hot felt like — Charleston could be a bonfire — but I'd been north at college in Vermont. Now the humidity felt like a thick sweater, as if I'd never felt it before.

I kept thinking I was lost, because in Watersend the curvy roads changed names without warning as if a drunkard had planned the place. I checked the little hand-drawn map and saw I was exactly where I was supposed to be — one more left and then downtown. Along the way, there were cedar shake houses with wide porches and front lawns with wildflower gardens and iron gates hinting at hidden secrets. It made me think of *The Secret Garden,* but then again, Ryan (my ex) made fun of me because he said everything made me think of a book. I was a weirdo. Which he once thought was cute, but not so much anymore.

The river scooped around the town like a hug (I couldn't believe I thought something so sentimental and sappy). And everything — the town, the houses, the streets and stores — sat in the curved arch of the bay.

If the river overflowed, or decided to swallow the town, it would all be gone in an instant, absorbed into the green and gray and oyster-dimpled basin.

These were the things I thought about as I strolled into town because I was doing my very best not to think about Ryan. And how much I loved him. And how he'd chosen Hannah over me even though I'd offered him everything and how he was backpacking through Europe with her this very second and how he posted things on Instagram like "View from here" and I could tell it was from the bed where he lay with her. He was my "first," and although I'm not a big enough idiot to believe that the first is the last, I loved him so much that I couldn't *stop* believing it. It was horrible knowing something wasn't true but believing it anyway.

My chest felt bruised even though he'd never hit me. And to add insult to embarrassment, there I was dragging one of those ridiculous wagons with the big beach tires because "everything is walking distance."

My cell phone dinged. I glanced to see who had texted or e-mailed or Instagrammed or Facebook messaged or Snapchatted or . . . anything at all. But it was just Mom asking how it was going.

It's going, I texted back. On the way to market. I rounded the corner to downtown and it was charming for sure. My grandma, she would have said, *Golly!* And sometimes I say it just to say it, which I did right then.

Downtown had the only straight street so far: the town planner had finally sobered up. The shops were decked with brightly colored awnings — yellow, blue, pale pink and garish orange. The rows of attached shops were separated only by paint color and awning designs. Benches, black iron with curved backs, lined the street and I spotted a retro movie theater, its marquee bright red. Gas lanterns burned, trying to outdo the sunlight, which today was impossible. Faded white lines marked the parking spaces and most people obviously ignored them, parking any which way they chose.

I glanced at the grocery list, which was on a pad of paper with a ridiculous dolphin on the upper left-hand corner and the name of the house typed below: Sea La Vie. *Dumb name.* Even though I failed French (eight a.m., were they serious?), I knew that La Vie meant "Life."

The Summer Sisters' shopping list was like a Rorschach test of food.

Mom, the OCD ER doctor: Chicken cutlets. Asparagus. Eggs and cheese. Like she printed her list from the *Cookbook for the Boring.*

Lainey, the artist: Chardonnay came first. That told me mostly all I needed to know. Then health food after that. Which was frankly quite the contradiction, but who was I to judge? "Vegetarian," it said at the top of the e-mail. Guess Lainey was oh so California now. Her kids couldn't have anything processed, packaged or pumped with hormones.

Guess chicken nuggets, macaroni and cheese and Goldfish weren't good enough for her kids even though I seemed to be alive and well after being fed that usual fare in my childhood.

I tucked the list into the back pocket of the cutoff jean shorts that Mom would most definitely tell me were too short. Then I stopped because I saw one of my favorite things: a bookshop. It was small, tucked between a gift shop called All Things Seashell and a knitting store, Top Knot. It was a slim doorway, almost something I'd pass if I were in my usual state of rushing, which I wasn't because what was there to rush to do here? Nothing. Nada.

Title Wave, the sign read.

Coastal Theme overload here. The bright blue awning yawned over the window where, in smaller print, was the subtitle *Purveyor of Imagination.* The window display held an antique desk covered in books. An old Underwood typewriter squatted in the middle of the desk with its little letter-stamped faces looking at me, and I couldn't help but see a book hidden in the promise of typing.

I left the cart outside and a blast of arctic air washed over me as I opened the door. A small bell jingled my arrival like some fairy announcement. I took a quick glance and saw that it wasn't a well-organized store, but the disarray felt welcoming. Music played, a whisper in the background: "Fly Me to the Moon." A long counter made of old shutters ran along the right side of the store and was covered in pamphlets, book-marks and tiny reading lights — all the things people would buy without thinking as they were checking out.

"Welcome," a voice said, and I glanced around to spy an old woman behind the counter, her white hair fluffed into a cotton ball slightly dented on the right side. She wore red cat-eye reading glasses secured by a purple string that looped down by her chin and disappeared behind her neck. "Make yourself at home," she said, but she squinted at me like she didn't really see me as much as know I was there.

"Thanks," I said and wandered farther in, the door swishing shut behind me. I wanted to make myself at home. The store was bigger than it appeared from outside, with cozy white oversized chairs that just begged to be curled in and green metal café tables with matching chairs scattered around as if a party had just ended. There wasn't a coffee bar or sweets shop. Just books stacked to the ceiling and wall to wall and piled on the floor.

Suddenly I knew where I would spend the time hiding from Mom, Lainey and the kids: here. Right here.

Books. They were the only place in the world where I could be Piper and not Piper at the same time. I didn't have to leave myself, but I could be someone else entirely, without the hangover.

I know. I know. I took Psych 101. It sounds like escape is my go-to thing in the world — to be drunk or to disappear into a story. And maybe it's true, but I didn't see it that way. I just didn't, right then, exactly like being Piper Blankenship. I believed I would like myself again. Or I hoped I would. But I didn't today.

I wanted to unzip myself and let the real Piper out to go find another life. And I could do that in a story — a good one, anyway.

I slipped into the fiction section and ran my hands along the book spines but didn't choose one. Instead I went to the poetry section and picked out a Marjory Wentworth book. I checked my cell for Ryan again, which was ridiculous and slightly embarrassing, like I had a tic. I approached the checkout counter and the old lady with the white hair glanced up from her reading.

"Did you find what you were looking for?" She stared at me funny, like there was food on my face or toilet paper stuck on the bottom of my shoe and she didn't know how to tell me.

"I did find exactly what I was looking for. This is a great bookshop."

A little chitchat about this and that, and about how she knew my mom and Lainey when they were little girls, and I was back outside in the sweltering heat. I rolled the wagon for only a half block and then stopped under the yellow striped awning of the grocery store. The Market, it was called. At least something here wasn't trying to be too-too cute.

Hand-painted signs announced: *Organic! Fresh!* On the sidewalk, zinc buckets spilled over with fresh wildflowers — zinnia and thimbleweed, doll's eyes and bellflower. I knew my wildflowers; Mom was obsessed (when Mom loved something she didn't just love it, she obsessed). Then there was the fruit, plump and seductive, resting in large wooden crates. I lifted a peach and my fingers dented the skin. Juice trickled along the side of my hand and quickly, without thinking, I licked the side of my wrist. The sweetness of the fruit filled my mouth.

"You planning on paying for that?" a deep voice asked.

I peered up, embarrassed, at the face of the best-looking boy I'd seen in months — a rugged guy who looked like he'd just played a soccer game on the beach, all smiles. He was African American, and as beautiful as if he'd been carved from the air he misplaced. His dreadlocks were long enough to almost touch his shoulders, but not quite yet.

"Honestly?" I said. "I was hoping to eat it before anyone noticed."

He laughed and then tried to appear serious. "Maybe I should call the very bored Watersend police on you, give them something to do."

"That'd be great," I said. "Perfect way to start the summer."

He stuck out his hand. "Hey, I'm Fletch.

And this is my parents' place. You new here?"

I noticed everything about him in one flash: His left front tooth was slightly crooked, slanted toward the middle. His T-shirt was a faded green and advertised a long-gone county fair. His face was clean shaven, and then, stunningly, there were his eyes, blue and so bright they seemed to be made of the sky.

I looked away because I realized I was staring too hard and too long. "Yep. I'm new around here." I faked a thick southern drawl. "Just for the summer." I took a bite as if to prove my point. "Thank you for not arresting me. And your folks, too, I guess. I'll pay for it with the groceries. God, this is a good peach."

"We know how to make 'em around here," he said, imitating my fake accent but with a much better drawl. He jostled the bag to his other arm. "Let me know if you need any help." He disappeared inside and I took another bite, allowed the juice to roll down my chin before I wiped it off with the back of my hand.

I took inventory of my morning — the river coursing behind the house, the beach only steps away through a wildflower-strewn pathway, a bookshop and a market with fruit so fresh it burst from the skin. So far, not quite as crappy as I'd imagined. But there was still plenty of summer left.

CHAPTER 7
BONNY BLANKENSHIP

It was time to go. After all the planning and fixing and painting and packing, it was time. Piper was waiting for me in Watersend and Lainey would arrive in two days. I threw my suitcase on the bed and the corner of it smacked into a framed photo of last year's family Christmas card. It was a card that portrayed the kind of holiday glee advertisers post on their websites to sell cards — that's how family-idyllic we appeared. The frame tumbled facedown with a crunch, catching the edge of the nightstand and toppling onto the carpet.

Christmas card framing — it was just one of our many traditions. We kept the card framed until the following year when a new one would be displayed after January first. If we took a photo today it would show me, once Charleston's top ER doctor, broken-hearted and jobless, so consumed with panic attacks and anxiety that even a ringing phone sent me to deep breathing. A woman who often dreamed of the night Mr. Rohr died, although the patients changed into people I knew.

Lucas? He certainly wouldn't pose for the photo now that I'd finally told him I was leaving. I couldn't give him the absolutes that he wanted — the bullet point plan — because all I knew was that I was going to Watersend for the summer, where I would wait to hear about the job in Atlanta. I couldn't tell him anything after that, not because I was keeping it from him but because I had no idea at all. And Piper . . . well, she might be in the photo, but she would not be smiling. Definitely not smiling. Maybe we could add her campus police mug shot.

That's how, lickety-split, as my mother would have said, life changes.

I packed while Lucas was on a business trip that wouldn't bring him home until the next day. I'd told him about Atlanta, but that I might not have the job at all anymore. Meanwhile, I was headed to our rental in Watersend with our daughter until I knew the next steps we needed to take. A timeout. A reprieve from the pain. This news was received about as well as one could expect — meaning he ranted, gnashed his teeth, threatened to "clean us out" and not to allow Piper to go with me.

He also believed I'd change my mind when I calmed down. "Don't make a permanent decision based on a temporary emotion," he'd said. As if any of this was temporary.

The bedroom was in shambles. It occurred to me that we didn't really know what was in our drawers until we threw that drawer across the room. Which was what he'd done as he'd packed for his trip. I hadn't picked it up yet. In fact, I wasn't planning on it.

I wasn't mad that he tossed his top dresser drawer across the room. I understood. But that didn't mean I didn't think it was a crappy thing to do. Vengeful. And I didn't have much patience for vengeful from anyone else because I was punishing myself enough as it was.

War zone as the bedroom was, it was still achingly familiar: Painted a pale blue with all-white linen bedding. Silver lamps and frames sat on the bedside tables where I'd placed them. A faded Aubusson rug covered the hardwood floors, and photos of our wedding and of our daughter at various stages of life hung on the walls. A candle, gardenia scented, now burned to the bottom of its glass container, was on the bedside table along with the endless pile of books I'd been meaning to read. When I allowed myself to dwell on the energy and time and effort I'd invested into making this home what it was for us, and then when I registered its undoing, it was enough to make me feel nauseous and free-falling, as if I were stuck on a thrill ride at a cheap carnival.

Focus, I scolded myself, and I glanced at the packing list I'd made the night before in a fit of organization. But I couldn't focus. I just wanted to get out of this house, a house I'd designed and built and decorated and thought I'd never want to leave.

I tucked my folded shirts into the corner of the suitcase and had just grabbed a pile of shorts when I heard the chime that signaled the opening of the front door.

God, I thought with a begging need, *I know I don't deserve it, but please let it be a friend.*

"Bonny?"

It was Lucas. God was definitely not in the business of granting me any wishes.

"Up here," I called.

His footsteps, the ones I'd heard for twenty-two years, sounded on the hardwood stairs. Each family member had a distinct footfall. Piper was light on her feet, almost like she was dancing. Lucas, he had a bad ankle and his steps were heavy and uneven. My stomach rose in fear. He was going to light into me again. How quickly, how very quickly, what had once caused me to smile — his approach — now sent the fight-or-flight adrenaline flowing. My throat constricted like someone had a stranglehold on my neck. I sat on the bed and waited. I held my own hands; wound them together in a knot.

He threw the bedroom door back on its hinges and stood there with his hands balled into fists at his sides — a parody of the angry white male in his professional clothes and ruddy complexion turning ruddier.

"You just left it like this?" He pointed at the cuff links, receipts, golf scorecards, loose change and socks scattered from rug to hardwood floor.

"Yes." In the past few years, I'd learned better than to say more than a word or two of defense, as it only enraged him more. I would let his accusations pass over me, water over rock.

He shook his head in disapproval, which used to bring me to tears but now only made me want to throw the lamp at his head, which of course I wouldn't do. He squinted as if I blinded him. He hated me — I'd deceived him, kept the truth of my leaving from him. He was both humiliated and hurt.

"I'll be gone in an hour. I'm so sorry," I said for the uncountable time. *I'm sorry. I'm sorry.* It was a mantra.

And I *was* sorry.

Lucas stomped to the dresser and opened it with such rough hands that the drawer popped out and landed on the carpet in a spew of T-shirts and boxers.

"Fuck," he cursed.

I didn't know him.

Once, at a cocktail party, I'd heard a woman in a sparkling gold-beaded dress say, "You don't really *know* your husband until you divorce your husband."

It had seemed inane, red wine nonsense. *Of course you know the person you live with,* I'd said. But that sparkling woman was right, because Lucas was like a raging animal now, and any approach caused harm.

He whirled toward me, his face contorted. "I know I've said this before, Bonny, and I guess I'll keep saying it until I believe it. But I can't believe you're doing this to our family."

I opened my mouth and then closed it. What could one more explanation possibly do? I'd tried so many times that I could bury us both in all the reasons. If words could have healed, if all the thousands and thousands of words we'd said could heal, they would have done so by now. If I could apply sentences as I did bandages and medicine in the emergency room, we would be well. But we weren't. We were broken.

"You have nothing to say?" He turned back to his dresser and opened the second drawer without spilling it this time.

"I think I've said it all, Lucas. This is what you wanted all those times you were mad at me and you said you wanted out or when you were disappointed or frustrated. Now it's here. I have no idea what to do or say now. I'm empty."

"I'm sure you are." He turned to me again and pointed at my suitcase on the bed. "You're running away. Can't even stick around to face the hospital verdict or repair our life."

I twisted my wedding ring, which I hadn't yet removed. "That's not fair." I shifted my eyes to his. "Lucas, I know you hate me. I know you're angry. I know. But please, I'm begging you, don't be so cruel. I have so little reserve. I can barely . . ."

His body deflated as if he'd been blown up by the anger and then someone had opened the release valve. I watched as his face fell and his eyes filled with tears. Maybe the anger was better because the hurt that puddled in his eyes made me dizzy with shame and regret — these were the times I saw the hint of the man he used to be, the man I'd fallen in love with. I turned away.

"Bonny." His voice cracked with anger or sadness, I couldn't tell which. Then he went for the jugular — not his disappointment, but my parents. "Your parents. Do you think they'd approve? They never wanted you to go back there."

"Their reasons aren't my reasons, Lucas."

"You're not being logical. You aren't listening to reason," he said. "You can't start over without bringing the past with you. You can't just throw it all away because you want something new. It's juvenile, Bonny. And Percy, what does he want?"

My brother, Percy — he lived in Austin, Texas, and coached high school football. He'd been so very young when we'd gone to the river house that his memories were nothing more than cloudy dreams. The house meant nothing to him beyond what monetary value he would gain when I sold it.

"He doesn't care, Lucas. You know that."

"Then why should you? Let me ask you

something, Bonny."

"Go ahead."

He leaned forward and tapped his chin as if in some exaggerated courtroom gesture. "Were you fixing it up to sell it or to move there?"

"What?"

"If you were planning on taking a job I didn't know about. And moving to Atlanta, which I didn't know about. Were you lying about fixing that old piece of shit to sell or were you planning on going there all along?"

"I'm still planning on selling it. Just like every other one of Dad's rentals." Even as I said it, feeling its rounded truth, I also wondered if underneath the truth there was a subtle desire to keep it. Why had I saved it for last?

"I don't believe you," he said.

"I can see why you wouldn't believe me. I get it, I didn't tell you about Atlanta, but . . ." I glanced at the broken family photo, at his paraphernalia scattered on the floor. "Do you want to keep living this way? I don't. I just don't. I decided to leave when I applied for that job. And now I can't stay, Lucas. Not with us this way, and I don't want to sit here in this angry house waiting to find out if I killed a man. I don't know what will happen . . . I'm going there to wait until I know more or find out about my job."

"God, I hate who we've become," he said.

"Me, too. That's why I'm leaving."

"I don't know what to do, Bonny."

"I didn't either," I said and forced myself to meet his eyes. "But I do now. And it's done."

He came and sat next to me on the bed. Gus, our lopey terrier, slobbered and circled the room as if he knew something terrible might happen. I clicked my fingers and he came to sit next to me. I buried my fingers in the fur of his neck and scratched while we talked.

"Tell me again *exactly* what you want," he said.

I'd told him so many times that I could have done it in my sleep. I could say it all backward. "I'm drowning, Lucas. I don't want the old bitterness that has eaten away at our life. I want to find some balance. I want to continue to be a doctor, but I don't yet know if I can or how I will or even where. And most importantly, I want to help Piper. She failed her freshman year and she has an obvious problem with her excessive partying. She can't go back to school . . . We have to figure out what to do."

"And you think all of that will happen in

86

a mythical childhood home."

"No. I think all of that will happen day by day."

"I will never forgive you if you leave now," he said in a voice as calm as if he was saying he'd stop at the market for dinner on his way home from work. "If you change your mind and come back home, I won't forgive you. When you get your job back and need to be here, it will be gone. If you leave for some sappy childhood memory . . . This foolishness is absurd. I never meant it when I said we should divorce; it was just words in anger. You *knew* that. This is our home. We raised our daughter here. We built a life. You will destroy what's left of us."

"I don't want to destroy anything. I want to build something new."

What I didn't tell him was that I was scared. Scared to be without him. Scared to be without my job. Scared to leave. Scared to stay. Scared as hell.

"How could you . . ." His voice trailed off because we both knew we'd had this discussion too many times. At home. In the counselor's office. In the car. In the backyard where we thought Piper couldn't hear us. We could talk about it again, of course we could. I'd tell him of all the ways he'd hurt me through the years, and he would tell me how he could change. I would tell him how the mistake I'd made in the ER had destroyed me and the fear haunted me both day and night. He would tell me it didn't have to. We could talk of my deception in making plans to move without him, and I'd apologize again. Image and money were more important to him than my heart, I would say. And to that, he wouldn't have an answer.

But I did try one more time. "Lucas, I might have killed someone. A life is gone and it might be my fault. I have spent my entire life *saving* lives. Now I can't sleep without nightmares. The slightest sound sends my adrenaline into overdrive and I can't think or breathe. I feel like this . . ." I paused, feeling the wings that began in my chest before I wept. I wanted to give him a visual of my internal world, the one that spurred me to go find peace. "I feel like I'm at the top of a roller coaster right before it plummets. And I can't get my harness fastened. That's how I feel." I'd done it; I'd told him how I felt. Now he could respond. I almost held my breath.

"You're a doctor. You know that will pass. You have to stay here and save your life. Save mine. Save ours. *Do* something about it."

"I *am* doing something about it," I said, resolute with a deep breath. "But here's the thing, Lucas — I have spent so long trying to keep my life and home safe that I didn't keep my heart safe."

"You're pitiful," he said.

It was so cruel and so true. The anger seeped out of the room, leaving us both silent. He took what he needed and didn't say good-bye as he closed the bedroom door. My natural instinct was to run after him, as I'd done all those times before, and fix it, make it right, save us.

I dropped to the soft carpet and placed my arms around Gus's neck for as long as he would let me. "Sorry, old buddy. But you'll be fine here with your dad. He loves you." Gus licked my face, and the last of my tears. I scratched behind his ears and whispered, "We'll come back for you. I promise."

After Lucas was gone, I loaded my car. On the way out, I plucked a piece of Lainey's art from the living room wall — a mixed-media encaustic of a mother and child. It was my favorite piece in a house full of fancy oils and family portraits. I shut the door with one final thought: sometimes you had to leave home to finally find it.

Chapter 8
Lainey McKay

Petaluma, California

The canvas had become a mess, globs of wax settling like pimples across the surface. The iconic photo of Albert Einstein sticking out his tongue was now layered with quotes about genius, pictures of electricity and then black swaths of paint over the quotes and . . . well, nothing was working. Mixed-media art became mixed-up mess and I took it from the easel and set it on the floor, then turned to pick a fresh canvas to begin again. If there was one thing about art I'd learned to accept — it was *always* begin again.

This studio was my haven. I'd built it for myself out of an old Airstream trailer I'd bought at a car auction in L.A. I'd had the silver and blue bullet towed here to the backyard of our little house in Petaluma, California, and outfitted it for my studio. If there was something I loved — a rock, a crystal, a feather, a small scrap of a poem or even a vial of dirt from a trip I'd loved — it was in here. But mostly it was filled with canvases, art supplies, printers and paint. It was more home than my home a few yards away.

I'd just dropped the new blank canvas on the easel when the Airstream door opened and the face of the man I loved peeped around the corner with a grin. "Hey, baby."

Tim. My husband.

I loved Tim as much as anyone I'd ever known. We lived together in a San Francisco Craftsman home built on the side of a curved road in Petaluma. He was my best friend and my partner. I loved all the things about him — the way the wrinkle between his eyes furrowed when he tried to under-stand me; the stubble that bloomed only hours after a shave; his laugh so quick and bursting out of nowhere like a hidden cymbal suddenly ringing out. His almond-shaped green eyes were crowded and sur-rounded by dark eyelashes. It was the first thing I'd noticed when I met him and the first thing I'd seen every time after, includ-ing now. Sometimes I didn't notice anything else, like whether he'd gotten a haircut or changed his eyeglass style, whether he was dressed up or wearing his jeans and a

T-shirt. But that day I noticed Tim was filthy, his shirt and jeans striped with mud.

"What are you doing?" I asked as he strolled into my space.

No matter how much I loved him, and I did, I still felt defensive and intruded upon when he burst inside my private space, all energy and fresh air.

"Weeding the summer garden and realizing that you won't be here when the tomatoes ripen, that I'll have to eat them all myself or find someone to share them with," he said with a grin.

"Funny."

"Seriously, Lainey." He dropped into a lounge chair with faded flower chintz and a deep seat. "How could you possibly leave with our kids, and why? Tell me again and maybe this time I'll understand." It was a fake pout but a real question I'd already answered.

I dropped my paintbrush and moved closer to him. "Because my childhood best friend's life is unraveling and she's asked for us. Because I can work almost anywhere. Because Bonny and I promised each other that we'd be there for each other through anything. Because it will be fun for the kids to go to the South."

"Because you want to leave me," he said

and slumped deeper into the pillows.

I leaned over, placed my hands on his shoulders and touched my forehead to his. "That's insane. I'm sick about leaving you. And I really, really hope you come visit. At least once. I'd love for you to see everyone and you've never been to the real, real South."

"South Florida doesn't count?" He pulled me close to him. "I just don't want you to leave."

"I know. Part of me doesn't want to leave either. But Bonny needs me. All those years and years ago, we promised that if anything really bad ever happened . . ."

"In your little witch ceremony." He tried to smile; I saw the crinkles begin to form but then disappear.

"It was anything but." I kissed him full on the mouth. "And what a terrible godmother I've been."

"I believe you've been a little busy being a mom to our own kids."

I held close to Tim and hugged him before asking the favor. "I need to pack a box to send to Watersend. I *am* going to work while I'm there. Will you send it to me?"

"You pack it and I'll send it tomorrow after I drop you off at the airport."

"Thanks, sweetie."

"I have to clean up and stop by a construction site. I'll let you finish that beautiful piece of artwork you've dropped in the corner like it's in time-out."

I awarded him a playful pop on top of the head with my palm. "You weren't supposed to notice that."

He smiled and kissed me again. "I know you hate talking about this, but we must before you go."

The electric pulse under my lungs sparked. "My mom," I said.

"Yes."

"There's nothing left to say, Tim."

"Yes, there is. I'm worried about you going there again, tearing into old scars, poking into old fears. It's something you seem to have finally let go of — searching for her and wondering — and now you want to go where it all happened?"

"Going there isn't going to make it any better or any worse. I'm not going to miss her more by going. Or less. I'm not going to wonder more if I go. Or less."

"I don't think that's true," he said and began to pace around my studio, picking up brushes and paints and setting them back in absentminded motion.

"I guess then you'll just have to believe me. I haven't searched for her in a year. I haven't stopped my life or my art . . ."

"Yes, you have."

"Do you really want to fight about this right now before I leave with the kids and won't see you for weeks? Is this how you want me to exit?"

"No. Of course not."

He stopped pacing and faced me, a hard block of wax in his hand. He tossed it back and forth and I felt the irresistible urge to grab it from him and scream, *That's mine!* I also wanted to say the same about this trip and about my life and about my studio, but the truth was that I shared my life with Tim, and I *wanted* to, but he doubted my commitment to stop looking for my mom.

"Then what do you want?" I asked. "I'm not going back there to dig up the past, but to help Bonny find a new future."

"Tell me that you haven't contacted the private eye or looked online or searched . . ."

"Stop." I took the block of wax from him. "Stop now. I haven't contacted him. I haven't Googled her name. I have let it go."

"Lainey," he said in that soft voice that let me know he didn't believe me.

"Well, maybe a Google or two." I tried to smile.

This was a hot spot in the corner of our marriage. Too many times I'd spent money we didn't have, and disappeared for long weekends without calling, with only a whiff or scent of the possibility of finding her — finding the mom who'd disappeared in Watersend, South Carolina, after putting her young son in the hospital, the mom who'd walked away from her family. I'd promised to stop looking, and Tim took it personally — believing that our family didn't make me feel complete. I didn't know how to explain that it did, but still there was a gaping hole where a mom should be.

"I'll be back in a couple hours." Tim lifted my face to his and kissed me. "Listen, I don't want you to go, or take the kids with you, but I understand. Please just don't go for long."

"Okay." I kissed him in return before he walked out, gently closing the door.

I'd believed I would never return to Watersend, but ever since Bonny had called, I'd felt as if part of me was still swimming in that river, running on that beach, laughing in that house, as if a broken and living piece of me was still there and couldn't catch up to the present. Maybe in traveling to Watersend I could find that fragment of my soul and carry it home. Maybe the emptiness inside of me didn't have anything to do with finding Mom, but finding what was left of me.

I picked up my Einstein canvas and apologized. "That wasn't the best way to handle that situation."

Yes, I talked to my art, and to the muses and to the empty room. Because it was how I spent most of my days — interacting with an unseen world, the world that wanted to come into the physical world. I played with the ideas and inspiration and creations that wanted to move from there to here.

I'm an artist. I still covered my mouth and whispered this when I was asked what I do. How on earth did I get to call myself something so worthy or wonderful? I made things out of things, and then I sold them. That was it. I'd tried all the art forms but my specialty was mixed media. I used vintage or iconic photos as the base. I then added text, newspaper clippings, pictures, paint — almost anything that struck me as part of the overall impression the photo meant to be all along.

I placed Albert back on the easel and squinted at him. Why wasn't it working? I'd heard it said that some writers don't know what they think until they write. I often didn't understand what I was making until I was done making it, but this one was especially eluding me. Was it about genius?

Creativity? Electricity? Madness? I didn't know yet. But I also knew better than to force it. That was where the worst of my art came from. Maybe the worst of life also.

It didn't take long, but I formed a pile of the art supplies I wanted sent to South Carolina and then I gave my studio one more glance before locking up.

Back inside the house, I tossed my satchel on the bed and began piling the books I wanted to tote along with me. Daisy, eight years old, and George, six years old, would be home from school in thirty minutes, clamoring off the bus and running along our lane with their backpacks bouncing against their shoulder blades and their flip-flops smacking the pavement. They would fly through the door like sun rays and the world would, for a heartbeat, seem perfect.

I was in my forties when I'd decided to have kids. I'd waited, always afraid that living without a mom didn't qualify me to *be* a mom, scared to death that I would repeat her patterns and abandon my children when they needed me the most. Until Tim lovingly and slowly made me realize that we were our own family, and patterns were shattered with love.

When I watched the twenty-something

moms on the playground, I was in awe of their energy. But I didn't envy their frantic need to outdo, outrun, out-PTA, and out-dress each other or their kids. Daisy and George were simply their own little wonders and I didn't know how I could ever live without them.

I smiled when I thought of showing them the Lowcountry of South Carolina. Although I'd visited Charleston a few times to see Bonny, I'd never taken the kids with me. The South to them sounded as exotic as a faraway planet.

Like Bonny, I'd grown up in the suburbs of Atlanta, so it appeared that I'd taken out a map and stated with intent, "Where can I go that will geographically separate me farthest from my past?" I didn't really do this. In reality I'd never done anything with that much forethought or planning. So through the years, I'd had to find a way to make a house a home, to make my surroundings soothing. Feng shui was the answer. And because I knew what memories houses could keep, I knew what the river house in Watersend held, and yet I was willingly returning.

Wondering about Watersend was just another one of the aching moments when I wanted to talk to my brother, when I needed

Owen to at least answer his damn phone. But although he was here in the world, he wasn't in *my* world. He lived in Colorado, but I use the word "live" lightly. He had a home there, but he owned an adventure company and traveled all over the world finding new and frightening ways to keep the adrenaline pumping. He was certified in every kind of rescue, from mountain to sea to fire.

When he did show up, I always had hope that he'd stay, but he never did. Somehow our mother's absence had sent him out into the wilderness, as it had sent me to find one faraway place and root down. Same broken hearts; opposite reactions. I ached for him sometimes as much as I did for Mom, for what we'd all lost. Meanwhile, when we were young, I'd fantasized about Bonny and I becoming sisters — more than Summer Sisters — where we could share a last name. But when that hadn't happened, and I'd realized that Owen was drawn to her more than his own family, resentment had grown. Of course I'd never told either of them how I felt — it was petty and ridiculous. We love whom we love.

I hadn't yet told my brother that I was boarding an airplane to fly across the country to see Bonny with my two bundles of energy in tow, because, like Tim, he would use his powers of persuasion to try to talk me out of it. But his eager missives wouldn't work, because I'd tell him (if he'd answer his phone): there's power in that river, in that long-ago night and in my sisterhood with Bonny. A promise made is a promise kept.

■ ■ ■ ■

LAINEY MCKAY'S RIVER WISH

■ ■ ■ ■

I wish to grow up and be an artist, a
famous artist.

CHAPTER 9
BONNY BLANKENSHIP

The tropical storm warning had been on every TV station, but then the weather had inched its way north. Still the rain fell and gathered itself too quickly to be absorbed by the roadway's drains and the earth's soil. The roads were shallow rivers, but my SUV cut through the water as surely as a boat. The windshield wipers slapped frantically. Palmetto trees bent toward the ground while branches broke loose and skittered along Highway 17 like something alive and running. The bridges over the marshland blurred into the landscape, and it felt like I was part of it all — the wind, the rain and the rising tide.

I turned off the radio and allowed rainfall to be the music. My heart rate slowed as I drew closer and closer to Watersend. I would absorb myself in painting and furniture and fixtures. I'd spend time with Lainey and Piper. I'd disappear into the remaking of a house while I waited to discover how to remake my life, while I waited for clarity, for the call from Emory (they were waiting on the verdict and holding the job for me, they'd told me) or for a solution to problems that seemed insurmountable.

The panic had grown worse since Mr. Rohr's death. Every time the phone rang, every time the e-mail dinged, heat flashed through me like electricity. I'd learned to breathe, to move my attention to something else. The thought of being in the river house saved me from descending into the labyrinth of that horrible night where there was nothing but dead ends, and my fatal mistake waited like the mythical Minotaur around every corner.

I'd made a notebook with a list of things that needed to be fixed or painted or caulked or replaced in the house. And with each duty crossed off, I knew I would feel a little more in control, a little more like life could be handled even when of course it couldn't.

Ten miles from Watersend, an ambulance roared behind me with its lights flashing. With the siren's wail, the world shriveled to the size of my car, the red lights bouncing off the side mirrors and streaking into my backseat through the rear window. The ambulance was in my car, in my throat, in my head. I couldn't think. I couldn't drive. I forgot what to do. A great horn blew and a calm voice inside of me whispered, *Pull over. Now.*

I jerked the car to the side of the road and slammed on my brakes. The wheels skidded into the soft mud of the road's shoulder and my head lurched forward. The ambulance passed, but the sound and the fear remained, echoing like a war cry inside my chest. My heart beat high and into my throat. I couldn't take a full breath, and my head floated. Gasping for air, I opened the car door. I bent over my knees.

Deep breaths. I'd learned this. Breathe in for four. Hold for two. Out for six. Slow. Slow. Wrap my arms around myself. Mantra: *All is well. I am safe.*

Even as I knew what was happening — a panic attack — I couldn't make it disappear. Knowing what it is doesn't cure it. Slowly, and I didn't know how long it took, I gained some control of my breathing and my heart. I closed the car door, leaned my head on the car's headrest and allowed the tears to rise. This had to stop. I would never be able to be a doctor again, no matter the verdict, if I couldn't stand the sight or sound of an ambulance or phone or bell.

My mouth felt parched, but the water bottle next to me had been drained miles back. I was only a few miles away from the place where I could sit on the dock and watch the river, find my breath again.

Pulling into town, I drove to the Watersend sign, weathered and wooden with carved letters that stated, *Welcome to Watersend, South Carolina,* and parked. The ubiquitous South Carolina flag symbol — a palmetto tree and a crescent moon — was carved into the wood, dark blue and fading in places.

I stepped out of the car and walked to the sign. The unrelenting rain smattered against my glasses, so the world showed dimpled and misty. Rain pecked at my bare skin and slithered down my shirt. I touched the sign in the same ritual my parents had done when they left each summer, believing it meant they would be back soon. An omen. A touchstone. The wood was warm and wet, softened by years of sun and weather and generations of families stopping their cars at the bend in the road to rub their hands across its edge.

With that touch, I was thirteen years old again, on the cusp of all the good things in the world, all the possibility and wonder and million chances for happiness. Blue Popsicle juice stained my cheeks and sand was crusted on my hands and the soles of my feet. My skin was prickly and tender with sunburn while I sat around a bonfire and whispered secrets with my Summer Sister, Lainey.

CHAPTER 10
BONNY BLANKENSHIP

Landscape was memory or maybe memory was landscape. This was what I thought as I drove along the short road to the old house.

Our three childhood summers in Waters-end had been more than sun-soaked ellipses between school years, more than vacation. Those days held the making of me. Summers in the river house had cracked me open. I'd fallen in love for the first time; I'd found my first best friend. I'd come to love books as something more than words. I'd seen my parents as people instead of just parents. For the first time, I'd deeply felt the pain and irreversible despair of losing someone.

So, there I was again: *the river house.*

The rain spit its last as I parked in front of it. I'd spent my early summers inside this marsh-soaked seascape, in this rambling old river house. I was eleven years old when we'd come here for the first time. Mom and

Dad had inherited some family money when Granny passed. It hadn't been enough money to allow them to quit their jobs as a second-grade teacher and an advertising exec, but enough to buy a small house where Dad could come from Atlanta to fish, net shrimp and drive his little johnboat; where Mom could read her paperbacks on the porch and invite her friends to hang out; where my little brother and I could run free and safe during the stifling days of high summer. It had been an escape from the city in a town no one had yet discovered.

So much time had passed and all the while the old river house had stood watch over an ever-changing marsh, which was held together by sand and tidal mud. The same front porch, where we used to play checkers, still spread across the front and then bent around the left side. Rocking chairs painted white and blue were scattered in little clusters across the warped planking like gossiping old ladies. The front door was the same color my parents had painted it all those years ago. Haint blue. It was a white one-story beach cottage with a high-pitched roof. It spread both wide and deep, the back end stretching as if reaching, as we all did, for the river. The windows were open to every view, unblinking.

This sanctuary was a living heartbeat between the river behind it and the ocean across the street, a halfway point. It wasn't *just* wood and shutters and doors and porches. It had its own thoughts and memories, as if we shared something whispered and secret. It remembered me just as I remembered it; I was sure.

Lainey had always told me that houses breathed just as we do, that they held secrets and energy and molded themselves around their owners. Or was it that their owners molded themselves around the house? I couldn't remember.

While I stared at the house from inside my car, Piper opened the front door and came onto the porch with her hands on her hips like an irate homeowner waiting on a late delivery. I'd imagined her seeing Sea La Vie and loving it as I once had as a child. I'd imagined her eyes lighting up at the way the house seemed to reach for the river and open its front door and windows. "Mom," she'd said in my musings. "It's so perfect."

Yeah, right.

I eased the car down the driveway of gravel and stone to the garage. To my surprise, as I shifted the gear into park and stepped out of the car, Piper came to me. To me! I didn't have to go to her. And she

112

hugged me. "Hey, Mom."

"Oh, Piper. You look so lovely." Her chestnut-colored hair was nature-painted with sun-blond strands, and her ponytail fell loose over one shoulder.

"Oh, right, Mom. Whatever."

"God, it's humid today," I said as the last of the cool air from the car's air conditioner faded away. "That rainstorm makes everything feel like a sauna."

"Mom, it's June. Yes, it's hot. I think it will be for a while."

I hugged her again, and this time I held her until she let go.

"Help me carry in my luggage?" I asked.

"Sure thing."

Together we carried in my suitcases and then faced each other in the kitchen. "We can empty the rest of the car later." I touched her cheek. "Beautiful you," I said. "I'm so glad you're here."

"I had a choice?" She smiled but suppressed it quickly to add an eye roll. She lifted a Coke bottle, sweating in the heat of the kitchen, and chugged it like water. I ran my hand along the worn table, a long farmhouse table, made from reclaimed wood, which I'd found at an antique mart. The aroma of fresh paint and oiled wood seeped into the wet air. Everything here was

113

new and old at the same time.

"So, you've been here two whole days already. What do you think of the town?" I asked. "Do you just love it?" Hope, it springs eternal or something like that.

"It's okay." Piper shrugged. "I mean, all I did was drag that ridiculous cart into town to grocery shop. I've cleaned up and made the beds. You know, all the things on your infernal list. It's not like I've had any fun or anything."

"Have you seen the beach yet? Or gone to the dock?" I glanced out the kitchen window into the backyard. There it was — the blue-gray ribbon of river that haunted my memories and ran through my dreams.

"I went to the dock. That little metal boat." She pointed in the general direction. "Is that ours?"

"Yup."

"It's kind of a mess."

"It works," I said. "We just need to clean it."

"And when you say 'we' I bet you mean me. I bet that's part of my job, too. Clean scum. And the doors that don't close? And the broken spindles on the porch? And the missing cedar shakes and . . ."

"Yes," I said. "We will save it all."

"You mean fix, right?"

"I mean both." I took Piper's face between my hands. "I mean both." I kissed her forehead.

She shrugged away from me and then reached for the refrigerator door, opening it. "Voila."

There it was — four shelves labeled and organized like a photo shoot for a Martha Stewart exhibit. Small pieces of paper were each inside a Baggie taped to each shelf: *Mom and Piper, Lainey, Kids* and then *Condiments.*

"Piper. It's perfect."

"Right-o, Mom. And p.s., your phone is blowing up over there." Her lips pressed close together and turned downward. "And *who* is Owen?"

A beat or two passed before I could answer. I'd turned off the sound, but the screen was lighting up with his name. "An old friend," I said and concentrated on moving slowly. My hands shook, and I took two steps to the kitchen table and my phone.

I hadn't spoken to Owen since the "incident." I couldn't. He'd tried to contact me numerous times over the past weeks, again and again he'd tried, but whenever I thought of hearing his voice, I felt sick with panic, the night coming back to me as a living nightmare.

"An old friend?" Piper crinkled her little forehead like she did when she was confused with her homework. *An integer? A chromosome? A mitochondrion?*

"Yes." I turned off the phone. "Obviously I don't want to talk."

"I'm sure," she said.

"Let's take a look at our little palace. I'm so proud of you for getting everything ready." My voice sounded canned, like a voice-mail greeting at a lawyer's office. *Leave a message at the beep. I'm so proud of you.*

That was the problem with Owen, or just his name — it threw me off balance, like a sickness or a shot of tequila.

Together Piper and I went from room to room, and I yanked my thoughts back; they were like a stray puppy jumping around barking, *What does he want? Where is he? Is he okay?*

"I washed all the sheets, in that soap you sent with me, and made the beds." Piper opened the door to the first bedroom and spread her arms wide to show me the room with the all-white linens and comforter. There were two bedside tables with silver lamps and little white milk glass vases with a single peony in each: simple beauty. We went through each room as she described what she'd done to get it ready.

"When do Lainey and the kids get here?" she asked.

"Tomorrow."

"If this is all you need until they show up to further ruin my life . . . I'm going to the beach. Finally."

"Ruin your life?" I bit back my internal comment. *You seem to be doing that just fine on your own.* Instead I smiled because that was what I did when the alternative meant another awful confrontation. "Before the beach, why don't we run into town and eat lunch?"

"Well," Piper said, "there's the café right next to the market. But I've been there already."

"Really?" I smiled at her. "Sounds like you've got it all figured out in only two days."

"Mom. Seriously? The town is about as big as my hand. Not much to figure out."

"Well, then let's go. Beach, river and unpacking after we eat. Okay?"

Piper hesitated in that way that let me know she had something to say but just wasn't sure how to say it. "Where's Dad?" She risked a glance at me. "I mean . . . is he okay?"

"I don't know, sweetheart. I don't know.

But I know he'd love to hear from you."

"This is weird. You know that, right?"

"I know."

"There's no way, no matter what photos you bring here" — she gestured with black-polished fingernails, to the wall where I'd framed and hung pictures of us from various stages of life — "or what candles or what linens, that this will ever feel like home."

"We won't be here long, sweetie. I have to sell it soon. I'm just doing the best I can to make it feel as much like home as possible for now."

"And you left Gus at home. How mean is that? Couldn't you have at least brought him?"

"Dad would have come to take him back. I had to leave Gus. You know that." I reached into my bag and pulled out a leather-bound folder I'd been carrying around like a talisman. "Here's our to-dos."

She glanced down and then opened the binder. "Paint the sitting room floorboards white. Replace rotten cedar shakes. Replace porch spindles. Most definitely fun, Mom. The best ever." She read on. "Replace doorknobs. Are you kidding?"

"No. I found some cut-glass ones at the antique show and . . ."

"God, Mom. This is ridiculous." She rolled her eyes but her empty stomach won her over. "Gimme twenty minutes. I'm going to shower and change," she said. "Then we can go to lunch. I guess."

"Perfect."

In my bedroom I plopped onto the bed and pulled out my phone, turned it back on. I leaned against the simple pine headboard and, along with a bone-weary fatigue, I felt the house embrace me.

"Do you remember us, too?" I whispered to the empty room. Sitting there, about to call Owen, I knew it did.

CHAPTER 11
BONNY MORELAND
ELEVEN YEARS OLD

June 1976

It had all been done in secret, whispers behind closed doors because they'd wanted to surprise us. I was eleven years old so I had everything figured out. I was unruly and made of bent twigs, tripping over both myself and also everything else. My five-year-old brother, Percy, was all adorable, constantly amazed and alert to changes around him.

The air conditioner in the woody station wagon was broken and although the windows were open, the breeze only circulated the muggy air. Percy lay on my lap in the backseat and I tried not to move. Mom was in the front seat, singing show tunes one after the other, and Dad was in such a good mood that he didn't even ask her to stop.

"What do you think it is?" Percy asked, wiggling his fingers through mine, winding and unwinding.

"Obviously they rented a house for the summer," I said. "The car is full of beach toys and stuff."

"Oh," he said and curled on his side, his eyes already closing as the lull of the car sent him to sleep.

I held on to his hand and wished I could rest. Instead I just felt carsick, a low, nagging feeling that only sleep could cure. I closed my eyes, wishing I could read my Nancy Drew book without throwing up. It would wait. If we really were going to the beach, as I'd confidently told Percy, I could read all day every day.

The car rocked and Mom and Dad whispered and sometimes Mom laughed with a simple sound that made the world seem rounder and softer. I must have drifted off because I awoke to the lurch of the stopping car. Startled, I sat up.

Dad had pulled the car over and stepped out into a patch of grass on the side of the road.

"What's wrong?" I asked. Blurry with sleep and the slight sway of nausea, I opened the car door to get out, too. Maybe this was it. The Big Surprise.

"Nothing's wrong, Bee," my mom said. "Nothing at all." That was what she called me: Bee for Bonny Bee.

With the door open, I swung my feet onto the soft grass. Dad's back was to me as he stood in front of a wooden sign. *Welcome to Watersend.* He ran his hand across the top edge of it. We'd never been here; I'd never seen this sign, and my heart did a quick step, just like I was scared, but I wasn't. I was happy. This was a new something in the world. But I didn't know yet what. There was an expectation like I was at the edge of a cliff and I would soon be able to fly.

Dad turned then and saw me, and he smiled. "Welcome to Watersend."

"What is Watersend?" I asked, stretching, inhaling fresh, wet air.

"A town. Our town," he said.

"Ours?"

"Yes." He sauntered over and picked me up and swung me around in a circle with his strong arms under mine. The air felt different, unlike the beaches we'd visited before. And I gulped it like water. It was ours, Dad said. *Ours. Belonging to us.*

Back in the car, Percy and I watched the town breeze by our open windows. Cedar shake houses. Green lawns and water of every shade — blue, gray, greenish, sparkling, dark and clear — everywhere water twisted past, disappeared and then surprised us around another corner. This town seemed an island without a bridge. I was Peter Pan, or maybe Wendy. I was Jim Hawkins on Treasure Island. I was Lucy in Narnia. All adventure was mine. We'd left Atlanta only four hours before, in the late morning, and arrived in the middle of the day, but it still felt like a new day, another world.

The car made a slow turn onto a side street and stopped in front of a sprawling white house. An orange moving van was parked out front, its back end open. Inside was a puzzle of furniture and lamps and boxes.

Dad and Mom climbed out of the car and stood next to each other, facing the house. They linked arms. They didn't usually link arms, and this was an anomaly I didn't really understand, but I was willing to suspend my judgment to see what needed to be seen. So *this* was the Big Surprise?

Percy and I fell out of the car — well, he fell out of the car and I lifted him and propped him on my hip. We stood next to Mom and Dad.

"What's going on?" I asked.

They unlinked their arms and turned to us. Dad took Percy from me and shimmied him onto his shoulders.

"This," Dad said in his loud proclaiming voice, the kind he used when he had a surprise or great news. "This is ours. Welcome to Sea La Vie, our new beach house."

"There's no beach," Percy said. "Just that river there." He pointed behind the house to where a sliver of blue water ran like a ribbon. Tall grasses lined the banks, swaying like someone was running their hands through them.

"Yes, that is the river, son. Where we will keep our boat and go fishing and shrimping and digging up oysters. So yes, let's call it our river house." He gestured across the street. "That," he said, "is the beach, just one block thataway, up and over those dunes. Just a little path between us and wide open beach."

"I'm confused," I said.

Mom placed her hands on my shoulders. "This is *our* new house."

I looked at the house again and with new eyes. We weren't staying here for a week and running through its rooms seeking treasure (a game we played at beach rentals). That U-Haul — it was full of *our* stuff for *this* house.

"We're moving here?" I didn't know how to feel about that yet. It was all too new, too soaked with possibility.

Mom laughed, which she didn't do very much or very well, so I laughed, too.

"No, it's our summer place, silly. Our home away from home."

It's a different thing to know something is yours when only a moment ago you didn't know it existed at all. Percy and I, as if on cue, ran toward the house with the kind of glee we saved for rare snow days or Christmas morning.

The house was empty that day. We ran from room to room, calling out each other's names and proclaiming, "This is so cool. So cool. So cool."

By the time we came back outside, Mom and Dad were walking toward a car that had just parked next to ours. A family poured out of the car like a little replica of our family, except the boy was older than the girl. The boy was drowsy like he'd just fallen out of bed. His brown curls couldn't decide which way to go and his smile was aimed directly at me, all lopsided like he knew a secret he wanted to tell. My stomach did a little flip like I'd come down too fast off the seesaw, and I avoided his gaze. The little girl was blond and dressed for a birthday party or church in her sundress, her pigtails so tight they must have been painful. I smiled at her, ready for a friend. I wore a little wrinkled sundress covered in white and yellow daisies — it was my favorite but suddenly felt babyish and silly.

Using his proclamation voice again, Dad took my hand. "The surprises aren't over yet," he said.

Percy jumped over and over, twisting like a five-year-old cyclone. "It's the best house ever, Dad. Ever. There are all these little places and the floors are wood and the fireplace is huge. I can fit inside it . . ."

Dad held his fingers to his lips, which meant shush.

"I know, son. It's perfect. But I want you to come here and meet the McKays. This is Clara and Bob, and their kids . . ." He faltered.

Mrs. McKay spoke. "This is Owen; he's thirteen. And this is our daughter, Lainey. She's eleven."

They appeared so exotic, dressed as if they were going to a party, and yet they'd climbed out of a station wagon just like we had. The dad, Bob, looked like Burt Reynolds in that movie where he stole a car.

Then there was the mom, Clara. She was like a glitzy model from a magazine. Her flowered sundress matched her daughter's, and her platinum hair was piled high in a ponytail. Her large round sunglasses covered half her face and her scarlet-painted lips were smiling in that same way as her son, secretive and amused. Who on earth was this family and why were they parked in our front yard when I wanted to scream and yell and do cartwheels because we had a river house and it was all ours? I couldn't act like that in front of glamorous strangers.

I wanted to hug Mom and Dad, go crazy with happiness. Instead I tried not to stare at the drowsy, rumpled boy who made me feel self-conscious and nervous. They needed to hurry along wherever they were headed — probably a perfect house that should also be in a magazine.

Mom sprang forward and hugged the woman so tightly that I wished she hugged me that way. "Isn't this all so exciting? Just like the old days when we would road-trip together. Clara, I'm so happy you're here."

Dad did this weird half handshake, half hug with the Burt Reynolds lookalike. "Welcome."

Mrs. McKay lifted her sunglasses and stared at the U-Haul. She swished her hand, with its bright red fingernails, through the air as if she were swimming. "Looks like we have our work set out for us."

Nothing was making sense. Did they own the house, too?

Dad lifted Percy, who had started to make his way to the backyard, the one place we hadn't yet explored.

"This is our son, Percy." Dad threw him in the air and then caught him. "And our daughter, Bonny." He ruffled my already tangled hair. I swatted his hand away.

"Kids, say hello to the McKay family. They're our best friends from college and they're here to help us unpack and to stay for a while."

Mrs. McKay lurched toward the house in tiny high heels, almost like the plastic ones my Barbie doll wore. When she stepped onto the porch, she swayed the littlest bit, like there was a strong wind coming from inside. She peeked over her shoulder as if posing for a photograph. "This is dreamy. Very, very dreamy."

We all watched her like it was a TV show and she was the star. Maybe she was. Or would be. *Me,* Clara McKay seemed to say. *Look at me.* And we did.

CHAPTER 12
BONNY BLANKENSHIP

I looked at my phone. Six missed calls. Owen hadn't ever called that many times in a row. I slid my thumb to voice mail and clicked, but he hadn't left a message.

Text messages. I checked those. One.

Call me.

I texted back. I can't talk right now.

Find a way.

I slipped into the bathroom and shut the door. I was behind two closed doors, and still I knew the house well enough to know that voices traveled through secret passages — the floorboards or a vent or a crack in the walls. I'd covered the old drywall with clapboard bleached oak, which was beautiful, but definitely not soundproof.

All through childhood I'd heard things I wasn't supposed to hear, little snippets disconnected from the context, severed from the sentences that came before or after, and I'd always been left to guess what the adults really meant.

Owen answered on the first ring. "Hey, you," he said.

I fell into his voice. It was a surrendering, like exhaling, like falling asleep when you thought you might not. But I hid this from him and asked right off, "Are you okay?"

"I am. Are you?" he asked with a laugh.

"I'm in the house with Piper and . . ."

"That's why I'm calling. What *house* are you in?"

"Watersend."

"That's what I was afraid of," he said with an exaggerated exhale. "You're there with Piper?"

"Yes. How did you find out?"

"Lainey."

"You've talked to Lainey?" I asked.

"Well, not really talked. She e-mailed me and she said you might be going back . . . but I haven't checked in with her again."

"Of course you didn't. Why would you keep in touch with her or . . ." I stopped. This was the rabbit hole I'd promised myself I would never go down again — where I battered us both with past mistakes, tried to solve them, pushed and prodded and attempted with sheer force of will to make things come out the way I wanted them to come out, to change what had

130

already happened. I bit my tongue and tasted the metallic regret.

"I miss you," he said.

"Owen . . ." I closed my eyes. "I know that's not why you called."

"I just wanted you to know. And I've been trying to call you. You never came back to check on me after the surgery and every time I asked for you, they said you were off that day. I thought you'd at least . . ."

"Things really fell apart after that night, and I'm not working right now. I'm on sabbatical."

"You have to tell me what's happening, Bonny. I have no idea what's going on. Lainey wrote that you were going back to the river house, but that's all she said. Are you ticked off that I didn't tell you I was in town?"

"You mean, am I mad I discovered you were in Charleston when you rolled in on a stretcher? No, that's not it."

"I didn't tell you because you told me not to contact you anymore. You told me to stay away. And I was doing what you asked."

"Kite boarding a few miles from my house is staying away?"

"It was a competition. It could have been anywhere. I've done what you asked . . ."

"That's not it."

"Then what is it?"

"It's what happened that night. Owen, it's a mistake that cost a life and a job I desperately wanted." I stopped and slid to the tile floor in the bathroom, my knees drawn in a tented V where I could rest my forehead.

"I don't understand."

"I can't talk to you about this. I just can't. I'm here to try and gain my footing again. To save my own life."

"Okay. But you can't go running back there to that old river house. You have to tell me what happened. Right now you have to tell me if it had anything to do with *me.*"

"It wasn't you. Or maybe it was, but it wasn't your fault. I made a medical error, Owen. I gave another patient the same pain med I gave you, but it wasn't . . . right. The dosage might have been off and he'd already had some and . . ." The electric panic started to bloom under my chest and I closed my eyes, took in a long breath. "I can't talk about this. Not now. Not with you."

"Bonny, let me come to Watersend. I can be there by tomorrow."

"Please don't. I'm here with my daughter and you are the last person I need to see."

"Don't stay there, Bee. Don't stay in Watersend. You can't go backward like that.

It's not a good place for you or your daughter."

"I'm doing everything I know to do to save myself, Owen. Everything. And part of that is letting go of you. Of us."

"The place where my mother found herself in jail and then disappeared? Bonny. You could go anywhere, literally anywhere else. That is *not* the place for letting go."

"It is for me. You can run to the wilderness, or another country, or an ashram or an island, but I can't settle into an old house?"

"I just don't want you to make things worse. You've said a million times you don't understand why I am the way I am. Part of that reason is because of what happened there. What we lost there . . ."

"But there was also goodness and simple beauty. And I'm here for that."

"There are other ways to build a new life. You don't have to chase an old one." His voice changed, the softness and need fading.

"Owen, this is too hard for me. I have got to go."

"I love you, Bee. I miss you all the time."

He was the only one who called me Bee now. A secret language. A single-word tell-me-everything evoker. I had my defenses, the phrases I wanted to shout at him. *If you loved me, you wouldn't have disappeared when I needed you the most. If you loved me you would have left that wandering life for me . . . if, if, if . . .*

And that was where I stopped because somehow I'd always believed that if he loved me he would sacrifice his chosen life to be with me. It was a wrongheaded belief. And absolutely right. It was everything all at once.

Silence was like the rain I'd driven there in, the slip-slap of it drowning out all thought until the ambulance had roared past.

"I have to go," I said.

And then I hung up without waiting to hear his good-bye, with an echo of the questions I'd wanted to ask: *Where are you? Will you come here if I ask?*

As a child in the river with his sister, I'd thought that it might be cheating to make two wishes, but there were only two things I'd wanted then, two things I'd thought I'd ever want: Owen and being a doctor. Of course my wishes would be different now, if I believed in wishes at all.

CHAPTER 13
PIPER BLANKENSHIP

Mimi stood on a ladder, shelving a handful of hardcover books in the "Local History" section, when the jingle of the door announced our arrival and she turned. Her face broke into a huge smile, and I almost wanted to run under the ladder in case her happiness made her fall.

"Oh, Bonny Moreland. Welcome back," she said. "And hello there, Piper."

She took a step down and headed toward us, and she hugged my mom, who looked stunned and frozen with her arms by her sides as hard and straight as branches.

"Ms. Mimi," my mom said. "You're still here." And then Mom seemed to regain the use of her body and she hugged Mimi back.

"You're surprised?" Mimi asked with a laugh.

"No . . . I mean, yes. I guess I am."

"Well, look, you're here now. I met your lovely daughter yesterday so I knew I'd see you eventually. When I first saw her all I could think about was your little Nancy Drew Club. She looks so much like you."

People often coo that I look like Mom, but I don't. She's prettier even though she's older. She has such thick brown hair, all scattered with blond streaks like she colors it even though she doesn't. Her round, dark blue, almost purple eyes look like they've been painted on, and I'm glad I have the same ones. She has this way, this kind of quiet way, of not drawing attention to herself in a crowd, and yet she will always be the one you remember when you leave.

"You met?" Mom asked me.

"I meant to tell you," I said. "But we just kept talking about other things. But Mimi said she remembered you and Lainey — the Summer Sisters."

"Summer Sisters," Mom said with a bit of sadness caught in her voice. "I thought I was the only one who remembered that."

"Oh, I don't think you're the only one." Mimi rubbed her hands together in a swish-swish movement as if wiping dirt from her palms.

"The store looks great," Mom said. "I love how the books go to the ceiling now." She pointed at the rolling ladder attached to a metal track above. "Is this the same space?"

"Yes, same space, but in between your childhood and now, it was a couple other things before it was a bookshop again. I lost the store and started it back about two years ago."

"Thank goodness you reopened," Mom said. "How did that happen?"

"A story for another time," Mimi said. "But it involves a movie producer, a love story and a little bit of magic."

"Wait. Yes. I heard about that," Mom said. "Some movie was both filmed and premiered here a couple years ago. Some hotshot from California fell in love with a local girl or something."

"Yep. Ella and Blake. They still live here, and they helped me reopen the store. So, let's do our best to keep it open." She headed toward the counter. "What can I get for you today? Is there something you're looking for?"

"No. I always trust your recommendations." Mom seemed to have a secret language with Mimi, as if they both knew something I didn't.

"How about a good mother/daughter story?" Mimi nodded at me.

Then I remembered something Mom had told me once, a long time ago. We'd been at the library in Charleston and she told me about a woman who had known how to give her customers books that hinted at something they needed to know.

"Sure," Mom said. "Sounds great." She reached over and pulled me into a one-arm hug.

"Hold on," Mimi said. "I'll be right back."

We waited as Mimi roamed in search of the perfect title. I picked up books and bookmarks and then placed them back down. Then I lifted a leather journal, bound together with a string and clasped shut with a green sea glass pendant. "Mom. Look at this."

"It's gorgeous," she said. "Want it?"

"I do."

"That's what I . . ." Mom started to tell me something and then brushed her hand through the air like she'd already forgotten what it was. "I just can't help but think of any blank notebook as a promise of adventure."

"All right, then," I said as Mimi returned.

"Here you go." Mimi extended a paperback with a bright cover showing a woman in caricature with oversized sunglasses. "Great book for both of you. It's fun."

"Well, I definitely need fun," I said.

Mom came to my side and laughed. "Maybe that's exactly what you don't need."

And see? Right there was why Mom was such a pain in the ass. There was no reason for her to say that and embarrass me when everything was just fine. Now Mimi knew that I'd had *too* much fun. My face turned red just like it did when a teacher called my name or Ryan told me that my outfit looked slutty.

Mom saw this because she sees everything, and she cringed. "Bad joke."

I was set to leave just as the bell jingled over the front door, and we all turned to see a woman enter. I barely noticed her beyond the obvious — she was tall and wore a tennis outfit, one of those cutesy pastel skirts and a tight athletic top. Her brassy blond hair was pulled back into a ponytail and she wore a white visor and sunglasses.

Mimi toddled over to the woman and greeted her, but the woman stared at Mom.

"Bonny?" she asked out loud. She'd taken off her sunglasses and was glancing between Mom and me, taking us in.

"Yes."

"Bonny Moreland?"

"Well, Blankenship now, but yes . . . Do I know you?"

"You did." The woman stepped forward. She seemed to be my mom's age but better preserved, if that was the polite way to say it. In other words, she'd had some work done, and not good work at that. Her lips were too big and slightly lopsided. Her forehead was smooth but lifted high so her eyes seemed too large and stunned. "I'm Margaret Edgars. We played together as kids in the summer."

Mom does well under pressure — otherwise she wouldn't have made it a month in the emergency room — but she just stood there. Finally she said, "It was all so long ago."

"When did you get to town?" Margaret asked.

"Just now, an hour ago . . ."

"Well, it's really good to see you."

Mom tried to laugh but it didn't sound right at all. "How do you remember me? I can hardly remember last week."

"Oh . . ." The woman looked at Mimi as if she might help. "I saw you on TV. That's all."

Poor Mom, it was bad enough that she might lose her job, but her biggest mistake had ended up on the news. At least my biggest mistakes stayed private, or on Facebook only.

"TV." Mom didn't ask this but stated it. "Fantastic."

The woman laughed. "It's nice to have

you back in town. Let's all try and get the old summer crowd together. Who was your little best friend?" The woman closed her eyes. "Elaine?"

"Lainey," I said. "She's a famous artist now." I didn't know why I felt I needed to explain, but I wanted to shift the conversation somehow away from Mom.

"Oh, I bet she is," the woman said. "Well, I have a million errands. I just needed to grab a book for my little niece. I hope to see you around." She walked toward the back of the store and Mom took a couple tentative steps to the checkout counter to buy my journal and the book Mimi gave us, which now I wanted to throw on the front table so we could just leave.

"God, I was hoping I wouldn't be recognized here," Mom said. "So much for that." Embarrassment crawled all over her like a rash.

"TV?" Mimi asked. "You were on TV?"

I felt the shudder of shame for my mom.

"I'm an ER doctor in Charleston," Mom said. "And there was an accident . . . it's being investigated . . . and it's been on TV." This was the shortest explanation Mom had. I'd heard her give it before. If I were her I'd be shouting, *I have saved a gazillion people and I didn't do it on purpose and leave*

141

me the hell alone. But not Mom. She just took it.

"Oh, Bonny," Mimi said. "This must be a terrible time for you."

"It is," Mom said. "All I've ever meant to do, or wanted to do, was save lives."

"Ah." Mimi glanced upward as if trying to find something. "What was it our beloved Flannery O'Connor used to say? Oh, yes. 'The life you save may be your own.' "

As usual, I blurted before thinking. "It's all bullshit. Mom is the best doctor in the world."

Mimi glanced at me and with a smile said, "Language."

"Sorry." I cringed, suddenly ashamed of the words both inside my head and coming out of my mouth. "It's just infuriating."

Mom deflected. "I don't remember Margaret at all. Isn't that awful?"

"She was one of the little girls you played with back in those days. Her daddy was the mayor. Her mom was the real pretty one who always had all the parties during the summer."

Mom lifted her eyebrows and made that aha sound she sometimes does. "Oh, the rich, pretty girl with blond hair and a pony. A pony!" Mom shook her head. "And a huge backyard with a white picket fence."

Mom laughed and I felt the relief.

We chatted a little more before exiting into the blazing heat. We walked in silence until she passed me and I called out, "Mom!"

She stopped on the sidewalk and turned to me because she had roamed past me in some kind of daze. "What?"

"Wake up. The café is right here. You missed it."

Inside, we sat at the table under a fan. The little café must not have been redecorated in a hundred years or more. It was like something in one of those old movies. Booths with red shiny material on the seats, tablecloths decorated with a tiny flower print and covered in some kind of oily coating. The salt and pepper shakers had tiny silver tops that looked like bullets. The menu was printed on a trifold piece of paper, stained and crinkled. "So what is all of this about the Nancy Drew Club?" I asked.

"The Nancy Drew Club," Mom repeated. "We didn't call ourselves that. We called it the Girl Detectives Club. But yes, Nancy Drew inspired it. Back then, we didn't have the Kardashians."

I did laugh at that. "I thought you were the Summer Sisters. Vowed to be there for each other forever. Girl Power and all that."

"We were both. All of the above." She lifted the menu to glance at it and then back at me. "Anyway, we would run around town, find all these little mysteries and try to solve them. We had a notebook and we wrote about everything we saw. We nosed our way into things that weren't any of our business and giggled and believed we were true snooping detectives." She shook her head. "We had no idea that adults kept things secret for a reason."

"Not just adults, Mom."

"No, not just adults." She seemed so sad, but then she smiled at me. "I wonder where that notebook is. I hadn't thought of it at all until it was time to pack to move. Maybe Lainey has it. It would be fun to have it here and show you."

"I can't believe Mimi remembers so much about you," I said.

"Well, we practically lived in her bookstore for three summers." Mom's face relaxed, which I hadn't seen it do in weeks. "She always gave us the exact right book. And they weren't just books to tick off a summer reading list — they were books *meant* for us. *Little Women, Pippi Longstocking, Little House on the Prairie.* Books that took us out of our small, small world and into larger ones, adventurous ones, where little girls could carve out their own fate. Books where girls weren't just cute and nice, but maybe a little too loud, a little too much. Mimi offers you what you need, not what you want."

It was good to see Mom animated and talkative, and for the first time since "the mistake," I felt some hope for her. She fanned out her menu, and I quickly glanced at my phone. I'd mastered the art of peering at the phone without being noticed. Or so I thought.

"Sweetie," Mom said, "I'm sure whatever that is, it can wait."

"Okay."

"What's wrong?" she asked, and I hated and loved that she could read my hurt expression so quickly, so easily.

"It's Ryan," I said. "He's . . ." I couldn't say it; the truth was too much out loud. Mom had met him. We'd dated for almost a year and I'd brought him home one fall break. But I didn't need to finish the sentence for her to know.

"Oh, sweetie. I know it hurts. I know . . ."

Just then, the front door opened and a blast of hot air rushed in. This town sure was small. Fletch, the boy from the Market, saw me first. He strode toward us and waved even though we were right in front of him. It was an endearing nervous gesture, which made me grin. "Hi, Fletch."

"Hey!" He stood at the table and glanced between Mom and me. He carried a basket of tomatoes under his arm. Those damn eyes were killing me. "How's it going?"

"It's going," I said and placed my phone upside down on the table. "This is my mom. Mom, this is Fletch. His parents own the Market next door."

"Hello," Mom said. "So lovely to meet you."

"Fletch helped me that first day when you sent me on that Sisyphus errand to get groceries."

He laughed. "Nothing like a good mythology reference."

I wanted to crawl under the table and pull the oily tablecloth over my head. Who talks about mythology in the middle of a casual conversation? He took a step back and then forward, trying to decide where to stand. "It's true," he said. "That's why we have a market. Just like poor Sisyphus pushing the boulder up the mountain, only to have it roll down again, for all eternity, you finish shopping only to start again."

"That market wasn't here when I was young." Mom smiled at Fletch.

"I think it was a hardware store, or so I'm told." He shrugged and then shifted the basket under his arm.

"Is your family from here?" Mom asked.

"Mom." I flipped over my menu. "Stop interviewing him." I peered up at Fletch.

"No worries," he said. "This is what it's like to live in a small town." He addressed Mom. "We moved here about ten years ago so Mom and Dad could open the store."

"I bet you love it here," she said. "It's such a beautiful place to live."

"It is," he said. "And now I'm off for deliveries. It was nice to meet you, ma'am."

The waitress approached to take our order and greeted Fletch. He handed her the basket of tomatoes. "For Beatrice," he said. "She had a tomato emergency in the kitchen." He moved a step backward as if to leave and then threw me a parting gift. "See you soon, I hope."

I twisted my hair behind my neck and wrapped a rubber band from my wrist around the bunched tangles. "Oh, I'll be around. Where else would I be? I'm trapped here all summer."

Mom waited until he was gone and we'd ordered and then she said, "What a nice kid. The most beautiful eyes I've ever seen."

"Yes, he seems nice so far. It's not like I know him."

"And you're trapped?"

"Yes. Totally trapped. Mom, come on. I couldn't leave if I wanted to. That's the definition of trapped."

"Do you want to leave?"

"Not sure. I'll let you know when I decide."

"It's going to be okay, Piper."

"What's going to be okay?"

"Everything," Mom said.

"Right, Mom. Just run away to an old house and that will fix everything. This wasn't one of your best ideas, you know."

"It might be. Let's give it a chance." Mom took a deep, deep breath like she needed air in her toes and then said, "I need to tell you about Lainey's mom before Lainey gets here tomorrow."

"Because people in town know about it? Is that why you asked if he was from here?"

"No. Because I want *you* to know."

"Okay."

I'd heard hints through the years. I loved Lainey whenever I saw her — a hippie with the slight aroma of incense and oil paint surrounding her, and I'd wondered how she'd finished growing up without a mom. I hadn't seen her since my freshman year in high school when she'd come to visit Mom for a weekend.

"You know she lost her mom, right?"

"Yes. But, I mean, is she dead or did she leave them or what? Nobody's ever told me."

"We don't know. When we were kids, thirteen years old, she left a note that said she was leaving and that was that. They never heard from her again."

"Literally never heard from her? That's impossible in today's world."

"No, it's not. When you want to be gone you can be gone. And remember, it wasn't today's world. It was almost forty years ago."

"What happened?"

Our chicken salad orders arrived with little tomato aspic blobs on the side of the plate wiggling like Jell-O. I poked my fork into it but didn't take a bite yet. Mom pushed her plate aside as if she needed to tell this story without food.

"Ms. Clara was so beautiful, and I adored her. I wanted to be like her. But she was an addict, frantic, always trying to find stillness and never able. I don't know her history, and neither does Lainey, but something terrible must have happened in her childhood. She was diagnosed with anxiety, but it had to have been more than that, and she took Valium. And she drank. A lot."

"Maybe that's why you're so crazy sensitive about me drinking."

Mom smiled, but it was sad. She took a sip of her iced tea. "No. I'm crazy sensitive about your drinking because you're my daughter and I don't like you spending the night in the tank."

I blushed. "Got it. Go ahead."

"It got worse and worse — her drinking and her addiction and her outbursts. She went from manic to quiet. Then she stopped taking care of herself. I remember one night we all went out to dinner at the Crab Pot and she wore her nightgown, saying that everyone would think it was a sundress. She just stopped . . . caring. But then this awful night happened — there was a car wreck that was her fault, and she and her husband got in a terrible, terrible fight. We heard the whole thing. We'd seen and heard the fights before, but this time was the worst and he shouted something at her that no one will ever forget."

"I hate you?" I asked, knowing that might be the worst that could be said to me.

"No. He told her that they would all be better off without her. And that was after he'd threatened to send her to a facility for help. And in 1970-something that meant shock treatments or worse."

"What the hell?"

"Language."

I smiled.

"After he told her that horrible, untrue thing, Ms. Clara wrote a note and left in the early morning while everyone was asleep. She took her clothes and some cash from the jar in the kitchen and that was that."

"God, poor Ms. Clara. Poor Lainey."

"And her brother, Owen."

"Owen is Lainey's brother?" I'd never made this connection before. Now it made sense why his name appeared on her phone.

Mom nodded.

I took a bite of my lunch, and it felt like a piece of Styrofoam had been stuck inside my mouth. I wanted to spit it out, but I swallowed and chugged my Coke. "If someone told me they were better off without me, I would die."

"That's what we think happened."

"Why?"

"Lainey has hired detectives. She's searched and searched. But she's come up empty every time."

"That's terrible," I said.

"Yes, it is." Mom drew her plate forward and stuck a spoon into the salad, but only twirled it around. "When we were kids we used to make a list of all the places Clara might be. All the things that might have happened to her. It's in our Girl Detective notebook. Who was she? Where was she? Another country? The bottom of the sea?"

"That's so awful and sad."

"They were all just guesses and we were kids. It was the year after the Son of Sam, and our minds were crazy with horrid possibilities. Lainey's dad could have sent her away. She could have run off with the man who was fixing the roof — he disappeared at the same time. She could have overdosed, of course, and that was the most likely. But we had better scenarios." Mom trailed off, her ideas gone.

"Now all someone does is push the Find My Friends app and there I am. Or there Ryan is. Or there anyone is."

"Well, we didn't have a find-your-friend app."

I laughed and Mom smiled, but Ms. Clara's despair hung over the table, swirling under the ceiling fan like smoke. "That must have been awful. Is that why Grandma and Granddad never came back here?"

"Yes."

"But you did."

"Not until now." Mom nodded. "I loved it here. I'm giving it a chance."

"A chance," I repeated.

Mom glanced at her food and I reached

into my back pocket and once more scanned my phone. I searched for the one text that might convince me that Ryan missed me and loved me best. And even as I hated myself for caring, I couldn't stop.

Poor Clara, not able to stop taking drugs, and not able to stay. To be told that the world would be better off without you might be the worst I could imagine. I glanced at Mom, but she was staring off across the room, lost in her own story by then, as I was in mine.

CHAPTER 14
LAINEY MCKAY

June 1977
The Second Summer
Watersend, South Carolina

The day my parents told us we would return to Sea La Vie again the next summer, I hung a Donny Osmond calendar on my wall. In Magic Marker, I crossed off every day that passed until we would return to the river house. I added doodles and pictures and noted the dwindling blank days, which was what they were to me — blank. Life began again when we drove those four hours from Atlanta to Watersend, when I saw that long stretch of palmetto trees and live oaks, when I felt the frigid air of the bookshop, when I sat up all night with Bonny scribbling in our notebook, when I sank into the coarse sand and dug my toes in to find the cooler sand, when I jumped into the river and held my breath for as long as I could under the blue-gray water.

For the first few months after returning home the summer before, I'd been afraid that the Moreland family wouldn't invite us back, that my mom had embarrassed all of us enough to prevent another invitation. But I'd heard Dad on the phone talking to Mr. Moreland about plans and dates. Even before he told me, I knew.

I didn't get to see Bonny at all between summers. Our parents went out together, but we lived towns and towns apart. Atlanta wasn't like Watersend, where the name of the city meant you knew the names of the people in it. We lived in Buckhead; they lived in Marietta, which was only thirty minutes by car but might as well have been Alaska for twelve-year-old girls in the seventies. But we talked on the phone. A lot.

My brother, Owen, didn't pay much attention to me that year when I was twelve years old. He had his first real girlfriend, a prissy girl from some rich family on Tuxedo Drive. He spent all of his time there and came home rumpled and stoned. (Yes, I knew what stoned was at twelve. You would, too, if you had Owen for a brother and my mom for a mother.) I was lonely in that angst-ridden, end-of-the-world way that a twelve-year-old girl can be. Everything meant *everything.* Poems. Short stories. Art.

They all made me cry and believe that I was the center of the universe and everything was created on earth just for me or against me. Me. Me.

That was when I found Mod Podge — the glue sealer that dried clear and let me make collages. I covered everything in images — notebooks, dresser tops, frames, boxes, or anything wooden I could get my hands on and Mom wouldn't be upset about. Then I painted on top or added words. Who ever knew that what I did then to quell the anxiety — and what got me in trouble — would turn out to be how I made my living?

Finally, one June morning a year later, we packed for Watersend and I filled a box with my clippings and artwork. I wanted to show Bonny. Before boys gave me butterflies, before I dreamed of someone saving me with a ring and a white horse, I wanted Bonny to love me as much as I loved her.

So I packed the box and I picked out my cutest sundresses and the polka-dotted bikini Bonny's mom bought us all last year so we could match and sing the silly song ("Itsy Bitsy Teenie Weenie Yellow Polka-dot Bikini"). Our station wagon was parked in the driveway and Mom stood leaning against the car, smoking her millionth cigarette of the day. Owen was hanging all over Polly, his ridiculous girlfriend, and they were making out while she cried about him leaving.

"Mom," he called out. "Come on. Just let her come for a week."

"Don't ask again," Mom said. "It's family only."

Mom's voice had that recognizable slur to it. I could gauge our family fun by the way Mom pronounced words. Slurred: a nice quiet trip. Staccato like a tap dance: arguments from here to there, wherever the "here" was to wherever the "there" was. Singsongy: watch out because cursing was next and flung at anyone who crossed her path. I planned my hours on her tone. This should be an okay trip.

I stepped forward to help Dad, who swore under his breath. I knew the words, but I'd never heard him say them out loud, only mumbled, which was how I came to learn: if you have something awful to say, mumble it.

"Let me help," I said, always the mediator. I wanted nothing, absolutely nothing, to ruin this trip. We were finally on our way. I wanted the calendar to pause. I wanted to fold Donny Osmond up and tell him to stop the days because it was finally summer.

"Don't worry, pumpkin," Dad said. "I've got this, but thank you for always being the helpful one." He tossed Mom a wry, mean glance as she stood there in her huge sunglasses and flowered dress. *He hates her,* I thought again. I'd thought it a lot lately, but it was one of those thoughts that couldn't even be mumbled.

When Dad was finished, the back of the station wagon was a puzzle with all the pieces in the wrong place, but still it fit into the frame. Except for one piece — my art box. He set it on the lawn like discarded trash.

"My box," I said and pointed to it.

"It won't fit, sweetie. Do you really need it?"

"I do," I said. "Take out my suitcase."

He pointed to my round pink case, the one Nana had given me for Christmas with the little kitten on it. "That has all your clothes. You can't leave that."

"Yes, I can. I'll wear this the whole time," I said. "I don't care."

Mom ambled up then and pulled her sunglasses off her face so we could see her hooded eyelids covered in so much blue eye shadow that it creased with every blink. "Do not be ridiculous, Lainey. Please can we just go before the summer passes in this god-awful driveway?" She kissed both my cheeks and then sidled around the car and opened the passenger-side door to sit. She propped her legs through the open window. "I'm ready."

"Dad, I'll put it on my lap. I'll carry it. I don't care. But we aren't leaving it here."

"Leave me here," Owen called from the yard, where Polly had him wrapped like the kudzu vines on our fence.

"Get in the car," Dad hollered in a voice that made my stomach flip over.

And we all climbed into the car. I plopped the box on my lap; Dad turned on the talk radio station and Mom closed her eyes immediately, her head lolling back on the seat.

"Clara, put your feet in and close the window," Dad said.

She didn't answer and a soft snore escaped.

He mumbled curse words and then leaned over her sleeping body to yank her feet down and manually roll the window up before backing out of the driveway.

"What is that?" Owen pushed at the box on my lap.

"Stuff," I said. "What do you care? All that matters to you is Polly."

"Oh, Bug, that's not true." He moved closer to me and wrapped his arm around me, then shook me with a little hug. "I love you best."

"You do not." I pushed him away. I made kissy faces and he laughed. He always laughed. No one was happier than Owen. It was infuriating. Didn't he feel the way the world could fall apart at any minute? Didn't he know Mom was crazy with whatever pills she took? Didn't he know Dad hated her? Didn't he feel the sadness in the world that clouded everything?

"I do, too, love you best," he said. "Cross my heart." He let me go and scooted to the other end of the bench seat, where he dropped his head onto the window. "I'm glad Polly can't come."

"Then why did you pretend you wanted her to?"

"So she'd stop crying," he said. And he patted the empty space between us. "I don't care if you put your box there."

Eventually we all fell asleep, except for Dad, of course. I was lulled into and out of a half sleep by the radio turning to static and then Dad finding a new station, or by the sway of a turn or stop. I woke once to Dad's whispered words, ones I'd heard before but knew he never meant. "Clara, if you can't stop, I'm going to have to send you somewhere to get help. You have to stop." I kept my eyes closed and slowly drifted back to sleep.

It wasn't until we took the sharp left into Watersend that I fully woke. My little bag of snacks and the Thermos of lemonade that Dad had given us rolled untouched on the floor.

Owen and I stirred and rubbed our eyes as the car pulled in front of the house. Bonny sat on the front porch reading a paperback. When she saw us, she jumped up and ran down the pathway toward our car. She reached us just as I climbed out and we threw our arms around each other and screamed, "Summer is here!" as if we'd planned it, as if we'd known what we'd say when we reunited.

She looked like those girls in *Teen Beat* magazine. Her curled eyelashes and almost purple eyes; her long legs and straight brown hair; her round lips and — oh, my God, she had little boobs now. I tried not to stare, but there they were, two tiny bumps under her halter top.

Owen crawled out of the car in his rumpled, stony way and stretched like he was unfolding. He let out a loud noise like a tiger waking up and then popped his sunglasses on before turning his gaze to Bonny.

"Hello, little Bee," he said, which was

what he'd called her that last summer after hearing her parents call her the same. But that was when she was littler.

"Hi, Owen." She turned away as if he'd said something weird to her and went to my mom and dad as if she were the mistress of the house.

"Welcome, Mr. and Mrs. McKay. It's so wonderful that you came back this year. Mom is at the market, but she said to tell you to take the same bedroom." She grabbed my hand. "Lainey is with me in my room."

The first night of that summer we didn't sleep. We stayed up and I showed her my art and we read our Girl Detective notebook from the summer before and she told me that she still hadn't kissed a boy. Those were the things we talked about; those were the things we cared about.

Until later.

I parked in front of Sea La Vie but didn't pull into the driveway at the side. Both Daisy and George had fallen asleep in the backseat, and I didn't want to wake them: it was my prerogative to have five more minutes of peace, right? We'd colored and read and watched movies across the country and my eyes burned with fatigue. A five-hour flight from San Francisco to Atlanta, with a three-hour layover before the quick thirty-minute flight here. The rental car. The forty-minute drive. And finally we were at Sea La Vie.

I pumped up the air conditioner in the car and stepped out with the car doors open. The world was brighter in Watersend, too bright; it always had been. How had I forgotten? The light was sharper, razor edged. It bounced off the river and the ocean, doubling its glare. I reached for my sunglasses and realized I already wore them. With a couple deep breaths, I leaned against the rental car, a compact that had felt like a tin can on the drive from the Savannah airport.

I took out my cell phone to try Owen one more time. I hadn't informed him that I was coming here — I wanted to tell him on the phone, not by voice mail or e-mail. The phone rang the obligatory six rings and then his voice told me to leave a message. There were plenty of messages that I wanted to leave, but I hung up without saying a word.

The last time I'd heard from him — three months ago — he'd been in Wyoming, climbing in the Teton Range and doing something so awful that when I Googled it, I felt sick. "Freebasing" it was called. It sounded like a drug thing, but I knew Owen would never touch them. When your mom destroyed her life with drugs, you definitely found an alternative. Owen's addiction was adventure sports, extreme sports where death was the result if the tiniest thing went wrong. He owned an adventure company that coordinated this for others. And free-basing — jumping off a cliff and opening a parachute that has wings (freaking wings!) — was his latest offering.

He wouldn't like it that I'd flown across the country with my two little bundles and without Tim. He would never, under any circumstance (his words), step foot in Watersend again. It was a town full of ghosts and crazy (again, his words).

After that last summer, when Mom had been released from jail, and Owen from the hospital, Mom had left us. We'd stayed only another week in Watersend for the unrelenting search, but eventually Dad had packed us to leave. The police had been called and the beaches combed and the tears shed, and the press notified, and without a clue where Mom had gone, we went home. Maybe, as I'd thought before, death would have been better than disappearing. At least there was an ending to death. *This* wondering never ended.

Once back in Atlanta, Dad had decided that what with his travel schedule and all the childhood duties, it would be best if we moved in with his sister Anna-Marie until Mom reappeared. So we shoved our favorite things in boxes and bags and moved to Anna-Marie's little house in midtown Atlanta, where she lived her single life. And although she was as sweet and kind as could be, it was about the same as being raised by an adorable golden retriever. Owen and I figured out how to raise ourselves, and then when he graduated from high school and threw his childhood room into the back of a beat-up pickup truck for the University of Georgia, Dad sold our house in Atlanta and shipped me off to boarding school in Connecticut. He moved to Arizona, which meant that any break I had at school, I didn't go *home* because I didn't have a home or a mother. I slowly, through the years, learned to make a home wherever I was.

Dad had never remarried because technically he was still married, but the slew of women in and out of his life made me believe he'd never have done so anyway. Freedom was salvation to my dad. Freedom was disastrous for my brother and for me.

I'd gone to college in San Francisco and

had never left. I couldn't, even if pressed, tell you how many places Owen has lived since he left Georgia. Always out saving someone or skiing something or backpacking somewhere. It didn't matter whether he would approve of me being here or not. If he wanted a say in anything of my life, he should answer his phone.

The house in front of me seemed the same but updated. The doors and shutters still that brightest blue, meant to scare away anything evil. So much for that little fable: evil had arrived anyway. Valium and vodka.

I'd promised myself that when I arrived at the house, I wouldn't think about *Mom,* yet there she was — a mirage wavering on top of the present moment. The house was offering me a memory montage and I didn't want it. I refused. What pains and energies was that old house still carrying? Or maybe the worst parts of our summers had been burned off with new families, new memories and the scorching heat of many Augusts.

I shivered in the heat and spoke out loud. "Stop, Lainey. Enough. It was a long, long time ago." I peeked into the backseat at my sleeping children, took a sustaining breath and opened the door. "Wake up, sleepyheads. We're here."

They stirred slowly until Daisy let out a

squeal. "George. Wake up. Wake up. We are here. *In the South!*" Daisy unsnapped George's car seat buckle and then her own seat belt and together they tumbled out of the car, falling first to the ground and then popping to their feet. This was my family now. The one I'd made and the one I'd keep.

"Look," she said to her brother. "It's just like the picture."

George's sleepy face broke into a smile.

The three of us walked to the front door, which was ajar with the screen door closed. We entered and stood in the hallway. Even as a kid, I could have been blindfolded and known what friend's house I was entering just by the aroma. Homes were extensions of the souls that lived in them, and I could feel Bonny everywhere. Each room held its own personality. Bonny had made the place her own again.

She'd sent me a layout of the house and I'd divided it into the *gua*s of feng shui, giving her little "cures" to set in each section. I noticed she'd placed a piece of artwork, a charcoal drawing of an antique medicine bottle, in the "Life Purpose" section. I smiled.

Through the hallway and into the kitchen, my littlest loves trailed behind. My sight wandered slowly across the shiplap walls, which she'd painted white, the dark hardwood floors covered with scattered rugs. One of my favorite art pieces, which I'd given to her on my last visit to her in Charleston, hung in the hallway: a photo of a mother-daughter pair painted in wax with the mom's face partly blurred out and the daughter staring out with a wide-eyed expression. I ran my hand over the corner of the canvas. Bonny had even hung it in the "Family" *gua,* as if I'd been there to tell her what to do.

The kitchen, which had once been secured off from the rest of the house like an embarrassing relative, was now open to the living room, the wall gone and a large exposed hardwood beam above. I picked up a red candle and moved it to the table running along the back wall in the "Fame" *gua.*

Bonny had pasted a little note on the door of each of the two back bedrooms — *Lainey* on one and *Kids* with a heart on the other. Mine was our childhood bedroom and just so happened to be in the "Creative" corner of the house — middle right side. In the days when I'd shared it with Bonny, it had two single beds with pink chenille bedspreads and baskets that slid underneath to hold our clothes. In a flash, I saw the three of us — Bonny, Owen and I — knotted together in one bed, waiting to discover if Mom was okay. In a way, we were still there knotted together, forever not knowing. I blinked away the image.

I needed to leave. I shouldn't have come.

I could throw my suitcase back in the car, buckle the kids in their seat belts, speed back to the airport and jump on a plane. Tim would be waiting for us, joyous.

Then the back screen door slammed its summer song and Bonny's voice called my name. The chance to escape had come and gone.

"Bonny?" I called out. And then there she was in the doorway of the bedroom, her hair wild about her face as if she'd run there, her smile radiant and her arms spread wide for a hug. I loved her so. I always had. Even in memory, and now in person, she always seemed surreal, a living painting.

She took me in her arms and I held her so close, feeling her tremble below her thin T-shirt. She released me and yet we held our arms out, our fingers still entwined.

"Look at you, just look at you!" she exclaimed. "Here."

"I'm so glad I am," I said, and I let go of her hand to wipe away a quick tear, shocked that I suddenly really did feel happy to be back.

"I know it's all mixed, Lainey. The good, the bad, the fun and the terrible. I was so afraid you'd change your mind."

"I almost did," I said. "If you hadn't shown up right when you did . . ."

She threw her arms around me. "You can't go anywhere. I've already decided: we are going to remember the good stuff, and there was so much of it! We are going to make all new and wonderful memories." She then leaned down to the kids, who hung back holding hands with each other and watching us.

"Hi, Daisy. I'm Aunt Bonny. I know I haven't seen you since you were four years old. Hi, George."

They both stared at her until she ruffled Daisy's hair. "You hungry?"

"He's always hungry," Daisy said and pointed at her brother. "Always."

"Then let's get something to eat. And then we can go to the beach."

"The beach?" George asked. "Let's go there now."

From the far side of the house a door creaked and then a voice, so like Bonny's but raspier, called out. "Mom?"

"Back here," Bonny said.

Piper took hesitant steps into the room as if trying not to be seen, a slip of a girl but tall. So like Bonny that I expected to see a 1976 puka bead necklace around her neck and a neon peace sign embroidered on her jean shorts. She smiled at me, but there was reserve in that smile, something essential held back, and I didn't know if that was her way or her way with me. It had been four years since I'd last seen her, and now she stood there, a woman instead of a young child.

"Hi, Lainey," she said and reached back for her ponytail, yanking out a rubber band and letting her hair fall over her shoulders.

"Hello, darling," I said to her. "You are so grown-up I can't stand it." I hugged her and then she bent to smile at the kids.

"Hi, I'm Piper. You must be George and Daisy."

"I'm Daisy. And this is George, in case you're confused." Daisy attempted a grown-up voice that made my heart feel pulled to a future I wasn't nearly ready for.

"Phew, thanks for telling me," Piper said and then looked to me. "Want me to show them around?"

"We have to eat food first," Daisy said in the voice Tim called Miss Priss.

"Then let's do that," Piper said and she held out her hands, one for each child. I watched my children take my goddaughter's hands, and I felt the house settle as if it took one long exhale of relief.

CHAPTER 15
PIPER BLANKENSHIP

Lainey and the kids arrived in mid-afternoon, just when the sun was at its fiercest. Mom and I were settled on the back screened porch watching the river do its river thing — moving slowly to wherever it goes and then coming back again. Small johnboats and kayaks passed; herons sat on the marsh edge and posed as if for a portrait; dolphins nosed up and then back under, showing off with their sleek backs and flipped tails.

The front door screen opened and then slapped shut.

Here we go, I thought. *Here we go.*

Mom jumped from her chair but I waited, not wanting to yank myself from the story I was reading and back into the real world. It took me a minute sometimes, the moving from one world to the next so quickly.

When I entered the bedroom to see the kids, they hung back while Mom and Lainey did that best-friend-hugging thing. There was the boy, George, with a head full of hair so white it glowed, and then the girl, Daisy, a little older and taller, with the same hair but longer and tangled with curls.

Mom hugged Lainey with a squeal as if they were teenagers who had just won Homecoming Queen. I was embarrassed for Mom, acting so silly and young. She was telling Lainey everything she'd done to the house — so proud of what she'd accomplished. And she should have been. She'd taken it from a ramshackle mess to cottage-cute. I could be as mad at her as I wanted, but I would say this — she knew how to make a house a home.

Now we left the bedroom to explore. I followed them — I had no idea how much eight- and six-year-olds could do alone. I knew nothing of kids. I could have taken a summer job designing rocket ships to the moon and have been just as prepared as I was following the kids.

"Piper," Mom called, "will you keep an eye on the kids while I get us some lunch? We'll be in the kitchen."

"Got it," I called back, with absolutely no idea of what "got it" could mean in this context.

"You're our babysitter?" George asked.

"I am."

"We didn't want to come here without our dad," Daisy said and pulled a stuffed rabbit she'd taken from her mom's bag closer to her, one ear dangling and one tucked.

"Well, that's funny. Can I tell you a secret?" I asked and bent, my hands on my knees.

"What?" George asked, wide-eyed and reaching for his sister's hand.

"I didn't want to come here either."

"Really?" Daisy smiled.

"Really." I nodded. "But I've found some fun things to do. There's a beach to play on, and an ocean to swim in, and a book-shop . . ." I hesitated. A bookshop might not sound all that fun to them. "And a movie theater with real popcorn, and a candy store and . . . I can teach you card tricks." I was pulling stuff out of thin air now. I didn't know how to do card tricks. But look, we'd made it five minutes into the summer and I hadn't lost them or made them cry.

"I want my mommy," Daisy said and peered around the room as if surprised to find it empty.

"So do I," I said. "Let's go find her."

Daisy put out her hand for me to take, and I did, her little fingers winding through mine. She pulled me forward. "Let's find her." As if we were in it together.

I entered the kitchen with Daisy holding fast and George trailing behind us, singing some song about a spider. Lainey and Mom were setting out lunch — peanut butter and jelly sandwiches, chips and juice boxes for the kids and shrimp salad for us.

"Well, look at you," Lainey said. "Already the pro."

I laughed because if I was anything at all it wasn't a pro.

"Let's eat on the porch," Mom said, "and then we can all go to the beach for a while."

Lainey stepped up and took Daisy from me.

"Tell you what," she said. "I'll sit with Piper and go over the kids' schedules. Then we can have fun from here on out."

Fun from here on out. Right-o.

Lainey sat at the kitchen table and I sat facing her while George climbed into her lap and Daisy into mine. It was a comforting feeling, a child in your lap. Lainey placed a folder on the table.

"I really want to thank you for helping with the kids this summer. I don't get much of a break at home. They were late-in-life babies and just when I thought I might never . . ." She smiled and glanced at the kids as if making sure they were real. "Anyway, thanks. This folder is full of lists . . . Just bear with it because I made it in a spurt of uncharacteristic organization."

I opened the folder. Sure enough it was full of lists. Their favorite foods. Their favorite games. Their favorite everything: colors, clothes, songs. And their schedule.

"And George, he runs off. You have to keep an eye on him all the time. He just . . . takes off without thinking. Daisy here will always stick by you, but George forgets that the world is too big." She exhaled as if this big world was her biggest problem.

"I'll read it all," I said. "I promise."

"And I don't expect you to have them all day every day. I love being with them. Honestly, I just need some quiet to work a few hours a day."

I saw those hours in my mind like a pie chart, a piece of the day so large that the bookshop faded, the little boat on the river became obsolete and swinging in the hammock for no good reason drifted away.

Mom piped in. "She's fine with that and even more if we need it. Come on. Lunch on the porch. Everyone grab something."

"I think I'll stay here and read through this folder," I said. "I'm not hungry anyway."

"Nope," Lainey said. "Lunch together. It's mandatory because I said so." She laughed with the statement, as if she was the one who was nervous instead of me.

So off we went onto the porch and I had a feeling that it was a lot less about all being together than me watching the kids while they talked. And I was right. Like Thanksgiving when you're stuck at the kids' table. George, Daisy and I were at the card table and the ladies sat at the picnic table.

"Okay, Bonny. How are you really doing? You hanging in there?" I heard Lainey ask.

"I'm okay. Better now that you're here."

"Of all the places to come to," Lainey said quietly. "But I'm not complaining. We needed a getaway in the worst way. You've made the house feel like it used to, but better."

I pretended to be interested in the way Daisy needed her crust cut off, or the way George wanted to run out to the dock, but really I eavesdropped.

Lainey glanced at us and then stretched her legs across the picnic bench. She was so fluid. Ever since I was a little girl, I'd wanted to figure out how she seemed so calm and peaceful. It was like watching a bird, a graceful one that stretched and then settled and slowly took in its surroundings.

She wore her hair loose and over her shoulders and never fidgeted with it or piled it up or down. I was always running my hands into and out of my hair. She kept the littlest smile even when she thought no one was looking. Her oval face was topped off with a fringe of bangs, which I heard her jokingly tell Mom was "cheap Botox." Her eyes, makeup free, were surrounded by the longest eyelashes, dark brown and curled upward.

She caught me staring and smiled widely. "I remember more about our summers here than I do about any of my childhood days at home or at school. I bet you'll love it, Piper." Lainey lost that smile for a minute and then looked off toward the river. "I wonder where Owen is right now. I wonder what he'd think about us all here together."

Owen. That name on Mom's phone. The call she didn't want to take. I took a quick glance at Mom and she, too, stared out to the river and then cleared her throat, as if wiping tears from inside.

George broke the reverie as he pointed to the river and hollered, "A fishing pole."

"Yes," I said. "Want to go down there?"

But he was gone in half a heartbeat. His bare feet padded across the wooden floors and the screen door slammed behind him. I jumped up and ran after him as Daisy hollered, "Wait for me!"

"Life jackets," Lainey called as I caught George and grabbed his little hand.

"Whoa, buddy. Slow down. Your mom says you have to wear a life jacket near the water."

"No, I don't. Dad says I don't. I know how to swim same as Daisy."

"Well, it's just safe." I didn't have any idea how to negotiate or argue with a six-year-old and I sure as hell wasn't going to say, *Because I said so.*

I reached the dock and opened the bench storage to pull out two orange jackets. I fastened them on first Daisy and then George before I took out the rusted bait box.

"So who knows how to fish?"

The voices from the porch were muffled and I was sure Mom would go deeper now; maybe even tell Lainey how I'd been in trouble. The horrible, vortex-sliding feelings came back to me so quickly, so easily. One minute I was feeling like I could handle this summer, find a slow way into it while reading and making a new friend in Fletch, while being in a quiet house with nice people in a small town. But the frantic need to *not be me* found me again. Not the girl in trouble, not the girl who had failed at school, not the girl whose boyfriend had left her for another.

I baited a plastic worm on a hook for George and made funny faces, but I wasn't fully there. The estranged feeling crawled over me with its need to remind me that everydamnthing was wrong.

The tears came no matter how I tried to stop them. Why couldn't the good feelings last? I could use a nice night out with a few beers or a shot or two of Jack Daniel's, just to take the edge off this longing and regret. While George and Daisy tangled their lines and bickered, I glanced at my cell phone.

Nothing. Absolutely nothing from Ryan. As if I'd never existed. I clicked over to his Instagram and scrolled through the photos. He was in Venice. How very nice for him. Tears rolled down my cheeks and I was hot with shame and sadness. I felt a tug at the edge of my T-shirt and I looked to Daisy. The life vest had ridden up and her round cheeks were resting on the orange fabric. "Why are you crying?"

"Oh," I said and wiped at my face. "Oh . . . nothing. I'm fine." I squatted and readjusted her jacket. "Just fine."

She took her hands and placed one on each of my cheeks. "Don't cry."

"Okay," I said. "I won't."

I glanced to the porch and saw Mom and Lainey huddled together, laughing.

Life was so fragile, everything easily broken — a mood; a chance; a life. I hoped it would be a long, long time before George and Daisy understood. Without thinking, I planted a huge kiss on Daisy's round cheek right there on the dock while that river flowed past us.

CHAPTER 16
BONNY BLANKENSHIP

Lainey hadn't yet emerged from the bedroom that first morning, and I needed a distraction. Piper had taken the kids to the beach to let Lainey sleep in. I opened the leather to-do folder. I picked one thing from the list every day, finished it, and then another and then another and . . .

Paint wicker furniture.

The two chairs and table were part of a set I'd found at the flea market, which someone had painted what I called poop brown. I'd bought a spray paint as close to haint blue as I could find and this task seemed as good as any.

The chairs and table were stashed in the little garage and I dragged them out to the back lawn and set them on a large tarp, sweating as if I'd run ten miles in that formidable heat. Changing one thing into another made me feel like I had some control over at least the littlest things in my world, when I had no control over much of anything just then. I knew, logically, that painting an old wicker set would no more set things right in my life than making wishes inside a river under a full moon. But it was worth a shot.

The little ball inside the spray can clacked around as I shook it, a satisfying sound. With one step back I pushed the button and blue paint spewed out, covering the wicker in slow swipes of paint, obliterating the brown color completely. An armrest. A leg. The seat. My heartbeat slowed, and the low hum of fear settled down for a siesta in the morning heat.

"Bonny," I heard and startled. The spray paint came along for the ride as I spun around to see Lainey standing there, sleepy and disheveled. The blue streak spread across the air and then across her white T-shirt and onto the green grass. Lainey hollered and jumped back, and then glanced at her shirt before looking back to me.

I stood stock-still, holding the paint can aloft. "Oh, my God." I slapped my free hand over my mouth, stifling a laugh.

Lainey, too, burst into laughter. "What are you doing?"

"Painting," I said.

"Obviously, but I mean what are you *doing*?"

"Waiting for you to wake up."

In a playful move, a duck and dive, she grabbed the paint can from me and held it toward me like a gun. "What's fair is fair," she said. With that, she pushed the button and a streak of blue materialized on both my shins, up and over.

"No way," I screamed and dove for the can.

She dropped it and ran straight for the dock and river. Without a glance backward, she tore off her ruined T-shirt and slid off her pale blue shorts. In a move so swift I couldn't even holler after her, Lainey jumped in. I ran to the dock and peered down. There she was, holding on to the warm edges of the wood, shaking her head to scatter water drops that caught the sun like crystals. Her movements on earth were the same as they were in the water, always fluid. Her hair was once blond and now was darker, a few light streaks scattered like memories of the past.

"Get in," she said.

"No way." I shook my head and tried to back away, but she'd grabbed my ankle.

"Come on, Bonny. You're the one who always made us jump in."

"I was thirteen." I laughed and shook my foot free from her grasp.

Lainey pushed off from the edge of the dock and floated on her back. The tide, going out, pulled her sideways. "You're going to get hit by a boat or end up in the ocean," I hollered. "The tide is going out."

"You're *so* much fun now," she said to me, shaking her head to negate her own words.

And then I was thirteen and not to be outdone by Lainey McKay, who could do and be anything she wanted. I would not let her have more fun than me, or be braver than me, or anything at all more than me. Without shedding my clothes as she'd done, I flipped off my sandals and jumped in after her. I hit the water and hollered just as I went under, swallowing a mouthful of brackish river. I came up sputtering and laughing both. Lainey was at my side and we grabbed on to the dock together.

"See?" she said. "I can't believe I forgot how great this water feels. It's like silk; it's like something smooth and warm washing past you, full of life."

"And fish and sharks and stingrays and . . ." I kicked my feet below. "We never thought about that when we were kids."

"Then don't think about it now," Lainey

said and dove back under, flipping over so her feet came up like a mermaid's tail.

"Right," I said to her when she rose. "I just won't think about it."

"I've been told denial is my finest quality," Lainey said.

"It's definitely not mine," I said and lifted my face to the sun, my eyes closed. "All I do is think about what I've done, the damage I've done, how to fix it, if to fix it, when to fix it . . . what I should do, can't do or . . ."

"Stop!" She held up her hand.

I kicked my legs under the water against the tide.

From the back porch came the slam of the screen door and then Piper's voice. "Mom?"

"We're here. In the river," I shouted.

Piper's face appeared above us and she glanced back and forth between us. "I'm seriously worried about you both," she said. "You two are very possibly crazy. I'm not letting the kids see you swimming in there because then they'll want to get in that water." And with that, she ran off.

Lainey and I stared at each other, our eyes widening.

"She may be right," I said. "We may be crazy."

She tugged at my hair and we smiled at each other as if this was any other summer, another one that had come directly after the one before instead of arriving as it had, years later.

We hauled ourselves out of the water and were heading into the house when my cell phone on the outdoor picnic table rang. I almost didn't answer or even look, finally feeling a sense of calm start to settle around us. Then I saw the 404 area code: Atlanta.

I answered breathless and still damp from the river as if the brackish water itself would protect me from bad news.

"Dr. Blankenship?"

"Speaking," I said and wiped my face with a rag from the spray-painting project.

"This is Morgan Ingram, from Emory's Human Resources. I'm calling to inform you that we need to cancel your job offer. MUSC has not released the results of their investigation and we need to move on."

The ground shifted beneath me, and a sweeping panic rose from my chest. If I'd expected this to happen, I hadn't let myself feel it.

"No," I said. "There is no reason to postpone employment."

"This isn't a postponement, Dr. Blanken-ship. This is a cancellation of the job offer.

We can't employ a physician during an active investigation."

"It will be over and settled soon," I said, although I didn't know if this was true. I reached for a life preserver as I sank into the waters of panic, and there was nothing there. I went under.

"We wish you the best," the voice said.

I must have said some sort of robotic, well-mannered good-bye, but I don't remember. I was drowning. Or was I dizzy? I didn't know. I sank to the grass and dropped my head between my legs, gulping for air.

Lainey ran to my side and crouched down. "Are you okay? What is it, Bonny?"

"They canceled their job offer." And then it happened — the withheld tears burst forth. A retching noise came from someplace deep and my throat felt raw with its power. The tears came and there was nothing, absolutely nothing, I could do to stop it. For all the times I'd held back, for all the times I'd kept control, there was a break inside, a crack that widened.

Lainey dropped to the grass and wrapped both arms around me. "Bonny, it will be fine. The results will come back and . . ."

"No, it's over," I said. "Even if it comes back okay, that job is gone." My voice was garbled.

"Anyone would hire you. Anyone."

"What am I going to do now?" I asked. "What?"

"We'll figure out something."

"Return to Lucas? To that life? God, Lainey, I can't. Even though I just now left physically, I left a long, long time ago emotionally. And I don't know how to go back to the dismissive coldness, to the angry rebukes, to the husband as a boss instead of a partner. I was alone even in the middle of the marriage. That's worse than being alone by yourself." I took a couple deep breaths and my body slowed. I wiped my face and sat straighter.

"You don't have to go back there, Bonny. Just because Emory rescinded doesn't mean you can't do something new."

"Do you know how long it took me to get that job? A year, Lainey. A year. And they don't just pop up every day for the grabbing." I wiped at my face, tasted the river and the salt of my tears commingling. "I've made decisions, one by one by one by one, and they've added up. Now here I am. We can't subtract a decision or undo it."

"No, we can't. But you can make new ones."

"I have no idea, absolutely no idea, what those could be." Anger forced the words in

190

staccato-like sentences stomping across the yard. "It took me so, so very long to make the decisions I did. Meticulous planning. Outlines and checklists. And I don't know how to do it again." I exhaled and gazed toward the river. "What I'd give to go back to 1978, change my wish, change my life. Make new decisions. Start over." I turned my attention back to Lainey. "Don't you ever feel that way?"

"Of course I do. What if I'd come out of the bedroom and stayed with Mom through the night? What if I hadn't written all her wrongdoings in our stupid notebook? What if I'd been a better girl . . . what if, what if, what if . . ."

I leaned into Lainey and our weight fell hard against each other as we gazed out toward the river. And it didn't need to be said: there was no changing the past.

CHAPTER 17
BONNY BLANKENSHIP

June 1978
The Last Summer
Watersend, South Carolina

That summer of 1978, when the world was dancing to disco and we shook our Polaroid photos, Lainey and I unpacked the new dishes Mom had brought to the river house, organizing them into the cabinets.

"You should have seen Mom freaking out this morning making us all get so dressed up just to sit in the stupid car. She was so worried we wouldn't look good for your family," Lainey told me.

"Well, I like your sundress," I said. "I don't have one that nice."

"Mom got it at the church rummage sale. I hate wearing it. It itches and I don't know who wore it before me and I keep thinking that I'm going to be somewhere and some little girl is going to scream, 'That's my dress.' And I will die a thousand times over."

"Well, go take it off and put on some shorts. Then let's sneak away to the beach," I said, feeling bold because Lainey was finally back with me.

"I will get in so much trouble," she said. "*So much.* We have to help before we can have fun. Dad told us that six million times on the way here."

"That's stupid," I said.

"I know."

Owen sauntered into the kitchen while we stood jumping to crush the box we'd just emptied: a victory dance. He laughed at us, and the sound echoed below my heart. It was an odd feeling, like he was loosening things inside, like something stretched and wiggled under my ribs. It was a nervous feeling like when I needed to speak in front of the class or when I'd lied to my parents and was about to be caught. I didn't want to be around him, but I did. No, I didn't.

"Look what I found," he said and gently placed a record player on the kitchen table. It was a black box I recognized from the attic at home, an old record player Dad had brought to the river house.

"Awesome," Lainey said. "What are we supposed to do with it now? You got any records hidden under that fancy shirt?"

"Oh, dumb sister," he answered, but in

this soft, funny way, like the word "dumb" meant something different to them. "There's a second box. Hold on." He marched out of the kitchen and I wanted to follow him or make him return.

"You don't get in trouble for calling each other names?" I asked. "I'd get a spanking and be sent to my room."

"Spanking? Your parents hit you?" Lainey's eyes opened wider.

I'd never thought of it this way. Here was this girl, Lainey, with her prissy sundress and her truth-telling humor, telling me that my parents hit me.

"Spanking isn't hitting. It's like a punishment for doing something wrong."

"No," Lainey said, "it's hitting."

Technically, she was right. Suddenly I felt a little sick and a lot embarrassed at my parents, who hit their children. I felt like apologizing for them, but then Owen came back and placed a box on the floor. "Records."

"Yes," I said. "That's my parents' collection. You better be careful. Dad will go crazy if you scratch one."

"And hit us," Lainey said.

"I'm not scared," Owen said, and he did this Popeye move with his arms, pulsing his biceps muscles. I wanted to laugh, but I was too busy staring at him, at the way he thumbed through the records as if he didn't care what he scratched or how. He yanked *Saturday Night Fever* from the box but then slipped the record from its cardboard envelope gently, holding the edges with his fingertips. It dropped like air onto the turntable, a soft whooshing sound as it settled. Owen lifted the arm and bent, eye to record, to settle the needle onto the first groove.

He switched it on and there we were, dancing to "Stayin' Alive" when we were supposed to be unpacking another box. Laughter spilled out and filled the room, and I was someone I'd never been before, even though I didn't have a word for it yet. I was someone who moved to music and felt looser in my body, like my limbs were made of rubber bands. A hummingbird, the kind that flittered outside our window in Atlanta, now lived inside my chest, tickling me.

" 'Stayin' alive. Stayin' alive. Ah, ha, ha, ha,' " we sang together, a trio, out loud. Owen grabbed my waist and spun me around, lifted me off the ground and then set me gently back down on the crushed box we'd been stomping. He lifted Lainey next and she squealed, let her arms fly to the sides like airplane wings and lifted her face to the ceiling as if it was a sky full of all the stars.

I wanted to reach for this boy and yank Lainey from him. I was annoyed, the way I was when Dad parceled out a bigger piece of his grilled cheese sandwich for Percy, or the way I was when Sara at school let Millie sit in my saved seat at the lunch table. But also differently, with an ache. Which didn't make sense because this was his sister and it was the most perfect day.

Later that night, when we were all so tired we could hardly speak, Dad ordered pizza. He swayed across the room, loopy steps like one of those clowns hamming it up at the circus. But he wasn't trying to be funny, although he was laughing. His arms swayed in front of him like they were too heavy and his words were thick like he had taken too big a bite of bread and couldn't chew it all. Lainey and I were sitting at the kitchen table so happy to be back together, and Owen sat across from us.

We played Clue. I knew it was the candlestick in the library by Professor Plum, but I didn't want the game to end, so I didn't guess yet. "Hello, kids," Dad said. "How's it going on your first real day of summer?"

"Just fine, sir," Owen said and rolled the

die for his turn.

Dad left us the pizza and then picked up a bottle of Jack Daniel's and headed back for the living room, only a few steps away. I could see the parents from where I sat. Cards were scattered across the table and they played poker, using the red and black wooden checkers pieces to bet with. Lainey's mom smoked cigarettes and there was an ashtray stuffed with lipstick-stained butts and dark ashes falling over the edges. Twice I'd seen my mom reach over and take a puff. The first time I almost screamed out, but then I just watched, amazed, like Mom had turned into something other than Mom.

I did my best not to stare directly at Owen because when I did there was this weird thrumming feeling under my chest and I sort of felt like I was going to throw up. But then again, I wanted to stare at him so hard that I memorized his entire face, which seemed like nothing I'd ever seen before even though this was my third summer with him. His mouth turned down at the edges in a sleepy way, and his chin was squared off like he'd drawn it. His eyes, a brown so brown they melted into his pupils, and eyelashes longer than any pretty girl's. Every time I did stare at him, he stared back and did that mean thing that boys can do —

where they widen their eyes and stare back real hard as if to say, *What the hell do you want?* and then I felt dizzy with embarrassment.

"This is so stupid." Owen pushed the game away.

"But this is fun," I said.

"No" — he leaned across the pine table — "it's not. Let's go explore outside."

Lainey didn't even glance up from her sketchpad, where she was drawing a dolphin. "You go ahead."

"We're a team," I said. "Let's all go."

Owen smiled at me and I blushed, which was more embarrassing than burping because at least you could laugh about that. Blushing was a dead giveaway that I didn't know how to talk to boys, which I didn't.

The parents turned on their own music then and we huddled together in the kitchen, peeking out to watch them. It was dance music that my parents listened to all the time, "Sweet Caroline," and I knew the words and I started to sing them. Lainey shushed me. "Shhh. They'll make us go to bed."

I leaned against the framed opening and watched in astonishment. I'd never seen my parents dance with each other, or switch partners. Lainey pulled at my arm. "Move," she said. "Don't stand there and watch."

"Why?" I twisted away from her grasp and peered into the living room.

"Because my mom is embarrassing. That's why." Her voice cracked.

"It's fun to watch them. I've never seen my parents like this."

Owen idled next to me and his arm brushed against mine. I wasn't ever going to move if he'd just stand there with me. "We see our parents like this all the time. Trust me, it's not fun to watch."

I averted my gaze from Owen and back to the scene in the living room. What was embarrassing about Mrs. McKay? She was so beautiful. I'd already decided I would try to walk like her, with that little swing in her hips. Her lipstick never faded off and her hair was piled high on her head and small pieces fell onto her shoulders. She was so dreamy. And she lived like she was in a dream. The sleeve of her sundress had slipped and a red bra strap stretched across her shoulder. Every few dance beats she would twist down and take a sip of her drink or drag of her cigarette without ever missing a step.

Dad was dancing with Mom, swinging her in a wide circle, when Clara cut in and took his hands. Her dress twisted around her body with every movement, and her boobs swung against my dad's chest, where she planted herself and stayed. I was shocked in the kind of way where I couldn't tear my gaze away. It was too interesting and too weird.

It happened so fast, the way Mr. McKay grabbed his wife and twisted her around to face him, his left arm around her waist yanking her tight against him. He dragged her the few steps toward the kitchen and Owen pulled me backward into the room and to the table where we couldn't see them, but I heard them. We all heard them.

"What do you think you're doing, Clara? It's our first night here and you're drunk as hell, flirting with our host."

"I'm not flirting," Clara said, but her words were so slurry, like a child lisping.

"Don't you fucking ruin this vacation. I won't say it again. If you can't stop, I'm sending you somewhere that can make you stop."

"I'll stop. I have stopped." She was crying, I could tell. "I'm just having fun."

"Let's go to the dock," Owen whispered close to my ear, and he moved quickly to the back door. "Come on."

I followed him and so did Lainey. We always did.

CHAPTER 18
PIPER BLANKENSHIP

Everyone in the house was in bed, not one light on, so even the house itself felt asleep. Nighttime was always the worst for me. The jagged feelings returned — the awful me again. And I wanted escape. I didn't know what mattered. I didn't know who mattered, and the rest of the world *did* seem to know. I could be witty with old myths in a café, or tell you my favorite books, or look cute in too-short shorts, but I didn't know what the hell *really* mattered. What was the deal with Owen and Mom sneaking phone calls like a cigarette? And Lainey, missing him so badly that I heard her cry?

I knew I wouldn't sleep, and the sea called to me like it wanted to tell me how to fix whatever it was that was wrong with me. I slipped on my shorts and a T-shirt, and carried my flip-flops as I tiptoed out of the house. I held my hand on the screen door and guided it back into its frame to avoid the bump-slam that might wake someone.

The flashlight app on my phone and the crescent sideways moon guided me across the street and over the dunes, past the prickly bushes and onto wet, packed sand. I heard them before I saw them — a group of teens around a bonfire. Loud country music vibrated across the sand. Coolers of all shapes and sizes were scattered about the beach, some open and some being used as chairs. Aluminum beach chairs, bent and pulled close to the fire, were full of kids and couples. I stood still, about to turn around, when I inhaled the sweet aroma of someone's joint. Yes, that would definitely help.

I dug my toes into the warm sand that held the leftover sunshine of the day as if the beach didn't want to let the day go. I wandered close to the bonfire: girls in shorts, boys in baseball caps, beer cans scattered and a guy with a guitar butchering a Kenny Chesney song about a blue chair. It felt like I'd been dropped into a country music video.

I stood still and quiet, trying to decide whether to bolt or make the first move, but I didn't have to because it was then that a guy with curly dark hair and a scruffy beard came over to me. "Hey," he said and tilted his head as if questioning me instead of greeting me.

"Hey." I smiled and glanced at the joint in his hand. "I'm Piper. I don't mean to crash your party, but I heard y'all and thought I'd come down here."

"A pretty girl like you can crash anytime. You a vacationer?"

I laughed. "I didn't know that's what we were called, but yeah, I guess I am."

He bowed in a silly gesture and pretended to wave a hat. "Welcome to our small boring town. I'm Lyle."

"Nice to meet you."

He held out his joint. "Want a hit?"

"Absolutely," I said and took it from him, inhaling the sweet, pungent smoke that would burn and then soothe. It would happen quickly — the fluttery fear would settle down and leave me alone. I would be fine with who and what I was. I took another hit and then tried to hand it back to him. "Keep it," he said. I tapped it out on the sand and slipped it into my back pocket for later.

Soon a few of his friends joined us and I met local kids with names that blurred together like watercolors. I sat in one of the empty aluminum chairs and stared into the flames, watching them lick the sky and attempt to join the stars.

A slow fuzziness descended and the warm night soaked through my skin and my eyes closed. I sank deeper into the chair and felt my body melt into it. Who cared if I didn't know what mattered? I would figure it out. Who cared if Ryan was with Hannah? Who cared if I lost my virginity to a guy who didn't give a flying F-word about me?

I couldn't feel my teeth, which happened when I got stoned, but I could feel the hot sting of heartbreak. I opened my eyes and stared out to the sea. Then I stood and stumbled to the edge of the ocean to sit and dig my feet deeper into the sand, burrowing for something solid.

"Piper?" My gaze wandered, languid and tired, to my name. A flicker of familiarity crossed my mind: Fletch from the Market.

"Fletch," I said, peering over my shoulder. "Hey there."

"You've got a little fan club up there. You've already made friends and you've been here for, like, a minute." He laughed and plopped down next to me.

I was not in the mood for this — making small talk with some guy I didn't know while I was stoned and wanted to be alone. And cry about Ryan. And stare at the waves. And think about my life. Everyone thought I didn't care about anything. Like Dad saying, "Why don't you care about *anything* at all?" when he found out about my failing grades. But how could I ever explain that it wasn't that I didn't care about anything, it was that I cared about *everything.* Too much. The world poked at the softest places inside of me all day long. I didn't fail because I didn't care. I failed because I felt too much, and then avoided all the things I was supposed to do.

But there was no way to explain all of that, to my parents or the teachers. It sounded ridiculous.

I smiled at him. "You sure get around." My words were slow and soft around the edges. I tried to articulate in that awful way people do when they're trying to prove they're sober.

"Not much to do around here. This bonfire?" He pointed back at the crowd. "Happens almost every night even though any minute now the cops will come and tell us it's illegal and to pack it up. Then we'll do it all again tomorrow night." He paused and ran his hand through the sand. Finger trails wavered like tiny rivers. "You okay?" he asked.

"I'm fine," I said. "Just fine." I shifted on the sand. "Can I ask you something crazy?"

"Anything."

"Why do you have blue eyes?"

His laugh was so deep and resonant that I actually felt it rumble across the sand. "Do you mean why am I a black man with white man's eyes?"

"I wouldn't have put it quite that way . . ." Embarrassment needled at my softly stoned conscience. "It was a stupid question. I'm sorry."

"I get asked that a lot. And the answer is simple. My dad, Hayden, is white and has these exact same eyes. He's from North Carolina, but his family vacationed here one summer when he was a kid and he never forgot this place. My mom, Keke, is black, with some obvious recessive genes in her DNA. They met and married in college in D.C., and that's where I was born. But Dad wanted to come back here to open an organic market. I think Mom was worried about coming to South Carolina, all the Old South bullshit, but it's never once been a big deal. Life is one big adventure for the two of them, always wondering what might happen next."

"Well, your eyes are so beautiful that when you leave I want to see them again." I again lolled back in the sand and cringed. What the hell had I just confessed?

He twisted toward me and laughed. "That

is literally the nicest thing anyone has ever said to me."

"Don't count on it again." I tried for levity and failed.

"Don't you want to come join the party?"

"Maybe in a minute," I said.

"You too busy staring at the ocean?"

"Yep. Staring at the ocean is on my to-do list this summer."

"It's a very good to-do." He leaned back on his elbows, staring at the sky. His dreadlocks caught in the breeze, tangling. His voice was low and husky, a just-woke-up kind of sound.

"My mom's best friend came yesterday," I said before I knew I said it, like I always do. "And her mom disappeared here years ago. On purpose."

He sat up and turned to me. His face was in half shadow, and still I could see the sympathy, eyebrows drawn together with concern. "That's horrible."

"Why do you think Lainey would come back to the place where her mother disappeared?" I asked Fletch as if he'd know. I rested flat on the wet sand. "Shit. I don't know why I'm asking you. I don't even know you. I don't understand anything."

"Neither do I," he said. "So look there, we already have something in common." He lay down also and we turned our heads toward each other, our hair splayed on the wet sand like seaweed.

I spoke so softly, but I was sure he could hear me face-to-face. "Sometimes the ocean makes me feel like everything is going to work out and be fine, and sometimes it makes me feel like the world is too, too big and nothing will ever be right because there's too much of it all."

Fletch laughed, but it held sadness underneath it all. This was not what I wanted. I didn't even know him — why would I want his pity?

"Forget I said anything."

He grabbed my hand and pulled me closer, not to kiss or even touch me, just to have me there on the sand next to him. He released my hand. "You should stay right there until you know it's the first option. Until the ocean lets you know that everything is going to be all right."

"I'm not sure that's going to happen. There's just . . . too much that's messed up." I knotted my hands behind my head and felt the gritty sand in my hair. I almost listed it all for him: failing out of college; court date for public intoxication; Mom leaving Dad; Mom's mistake at work . . . but then decided that a boy I barely knew didn't want to hear it all.

We were silent for a minute, only the background noise of the crowd and the music, bursts of laughter and a squeal. Then someone called Fletch's name, a girl's shrill voice.

I turned my head to him. "Someone is looking for you. A girlfriend?"

"An ex." He smiled at me in the half-light. "This is usually about the time she wants to talk about 'it' again. Right after her third beer."

I laughed and it felt good, and I wished I hadn't taken a couple hits off that joint. I wanted to feel the laughter fully.

"You have a boyfriend?" he asked. "Back home waiting? Is that why you're here pining away?"

"Nope," I said. "He ran off with a girlfriend of mine to jaunt around Europe for the summer." I tried to say it with a jovial nonchalance, but my attempt failed miserably. I sounded as sad as I was.

"He's a fool," Fletch said and wiggled his fingers up the sand to give my hair a little pull.

"The perfect thing to say," I replied.

We smiled at each other and then a spotlight hit the sand and the police made their nightly visit and someone threw water on the bonfire. It all ended that quickly, like a dream that ends when the morning alarm blares. Fletch stood and held his hand out to draw me to my feet.

"You should head home. They don't arrest anyone, but don't hang around." He rubbed his hands on his jeans, brushing off the sand, and then drew his fingers through his hair.

It would be nice, I thought, to rest my head on his chest, let him run those same fingers through my hair. But those were stupid thoughts of a stoned girl, and I didn't want him to know I was stoned.

I nodded and waved my hand through the air. "Go on. I'll see you in town."

I didn't watch him leave, but I continued to observe the water. I could do things to make the world fade, but it would come back. Always, and sometimes worse.

I walked to the shoreline, where tiny shells crinkled under my toes, and I threw the rest of the joint into the waves. It bobbed like an oblong, tiny white fish and then sank with its own weight. I again dropped to the wet sand where water met beach. I thought about Lainey's mom, about being desperate and sad enough to disappear from her life and her kids, maybe even sink to the bottom of the ocean. And I cried.

CHAPTER 19
BONNY BLANKENSHIP

The next few days passed just as I'd hoped they would — with food and laughter, trips to town and lazy afternoons on the beach with margaritas in a Thermos and forays to the movies and bookshop. In the times when Lainey left us to walk alone or play with the kids, I opened the leather binder with my projects around the house to keep me occupied. Still no news from MUSC. Still no decisions made. The quiet hum of the river and ocean was on either side of me as I worked my way through the checklist. I didn't forget about Nicholas Rohr or the job loss, or my impending divorce or Owen. No, those things still battered at the edges of my heart and mind, but for a couple days I did settle into what mattered most — my daughter and my best friend.

Mosquitoes and no-see-ums bounced against the screen like drunken men approaching a bar. I snuggled into the brand-new cushions on the now blue wicker furniture and lifted my face to the ceiling fan doing its best to circulate the humid air. Lainey sat across from me, leafing through a magazine, her kids watching a Lainey-approved movie on my iPad. Piper had gone for a walk on the beach, needing to get away from us, I was sure. Sage incense, Lainey's contribution to banish all bad energy, burned in the far corner.

"Bonny," Lainey murmured softly.

"Yes?"

"Do you remember that time Owen took us out in the little johnboat and we ran out of gas and had to try to paddle home using dead palmetto branches?"

Lainey and I had both been doing this the last few days — throwing out random memories like confetti.

"I do," I said. "And Mr. Moreno saved us. He was out fishing and . . ."

"We were so sunburned when we got home that we had blisters on our shoulders that night. Mom rubbed aloe all over us." Lainey's voice caught on the last word, like a nail snagging on a sweater, pulling at a string that might eventually make a huge hole.

"And Dad gave us baby aspirin and Owen tried to sneak us the vodka bottle, saying it would cure us all," I said.

"He was fifteen," Lainey said. "Already a mess, a troublemaker even before Mom left." She hesitated, and I thought she'd fallen asleep or become lost in thought, when she said softly, "Can we talk about the night Owen came to your emergency room?"

I nodded, but she wasn't looking at me; she stared out toward the backyard. She took my silence as acquiescence.

"How much have you seen him and talked to him since then? Or even before then, Bonny? I've missed him so much and he never calls or answers me. But he talks to you?"

These were the fragile bones of our friendship. We'd avoided talking about him ever since my marriage. I trod softly. "He doesn't talk to me much. I hear from him same as you — when he feels like it. The last time I saw him was the night before my wedding. You know this."

"It feels like there's more. Like there are things I don't know."

"No."

She folded and unfolded her legs. "Okay . . ."

"We talk every couple months or when something happens. He'll call out of the blue, or to tell me about a rescue in the Grand Canyon or a new adventure. We never see each other. He knows the milestones of my life, and he knows my marriage is rocky. We have talked. But not often, and I just knew I couldn't . . . see him."

"Did he know about your plans? The ones to take the job in Atlanta and leave Lucas? Did he know?" Her voice changed; it was tight with questions coiled inside.

"Yes."

"Did it have anything to do with him?"

"I don't know." I paused. "Honest to God, I don't know. I don't think so, but how could it not? I've loved him; you know that. But in the literal sense, no. I wasn't leaving for him. I decided to leave Lucas four years ago after that horrible night when I called you."

"The fight when he told you to quit your job — that his career was more important."

"Yes. I know people heal after things like that. I know. But not us. His anger and rage only grew worse and worse. God, Lainey, how many times have you suffered through listening to me? How long have you had to hash this out with me? I made those clandestine plans not to run away with your brother, but to get out. It would have been a nightmare to leave Lucas without leaving

214

Charleston."

"But it had *nothing* to do with Owen?"

"I don't know what does or doesn't have to do with Owen. It's like he's tangled in everything. But it's always on his terms, Lainey. He shows up whenever he wants — and this last time at the hospital, after twenty-two years of nothing but letters and phone calls? It was devastating."

"Yes, it was."

Our voices changed — the lilt and cadence of our friendship transformed into something stilted and unnatural. The subject of Owen did this to us, which was why we mostly avoided discussing him altogether.

"You're angry with me," I said.

"No. I'm confused."

"There's nothing to be confused about. I know you miss him, but I can't make him call you any more than I can make him stop calling me. I don't know what to say . . . I only know I love you and I want you here with me."

"There's nothing to say. I'm not mad at you. If I'm mad at all, it's at him. I promise." She then stood and stretched. "I'm going to try and get some good sleep."

"Lainey . . ."

"Don't say anything else. We're fine. It was just a question that'd been boiling around and . . ."

"I understand."

Alone, I sat on the porch. The candles burned low, puddles of wax surrounded the wicks and the incense stick dropped its last ash. My heart beat in one-two timing, a quick rap-rap against my chest. I understood that being there wouldn't banish Owen from my mind; how could it when this was where we had our first kiss, where I fell in love permanently and irreducibly? But I wanted to reclaim myself even in the place where he had claimed me.

Memories I usually avoided clicked into place, one after the other, of Owen coming and going. Would I ever be free of his memory? I rose to walk back inside the house, and then, as if he'd heard my wondering, my cell rang.

I didn't answer.

CHAPTER 20
PIPER BLANKENSHIP

Fletch arrived quickly after his text asking if I was going to be at the bookshop that afternoon. His footsteps came up the creaky stairs to give me time to adjust myself in the chair, fix my hair over my shoulders and pose in some content version of a girl who wasn't waiting for the boy, which she really was doing.

"Hey, you," he said, and I looked up from my engrossing story, pretending to be startled to see him standing there all wind-swept as if he'd just left the beach. This time his hair wasn't pulled back into a thick black rubber band, somehow making him even more beautiful than before.

"Oh, Fletch. Hi."

He glanced at the book, *Station Eleven,* in my hand. "So are you really into that book?" He pointed at my lap and ambled closer, his hands tucked into his back pockets.

"Very."

"Tell me your favorite line so far," he said and flopped next to me in the spot Mimi had just vacated.

"Easy." I lifted the book and flipped back to a page I'd bent over. " 'Hell is the absence of people you long for.' "

"Nice," he said and then shifted from foot to foot. "Not nice like it's nice to long for people, but a nice sentence."

"I know, right? Even though it ends in a preposition and isn't perfect on the outside, it is on the inside."

He laughed. "So I guess you're so into that story that you might not want to go run some Market errands with me?"

"You act like you want me to say no."

"Let me try again. Would you like to go run some Market errands with me?"

"Sure," I said. "Where we off to?"

"Deliveries."

"Okay. Let's go."

Fletch drove a Jeep, an open-air contraption that made me feel exposed and dangerous, like anything from the world could come in and grab us as we bumped along the dirt and pockmarked roads of peripheral Watersend. Because that was what I discovered — there were two Watersends: the one with the idyllic town square and the refurbished movie theater and quaint bookshop and then the one where people lived on the edge of poverty, but not quite tipping over. There the roads morphed into dirt and the picket fences were nowhere to be seen. The trailers began, and the dogs chased our Jeep, barking so heartily it seemed they were trying to tell us something.

"What kind of Market business do you have out here?" I hollered into the air and over the music from the radio — Grateful Dead, a band whose lyrics I could never make out.

Fletch downshifted and slowed, then turned the music low. "I deliver for a few customers. They either can't get into town or won't, so I just deliver them their weekly groceries."

"That's nice of you," I said and rested my head back on the seat and stared up at the sky.

Fletch took a right into a gravel driveway and I grabbed on to the metal pole over my head to keep from sliding toward the outside of the car. He reached over and grabbed my leg, although we both knew that I was held tight by the Jeep's harness belt. He kept his hand there for a moment and then shifted into park.

The house in front of us was so small I wondered if it was a storage shed. But it must have been a home, because there was a garden to the right of it, a square plot full of tomatoes and peppers drooping heavy and full on the green stalks, waiting to drop into the hand that might receive them. Flowers bordered the vegetables — wild reds and yellows, blues and purples. And behind the main garden, a passel of sunflowers, what seemed to be a hundred of them reaching for the sky, their faces lifted in ecstasy.

"I know," Fletch said.

"What?" I turned to him and it was then I realized that I was doing that thing I do — thinking all those crazy thoughts and some of them coming out in my voice.

"The flowers like faces lifted. I've thought that before," he said.

I smiled but I also blushed, because this was what Ryan hated — when I said such random things that made no sense and I didn't know I'd said anything at all.

"Sometimes I don't know when I say stupid things."

He took off his sunglasses and gazed right at me, like he wanted me to see the insides of his thoughts, right through his pupils. "That wasn't stupid."

I unbuckled the harness and mumbled, "Oh, well, thanks."

He took my hand before I jumped out of the passenger side. "I like the things you say. You see things other people don't see."

I squeezed his hand before pulling mine away. "So who is this we're delivering to?"

"Ms. Loretta. She's great, but she doesn't seem to like leaving this little square."

I saw what he meant. Everything about where she lived seemed square — the house, the garden and the two-foot-tall border of white bricks that outlined her property. "Weird."

He shrugged. "Not really. She's not weird at all. That's the funny part. Come on. I think you'll like her. Another woman named Rosie used to live here, but Loretta moved in a year or so ago."

I jumped from the Jeep and grabbed a bag from the backseat labeled *Loretta*. Fletch took the other bag and another one from inside a large cooler and carried one under each arm, like I did with the kids when they begged me to bob in the waves. He then stopped to glance over his shoulder at me with such a happy expression, one absent of critical assessment or disappointment. I still stood at the side of the Jeep, my hand resting on the back tire and my other hand holding a grocery bag. My heart tried to get my attention with a little flip.

Even on the drive here, I'd been thinking about Ryan and what he would and wouldn't want me to say or do in this situation. About how he was holding Hannah's hand or looking into her face after making love and telling her how beautiful she was. But when Fletch caught my gaze over his shoulder I didn't care so much about Hannah or Ryan or whether they were naked on a bed overlooking the Rhine River or wherever the hell her daddy's money took them next. I only wanted this guy, with grocery bags under his arms, to smile at me.

He nodded toward the door. "Come on, you. Her ice cream will melt for sure."

I followed him along the walkway of broken stone where moss and grass, dandelions and white clover weeds sprouted between the cracks. Fletch stepped onto the porch and knocked on the door. "Ms. Loretta, it's Fletch."

The door opened and I laughed, well, not out loud, but inside for sure. She was so cute. A little woman with springy white hair like corkscrews, which she tried to hold back with a very 1990s hot pink scrunchy. It wasn't taming her hair very well. She had a big wide smile and the darkest eyes I'd ever seen.

"Hello, Fletch my dear," she said and then

turned her attention to me. "Well, we have a helper today, do we?"

I had no idea why this lady needed us to deliver her groceries. She could do anything or go anywhere, as far as I could tell. She was like a little sprite. "Hello," I said. "I'm Piper."

"What a funny name for a girl," she said and laughed. "But aren't you just adorable." She pushed her back against the door to keep it open and nodded for both of us to enter. "Come on in."

"A funny name?" I asked and laughed out loud. "Really?"

"No," Fletch said. "It's a perfect name. Ms. Loretta, please don't scare off my new friend."

"Oh, dear, don't be scared. Sometimes I say things without knowing I said them."

"Me, too," I said. "I do that all the time."

Fletch entered and I followed him. Inside, Loretta's house was as otherworldly as she was. It was all one room — the kitchen, the dining room and the living room — together like best friends. The circular wooden dining table was covered in fabric and buttons and ribbons and thread, its top scarred and scraped. An old-fashioned sewing machine, a Singer, sat in the middle of the table. Everywhere there were nuggets of nature:

rocks and feathers, crystals and shells, driftwood and moss. A nest with a cracked-open, empty baby blue eggshell sat on the windowsill in the kitchen.

Fletch didn't seem to notice any of it as he placed the bags on the kitchen counter.

"Are you a vacation girl?" Ms. Loretta asked.

"A vacation girl?" I stared at a blue crystal that was set on the little window nook over her kitchen sink. I approached it and leaned over to gaze at it, a peephole into another universe. It was spiky and crystallized; small things could live an entire life in between the cracks.

"Here on vacation," Ms. Loretta said. "A girl on vacation. And isn't that beautiful? It's an amethyst crystal. It clears my space of negative energy."

Then I saw that it wasn't blue, but a purple so deep it had fooled me. "You don't even have any negative energy to clear," I said. "And, oh, yes, I guess I'm a vacation girl. But not really, because my mom actually has a place here. I should tell her about your crystal," I said and then felt stupid. "I mean, just because it seems like a couple bad things happened in the house and . . ." I looked to Fletch for help, but he only smiled.

Ms. Loretta smiled, too, and began taking things out of the grocery bags, one by one, settling them in very precise places in her cupboards as if everything had a home and just went straight into it. The tea, the canned corn, the noodles, the chicken broth, the tortilla chips, the pecans and cashews.

"So where is your mom's place?" she asked.

I tried to catch Fletch's eye, but he was organizing other things and putting them away in the freezer and refrigerator, like he and Loretta were an old couple who had unloaded their groceries a hundred times or more together.

"It's called the 'Sea La Vie.' I think it's stupid that people name their houses, but . . ."

She stopped her reach into the cupboard and then turned to me. Her eyes squinted like she was trying to hide them. "Naming things makes them yours."

"I guess so."

"Well, dear," she said to Fletch, "thanks so much for bringing everything. One day, soon I hope, I'll stop being such a hermit and putting such egregious demands on you to come all the way out here to me."

"It's not a problem," he said.

It wasn't until we were in the Jeep and on the way to the second house that I noticed we were driving along a beach road. To the left were the trailers and tiny houses, and to the right, over the hill and visible through a pathway in the wildflowers and thickets, was the beach.

"Stop," I said.

He pulled the Jeep to the side of the road. "What?"

"How can anyone not know about this?" I pointed. "This is, like, prime beach property. No one built here?"

"It's a nature preserve," he said. "Protected land."

I unlatched the harness and jumped out of the Jeep. I knew he'd follow, even though we still had one more stop. I ran through the pathway, my high-tops scraping past sandburs and red and yellow Indian blanket. I heard the waves and the secret sound of the place where earth met water. Halfway across the sand, I took off one shoe and then the other and ran to the water. Then into the water. The bathwater warmth of it wrapped around my ankles and then my thighs. Fletch reached me just as the sea came to my waist, soaking through my cutoff jeans shorts and tank top. A wave approached us and I laughed, jumping to let myself lift with it.

"What are you doing?" Fletch caught me, grabbed me around the waist.

"You have to jump into the ocean whenever you can," I said. "Whenever and wherever you can." The wave caught me in the chest and we both lost our balance and went under.

I stayed there for as long as I could; I always do. Waiting. Waiting. Until I have to rise. Until my chest burns and there's nothing to do but come up for air. We were separated by the wave, Fletch and I, and his legs dangled in front of me. Then his face as he dove back under. He grabbed at me and pulled me to the surface. We rose together.

I took a long fill of air and then said, "I like to stay under as long as I can. Don't you?"

He just looked at me, those very, very blue eyes as liquid as the ocean itself. "No."

"It's so peaceful," I said.

Our feet touched the sand below when the waves receded, and we stood there, bobbing, sometimes our toes fluttering against the shifting sea-ground and in an instant, for a moment, rising above it.

"Peaceful except that you can't breathe," he said and he held on to me, facing me, each hand on my waist.

"Can you imagine a time when we could? Before that first one of us decided to come out of the ocean and walk and breathe out here? To be able to breathe underwater, just in and out, in and out, in and out."

"The things you think about," he said and shook his head. His hair, wet and clumped, dripped into his face, onto his eyelashes.

"I know." The buoyancy of the day and the moment fled. I was flat and embarrassed. I realized, with sudden clarity of mind, that I was soaking wet and in the ocean with my clothes on, saying stupid things to a boy I barely knew. This was my problem. This was why I would never be normal. This was why Ryan left me, and why I didn't get into a sorority and why I would never, not in any way, fit into a life that other people fit into without even trying.

I took his hands from my waist and separated myself, then dove back under the water, where it didn't feel so peaceful anymore, where it felt stifling and as depleted of oxygen as it was. I swam toward shore, a smooth breaststroke like the days when I could swim past every kid on the country club swim team and take home my blue first-place ribbon.

A tug on my leg and then I couldn't come up for the next breath. I kicked backward and rose to the surface with Fletch still holding on to my foot. I gasped for air and he pulled me back under, face-to-face, inside the bottom of a wave. I blinked, the salt water burning, and he took my face in his and brought his lips to mine and kissed me as the water rose above us. It wasn't a regular kiss where you could feel each other's lips and open your mouth to search for how much more of a kiss you wanted. It was an underwater kiss with its own kind of thrill, its own kind of intimacy. I wound my legs around his waist and he pushed off the sand so we broke the surface of the water, and somehow, while still kissing, we took in a long, deep breath together.

We broke apart as the wave carried us toward shore and, tangled, laughing, we found our way to sit on the sand and face the water. A mutual embarrassment floated around us and I dropped my head onto his shoulder. He placed his hand on top of my head and we sat like that for ten heartbeats — I counted. Then he spoke. "That was the best first kiss of my life."

I made a single noise that was supposed to be a laugh but came out more like a sigh.

"Mr. Seaton is going to be very curious

why I'm delivering his groceries soaking wet and covered in sand."

"Let him wonder," I said. "Some of the best things in life we have to wonder about forever."

"You are brilliant, Piper."

"Oh, yes, I am," I said. "That's why I failed out my freshman year."

He wound his fingers through my hair and gave a little tug. "There's more than one way to be brilliant."

"My mom says that to me all the time. She's been saying it to me since my third-grade teacher conference, when they told her that I couldn't sit in my chair."

"Then your mom is right."

"She'd love to hear you say that." I closed my eyes and listened to the sounds of the earth, so very many sounds. "Can't we stay here for a while?"

"Sure thing." Fletch placed his finger under my chin and lifted my face to his and kissed me again.

Chapter 21
Lainey McKay

Shadows played along the edges of the bedroom ceiling as I lay flat on the cool sheets and stared up. The fan whirred and, outside, Piper's voice rose above my children's laughter. I wanted to be there for them every second, but sometimes this wasn't possible.

Before I'd had them, I'd had a fantasy of what a mom could be, what kind of mom *I* wanted to be that was the opposite of what I'd had. To me, the fantasy mom was someone out there ready and waiting for her child to say, "I need . . ." and that mom ran as fast as she could to her child's side. I played this game a lot after my mom was gone. *What would Mom do now?* I would ask myself when I was left out of a party or needed a dress hemmed or a boy picked someone else. This dreamy mom always did the right and good thing. Probably none of the things I did now, but I sure as hell was doing my best.

I stood and stretched, peering out the window. George was on the tire swing and Daisy held a tiny pink fishing pole over the river, wiggling it back and forth. Piper stood between them, her head moving back and forth as if torn over who to pay the most attention to. The doorbell rang. I turned away from the idyllic scene and went out to answer. There on the front porch, a box had been left, the big box that had made it across the country from my little art studio in California.

The edges were crushed and the top was slightly caved in, as if someone had sat on it while they read the paper during their cigarette break at the warehouse. A little thrill filled me and the lethargy I'd awoken with fell away. I dragged the box into the living room just as Bonny came from a bedroom with a screwdriver in her hand — replacing doorknobs, one by one, in the entire house. She never sat still; her leather binder with marching orders kept her moving. Maybe her way of keeping her mind busy with her body.

"What's that?" she asked.

"My art supplies. The ones I shipped from home. I thought it would take a couple days, not over a week." I knelt next to the box and started to tear at the tape. The top of it flapped back and I peered inside. "It's all here. Now I have no excuse not to work."

"Much bigger than that little box you used to carry with you in the summer."

"Not much different, though." I took out a paint palette. "But you're right — it's bigger. Like the supplies grew as we did."

We laughed and Bonny picked a canvas from inside the box, a square, cream-colored canvas stretched across a plywood frame, two feet by two feet.

"Where will you set up?" she asked. "You can choose anywhere you want."

"Ideally right there," I said, pointing to the right-hand corner of the living room under the large windows. "But I don't want my art stuff to hog the house and I don't want my wild injuns to get into the paint . . ."

"You know," Bonny said, "I had an air unit installed in the garage because I was thinking the new owner could make it into a bedroom one day. It's still raw and unfinished, but you could do what you want."

"Are you kidding? The garage has air?"

"It's not empty," Bonny said, "but we could shove most of the stuff to one side."

"This is so wonderful." I hugged her. "Be careful. I might not leave."

"That's my goal," she said and she squeezed me back, her arms tight around my shoulders. "To keep you here for good and all."

"You aren't staying here for good and all, Bonny. You aren't stuck." Her emotions, usually so hidden and camouflaged behind her beautiful smile and inspirational quotes, had been raw and out in the open since the Emory phone call. There was nothing I could say to help, but still I tried.

"I just meant I love having you here, that's all." She stared off toward the river and spoke as if there was another person at the far end of the room. "All my plans, lined like neat little soldiers, decided to mutiny. They've headed out to do whatever they please while I'm left standing here. I'm lost."

"You haven't lost everything," I said.

"Of course I haven't." She turned to me and there was that smile as if it had never left, so practiced. "I've just lost my mooring, my imagined future. I don't feel like I've lost *everything*. Not even close. Just what I wanted and thought I needed. I will go home and try again. Begin again, as they say." It sounded like she was giving a pep talk to a team about to head out onto the field to win the championship game and they were losing by too many points to win.

"You do *not* have to go back to Lucas."

"It might be the right thing to do — to try to fix the mess I've made." She shooed her hand through the air like her feelings were mosquitoes. "I don't want to talk about it anymore." She reached into my box to help me unload. Her hands emerged with a shoe box, which she set on the round entry table. "What's this?"

"Letters," I said and lifted the top. "All the ones I've written to Mom since the day she left. I stopped keeping a journal after Dad read ours. I could never write in one again. I kept seeing the Girl Detective book in Dad's hands, the way he read out loud all the things we thought were so private, and I never could get the words to flow again. But then I started writing to Mom and could get my feelings out that way."

"That night," Bonny said. "That horrible night when he read all the things we'd written about your mom out loud, how she hid her pills under the mattress, how she hid the liquor bottles in the fishing box, how she put vodka in her morning orange juice. Hell, if we hadn't been so nosy, thinking we were real detectives. He used us to shame her . . ." Bonny turned away as if the memory itself was trying to look her in the eyes.

"I've thought about that more times than I can count, but we can't blame ourselves. That's what I came to. Dad was going to shame her and say the same things to her even if he hadn't found our notebook. He was intent on getting her help or having her gone: I've never been sure which. But it wasn't our fault. Even if I felt it was for the remainder of my childhood."

I lifted a handful of the letters. Each one folded and inside a sealed envelope with a single handwritten word on the front: *Mom.* "I don't read them after I write them. It's usually when something has gone wrong or right." The urge to cry began as a weight in my chest and then rose to my throat. Tears puddled and I swiftly wiped them away. "I don't even know how many are here now. I started the year she left and the last one I wrote was only a year ago, after I promised Tim that I'd quit looking for her. I tried to put it all aside. Let it go."

"Oh, how could you do that? All that pain poured out onto paper. All that missing . . . Why did you bring them here?"

"I don't know." I scattered them across the table, a fan of envelopes representing years of aching sadness. "I just felt like this was where they belonged. That I should bring them here and find some way to get rid of them. Maybe even read them before I do. It's time to stop looking and wondering. I promised Tim."

"Don't you want to keep them? Keep them like you would a journal?" Bonny lifted a letter and held it in her hand like it was the very one I needed to save.

I shook my head. "No. I don't. I want it all to end. The wishing for a mom that never was. The absurd wishing to alter the past. What I'd give to make it different, to have her back. But I want that desperation to stop. So I brought them here. These" — I lifted a handful of them and let them flutter to the table — "are all I have left of her. Dad kept all the photos except one I have in a frame at home, and he passed all of Mom's jewelry to his various girlfriends. This is it."

"Why didn't you ask for some of her things?"

"I don't want anything," I said. "If I wanted anything at all it would be to have my brother in my life more than he is, not some jewelry or pictures. I'm not calling Dad and asking him for some leftover pieces of a mom I barely knew."

"I have an idea," Bonny said. "We could do some kind of ritual, some kind of burial or . . . I don't know. Do I sound crazy?"

"No," I said. "I love that. I'm all about ritual."

"Tim doesn't want you to find her?"

"It's not that." I sank onto the couch and rubbed my face as if waking up. "There've been a few times I wasn't quite as honest with him as I should have been. I spent money we didn't have on a private investigator. I've left the kids with friends while I flew to cities where she might be. When I find something that hints of her, I become preoccupied and irrational. It's been . . . bad."

"Oh, Lainey."

"Remember that time I came to visit you and left a couple days early to go home because I said one of the kids was sick?"

"Yes, the flu," Bonny said.

"I lied."

"What?"

"I went to Philadelphia, where there was a woman named Clara who had been found dead in the river. Do you believe that? Whenever the PI calls with some little hint, off I go like I'm an insane person. I've stared at dead, nameless bodies. Spied on women in shelters who won't give their names. Googled until my computer gives out."

"I had no idea." Bonny stood next to me, but I couldn't look at her.

I closed my eyes and let out a long breath, took in another and then opened them again to gaze at Bonny. "Only Tim has any idea and he needs it to stop."

"I can't say I wouldn't do the same thing. But how does one give up?"

"You wouldn't," I said. "It's untenable. You are more logical than this."

"Really? Because I don't see half of what I've done as logical."

"Yes, it is. Look at you when you decided to leave. You didn't just up and go. You planned and organized and put things in order."

"And you can see how well that's worked out." She tried to laugh, but it didn't sound right. "We do the best we can."

"Yes, maybe we do."

We ended the conversation when Daisy came running through the back door carrying a box turtle she'd found in the yard. She was always and forever wanting one more pet — our cat, Sasha, was never enough for her. I bent and focused on being a mom instead of talking about my own.

Once Daisy had run off to find George and Piper, I tossed the letters back into the box. I carried it all to the garage and then used my phone to video chat with Tim so he could see I was about to set up my studio.

"Hi, love," I said, trying to look at him and not myself in the top right corner. I plodded around the garage and held up the phone, twisting it to show him. "So this is my makeshift space for now. I wish you were here to help me unpack."

"Looks like home," he said. I instantly wanted to be near him and for a moment I regretted my decision.

"It's nothing like home. And I miss you terribly. Do you think you could come for a visit?" I asked.

"Probably not, sweetie. I'm dead in the middle of this new house renovation and even a few days will cost us. But hurry home. Get bored there. Miss me and come home early."

"I'll do my best," I said and kissed the screen. We chatted about the kids and his tomato plants and all the things we talked about twice a day. Then I promised him that I'd call back when the kids came inside.

"Sweetie," he said in that voice that meant he had something to tell me that I might not want to hear.

"Yes?"

"I have something to tell you, but you have to promise that you won't change your plans or do anything crazy."

"No promises." I winked at him through

the phone, but he didn't smile. "Shit, what is it?"

"Lorenz called from New York."

"The detective? God, I'd almost forgotten his name," I lied. "What did he want?"

"He said he has a lead on a woman in Texas named Kara Ellison. He sent me all the information on e-mail, but I don't want to send it to you . . . I don't want you to ruin your trip. And I told him to please stop looking."

"Why did you tell him that?"

"Because we agreed."

"We agreed. Yes. But 'Kara' is awful close to 'Clara' . . ."

"Don't." His voice was tight and I pulled the phone to my ear so he wouldn't see me cry.

"I won't. Being here, I know it's true. It's the living with the unknowing. If I just . . . knew." He was quiet until I asked. "Will you at least e-mail me the information?"

"Of course," he said. "This woman . . . she's in Houston."

After I hung up, I sat on a wobbly stool and felt the ache of missing him. I'd loved him so long and so hard that I felt like an essential piece of me was missing when he was away from me.

I dragged the box to the middle of the

garage. The air unit in the window emitted a growling noise and then clicked on, cold air pumping as I unpacked the box and set out my paints, brushes and encaustic medium. I lifted out the hot plate and the few blank canvases I'd packed. Inside a large glassine envelope were the six photos I'd sent myself, ones I wanted to work on. I placed them on the table in a neat pile.

"Hey, Lainey." Piper's voice startled me and there she stood in the doorway with her hands stuffed inside the front pockets of her shorts and her hair in a ponytail. She looked so very young. "Can I help you unpack?"

"Did your mom make you come out here?" I smiled and lifted a case of paints from the bottom of the box.

"No." She shook her head. "I just thought I'd see if you . . ."

"I'd love some help," I said.

She came toward me and then stopped. "Wait," she said. "We need music."

I set up the easel and she slipped away, only to return with a small round speaker. Soon Shelby Lynne's mournful voice eased from the speakers.

"Perfect," I said.

"You like her music?" Piper ran her fingers through a paintbrush I'd just set out and plopped onto a stool beside the workbench that ran along the far wall.

"I love her songs." I placed a set of charcoal pencils on the wooden work surface and dusted it off with a rag. "I saw her in San Francisco last year."

"You saw her live?" Piper's eyes widened and she leaned forward, the paintbrush pointed out as if she were about to paint me. "You are so lucky."

"I know," I said. "She was great. Every time I hear her voice I go back to that night."

"That's what a song does sometimes," she said. "Takes you back to that time you heard it first or best or whatever." She exhaled and stood.

For a long while unsaid words rested between us as we unpacked, the music playing in the background. It didn't take long before the right side of the garage was set up like a mini studio. The clean wooden work surface, meant for tools like rakes and hammers, was organized with art palettes, glue, a hot plate and other tricks of my trade.

"Have you always done this?" Piper broke the silence. "This kind of art, I mean?"

"Yes," I said. "Always."

"I wish I already knew what I was going to do. You're so lucky that you decided what to do and did it and now you still do it and I have no idea and . . ."

"You don't need to have any idea what you're going to do," I said. "I just loved art and I felt like it saved me. I didn't set out to keep doing it. It just kind of happened. I tried other things along the way. I went to college, and I've had loads of other jobs."

"Like what?" she asked.

"I've been a waitress, a vet's assistant, a secretary. I've worked in a nursing home and as an ice cream scooper, all along trying my hand at these projects. Art sometimes feels like a calling more than a job." I laughed. "By that, I mean when it calls, you don't have much choice even if it's not your 'real job.' Or at least that's how it was for me."

"Well, that makes me feel a little better. I mean, Mom? She just knew. I bet she knew when she was a baby that she wanted to be a doctor. And then everything she's done since that moment has made her a doctor. Like a beacon from shore that she just sailed toward. But I'm lost."

"You're not lost," I said. "It just feels that way."

I had no real idea what I was saying to Piper. Maybe she was lost. Maybe we all were. But I felt an instinctual need to help

244

her, to make her see that she was sailing her own boat to wherever it needed to go.

"We all take different paths," I said.

Piper lifted her face to the air conditioner. "The only thing I like to do is read and you can't make a living off of that." Her ponytail flew backward and waved as if in a photo shoot. Then the conversation shifted to things like concerts I'd been to, places I'd visited, what Tim was like and how we'd met.

I set out my yoga mat and she asked me about it. I told her she could join me in my morning yoga anytime she wanted. Eventually Daisy's voice called out for me.

"Guess they are done coloring in their new seashell book," Piper said and took a few steps toward the doorway.

"Oh, I'll get them." I gently placed a canvas on the work counter.

"Lainey?" she asked as I brushed past her.

"Yes?"

"I'm sorry about your mom."

"Me, too, sweetie. Me, too."

"I don't know how you could come back here, but I'm glad you did." She glanced at the doorway and then again looked at me. "I'll grab the kids. I promised them I'd build a sand castle when they were ready."

She was out the door calling Daisy's name

when I sat back on the stool and exhaled. *Houston,* Tim had said.

Maybe there was a time to stop wanting what you didn't have, and do just as Bonny said, to find what matters most and gather those things. But what if *Mom* was still what mattered? What if I couldn't stop making her matter? Tears formed in the curve of my chest and I swallowed them, setting off to join Piper and my kids in castle building. Yet on my way, I pulled up my flight app on the phone and searched for flights to Houston.

CHAPTER 22
PIPER BLANKENSHIP

We'd been in Watersend for two weeks and already there was a natural rhythm to the days, not a chaotic upheaval like at home, where anything and everything went wrong all the time. Dad slammed doors. Mom worked a night shift or cried in the kitchen. But here there was calm; maybe it was avoidance or maybe it was just a lull in the storm.

The morning routine went something like this. I woke to do yoga with Lainey in the garage. If you could call what *I* did yoga; mostly it involved falling and groaning. She would do it for much longer than I did because then George and Daisy were always waiting in the kitchen. We'd have cinnamon toast and fruit and then pack our lunches for the beach. If it was raining, we'd play old maid and color in coloring books.

I never thought I'd say it, but there was nothing cuter than these two kids at the beach. I lathered them with sunblock and they turned into little beach butterballs, rolling around in the sand, floating on their tummies in the tidal pools and building entire cities out of sand. They gathered treasures, which weren't anything more than shells and driftwood that the sea had washed ashore overnight. It was what they found between the tides that was their favorite — sand dollars and starfish, horseshoe crab shells and purple seaweed. We had piles of these in a bucket where we stashed them on the dock behind the house. But there was never enough treasure, always more to be found. Then we ate lunch and I was free until dinner when I had them again.

They loved to sneak into Lainey's art studio to see what their mom was painting, and since I loved to do the same, I went with them. I wish I'd known her better all these years, this woman who stayed so calm and spent hours arranging one tiny picture of scraps and made something important. But then again, I wished a lot of things.

At night, I listened to the women talk. Sometimes it was just a murmur in the background of the novels I read, and sometimes they thought I was reading but I was listening to every word. On these evenings, all the things I didn't know about my own mom always astonished me.

It killed me to hear Lainey talk about her brother and her mother — it took up a lot of her talks with Mom. And yet Mom just sat there not saying a word. I couldn't help but think that my mom had made a choice to leave Dad and Gus at home, while Lainey hadn't done anything that caused her to lose half of her family. She hadn't had a choice. I couldn't fix much in the world, and there was another situation beyond my control. I could only hurt for her, and love her.

One afternoon, I settled back in the bookshop chair, which I'd come to think of as *my* chair in Mimi's store, and opened my journal. Mimi bustled around downstairs, and I heard the little girl who sometimes hung out with her, Ava, chattering away like a bird, a small frantic bird in need of much attention. Ava was a neighborhood girl without a mom, clinging to Mimi whenever her dad would allow her to come to the bookstore. That was Mimi — protecting anyone who needed it.

Meanwhile, she had started writing quotes from her favorite books in her scratchy handwriting and then leaving them on the side table next to my chair. It's like she could read my mind and knew what I needed.

That day her quote was from a poet, Hafez, one of my very favorites. Did she know he was one of my very favorites? Had I told her?

Ever since happiness heard your name, it has been running through the streets trying to find you.

— Hafez

So melodramatic, Ryan would say. Do you have to be so freaking melodramatic?

Footsteps on the stairs let me know that either Mimi or Ava was coming to say hello. It was both of them. Mimi held out a cup of coffee from the Market. "This is from Fletch," she said and handed it to me.

I smiled just at his name.

"This is so nice," I said to Mimi and then looked to the little girl. "Good afternoon, little bug."

"Can I pick what kind of bug to be today?" she asked and jumped on one foot to the other end of the room. "Did you see that? I'm learning to jump on one foot. I might be a gymnast one day."

"You're pretty awesome," I said.

"Today," she said, "I'm a ladybug. Okay?"

"Perfect," I said.

"How was your morning?" Mimi asked

and motioned to my journal on the side table, facedown and open like butterfly wings spread wide.

"So far so good." I took a long swallow of the Fletch-delivered coffee. "I'm free until dinner. All my errands are done."

Ladybug disappeared down the stairs and I looked to Mimi with the coffee cup held to my face, obscuring my chin and lower lip. "Can I ask you something?"

"Of course," she said.

"Were you there the night that Lainey's mom disappeared?"

"Yes," Mimi said. "I was."

Mimi sat on the chair next to me. I tucked my feet under my bottom and found my way into what I'd really meant. "Mom told me all about it, but she was talking to Lainey about it a few nights ago. I just can't imagine what that must have been like. To wait and not know . . . and then . . ."

"Yes," Mimi said.

"Do you have any idea where she is? What happened? Do you even have a guess?"

"I do, but everyone does. Everyone has theories. It was terrible. No two ways about it."

"Yes, terrible." I paused and then hoped I sounded nonchalant, easy. "Did you know Owen, also?"

"Owen? Of course. We all did." Mimi glanced away as if she saw him coming up the stairs. "He was so special. A child who was more like a man. He was fifteen or so back then, and he seemed to watch over the girls more than their parents did. I don't know what happened to him, but I'm sure he's a great man now."

"I'm not sure." I shrugged. "Lainey hardly ever talks to him, and she misses him a lot. Mom talks to him . . ." I paused because I felt I was betraying Mom and yet I wanted an answer, a hint at what this could be that niggled like a hangover headache. Something, I knew. Something, and I couldn't quite touch it.

"They were very close. Like brother and sister," Mimi said. "I'm sure they've kept in touch."

"Oh." I fiddled with the fringe on the pillow. "But I think she knows more than she's saying to Lainey. It's kind of weird in a way. Mom is usually so open and all of that. I mean, they sit around and tell stories but not that one."

"Sometimes we tell our stories and sometimes our stories tell us," Mimi said and leaned closer like she does.

"What does that even mean?" She exasperated me sometimes, like a confusing puzzle that might show me something interesting if I took the time to finish it.

"So, why did you fail out of school when I can tell, right here, right now, that you are one of the smartest people I've come to know in all my years?"

I bristled, just as I did when Ryan told me that I was gaining weight or that my hair was too frizzy — he was good at pointing out those things that so easily go wrong, those things that mean I *am* wrong. Anger rose in a short burst of heat. "I failed because I hated it there. Hated every single thing about it."

"There." Mimi smiled. "You told your story by failing instead of by saying, 'I hate it here and I'm miserable.' "

"Oh." There are clicks inside when things make sense, like one of those old twirler locks on our school lockers. "I get it."

"But you can't make your mom or Lainey or anyone else tell their story." Mimi scrunched her nose in that little way of hers. "Some things can only be told by those who are living it."

"Well, I get that and all, but they better tell or it's going to tell them — like the clouds coming in with a storm fast behind."

"But it's not your storm," Mimi said.

"Maybe, but it is if I'm sitting on the

porch when it gets here," I said.

"Well, then, dear, you are right about that." Mimi laughed and stood. "Then I guess the best you can do is take cover."

The tinkling bell announced a new customer and I heard Ava say, "Hi, Fletch. How are you? How may I help you?" in a parody of Mimi, a young voice imitating an old one with such accuracy. Mimi threw me a knowing look and headed downstairs.

I closed the book and headed down the stairway myself, meeting Fletch, who was climbing up. At the stairway's curve we bumped into each other and both laughed, but uncomfortably, at that unexpected skin-on-skin contact. He took a step backward and gazed at me. "Guess you're ready to run those deliveries with me?"

With sudden impulsivity, I leaned forward and pressed my hands onto his shoulders and then I kissed him. "I'm ready," I said.

He steadied himself with one hand on the banister and one on the wall. I backed away and stood one step up, giving me the couple inches I needed to be face-to-face with him.

"Almost falling down Mimi's crooked stairs is a small price to pay for your kiss," he said.

I waved my hand. "So full of malarkey." I borrowed one of Mimi's words and imitated her voice as I shooed him down the stairs. "Now let's get to work."

His laugh sounded like his kiss tasted — warm and comforting with a little bit of adventure hidden inside.

"So I have a favor to ask," I said as I climbed into his now familiar Jeep.

"Which is?"

"Can I bring George with us? Lainey wants to take Daisy to the paint-your-pottery place and George would be a night-mare there."

"Lainey's okay with him in the Jeep?"

"As long as I buckle his car booster seat thing, she's fine."

"Car booster seat thing. Whatever that is, it sounds complicated."

"It's okay. We don't have to take him . . ."

"Piper, I'm kidding. Let's bring him."

Fletch's jam-band music played during the ride out to Mr. Seaton's house, where we left the deliveries in a cooler on the front porch, and then we were on to Loretta's house again. I peeked behind me to see that George's smile never once left his little round red face. He bobbed his head to the music and opened his mouth to the wind of the open-air ride. He spread his hands out like he was flying and laughed at nothing and everything.

In Loretta's driveway I unbuckled his six thousand buckles and he bounded out and ran for the garden. "Wait," I hollered.

George looked over his shoulder and laughed as if I'd told him to fly or do any other impossible task. He reached the sunflower garden before I could catch up to him. His small body disappeared into the tall stalks. I reached the edge of the flower-bed and crouched to spy his little bare legs. "George," I said. "This isn't our house. You can't just run into her flowers."

"Oh, yes, he absolutely can." Loretta's voice came from behind me and I turned around.

"Hi, Ms. Loretta." A hot, blushing embarrassment filled my face. There I was, I barely knew her, and the unruly child ran into something she'd worked so hard to make nice.

George popped out of the garden and held his hands to the sky, to the flowers' tops. "They are *so* big."

"I thought it would be fun to take him for a ride in the Jeep and then run on the empty beach. I didn't mean for him to bother you," I said to Loretta and took George's hand in mine.

Loretta bent her knees and placed her

hands, wrinkled and freckled, on them. Her hair was loose and it caught in the wind, silver and tousled. "Are you George?" she asked.

"Yes, I am," he said and stared at her with squinted eyes and intense focus.

She stood and smiled at me. "I heard you hollering at him. I thought something bad was going on out here, but it's actually something wonderful."

"I'm sorry if we disturbed you." Apologies poured out of me, another and another.

"Oh, darling," she said, sounding just like Mimi. "There is no reason for apologies. What great fun this is." She took a few steps closer to the garden and George shook free of my hand and followed her.

Loretta reached the edge of the sunflowers and wrapped her hand around a thick bright green stalk, then bent and twisted until it broke free. The flower's stem, two feet tall, dangled with ripped green fibers, and Loretta handed it to George.

His tiny hands wound their way around the stalk and he held it close. "This is mine?"

"Yes, it is," Loretta said. "All yours. Sunflowers are rumored to bring you good luck, and their little faces" — Loretta touched the dark inside of the flower —

"always follow the sun."

"Well, because they look like the sun," George said. He brought it closer to his face and rubbed the yellow petals across his cheek. "Thank you." His voice was suddenly deep and grown-up. Then he stepped closer to Loretta and whispered, "What does 'rumored' mean?"

She laughed and crouched to face him again. "It just means that 'some people say.' So some people say that sunflowers bring you good luck."

"Then you must be the luckiest old lady in the whole world." He pointed at her garden. "You have one million of them."

"I am the luckiest old lady in the whole world," she said and ruffled his hair.

Old lady. God, Fletch was never going to let me run errands with him again.

When she stood to face me, her eyes were moist with tears, and I knew he'd hurt her feelings. I should have left him at home . . . I should have . . .

"Are you okay?" I asked.

"Yes, dear. I'm completely fine. Sometimes we cry a little bit when we're happy."

"You're happy?" I asked, feeling the train of my thoughts switch tracks. I glanced at Fletch, who was carrying the cooler and grocery bags into the house.

Loretta's gaze followed mine. "Seems as if there is something that makes you happy, too." She winked at me and it made me laugh. And maybe turn a little pink.

"George," I said, "let's help Fletch bring in the groceries and put them away."

"Can I keep this?" he asked, clutching the flower tighter and drawing it closer to his body.

"Yes, you can," Loretta said. "It's all yours."

Inside, George sat at her table covered in fabrics and ribbons. While Fletch and I stashed her deliveries and chatted about the upcoming summer concert, she dug out some art supplies from a kitchen drawer and set them before George. "I always keep these around for my friend's grandchildren."

No one rushed to leave and Loretta poured us all a glass of lemonade. We leaned against her counter and talked of nothing at all while soft music — fifties crooners — played from a radio on the kitchen counter and the sun fell in honey-colored puddles across the table where George colored and ate frozen grapes covered in sugar. His flower rested on his lap and he bit his lower lip in concentration as he attempted to re-create it with colored pencils on thick white paper.

Maybe his flower would bring us all good luck, or maybe it already had.

CHAPTER 23
BONNY BLANKENSHIP

The Watersend Summer Block Party was already in full swing when we arrived. The police cars, lights blazing, blocked off Main Street, and music blasted on the street. Daisy and George clung to Piper's hands, one on each side. They'd attached to her like barnacles, always running next to her and keeping her within their sight. Sometimes it felt more like they were watching her instead of her watching them. I carried a cooler with homemade lemonade — one Thermos for the kids and one (adult version) for Lainey and me. When we walked past the silent flashing police lights, I turned my head away, but still the strobes flashed against the palmetto trees and pink-tinged sea grass. My heart thudded in double time.

"You okay?" Lainey asked.

"I hate it," I said. "Flashing lights make me feel queasy. It brings back that night in the ER and I don't know how to stop the panic that comes with it."

"How can I help?" she said.

"Nothing you can do about it."

"What if there *is*? I can teach you some meditation skills and there are some crystals that are really grounding for this kind of thing."

"Listen, I'll take a lit stick of incense and put it up my nose if it would help. Anything. Honestly. But I think it just has to pass."

Lainey tossed her arm over my shoulder and laughed. "No. I know you're the doctor and all, but panic doesn't just pass. You have to get it out of your body. Do something to get it out."

"Well, I'll do whatever it takes. When they say I can return to my job, I won't be able to go back to it if I freeze at flashing lights and blaring sirens."

"We've got time. Deep breath, my friend."

"God, Lainey, do you know how many times I've said that to patients freaking out? And not even believing it would help but just to say it."

"Well, now it's your turn, Doc. Do it."

We entered the tent, where Piper had already found an empty picnic table and dropped the kids' toys and coloring books on top to save it. Wildflowers filled vases on every table and exposed lightbulbs strung under the tent lent a festive atmosphere, like a wedding reception for the town itself. A wooden dance floor — just pieces of plywood laid end to end — was empty. The single guitar player sang a James Taylor song that hadn't yet brought out the dancing crowd.

Piper stood at the picnic table grinning at the stage and I glanced at the singer. "Oh, that's that boy from the Market."

"Fletch," she said.

"He's really good," I told her.

"Yes, he is."

"So much for Ryan."

"Way to mention his name, Mom. Perfect."

"As usual, not quite as funny as I meant to be."

Daisy pulled at Piper's T-shirt. "Come on, let's do the face painting, Piper," Daisy whined. Piper rolled her eyes and took George's hand as the three of them hustled off to the face painter in the far corner.

I should have known better. I know how just a single name can throw me off balance. And there I'd gone and tossed out Ryan's name as if I didn't know the pain Piper felt. Lainey sat at the table, unscrewed our Thermos and poured the spiked lemonade into two plastic glasses. We toasted,

"Here's to us."

The tent slowly filled, family by family, until every picnic table was full and another couple sat at the end of ours, too intent on each other to notice us. "Do you miss Tim?" I asked Lainey with a slight nod to the nuzzling couple.

"All the time," she said. "But I also really want to be here, and I'm happy here and the kids are having such a great time. So it's mixed."

"It's nice that you can miss him without being miserable."

Up on the stage, Fletch was introducing the upcoming band and we both paused to watch him. "Do you miss Lucas at all?" she finally asked.

"Not even one second. I miss the *idea* of our family." I pointed at a young family seated at the table next to us. "And I miss what I wanted it to be, but I don't miss him at all. Lainey, he never wanted me. He wanted the image of what he wanted me to be. I was . . . never enough for him. It's such a disheartening, sinking feeling that each time I dwell on it, I feel like I'm falling."

"God, that makes me so sad. You" — she leaned forward and took my hand — "are a wonder. You are a bright light and a full heart. You are enough and more all the time. I don't get why you even stayed this long if that's true."

"Family."

"Yes, that. I get that."

A high screech emanated from the stage and we both covered our ears as the sound system malfunctioned. A quick panic rose and settled in my chest. *Just a microphone. Just a microphone.*

I glanced toward the far wall, where the sweet aroma of barbecue flowed toward us. "Remember Billy's?" I asked. "Your dad went there at least three times a week to bring back ribs. He was obsessed."

"I do." Lainey took in a long breath as Piper returned with the kids. Daisy's face was orange and black, a lion, she told us. George's face was black and white, a panda.

Lainey drew her children close to her and squeezed them tight. "My little animals. I always knew you were wild."

"Mommy," Daisy said, "come make animal balloons with us. Come on."

When they'd reached the far side of the tent, where the clown made balloons into animals and flowers and dogs on a leash, Piper sat next to me. "They are exhausting. But adorable."

She reached for my glass and I held my

hand over it. "Nope."

She laughed. "I tried." Then she pointed across the room. "Mimi's here. And I think she has a beau."

"How sweet," I said.

"I'm getting us all some food." Piper stood up and walked away as the band started to warm up, a clashing sound of guitars, violins and a keyboard. We settled into the music and Piper returned with a plate of barbecue and Fletch by her side. Mimi headed our way with a tall, gray-haired man. Something about the way he moved and the color of his hair brought the panic bird to life and its wings flapped against my ribs, trying to get out. *Nicholas Rohr.*

Of course this man looked nothing like him, other than that he was tall and gray haired, but I'd never even seen Nicholas stand. He'd never stand again. I closed my eyes and took a long, deep breath. Held it for four and exhaled slowly. When I opened my eyes Mimi stood in front of me. "Darling, are you okay?"

I nodded and stood. "Oh, yes."

"I want you to meet my friend Harrington."

"Nice to meet you," the man said and reached out his hand. My breath caught below my chest as he took my hand, and then I knew why: it wasn't this gray-haired man who had set the bird to flight; it was Lucas. He stood five feet away, watching me, and my peripheral vision must have seen him and known. My body knew before I did.

I rudely dropped Harrington's hand without a word of greeting. Mimi and he glanced at each other and stood by silently as Lucas approached the table and faced me.

"What are you doing here?" I asked in a voice so quiet I felt I hadn't spoken at all.

"Dad," Piper said and moved a step away from Fletch.

He greeted her first with a hug and then turned to me. "I need to talk to you."

"Nothing good ever begins with 'I need to talk to you,' " I said.

"You're right."

He took my arm and led me away from Mimi and Harrington. Piper took one step forward and one back. "Dad, don't."

"Bonny?" Mimi asked.

"It's okay," I said.

But it wasn't. It wasn't at all.

"How did you . . . know where I was?"

"I saw the festival as I drove in, and when I found the house empty, I assumed . . ."

"Got it." I held up my hands as I backed

away. "I don't want to talk about us now or here."

"Well, you don't have much choice, now, do you? I'm here to give you these." He held out two manila file folders I hadn't noticed in his hand. "The first are the papers I'm serving you for divorce. The second are contracts to sell the house. I already put it on the market. The MLS listing goes up tomorrow."

"What?" Which was what patients said to me when they understood me but didn't want to hear the diagnosis.

"I think you heard me. And I told you this would happen if you left. This is obviously what you want. So here." He held out the folders, but I didn't lift my hand to take them. A breeze came by to join us and my sundress lifted and billowed around me like a parachute. I pressed on my dress and refused the folders. "No."

"It's what you wanted," he said. "So take them."

It was what I'd wanted, of course. But not with an ambush. I shook my head and then his lecture began — the long and arduous one about my lack of commitment and wasted money and not answering the phone. And it all ended with an assumption that I would have, by now, gotten over this ridiculous notion that staying the summer in an old family home would help me. It appeared, to Lucas, that I was beyond help.

"You ran away, Bonny. Now you'll have to learn words like 'summons' and 'complaint' and there are financial worksheets and affidavits . . ."

"Stop." I held my hand up. "I know you're trying to scare me. I can feel it all the way inside. And it's working. It's definitely working." I took the papers, gripping the file folders and feeling their edges dig into my sweaty palms. "Leave. Please. I'll go through these."

"I *am* leaving," he said and then his lip lifted over his teeth, a grimace of anger. "You're a fool." His anger moved like waves under his skin.

Maybe I was, but I didn't say a word.

"Aren't you going to say anything?" he asked.

"No."

This was obviously the wrong response. Twenty-two years of arguing and fighting back and defending myself had left him believing I would again engage. I saw how my reactions all those years had kept this going — he attacked; I defended; he increased the criticism; I increased the justification. But now that I didn't defend, what was there left to attack? My very being, obviously.

"You are ridiculous and absurd. I *am* taking Piper home with me."

"No, you're not."

"Who was that boy with her?" he asked.

"A friend," I said. "A very, very nice friend."

"Dear God, don't tell me she's dating a black guy."

"You," I said. "Do you see who *you've* become? Oh, God, Lucas." And I walked away, just like that. No more explaining. No more excuses. No more fixing. Before I reentered the tent, I opened the top folder and he was right — the paperwork was intimidating and frightening, and I didn't want to do it. But I would.

I'd loved him once. When I'd met him, his sense of adventure, his easy laughter and charm had lured me. The marriage death had been a slow undoing of kindnesses, and an escalation of dismissive disapproval. And now this: the End.

Inside the tent, the atmosphere had shifted to a more raucous party, and I watched Lucas walk away to the dirt parking lot at the end of the block. My heart hammered against my ribs and I wanted to go *home,* back to the river house and the porch.

Whatever I'd believed still waited for me in Charleston was gone. I'd ruined everything. This was my undoing and nothing remained. There would be no going back.

The band played, and the dance floor overflowed with families and couples and teenagers. Mimi and Harrington waited for me with Lainey and the kids at the table. I sat and took a long drink of the lemonade we'd brought — the adult version — and they sat with me.

"Where's Piper?" I asked.

Lainey pointed at the dance floor. "Dancing with that cute guitar player who is eyeing her as if she hung the moon, the stars and the majority of the planets." Lainey patted George the panda's head. "I think someone here is a bit jealous."

George sat cross-legged on the pavement, dejected and playing with a Tonka toy truck, which he ran over his legs and under the picnic table.

"Are you okay?" Lainey asked me. "Where is he now?"

I kept my sight on Piper and Fletch as I answered. "I don't know. He went home, I assume. I'm fine. Or not." I took another long swig of the lemonade and felt the vodka spike its way inside and then flow through my veins as surely as the Dilaudid had for Mr. Rohr. Back to *him,* always a return to that night with my mind looping ever backward. "Lucas gave me these." I held out the folders for Lainey.

She opened one, glanced inside and then closed it quickly. "Oh . . ."

"Yes, oh." I slid the folders back across the table and stuck them into my purse. "You'd think I'd be happy to get what I wanted — divorce papers."

"I know this is awful timing and . . ."

"There's no going home now," I said. "There is no home. No job. No husband. No house."

"Bonny . . ."

I ran my hand through my hair and closed my eyes tight against the forming headache. "No one took it away. I lost it. Or I gave it up."

"Lost what?" Daisy's voice asked from under the table. She popped up and jumped into my lap, wiggling her way to comfort.

"Not you," I said and kissed the top of her warm hair. "I'd definitely never lose you."

"I can hide really good," she said.

"I'd find you." I touched the tip of her lion nose and then looked at Mimi. Harrington sat next to her, although he looked toward the dance floor as if pretending he wasn't there at all.

Mimi glanced around the room as if searching for danger. "Did you know *he* was coming?"

I shook my head. "I didn't. But can we change the subject? I'm fine. This was such a beautiful night and I refuse to let him ruin it."

"Okay," Lainey said. "Change of subject." She turned to Mimi. "Is it odd to see us all here again? Like no time at all has passed?"

"Oh, time has definitely passed," Mimi said and laughed.

"I want you to tell us something about your life," I said. "I know there's more than just the bookstore, the bourbon and the pound cake. And Harrington."

"Oh, darling, of course there is." She tucked a stray hair into her bun and leaned forward. "I have a garden that will blow your socks off, full of every flower that will grow in zone eight. I have a host of hilarious friends, although I've also lost so many. I'm obsessed with the new movie theater and never miss the opening night of any movie, even if it's horror."

"Where do you live?" I asked, feeling my heart slow then, like Mimi's life could be mine. So beautiful. So simple.

"I have a little guesthouse behind another

house, only a few blocks away. But oh, darling, I've lived in so many places in Watersend. From the worst apartment to the nicest house. It's been a wild ride of a life."

"I bet there's very little you don't know about this town," I said. "You could write a book."

"I want to ask something kind of crazy." Lainey twirled her glass and glanced sideways at her kids before speaking in a whisper. "Do you remember my mom at all?"

Mimi's face changed so quickly that I could have sworn she was going to cry. "Of course I do."

"Do you think anyone in town remembers?"

"I'm not sure, dear." Mimi looked at the table and then reached to take Harrington's hand. "We don't talk much about it around here. Most people who knew her all those years ago are gone or didn't know her well. You know she didn't come into town very much unless she came to pick you girls up to go home. She stayed out at that river house or sometimes came to a party or two. I only knew her because she would talk to me when she came for you."

"I hate asking," Lainey said, "but I believe that one day I will say her name and someone will reply, 'Oh, yes! I saw her in

Houston,' or, 'I heard she was in Atlanta' . . . I know it's crazy. It's like a tic. She's probably gone." Lainey paused and then said what she must have wanted to say all along. "There's this detective I hired years ago. I stopped paying him — Tim begged me to stop. But the detective says he's never stopped thinking about this case — it burrowed under his skin. So every once in a while he runs another quick look, and he's called to say she might be in Houston, Texas."

"Texas?" Mimi asked. "Why there?"

"Wait," I said. "You heard from a PI. I thought you said you'd stopped."

"I did stop, but he called Tim. And I have no idea why Houston. But he does a sweep every few months in his database and I guess this woman turned up without real identification and she's the right age . . . I know I should ignore this, but . . ." Lainey looked at the twinkle lights and shook her head. "I even looked at plane flights. I've thought about leaving here to go to Texas. Just. In. Case. It's insane."

"Lainey, you are going there again — to that place you told me you wanted to avoid, to the place you promised Tim you wouldn't go, grasping at straws." I reached to touch her arm, a motion of solace and understanding.

Mimi shook her head. "But how could you not keep asking and looking? She's your mother. But I bet that if she's staying away, she has her reasons — and I know they aren't because she doesn't love you or your brother, if that's what you've been going through all your life believing."

Lainey laughed, but it was a choked sound. "That is such a Mimi-nice thing to say, but of course if she's alive she doesn't love us. I have children. There is nothing — not fire or hell — that could keep me away from them." She dropped her hand onto Daisy's blond hair where she now sat on the ground with George after she'd jumped from my lap to color in her mandala coloring book.

"I can see why you'd feel that way," Mimi said softly. "But sometimes we don't know everything there is to know."

"Well, that's enough about me, Mimi. I thought we were supposed to be talking about you. You've always been in Watersend, right?" Lainey changed the subject quickly.

"Where else would I go? This is home. Speaking of homes, I'd love to see what you've done to the old river house, Bonny." Mimi shifted on the bench closer to Harrington, who seemed still preoccupied by the dance floor.

The singer began to butcher an Alison Krauss song and I said, "I'd love for you to come see the house. At least it means I've done something. If I'm done saving lives at least I can save a house."

"You aren't done," Mimi said.

Harrington turned to us then, but he seemed absent at the same time. "You know, Mimi, I think I'm going to head home."

"Are you okay?" she asked.

"Just tired, my dear." He slurred his words and I wondered how he'd gotten so sloshed so early in the evening when I hadn't seen him take a sip of a drink.

Mimi looked confused and a low thrum began in my chest. Something was wrong. I wanted to bolt from the picnic table, head toward the fresh air. Was it Lucas again? I glanced around the tent but didn't see him. I stared across the table with white static filling my mind. The music reverberated, bouncing off the edges of my skull; the bluegrass violin's screech ricocheted off the edges of my consciousness. But underneath, in a small corner of my mind, the doctor in me screamed, *Do something right now.* But what was there to do? I didn't know. Dizziness and electric panic swirled through me like a storm.

"Harrington," I heard my voice say. "Smile for me."

"What?"

"Smile real big for me." I repeated myself, and the fog started to lift. I stood. "Now."

"What in the gravy?" Mimi asked.

But he did smile, and his gaze wandered away and the left side of his grin didn't lift. I moved quickly to the other side of the table. "Lainey," I said without looking at her, "call 911 and tell them to notify the hospital to have tPA on hand and ready."

"What?"

"Now," I said, repeating my instructions. I reached Harrington's side. He stood as I approached, and then he wavered, grabbing to the side of the table. "Sit," I said. "You're having a stroke."

"Hell no, I'm not," he slurred.

"Harrington," Mimi said calmly. "Do exactly as she says."

He looked to Mimi and his eyes softened and closed. "I don't feel right at all."

The sirens were far off and then closer and closer. I held his hand and Lainey pushed back the crowd, moving them to the far end of the tent. Mimi held his other hand while Harrington tried to convince us that he was just tired and hadn't drunk enough water, and that we needed to let him walk home. When the ambulance arrived outside the tent, and the paramedics rushed to his side, I rattled off his symptoms and then stepped away.

For a long while I stood still in the street, alone, unable to move until the sound of the sirens disappeared and the music started again. Something shifted inside, a slight tectonic movement that didn't yet change the landscape, but I was quite sure would.

CHAPTER 24
BONNY BLANKENSHIP

"You saved his life," Lainey said simply.

Back at the house, the little ones settled in bed, I sat on the back porch with Lainey and stared into the darkness. I couldn't see the river, but I knew it was there, pulsing and moving. Same with my life. I couldn't yet see it, but tonight had given me a glimpse into the darkness — I was going to be okay. Not yet, not tomorrow, but some-day soon I would be.

"I just saw the symptoms," I told her.

"You know, he was getting ready to leave. And if he'd walked off and gone home . . . I know enough about strokes to know it's all about catching it in the first hours. You saved his life."

"It was surreal, Lainey. We talked about your mom and the kids and home; I knew Lucas was gone; and then I was paralyzed. I couldn't do anything at first. I was frozen as solid as I have been for months. But some part of me, something inside, broke loose from the iceberg and took over."

"The *real* you."

I laughed. "Maybe."

"It was the woman who told Lucas you would not go back. The woman who saved a life. It is the woman who sits on this porch with me."

"We are never just one thing, are we?" I asked. "Never just this or that."

"Never."

"Where's our Piper?" I asked.

"Asleep in bed with Daisy," Lainey said. "Too adorable to even tell you." She paused and then asked, "Do you think Mimi was weird about Mom? I mean, defending her and all that."

"No," I said. "I think she was just trying to make you feel better. That's how she is." I settled back into the cushions and exhaled. "I know this sounds crazy, but sometimes when we're alone like this, and our kids aren't yammering around, I feel like your mom is going to walk in the door. Or my mom. That we have sand on our feet and we're rubbing aloe on our sunburns. That we're scribbling in our notebook. That we have a half-finished game of Monopoly on the kitchen table, and peace sign appliqués ready to stitch onto our jeans."

"Me, too, Bonny. Me, too."

We were silent for a time and then Lainey stretched and told me good night, leaving me alone on the porch. And, as if she'd summoned her brother with her voice, my cell buzzed and his name showed on my screen. I would answer this time — the need for him winning out over my strength to stay away.

"Hi, Owen." I tried to keep my voice calm, steady.

"Finally, Bonny. I've tried so many times. You know when you don't answer I think something terrible has happened."

"Nothing is wrong," I said. "Or everything is, depending on your take."

"Where are you?" he asked.

I laughed. "That is usually my question for you," I whispered and walked off the porch to the backyard, where I hoped neither Lainey nor Piper could hear me.

"I'm in North Carolina," he said.

"Tell me you aren't back in the air," I said. "Not with that broken collarbone and dislocated shoulder and . . ."

"No, Doc. I'm not in the air. My feet are firmly on the ground. Where are *you*?"

He repeated his question and a wash of realization almost made me smile. It was the first time he'd ever had to ask me anything twice. So willing was I all the time to give him exactly what he needed when he needed it. The urge when he arrived, always at that last minute, was to keep him there as long as possible, with the everlasting hope that "as long as possible" meant "forever," which I knew it didn't. But wouldn't it be nice if it did?

"Are you still there in Watersend?"

"Yes," I said.

"Are you okay?"

This was the chance to tell him that his sister was with me, that she was just a few hundred yards away in a room next to his niece and nephew. I didn't. "Yes, I'm okay."

"God, give me something. Tell me . . . I mean, have you heard about your job?"

"I really can't talk to you about any of it."

"Oh, Bee, why can't you?"

"Because it breaks my heart to share it with you. Because you shatter my heart. Every. Single. Time. And this time won't be any different. And I want to begin again, and I want to start over and I want to focus on the things that are most important to me. And when you are anywhere near me I forget everything else. You become the one thing, and I lose my way."

"That's a lot of 'and,' " he said in that light tone that came with a smart-ass grin and his hand coming to the back of my neck to pull me to him, to kiss me so anything I said and anything I thought faded. No matter how many years had passed, still that memory lingered.

"There's more of them," I said, "but none of that matters. You have to leave me alone."

"Tell me," he said. "Tell me — what are the most important things?"

"Saving my daughter and myself. Anything else comes second. Everything else."

"I'll be second. Or third. I don't care. Just don't take me out of the lineup."

"Like I'm a baseball coach." I laughed and felt our banter begin.

"Yes. I'm on the B team and you're trying to decide if maybe I need to be sent back to the farm team. Or worse, sent home."

"How could I send you home when you don't have one?"

"Good point."

There was a beat or two of silence, a time when we measured our own breath. I closed my eyes. I was falling into his voice; I always did. God, I always would. There was no way out. It was a magnetic force, a terrible gravity.

"Do you remember the night before my wedding?" I asked. "The night you showed up at my house?"

"Yes," he said, so softly I barely heard him.

"You begged me not to get married, but you said you still had to leave the next day. Just wait, you said. Just always and always wait. That's what you wanted. It's what you still want." My voice rose and I felt the sickness of his desertion again, as if it was that night and my wedding dress hung in the bedroom closet.

"But you married him," Owen said. "Then what was I supposed to do? I can't leave you alone. I can't ever give up."

"You gave up every single time you left," I said.

There was silence for a moment and I heard him gathering his breath, slowly.

"Can I come visit?" he asked.

"You've never asked before," I said. "Why now?"

"Because it seems different now."

"It is different, and you can't come. I'm with my daughter . . ."

"Well, there you go," he said. "It's why I've never asked before. Because you'll say no."

"I don't know what to say."

"Say that you miss me, and that you don't blame me and that you still love me . . ."

"I can't say those things." I closed my eyes against the lie, held my hand over my chest.

I did miss him. I didn't blame him and I loved him. But I couldn't tell him that because it needed to *not* be true.

"I understand," he said.

We hung up without good-byes, and it was a foreign feeling, keeping my heart hidden from him.

Inside the house, Piper slept and a fierceness rose in me, the kind of protective feeling I felt when someone else tried to hold her when she was a baby or when I placed her in the crib at night. A doctor knew what could happen between dark and morning light. It was a mother's lioness-protection that caused me to do anything, absolutely anything, to save my daughter from sorrow or pain. I'd wanted to set a dome around her — a force field where nothing harmful might penetrate.

I ached for her heart, and her safety, and for my mistakes. Why would she choose to drink herself into oblivion or skip her classes or choose a boy like Ryan who would hurt her in such awful ways? Where had I gone wrong? The Halloween when I had to work and so sent her to stay with friends? The fourth birthday party where I was so tired I barely got through the candle-wish-blowing before falling asleep on the couch? The lunch boxes I forgot to pack? The mommy group I didn't join. The mommy group I did join. The list was endless and formidable. I wasn't the woman, the mother or the wife I'd meant to be. If I'd meant to be one at all.

Loving a man who wasn't her father seemed the biggest sin so far and yet one she didn't even know about. I'd never *done* anything about it, unless you counted the one true fact that my heart was always with him, with the possibility of him.

Had I destroyed my daughter's concept of love, all the while meaning the best? I felt nauseated at the possibility of all my mistakes cascading down to her, invisible and as powerful as a waterfall. I wanted to prevent all heartache, all damage and all failure from touching her fragile soul.

I gingerly stepped across the damp and dark backyard, fireflies flickering and diving, and the moon high. I startled as I reached the porch and opened the screen door. Piper stood there with a glass of water in her hand.

"Hey, sweetie. I hope I didn't wake you." I kept my voice low and calm.

"No, Daisy was kicking me. Who were you talking to? Just now?"

"An old friend."

"Owen?" she asked.

Hearing the rounded sound of his name made my heart lurch and roll inside my chest. "Yes," I said. There was nothing else to say but yes.

"Isn't that Lainey's brother?"

"It is," I said.

"Why don't you tell her that you talk to him?"

"She knows I talk to him."

"She talks about him all the time, about how much she misses him."

"Yes, she does."

"I don't get it." The porch lights illuminated Piper's face and she squinted at me as if trying to read my own expression.

"I know. I don't think we get it either, Piper. He doesn't think we should be here after what happened to their mom. That's all."

"Whatever." Her face told me she didn't believe me, and she slammed the screen door a little too hard and left me alone.

How could I have believed my life was ever separate from hers? That we weren't inextricably tied together in a way that what I did affected her and what she did altered me? Our lives were mirrors, and tangled at more than the level of DNA. She was more than the sum of my parts plus Lucas's genes. She was all of herself and all of me and all of him.

CHAPTER 25
PIPER BLANKENSHIP

All drunken nights were different, but all hangovers felt the same. After that little tiff with Mom about being on the phone with Owen, sneaking around in the dark back-yard like a teenager, I woke in a damp sweat with the profound feeling that I was going to be sick. My mouth was dry and open; my heart raced. There was a spinning feel-ing inside my head, a roundness of thought trying to land on the *one* very reason I felt so badly. Then thoughts formed, one by one, like fog lifting off a jagged horizon so I could see small mirages of the things I'd drunk and the things I'd done, but not the entire knowing of it all. Tequila, no, it was Fireball shots. Sitting on a curb crying, no, that was last time, it was a bar stool and a stranger . . .

That was how it went every time until I dragged myself from bed and found a huge glass of water, some Advil and something

greasy to eat. Then after that, the awful realization that I was going to lose the day to
the feeling and, like being strapped in a bad
carnival ride, I couldn't do anything but
bear the sudden rises and drops, the terror.
Even sleep wouldn't help because I couldn't
sleep through this.

Finally, and this was the best part — my
vow — my eternal and blood vow:

I'm never going to drink again.

Last night I hadn't meant to get shit-
faced, obliterated, plastered, whatever the
favorite and best term is. It wasn't on
purpose. Was it ever? Yes, sometimes it was.
But last night it was not.

Here was how it usually went in Watersend: I'd tuck the kids into bed with *Good-
night Moon,* which I had now memorized
and could ad-lib and act out, making them
squeal with laughter. I'd pretend to find
another mouse, which there would never
be. One more book, their constant refrain,
and one more it was, until six books later
I'd say no, and either go join my mom and
Lainey on the porch, where they talked
about their lives, or to my room, where I'd
read and fall asleep with the windows open
and the hum of the moms' voices rising and
falling, their laughter like exclamation
points through the night.

But last night after slamming the screen door on Mom, I scrolled through Facebook and actually, to my own delight, deliberately avoided going to Ryan's page. I scrolled and felt that old I'm-not-enough feeling crawl over me, and I closed the computer, settled back on the bed and opened a novel to find the pages I'd folded to discuss in book club at Mimi's. Then my phone vibrated and I glanced at the screen. A text from my friend Childers. OMG, did you see the Insta from Hannah????

I knew better. I really did. But I looked. Even though I'd unfollowed them both (Ryan and Hannah), and had promised myself to never look again, I did. Another broken promise. There they were. Hannah's profile kissing Ryan's face. His smile broad and wide as he received her kiss, staring directly at the camera as if to say, *See? She loves me.*

I only wanted one sip of the Jack hidden in my bottom drawer, just the tiniest numbing of my feelings and my heartache. But it wasn't enough, and this was where the story got boring even to me, because there was nothing fun or interesting about sitting in bed alone drinking until the room spun and I fell asleep.

Then slowly a memory surfaced, a fuzzy

cell phone memory. *Oh, God.* Had I done this thing or dreamed it? *No,* my deep headache told me, *you did that.* I'd gone into Mom's room and, while she slept, I'd taken her phone, gone to her text messages and looked for Owen McKay. Sure enough, there he was in her contacts. I typed quickly.

Don't write back, but we need you here in Watersend.

And then, after I hit send, I erased it so Mom couldn't see what I'd done. Just like that — a dumbass-drunk move that had somehow seemed noble and righteous under the Jack haze. Let him show up so that Lainey could see the brother she missed so much. Screw what Mom wanted.

My anger at Mom had surfaced in one huge wave. She'd forced me to come to Watersend when I could be with Ryan (as if Ryan loving Hannah was Mom's fault). And then I'd gone and sabotaged her in some fit of irrationality.

Shit.

Then the little ones came in and jumped on my bed, and the day started and I wondered with headachy dread what I'd set in motion. What idiocy had prompted me to text their uncle? If Mom hadn't told him to come, she'd had her reasons. Then again, I'd had mine.

293

The book club I'd started was my idea, or I told myself it was my idea, but really it was probably Mimi's. I'd gotten it into my head the day I arrived and she told me there was a book club for everything. I wanted to read books about girls who weren't expected to do much and then surprised everyone because they did do something extraordinary. But there was no such category. So I just called it "Girls in Books." Mimi liked it; I taped flyers in all the downtown store windows and Fletch helped me.

It was the first meeting, and I arrived an hour early to set up the little space. I set out the crackers and cheese and fruit — all donated by the Market — and a pitcher of water with peach slices floating in it. I placed a bouquet of wild daisies that I'd picked off the side of the road into a vase on the kitchen table, and waited with tiny butterflies skittering inside — part hangover, part Owen dread.

Lately, time had passed so quickly that I sometimes forgot what day it was because they were all the same without school or schedules. It was a lazy feeling like everything would wait while I cut sandwiches for the kids and read books and delivered groceries with Fletch and fell asleep in the hammock. He'd taken me out in the little boat that appeared too rickety to keep us afloat and introduced me to the waterways and secret passages of the river and ocean.

Now I'd gone and screwed it up. But I'd made it this far through the day, and it was my first book club meeting. Maybe four people would show. Maybe two. Maybe none. But I was prepared.

Mimi arrived at the top of the stairs. "Look at you," she said. "I don't have to do a thing."

I shrugged. "Might be for nothing."

"Nothing is for nothing, right? You read a great book and tried for something. Who knows?"

I checked my phone. "We still have thirty minutes. I won't panic yet."

Mimi tilted her head before catching my gaze. "What's wrong?"

"I don't feel so well," I said.

"Oh, dear. Why?"

"Cocktail flu."

She laughed but stifled it quickly. "Oh, Piper."

"I know." I sank into a chair. "I'm not at all who I want to be. Why do I keep doing this?" I dropped my face into my hands.

"Seriously. There's something wrong with me. It's so stupid. Why do I act the exact opposite of who and what I want to be?"

Mimi sat in the chair next to me and I felt her hand on my knee. "We all do that sometimes. It has a really technical name to it."

I glanced up, so hopeful. "And what is that?"

"Being human."

I laughed and shook my head. Then changed the subject. "What if no one shows?" I asked.

"Twelve people bought the book, so that means someone will show. I promise. Two girls came in today to ask where we'd meet."

"Okay." I nodded and settled back into the chair to down another glass of peach water. At this rate, there wouldn't be any left when and if someone did show.

"I'm nervous," I said. "I so regret picking this to be the day to feel awful." I sighed. "I bet you don't have that many regrets."

"Where do you get these crazy ideas?" she asked.

"Crazy ideas?"

"That you are the only one who ever messes up. That you are the only one who doesn't do something you should or who does something you wish you hadn't."

"I don't know. I look around and every-one seems to have it together."

By instinct I pulled out my phone and scanned it.

"Look up, dear. Look up from that phone. Maybe you won't feel so brokenly special."

"You're right." I tucked my phone into my back pocket, turned away from the world of photos and images, of updates and film filters, and into her gray eyes. "The wrong places," I said with a smile.

Together we peered toward the stairwell as a man's voice said, "Is there someone who works here?"

"Oh, my." Mimi stood. "I didn't even hear the bell ring."

"Ms. Mimi?" the man asked, sounding astonished, as he reached the landing.

He was really handsome, even though he was kind of old. Dark hair that curled everywhere like Justin Timberlake in his boy-band days, and a tan that wasn't fake like those old politicians on TV. His dark T-shirt was untucked and he wore a pair of faded jeans, which ended in tattered hems over those hiking sandals everyone wore at my college.

"You look like your father, a time traveler," Mimi said and her right hand fluttered to her throat.

I wanted to guess who this man was to her. I wanted to stand and say, Wait, before you tell me, let me guess. Long-lost son? Old boyfriend's son? Ex-employee? But I just sat and watched with my dull headache.

"Ah, so they say." He grinned and closed the few steps between them with long strides. His hug enveloped all of her and he even lifted her an inch off the ground.

"It's so good to see you again. Just so good." His voice had lost the astonishment and was now on to gladness. Then he noticed me, his gaze catching on mine and sticking. I realized I was standing, still holding my glass of water.

"Oh," he said.

Mimi stepped between us and reached behind her back to take my hand. It was a protective move I didn't understand at first, until she spoke.

"Owen, this is Piper Blankenship."

The world scuttled out from underneath me.

"Owen," I echoed.

His smile shook even as he tried to hold it steady, and he glanced at Mimi for help, which she seemed uncharacteristically unable to give.

"Why don't we go on downstairs?" she said. "Piper here is waiting to start a book club meeting."

He nodded, but his feet were rooted to the hard plank floors. He moved his upper body as if to turn, but nothing happened. He stared at me and then looked away and then back again.

"Nice to meet you," he said in a weird, tight voice like those GPS-directions voices.

"You, too," I said. "Does Mom know you're here?"

He didn't answer and the air changed. I'm not making that up like some metaphor, a way to say something was trippy; it did change. It turned warmer and fuller.

"No." He stopped and scanned the room. "Is she here?"

"Not here," I said. "Here, but not *here.* In town, but not at this store right this second."

Then we all stood there in the most awkward moment of all my life. I've been in a lot of awkward moments — like finding Ryan on top of Hannah, or waking up on the wooden bench on the common, or seeing a picture of me dancing on top of a bar — but this won hands down.

I wonder what would have happened if this eager and beautiful girl with a singsong voice hadn't arrived at the top of the stairs with the book in her hand, asking, "Is this where book club meets?"

I turned away from Owen and said, "Yes!"

In the end, six girls showed. I'd seen some of them around town and I knew the one who didn't speak one word was Fletch's high school ex-girlfriend from the bonfire, and she was only there to check me out. But I didn't care because at least she filled a seat.

Two hours flew by and Ms. Mimi came upstairs to let us know it was closing time. We all exchanged phone numbers and friended each other on Facebook, and that was that. I'd had my first book club.

After I cleaned, I went downstairs, said good-bye to Mimi and went outside. Fletch was waiting for me and tossed his arm over my shoulder. We headed toward his Jeep, which was parked crooked like the rest of the town's cars.

"What is the deal with parking around here?" I asked. "No one parks in between the white lines. I noticed that my very first day."

"Oh, that." Fletch pointed at his Jeep. "They repainted the lines from slanted to straight about six months ago and no one pays it any mind." He pulled me close. "So, how was it?" he asked.

"Really great," I said. "And" — I elbowed his ribs — "Julie came."

"I saw her come out." He elbowed me back gently. "She's really nice. Don't be scared of my exes."

"I'm not scared," I said. "Just jealous."

"Jealous?" We'd reached his Jeep, and he threw both arms into the air. "That's the closest you've come to saying that you care even a little bit."

"Stop," I said, but I laughed. "You're embarrassing me now. Making a scene in the street. What will people think of you?"

He took both his hands, placed them on my cheeks and pulled me in for a deep kiss. "If you only knew all the many things they thought about me," he said when he pulled back. "But all that matters to me right now is what *you* think of me."

"What I think?" I stepped back and tapped my finger on my temple. "I think you're funny. And I love your Jeep. And you kiss like you've been practicing all your life. And you have the best hair when the wind gets ahold of it. And you make me feel safe. And when I'm around you I'm not thinking about anything else hardly at all."

Fletch drew me so close then that I felt my spine give way just the littlest bit, as if he was aligning me to him, making things right and straight. Then he kissed me again and we sank back against the Jeep. My body adjusted under his, the pressure of him. My limbs loosened and the air felt liquid. We were swimming and standing still. I wrapped my right leg around his calf, my flip-flop dropping off. He drew himself away from me and settled one finger on my lips.

"Let's get out of here," he said.

"Here," I said, coming to myself for a moment, remembering we were in the middle of the street in Watersend. And remembering that single word spoken only two hours before. *Not here,* I'd said. *Here, but not here.*

I fell back into my body, a clunky vessel now, with a sinking feeling that there was somewhere I was supposed to be; some catastrophe to avoid; some terrible something that must be stopped. I stepped away from Fletch, and then around the Jeep to the passenger seat. "I need to get home," I said. "I want to stay with you. I want to hang out longer, but there's something at the house, and I have to go home." It hit me how easily I'd come to call that house, Sea La Vie, home.

"I understand," he said, and he did that jump he does into the driver's seat. I climbed into the passenger seat beside him and buckled the harness.

Fletch started the Jeep and turned the radio on. Bob Marley sang about no woman, no cry, and Fletch smiled at me. "Are you okay?"

"I wish I could explain," I said, "I don't know if I can, but it's *not* you."

He nodded and we drove in silence for the few blocks to Sea La Vie. He parked in front and I glanced at the house as if it could tell me what I needed to know. Were things the same in there or had something unalterable shifted? Or had I been reading too many dystopian novels where the world ended with a single action?

Sitting there in Fletch's Jeep, with my hands folded in my lap, I felt like I was underwater and breathing through a straw. All the lights were on, each window ablaze, except the far right one that belonged to George and Daisy, who must be sleeping soundly. Music, soft, came from the back porch, where I knew Mom and Lainey were talking. Was *he* there?

I unhitched my harness and jumped to the soft dirt of the lawn. "Can I call you later? I just need to . . ." I tilted my head toward the house.

"You can call me anytime," he said with this little grin.

I walked around the side of the Jeep and onto the driver's-side running board to kiss him. "See you tomorrow."

He kissed me back. "You are a mystery."

"Not really," I said, "but it's pretty to think so."

"Hemingway," he blurted out.

"Last line in *The Sun Also Rises*," I said.

"Wow." He drew me close again. "You better be careful. You could make a guy fall in love."

"With Hemingway?" I asked and kissed him again before I jumped off the sideboard.

"Yes, that's exactly what I meant."

I laughed even though I felt that terrible sinking feeling that something was about to go very wrong. I waved over my shoulder and then jogged around to the back of the house. The women's voices were lyrical and normal, and I stood in the dark listening. I didn't need to know what they were saying to know that whatever it was, it wasn't about Owen and his arrival in Watersend.

I sank to the picnic table bench and lay flat on it, staring into the sky. It was a crescent moon night without cloud cover. The stars were so plentiful and clear I felt I could reach out and grab one, hide it in my back pocket, save it for the one wish I might want someday. Then one shot across the sky to loop downward and disappear into the dark blue nothingness. It was gone before I remembered to wish. Was it too late when it was gone? I closed my eyes and made a wish.

"Please let Mom be okay," I said.

It was the first time I'd ever wished for anything that wasn't for me. Or about me. Or of me. Or maybe it was about me because if she wasn't okay, would I be? I reclined there in the dark thinking of more questions than could ever have answers. How could Lainey have lived all her life without a mom? How could she live without knowing her brother? Should I tell Mom? And mostly, would Owen's arrival ruin the summer and the quiet beauty we had come to so easily in such a short amount of time?

My head lolled to the screened-in porch, where candlelight made the world dreamy and malleable. I wanted to stop time for as long as was needed for all of us to be okay, or at least okay enough to handle what Owen brought with him.

But this wasn't a book. Time would not stand still. I would not find a superpower to fix it all. And hearts broke all the time. All the time.

Chapter 26
Lainey McKay

Piper didn't know I could see her out there on the picnic bench, but I could. Her hair spread out under the moonlight. If I hadn't heard the Jeep pull up or the laughter, I probably wouldn't have noticed her. But I was looking and listening.

Bonny was curled like a cat on the far end of the couch, staring off into the world, so she startled at the ring of the doorbell.

"Who could that be?"

"I got it," I said.

What happened next seemed initially like the stuff of my dreams — of opening a door or turning a corner — and seeing *his* face. My brother was a piece of me that had disappeared and left a gaping hole. When he was near me, I'd find myself centered and calm, a surety in the world that wasn't there at any other time.

Here and then gone. Cut and run, Tim said about Owen.

But there Owen stood on the doorstep as if he knew I needed him more than I ever had, as if he knew to run to me in Waters-end.

I'd tried to describe my brother to people who hadn't met him, and I never could. I used vague and inadequate words like "rock" or "strength" or "safe," and I wanted to say that there wasn't really a word to describe him; it was more of a feeling he gave: a sense of rightness in the world or maybe redemption. But that was also like trying to describe a hurricane as safe. He was so many other things. Wild. Free.

There he stood. His feet planted wide and his smile broad. He held his hands behind his back and I thought he might have something in them. I said his name in a whisper so he wouldn't disappear, so the dream wouldn't fade. "Owen."

I threw my arms around him, rested my face on his chest and breathed in the wood smoke aroma of his shirt.

"Lainey?"

My name in his voice was exquisite and yet I noticed the question mark at the end; it quivered above us and I pulled back to take him in.

"Yes, I'm Lainey." I laughed. "Did you forget my name?" I kissed his rough cheek and brushed back the hair from his forehead in such a mom move that it felt like my own mother had moved my hand. "How did you know I was here? How did you . . . ? Did Tim tell you?"

He stepped back to look at me under the front lantern light. A breeze moved through the palm fronds in a sound like rain.

"Tim?" I repeated. "Did he tell you?"

He shook his head. "You look so great, sis. I've been so worried about you."

"Me? Seriously? You haven't answered any calls. I haven't heard from you. And you worry about me?" I punched him lightly on the arm, a remembered movement from the back of the car or the dinner table.

"I do. I know I'm a terrible brother," he said and hugged me again, this time tighter and longer. "I know that. I love you, though. I do."

"It's like you're a mind reader. You always know just when to show." I snuck a glance back inside the house and down the hall to see Bonny's shadowy figure on the porch. "I wanted to come here. I did," I whispered. "Bonny needed me and the house is so great and I'm working, but . . . it's full of ghosts, too."

"I don't know why you'd come back here, sis. I really don't."

"Because I love Bonny."

"I get that," he said. He held out his hand for mine and I took it. He closed the front door with his foot and guided me toward the street and a pickup truck parked in the grass.

"Don't you want to come in?" I asked. "Bonny will be glad to know you're here."

"Slow down," he said and dropped his arm over my shoulder. "I'm not going to intrude here."

"Intrude? Are you kidding? My kids will be so happy to see you — your niece and nephew. Bonny, too. Did you tell her you were coming?"

Cicadas conversed in their chirpy language; the ocean moved to its nighttime lullaby; the river rose over the marsh grasses with the sound of the wind. One lone frog bellowed out his commands. I would have stayed there forever with the sounds of the night, keeping Owen all to myself.

"Sis," he said, "I didn't know you were here."

"What do you mean?"

He didn't answer and a hot flush of embarrassment and anger flooded me. "You came to see Bonny. Not me." I took two steps back. "I was so excited you came for me, but it's not me you came for at all." He loved Bonny more than he loved me. He always had and always would. These truths hammered at my heart and it broke.

"Sis, I love you. I'm so happy to see you. I just didn't *know* you were here. I came because I thought she was alone with her daughter, and I was worried."

A hard knot inside me cracked open and whatever was there spiraled upward: betrayal.

"Tell me everything. You've been with her all these years? *Been* . . . with her?"

"No, Lainey. Not like that. I haven't seen her since her wedding, until the night in the hospital."

"Stop saying my name. Stop. Just tell me. I looked to you. You were all that was left of my family and you always ran. I understood, and I gave you that space, but then you had time and energy to call Bonny and confide in her? Talk to her?" All the pent-up anger, all the words I'd never said for fear of pushing him further away, poured out of me.

With the sound of a slamming screen door we both turned. Bonny stood on the front porch, her silhouette as stark against the house as a cutout. She stepped onto the soft grass and I moved quickly to meet her on the walkway with my hands held out in front of me. I didn't know what I was trying to stop or push or hold, but there I stood with my hands out and Bonny one step away.

"Stop," I said. I didn't know what I meant; I just spat it out like venom.

"Huh?" Her gaze met mine and she took my outheld hands. "Are you okay?"

I wrenched them away. "No, I'm not."

"What's going . . ." Her gaze unlatched from mine and found Owen. I saw the recognition the minute it happened, a widening of her pupils, an openmouthed joy, which she covered with her hand.

This, surprisingly, was worse than Owen's betrayal. Because I felt it — she loved him just as much. They loved each other more than they could me, or maybe anyone else.

"Owen." She whispered his name in the way of someone who has whispered it a million times, in so many other ways and in so many other places. I backed away from her. It was one thing to know they'd loved each other — she'd always admitted it — and another to see it and hear it. It was a reality that had always felt as foggy and far off as childhood.

On the way into the house, I slammed the screen door with such force that the door frame rattled. I sat at the edge of the bed, sick and wanting my *own* home. And in a flood of the past, I wanted my mom, our

311

mom, in that singular, desperate way of childhood when I would imagine her returning, throwing her arms around us and weeping that she'd never really wanted to be away for even one minute.

I thought of Bonny, of our years of conversations and times spent alone every year or so at each other's homes. For hours we'd discussed life and family. In our most private moments, even the question of divinity, of something greater than us. Like a replay of a bad movie, I remembered the times I'd cried to her of my worry over him, of how I needed him and couldn't reach him. I'd talked to her of how he was my only family and the only one who could ever understand the loss we had borne.

I hated her. I loved her. I wanted to scream and yet couldn't.

A memory, like the decay from the bottom of the river, bubbled up.

Summer 1978
Watersend, South Carolina

The first day of our last summer at Watersend, we went straight to the bookshop. It was exactly the same, as if Ms. Mimi had closed the door when we left the previous year and then waited for us to return before she opened it. I knew this wasn't true, of course, but it felt like it. Bonny and I entered and Mimi waved from the other side of her counter. "Well, well, look who's back. Welcome, Summer Girls."

"Summer Sisters," I corrected.

"Ah, yes," she said and came around to give us a hug.

We huddled in our corner, a stack of Nancy Drew books on the little table between us. We knew we couldn't buy them; neither of us had the money. The library was too far away and we were desperate. So there we sat and there we read, as if it was a library. Mimi never once stopped us.

"This year," Bonny said, leaning closer, "let's solve a really big mystery."

"I thought the book stealer was a big one last year," I said.

"Oh, it was. But something bigger. Something better."

"Deal," I said. I think I would have agreed with her if she'd suggested we run away or start a fire or steal our own books. I loved her that much.

Bonny had pulled out her notebook. It was really just a composition book from school, but she'd decorated it with stickers.

Bonny had always been the keeper of our Girl Detective notebook. It was never a question. She was the leader, without discussion. There were our little notes and drawings. We'd ask a question: Who stole *Gone with the Wind* from the bookshop? And then we'd list clues: long lists of things that might or might not matter.

Then there were other questions that weren't so much crimes as mysteries in our world, things we wanted and needed to know.

What's the best-selling candy at the Penny Candy Store? (Pop Rocks)
How is cotton candy made? (with air and sugar)
Why does Owen go out on the johnboat alone? (to smoke cigarettes)
When does Lainey's mom ever sleep? (during the day, after taking another blue pill)

We made a game of it all, listing our clues. Mimi came and sat to join us. "So how was your school year, girls?"

"Boring," I said.

"Great," Bonny said.

"You don't go to the same school?" Mimi sat back in her chair. She had the longest, prettiest black hair I'd ever seen. I always looked at it instead of her face. It moved and swayed and fell over her shoulders like water.

"No, ma'am," Bonny said. "We don't. We live kind of far away from each other."

"Oh, I thought you both lived in Atlanta."

"We do," I said. "But Atlanta is huge."

"Yes." Mimi patted her lap as if a small child sat there. "It is."

We whiled away the afternoon reading *The Secret of the Old Clock* and then wandered to the ice cream store, where we spent our pocket change. By the time we got home, Mrs. Moreland was cooking dinner and the adults were playing gin rummy.

Owen sat on the front porch staring out toward the beach, which you couldn't see for the dunes, but we knew it was there waiting. You could hear that ocean right across the street.

Bonny and I rode our bikes to the porch and he jumped up.

"Where have you been? I'm so bored." He sauntered toward us.

"The bookshop," I said.

"Not the bookshop again," he said. "Come on, let's get out of here."

My brother picked me up and tossed me over his shoulder like a bag of potatoes. "Stop!" I hollered.

"Nope," he said. "We're going to the beach."

"Let's go out on the boat instead," Bonny said.

I was stunned for a minute. Owen's suggestions were always the best, always the most fun.

But Bonny continued. "Dad bought a new crab trap. And it's high tide right now. We could go drop it out and maybe tomorrow have tons of crabs."

"Good idea." Owen placed me gently on the ground. "Let's go."

I glanced back and forth between them. Bonny had no idea what she'd just done in a quick second — changed Owen's mind. No one did that. Not Mom. Not Dad. Not me. Not Polly. When he decided, well, that was just that. Bonny could change his mind. Bonny could make Owen do things I thought he was incapable of doing.

Chapter 27
Bonny Blankenship

"Oh, God, what are you doing here?" I asked Owen.

He stood in my front yard, with his hands at his sides. An image I'd often dreamed of and dreaded. I took it all in like a photograph on the wall, something I could stare at that wouldn't change and I had all the time in the world to evaluate. I wanted to run to him, and my feet were already in motion before I stopped myself. I needed to go after Lainey, to explain, if there was any explaining to do. But Owen reached me first.

"Not the exact greeting I was hoping for," he said. "I think I just really screwed up, didn't I?"

I peered over my shoulder toward the house and then back at him. "Probably."

He reached to take me in his arms, where I wanted to be, where I'd always wanted to be, and yet where I could *not* be. Not right then, not right there. "Don't," I said.

He took two steps back from me. "Why didn't you tell me Lainey was here?"

"Why didn't I tell you? Seriously? Why are you here?"

"You texted me last night."

"No, I didn't, Owen. Why would I do that?"

"You said not to answer but just to hurry here. I wouldn't have just shown up like this." We both glanced back to the house as if the answer might rest there. He pulled out his phone and showed it to me. "See?"

Confusion swept over me like a cold wave. Had I done it in my sleep? Had I done it in a fit of missing him? Had I drunk too much? No was the answer to all of the above, and then I said it just as I knew it. "Piper."

"What? Why would she?"

I shook my head. "She's mad at me. And she asked me about you a couple days ago because she heard how much Lainey misses you, and she loves Lainey, so . . ."

"Screw Mom, right?"

"Exactly." I paused and then asked, "How did you get here so quickly?"

"I was in North Carolina helping a group start on the Appalachian Trail, and I came straight here."

"We can't talk about this right now. I have

to go inside, see Lainey."

"Maybe I should, too . . . She's my sister."

"You're right." I stepped aside.

My insides collapsed. There were so many better ways for this to have gone. I didn't know what those ways were, and if I'd had a chance at all to find those ways, I'd missed out. All those secret times that felt so closely ours, so absolutely only Owen and me, weren't any longer. We'd hurt Lainey with our closeness that had excluded her.

Owen entered the house, and I followed him. I wanted to reach out and place my hands around his waist, hide behind him, let him drag me to Lainey's room. But this was mine to face without protection.

We both materialized in her doorway. Her suitcase was on the bed, splayed open like a wound, and she threw clothes inside, unfolded and rumpled. Her face was wet with tears, anger contorting her features. "What is wrong with you people?"

"Everything," I said. "But it has nothing to do with you or loving you. Or . . ."

"Really?" She threw a pile of clothes into her suitcase and then turned to us. "Nothing to do with loving me?"

Shame tasted like bile. I moved two steps toward her. "I kept saying it was over, wanting to believe it was over. And it *has* been over for a long time."

"It wasn't to hurt you, sis. It was something we just could never get right," Owen said quietly.

I hadn't heard him say this before — how we could never get it right — but it was the simplest explanation, if not the best one.

"Please don't leave, Lainey. Please. Don't. Leave." I grabbed her arm as she reached for another dresser drawer. "I need you here."

She tossed my hand from her skin as if I'd burned her. "You need me?"

"Yes. You're the best friend I've ever had."

Owen stepped between Lainey and me. "Don't be angry at her. Be mad at me. This isn't her fault. It's mine."

"Oh, trust me, big brother, I'm mad at you, too. But at least you didn't pretend to be something you aren't. You cut and run. You hide. Bonny here was pretending to be real, to be honest and ready to find her 'one thing' and 'gathering what matters most.' Well, Bee," she said in an imitation Owen voice, "looks like you always knew what your 'one thing' was."

"Please just stop," I said and went to close her suitcase. "Stop packing. Stop . . . Just let me at least try to explain. There's nothing you haven't known. Nothing. I haven't lied about seeing him or anything."

"Try to explain?" Lainey sat on the edge of the bed and dropped her head into her hands. "I know the facts. Of course I do. But seeing you two, seeing how you, Owen, want her more than you've ever wanted what was left of your family, it's heartbreaking."

I sat next to her, my heart pushing in a race to find the right words to make her stay, to make her understand. I looked to Owen and he to me. Both our hearts were splintering.

"It's been like a sickness," I said. "The way we can't let go and then can't get it right."

"A sickness?" She looked at me and then directed her attention to Owen. "Do you feel that way also?"

"No," he said.

"I knew I'd screw this up," I said and closed my eyes to center myself, catch my breath. "He isn't the sickness. Me not being able to let him go, that's the awful part. In me. Not him."

"I don't get any of this," Lainey said.

"Okay." Owen's voice sounded tight, like he was on the edge of tears, which I'd only heard once, so long ago, the night before my wedding. "I have loved Bonny for as long as I've known her. I have screwed it up on every level there is. I have shown up and left. I've begged for another chance and not taken it. I have disappeared and reappeared at the worst times. I have done nothing good for her life. And nothing good for yours," he said. "Lainey, I'm so very sorry. This time, I meant to come here and make things right with Bonny. To help. To find a way out of the mess."

"And here I am," Lainey said. "To interfere with you two lovebirds. What I will do now is leave so everyone can live happily ever after."

"No!" I took her hand.

"No," Owen's voice joined mine. "I'll leave . . ."

"Of course you will," Lainey said. "It's what you do best." Then she grabbed a T-shirt from the bed and wiped at her face. "I'm being so mean. I don't know why I'm being so mean." She blew her nose into the T-shirt.

"I get it," I said.

"I don't." She stood. "I can't go anywhere tonight. What am I doing?" She glanced around as if waking and confused.

Owen took her hand. "I'm going to leave. I have a room in town. I will come back first thing in the morning and we will talk. I want to . . ."

"I don't know," Lainey said.

"If I'd known you were going to be here I would have come even sooner."

"No, you wouldn't have. You haven't come to see me in years."

"I hadn't seen Bonny until the kite-boarding accident and ended up in her emergency room. But it wasn't planned, Lainey — I had no intention of seeing her during that trip."

Lainey's eyes opened wide and she stood. "Oh, my God, *you* are the reason for her mistake, aren't you?"

"No," I said, too quickly, too loudly.

"Yes," Owen answered at the same time.

I turned to him. "No, you're not. Whatever mistakes I made were my own. You didn't do anything."

Lainey stared at me as if she didn't know me, which maybe she didn't. Maybe I didn't know me.

We backed out of her room as she waved us out, a dismissive move that felt like an indictment. Owen and I stared at each other and all our times together were water, drowning us.

"I'm a sickness?" he asked in a low whisper.

"No." I shook my head and my body

ached for him. "Yes. I don't know. I don't know."

"Bonny . . ." His voice broke.

"All I know is that even as I loved another, I wasn't able to stop loving you. I've tried. Oh, God, how I've tried. But you never *really* stayed away — you've always been there, even if not in person: your calls; your texts; our long phone conversations. You'd think that at least not *seeing* you for twenty-two years would have helped, but it hasn't. I don't know if that's a curse or a wish come true or all I ever wanted. Or a sickness. I just don't know."

He reached to pull me into his arms and I held mine up to ward him off. I'd heard Piper come inside and she was in her room down the hall. His sister was behind a closed door a few feet away. I needed the desire for him, for something that would never work, to end.

I turned away, walked unsteadily to my bedroom and shut the door. If only I could do the same with my heart.

I needed to remind myself of the truth: this had been his pattern — he'd arrive at just the right minute and then leave again while I was left waiting in the maybe; the possible happy ending; the could-be.

But he left; he always left. And even as he

stood outside my door there in Watersend, I could let him into my bedroom, but he would leave again. Lainey was right about that: it was what he did best. And it wasn't the coming that I couldn't handle; it was the leaving that was inevitable.

CHAPTER 28
PIPER BLANKENSHIP

Did Mom and Lainey think I didn't hear them last night, or that I was too stupid to get it? It was my fault Owen was at the river house. I was beginning to understand that there was just as much unsaid as there was said — Owen was there to see my mom. He'd just sauntered into the bookshop and turned the quiet summer upside down and inside out. I wasn't going to stick around that morning to see what happened next. That would be like watching a car wreck I'd caused.

Lainey shuffled out from her bedroom, her laptop held in her hands and open as she clicked away with one finger. She set the computer on the kitchen counter before she spoke to me. "Do you mind taking the kids to the beach for a couple hours? I have some things I need to do."

Her voice sounded taut, and on her screen was a travel search engine open to a list of flights to Houston, Texas.

"Are you leaving?" I asked.

She slammed shut her laptop. "Piper, I just need you to take the kids out for a couple hours. That's all." It was like someone had replaced Lainey overnight. Maybe Owen. He was a replacement specialist, turning Mom and Lainey into people I didn't know. I hated him.

"Okay," I said. "I've got them."

I gathered George and Daisy and took them outside, ready to go to the beach as we had every morning, already a routine. George was nearly at the street before I hollered after him. "Wait for us."

"I am," he said and stalked back and forth along the road.

In the cart were two beach chairs, one blanket, three towels, a Thermos of coffee and one full of lemonade and a cooler with snacks in little Baggies, which Lainey had made and labeled. Peanut butter on celery, raisins, trail mix with chocolate chips and sliced apples, which always ended up crusted with sand. There were buckets and shovels and plastic molds to make starfish and mermaids out of wet sand.

Daisy and I reached the road where George was now jumping from foot to foot.

"We did it," Daisy said, pretending we'd

had to sneak out of the sleeping dragon's house, a game I'd made up to let Mom sleep in. Not that I was courteous but I dreaded seeing her and explaining and apologizing for how Owen had surprisingly arrived at our front door.

"We made it out of the castle without waking the monster," Daisy said.

"You're stupid," George said and bent to pick up a beetle and roll it around in the palm of his hand. "There was no monster. Piper just told us that so we wouldn't wake up the moms."

"You're the one who's stupid," Daisy said and took my hand. "It was just a game anyway. So you're the stupidest."

George looked at the beetle in his hand, crawling toward his thumb, and then he flung his hand out to toss the bug onto Daisy's shoulder. She screamed, just as he meant for her to do, and I swiped it off. She clung to my leg and looked at her brother. "I hate you," she said.

I crouched next to her. "Boys. They do stuff like that."

"Boys," she said and stuck her tongue out at her brother.

I glanced left and right and we crossed the street together, a threesome who seemed like we had done it every day for all time, a silent amble across the street and then through the sand dune path to the beach beyond.

I spread the towels one by one in a row. The blue striped one for George, pink for Daisy, red for me and then the big ragged blanket on which I threw the beach toys and cooler. George made it to the water's edge first with his shovel, and he settled in to dig. I watched him with hazy laziness as Daisy sat next to me and colored in her mermaid book. The morning was uncharacteristically cool, or if not cool, at least not its usual ninety-eight degrees by sunrise. I drank from my coffee Thermos and stretched out my legs to dig my toes into the warm sand.

Daisy sang a little song to herself, the theme song from *Frozen,* permanently etched into my brain now. George made tractor noises from the water's edge. I closed my eyes and tossed through the options for what might have happened last night. Besides the fact that Owen had ruined what might have been a perfect night with Fletch.

Owen could have arrived here for a million reasons, but I was the one who'd brought him here. I groaned out loud.

"What?" Daisy asked, her little face lifting

to mine.

"Nothing, little nut. I was thinking to myself."

"I do that all the time," she said.

Like every other time, once the anxiety vine started growing I couldn't make it stop. So quickly it ran up my ribs and into my throat, and I wanted to cry, to find my way out of my body, which was betraying me with fear. It made me think of Ryan with Hannah, of Dad slamming doors, of Mom weeping in her bedroom, of the police flashlights on the common, of . . .

I took in a long inhale and stood from the beach blanket. I felt like I needed to run or jump in the water because, even though it was only seven a.m., what I really wanted was a drink. I looked to the ocean and George's shovel, the hole he was digging so far into the sand. Daisy, now my shadow, stood also.

"Where's George?" she asked.

The emptiness of the beach, which moments before had felt peaceful, now felt threatening.

"George!" I called out his name, louder than I ever had.

I ran to the shoreline and peered inside the hole he'd dug. A tiny Matchbox pickup truck floated in the bottom of the hole where seawater had soaked upward.

"George," I hollered again, peering into the hole as if there was a way he'd hidden in there.

"He does this all the time," Daisy said.

"Does what?" I turned to her standing next to me, my heart now inside my throat, threatening to strangle me.

"Hides on purpose to scare us. It makes Mommy crazy."

"George," I said to the empty beach, to the waves and to the sky. "If you are hiding, please come out now because I'm really scared and I'm about to call the police and you have to show me where you are. Right now. Right now. Right now." My voice rose with each sentence.

"Right now," Daisy repeated.

We stood together and she slipped her hand into mine and we waited for George to obey us, but nothing happened. No little boy popped out from behind the scrubby sand dune or the trash can. There was no place to hide.

I let go of Daisy and took her face in my hands. "Stand here," I said and splashed into the ocean. The tide was in, so there was a long stretch where George could have splashed and played without going underwater. It would be up to his little belly for twenty yards or more. I splashed through the water, scanning the sand below.

Nothing but scuttling crabs and shifting sand.

Had I fastened his life jacket on? I looked to the blanket and saw the orangeness of it sitting on the sand, a beacon. No, because he wasn't swimming. He was digging, not swimming.

I ran back to the blanket and lifted my cell phone.

"Fletch." My voice cracked as he answered the phone. I didn't know why I'd called him first. Because he was from there, because he might know what to do, because I was scared out of my mind and didn't want to tell Mom or Lainey, who had trusted me with her children.

"I need help. I lost George . . . I think he's hiding on me, but I don't know and I'm scared and . . ."

"Where are you?"

"The beach in front of the house."

"I'm calling the police and I'm on the way."

"The police?" My chest felt like it would explode. I couldn't take in a full breath.

"Yes, just in case. I'm coming."

"Should I go find Lainey and Mom?"

"God, Piper. Yes. Right now."

"But I don't want to leave the beach . . . just in case."

"I'm coming. Don't move."

I hung up and pushed the number for Mom. She didn't answer. Then I tried Lainey, but same thing, straight to voice mail. I held tight to Daisy, who had become completely quiet, her usual chatter gone. I bent to her, tears in my eyes. "Is there somewhere he hides that I can look? This is serious, Daisy. It's not a game."

She shook her head, back and forth. "I don't know. I don't know." She started to shake, her little face quivering.

"It's okay. You don't have to know. Help me look."

We held hands, Daisy and me. We ran up and down the beach. We called his name and we peeked behind the sand dunes and into the grasses. Lainey could not lose one more loved one to this beach or this town. Even though I hadn't known Ms. Clara, her absence settled around our house like an old curse. I needed to throw up, or faint, or float away: this couldn't be happening.

It was only minutes, but felt like hours, before Fletch came running onto the beach and I heard the sirens approach.

"Go get them," I yelled at him before he reached us. I pointed toward the house.

"They aren't answering the phone."

He turned around and ran as two police-men sauntered toward me as if they had all the time in the world, as if I'd lost a back-pack and we would now search for it.

I ran to them, words flowing so quickly that they felt like they weren't in the right order, tumbling like Scrabble letters onto the table.

"Whoa," the older man said and adjusted his sunglasses. "Slowly. Tell me what happened so we can start searching. I need a description and a photo if you have it."

From there, time took on a weird quality like someone had control of the button on a recorder and would push fast forward and then slo-mo and then normal time. Mom and Lainey ran out to the beach. Lainey screamed George's name, and Mom came to me and threw her arms around me the same way she had the times I was called into the principal's office and she was there to defend me. This time there was no defense, but that didn't matter — it was what she did, who she was. "This is my fault." I collapsed against her. "Also, I'm an idiot and I sent a text from your phone."

"I know, Piper. I know."

"But now this. It wouldn't have happened if I hadn't . . . or had . . . I don't know."

"I don't understand," Lainey screamed.

I looked at Lainey's pain. All I'd wanted to do was fix things for her, find her brother for her. And now . . .

She ran toward the water, kicking at the edge of the waves, looking down, and hollering his name with such panic that I felt dizzy. She picked up his tiny truck, still in the puddle, and clasped it so tightly it disappeared inside her fist.

"He was right there, digging that hole." I pointed to the hole. "Just digging. I was playing with Daisy. We thought he was hiding . . ." I kept saying the same thing over and over, the same ridiculous thing. *He was right there.*

Well, he obviously wasn't now. He was not right there at all. He was gone.

Soon, small groups were formed as more people showed up. Fletch's friends, more police and a few neighbors. They divided into three groups. One headed up to check the roads; one went north on the beach and one went south.

When the police didn't have anything else to ask me, and I felt I couldn't cry for one more second and the world was caving inward, sucking me down, I started to run north on the beach, calling George's name over and over. Fletch caught up with me and grabbed my hand.

"Slow down," he said. "You can't find him if you aren't looking carefully. I'm here with you. Slow down."

We paced the beach together and the only thing we said was George's name, over and over. We peered behind trash cans and ramshackle cottages. We knocked on doors, and every hundred yards or so I would drop to my knees in the sand, weak with the unknowing.

"What if . . ."

"Don't," he said. "Just don't."

"This place, it's cursed," I said. "We should have never come here. Ever. My mom is crazy thinking she could come back to some beach town and everyone would just be happy again."

"Stop, Piper. Stop. He's fine."

"You don't know that."

He lifted me from sitting and took me in his arms. "I don't know that, you're right, but I bet he's hiding or he went to find something he wanted. He didn't just disappear like Mrs. McKay."

"I won't let George be some legend here like her, Fletch. I can't. Because that would mean I'm part of a terrible story that will never stop being told. I can't have that. I won't. We have to find him."

"We will," he said. "Someone will."

I checked my phone every two minutes and called Mom every five to beg for news. Hours passed and the town was on the hunt, knocking on doors and searching in corners and boats and small hideaways. A hub was set up at the bookshop, Mom told me. Mimi was coordinating with the police and gathering the town to help.

I would not go back until he was found. I would not return to see Lainey and Daisy in their shattered pain. I would not face Mimi, who had believed that I could become who I wanted to become. I would not face Mom and what I'd done to disappoint her and how I'd betrayed her with Owen. I would not return at all, ever, if George wasn't found.

We walked for miles, maybe three, before I stopped Fletch. "He can't have gone this far. He's six years old."

"He might have. Hell, once when I was a kid, I followed a hobbled pelican along the beach for miles until my parents found me and dragged me home screaming that I needed to take it to the vet. Kids do this all the time."

"Oh, God, he's got to be so scared. Wherever he is, he's scared out of his mind. He has no idea where he is or if we'll find him or . . ."

"George!" Fletch hollered again and we continued our search, inch by inch, up the beach and through the grasses. We had hit the edge of the nature preserve, the area where we delivered groceries to Ms. Loretta and Mr. Seaton, and where we'd kissed in the waves.

"Let's go ask Ms. Loretta if she's seen anything," he said. "And you need some water."

We'd been searching and calling for hours, and my skin was pink and raw with sunburn, my lips chapped with heat. I didn't care; I deserved it. I'd taken off my flip-flops before I noticed George was missing, and my feet were now blistered. Thin lines of blood told of stickers that had scraped across my ankles and calves. We stumbled through the pathway toward Loretta's house a block away, and the tears started to rise again. I glanced again at my phone, but there was nothing there, nothing but stupid Instagram and Facebook notifications, which seemed an abomination compared to what I really needed, what I really wanted, to all that was important in the world. I was above all disgusted with myself, with ever caring about the things that now clogged my phone.

I held fast to Fletch's hand and hollered George's name one more time.

CHAPTER 29
LAINEY MCKAY

"George!"

I ran down the beach, tearing through the sand dunes and screaming my son's name. The police tried to pull me back, tell me that there would be a coordinated effort and he would be found. I needed to stay calm. But I can tell you that there is no one in the history of the world who has been *told* to calm down who has calmed down.

My God, if I hadn't been researching a ticket to Texas, and instead had been watching my children, this would not be happening. I'd created this. I'd betrayed my children and myself. In my own pain I'd turned to the sick obsession one more time, like an alcoholic to his drink, like my mother to her pills. When Tim discovered why I wasn't with our children, it would be the last of us, the last of his belief in me. My enslavement to this idea of finding my mother had wreaked its final injury — the loss of all that

340

mattered.

Piper had called four or five times and I'd ignored the calls — I'd thought she probably wanted some extra juice boxes or sunscreen — for my own preoccupation with a feverish need to find what was long gone. What if those minutes had made a difference? What if in needing to find my mother I'd lost my son?

"George!" I screamed again as the policeman tried to grab my arm, slow me down. I shook loose of him. "My six-year-old son is missing," I screamed. "And out there is an ocean. An ocean!"

The blue-uniformed man released me as I ran across the beach. And then I stopped — what if George had run the other way? I turned to bolt that way, then found myself frozen in the middle, weeping. Going one way meant giving up on the other way. He'd disappeared. How could this happen twice? My son. My mother.

I was thirteen years old and we'd all been downtown for the Labor Day parade — last day of summer. Mom had carried a little flask in her purse; she always did. We'd put it in our notebook: a clue to my parents' misery. Even as we knew what was wrong with her, we wrote about it like clues over which we

341

had some control. There was never control.

She drank all afternoon, her swinging hips and sultry speech magnified. My cheeks and Bonny's were sticky with cotton candy and our shoulders sunburned from the afternoon carnival outside without protection. Owen, at fifteen years old, was the first one to say, "Mom, maybe we should go home."

Of course she should go home; she was almost too drunk to walk. But this was when she was the happiest — when she was the drunkest. Her smile returned. Her laughter echoed across the fairgrounds. She held Dad's hand and hugged us close. Then Dad chimed in. "Clara, we must get you home before you do something embarrassing."

And that was when it fell apart for the final time.

She started crying. She usually did when Dad attacked her like that in public. Then she grabbed our hands — Owen's and mine. Mrs. Moreland pulled Bonny close to her. And off Owen and I went into the evening with Mom while Dad went to find the car.

He never found the car because Mom got there first, with Owen and me in tow.

"George." My voice broke and I ran toward the water, splashing along the high tide, looking for something, anything to give me an indication of which way he'd gone. The Matchbox truck dug into my palm like a talisman, a charm that would bring him back to me. I looked left and right and closed my eyes. *Which way did you go? Where were you going?*

He didn't answer and I bolted north on the beach, splashing through the high tide that was only an inch deep in water. He was prone to follow things, or to set a goal and forget where he was and why. He'd look for a single thing and forget all else. A shell. A horseshoe crab carcass. A severed crab leg. Who knew what he'd get in his head and go in search of with pure desire? I ran, screaming.

Mom's disappearance merged with George's, and I felt both of them, stumbling along the same beach the police had that night so long ago.

Mom put Owen in the front seat and I climbed, scared but glad to be with her, into the backseat. The day fought to stay, holding on to the light for the last few hours of summer. The pungent odor of smoke, teenagers with tightly rolled joints, wafted from behind the festival tents. Watersend felt an edginess that couldn't be named. This night felt different. More desperate. Everyone was grabbing at something — a beer; a joint; a girl; a boy; anything at all.

"Mom, let me drive," Owen said in his grown-up voice.

"That's silly." She laughed so beautifully, as if all the world was hers and she knew it. "I'm not letting my kids take care of me. I'm here to take care of my kids." She started the car and turned on the radio.

The song was "Just the Way You Are" by Billy Joel. She turned it all the way up and sang it at the top of her lungs like a wish, or a dream. We were rounding the corner to home when a dog ran into the road. It wasn't her fault, I'd said my entire life. The dog ran out into the road.

It wasn't her fault.

"Mrs. McKay!" a strange voice called and I turned, frantic.

"Stop," the young policeman said. "Your daughter needs you right now and we will search. The entire town is coming out to help."

Daisy.

Daisy.

I ran to her where she stood next to the policeman. I scooped her into my arms and held her so tightly that she squealed. "Ow, Mom."

"Where's Piper?" I asked, looking around, livid that she'd left Daisy alone. Had she been drunk, too?

No, that was Mom. This was Piper and it was eight in the morning.

"She is looking for your son with Fletch. They took off that way," the policeman said. He pointed north where I'd been going. "Ma'am, Mrs. Blankenship said there are headquarters for searching already setting up at the bookshop in town. You need to go there where things can be coordinated. We will find him."

That was what they'd said when Mom was gone: We will find her. Trust us.

The dog was a black mutt mix and the thump under the tires was so grotesque that we all screamed as one. Mom jerked the steering wheel and the light pole appeared. I could have sworn it wasn't there before — it just showed up when Mom turned the wheel too late.

The car lurched and slammed with a sickening crunch. I flew forward and slammed into the back of Owen's seat. He did the same, but into the dashboard with his arms held out. Mom, she slumped forward, limp like she'd just gone to sleep sitting up.

Owen howled in pain and then opened his

car door, fell out onto the soft dirt. I slowly lifted myself out of the car: I was fine, but my head hurt where I'd hit the seat. But nothing about me mattered. I, too, landed in the dirt and then crawled to Owen. "Are you okay?"

But he didn't need to answer because I could see that his arm shot out at the wrong angle and a small knob of white bone poked through the skin near his wrist. I turned away and puked into the thick grass.

Steam started to come from the hood of the car and Owen stood, rushed to Mom's side and opened her car door with his left hand, while his right dangled sick and bleeding.

"Mom!" I hollered out, wiping the spit from my mouth and crawling to the other side of the car.

The police were right; the bookshop was abuzz. I held tightly to Daisy and said, "What can I do right now?" to a policeman standing at the door.

Mimi came to me and held me so close. "Sit. I will get you something to eat and drink."

It was then that I realized I was still in my pajamas — drawstring pants and a tank top. My feet were bare. I'd driven Daisy and me here without thinking, like a drunkard just wanting to get home before he's caught.

"Call my brother," I said. And I rattled off his cell number. "Call him, please. I know he's in town, but I don't know where he's staying."

"I will," she said. "Lainey, we will find George."

"I've heard that promise before, Mimi. I've heard that before."

"This is different," Mimi said, and she placed her hand on Daisy's head. "George wants to be found."

She set me in a back room with water and toys for Daisy. She brought me a Title Wave T-shirt to slide over my tank top and held me close. "We will find him."

I needed to tell Tim. I needed to find George. I couldn't leave Daisy. My heart and my mind ricocheted like bullets with nowhere to kill. I didn't want to call Tim until they found our son, until I could say, "You just wouldn't believe what happened today." I didn't want to call him until it was over, until the good part started, until we found him.

But that wasn't fair, and I was jealous of Tim — I was jealous of the hour he hadn't known George was gone. The peaceful hour he'd had that I'd lost. The hour of unknowing.

I lifted my cell phone and pushed the button with his name.

Owen and I pulled Mom out of the car and onto the grass, where she groggily woke up. "What?" She sat, rubbing at her temples and then at the bump already forming on her forehead, a purple mass near her left eye. Her sunglasses were shattered and hanging crooked from one ear. Owen took them off.

I remembered the thump, the dog, and I bolted to the street, leaving Owen with Mom. He was whimpering — this little black dog with curly hair and big brown eyes looking at me for help. His back legs were bent, like Owen's arm, at the wrong angle, but he was trying to crawl forward with his front legs, trying to get out of the road.

A station wagon, much like ours, turned the corner then and I grabbed the dog and ran from the street to the side of the road. I stood next to our steaming car and Mom whimpered and Owen groaned. The other car slammed on its brakes; the smell of burned rubber filled the air. A man, tall and loud, ran to our side.

A second car then arrived, and it was the young woman in that car who went for help while the man stayed with us. I held the dog and Owen held Mom and the world slipped away from me in small increments of terror.

■ ■ ■ ■

Tim answered on the first ring. "Hello, sweetie. It's awful early here. Tell me you're calling to say you're on your way home because you missed me so desperately."

"No."

"What is it?" He was fully awake now. I could tell.

"George ran off on the beach. We can't find him. The whole town is out now looking." I stated the facts as if they were devoid of anything that had to do with me, or us, or our life.

"Is this some sick joke?"

I handed Daisy the book that Mimi had put out for her, *Winnie-the-Pooh,* and pulled her closer on my lap. "No."

"Oh, my God, Lainey. What happened? Where is he?"

"He was on the beach digging a hole and then he was just gone. Like he does."

"What were you doing?"

This was the moment when I could lie. I could tell him that I was asleep or working at my art. I could tell him that Piper was lazy and hadn't done her job. But the world was unraveling and my lies would only spiral us downward into a deeper hell. "I was on

349

the computer."

"What?"

"I asked Piper to take them to the beach so I could book a flight to Texas."

His voice changed. "I'm on my way."

Silence filled with the sound of rain there in Petaluma where my love was in his bed. I should have been there, with my children asleep in the next room. This trip was a colossal mistake on every front.

The ambulance roared away, screaming its siren call with Mom and Owen sharing the back of it on two stretchers. Bonny's parents arrived and hustled me into their car. The man in the station wagon wrapped up the little dog and promised to go straight to the vet. We returned to Sea La Vie, where I wept with hiccuping sobs until Dad walked into the house with Owen, who wore a white cast, like a stick of chalk, on his right arm and a dazed expression I'd never seen. He came straight to me and hugged me. Dad stood by with a set expression of such anger that even later in life when I imagined him, I saw that face.

"I have to go bail Clara out of jail," he said to Mrs. Moreland. "Please watch the kids."

"I've got it," Mrs. Moreland said, already moving toward the kitchen where she would bake something: her cure for all ills.

"Jail?" I jumped and ran to Dad. "Mom is in jail?"

Dad touched the small cut above my right eye. "Yes. She drove drunk. She hit a dog and an electric pole and broke her son's arm. Yes, she is in jail."

The sun had set by then, and the night was thick upon us. I couldn't bear to think of her locked in a cell alone. All alone.

"Go get her," I wailed. "Now."

"I am."

"The dog," I asked. "Where is the dog?"

"Lainey, I have no idea. Does that even matter?"

"Yes, it matters. It really, really matters."

Tim hung up on me and was headed straight to the airport. We had to find George before Tim arrived. We had to find him now. But hours passed, and I held to Daisy and listened to the squawks of the police radios and ate nothing and drank coffee with powdered creamer, and shook with fear. I started to mutter his name over and over, a mantra to bring him home.

George.

George.

George.

In silence we ate the warm chocolate chip

351

cookies that Mrs. Moreland had made and it didn't cure anything at all. Fear hung over us like a diseased cloud. Finally, Owen, Bonny and I went back to the bedroom because they told us to try to sleep. To just try. Bonny's little brother, Percy, was already asleep in his little nook, completely unaware of what had happened or why. I was jealous of him, of his unawareness. I wished I didn't know . . .

In the middle of the dark night, Dad arrived home with Mom, and when I tried to go out to the living room to see her, to rush to her, Owen and Bonny held me back. "No."

Mom and Dad screamed at each other, the broken sounds of blame and leftover rage. Earlier that week, Dad had found our notebook and leafed through it, discovered our notes about the blue pills, about the bottles hidden under the mattresses and couch cushions. He read our words out loud to her — a deafening accusation.

"The children, Clara. They watched this. They know. And worse, even worse than this? When I thought there couldn't be something worse — you could have killed them, Clara. Killed them. Not just a dog but my children."

A low mewl escaped my throat and Bonny pulled me closer. We curled on the bed like seahorses. "The dog," I said. "The little dog."

"They are my children, too," Mom's voice

wailed. "I would never hurt them. Ever. They are mine . . ."

"Not for much longer," Dad hollered in an animal voice, a growl of words.

"Don't say mean things like that, Bob. I can't bear it."

"I'm not saying mean things anymore, Clara. I'm saying true things. You will never see them again. You are an unfit mother and we'll all be better off without you. All of us. Every fucking single one of us. First you'll spend a little time in jail, and then you'll lose everything. You hear me through your haze of Valium, right? Everything. This was the last time."

Mom wailed in a cry so awful and shattered that I held my hands over my ears.

It was Mrs. Moreland who stopped the screaming with two words. "The children."

"Yes," my dad said. "The children."

Owen. Had Mimi found him?

The bookstore buzzed with activity and I finally worked my way from the back room into the crowd and asked how I could help. I needed to do something other than sit with Daisy and hear my own fear tapping out worst-case scenarios. It was just then that Owen burst through the door, his face full of the same leftover fear of that other night nearly forty years ago. I fully expected to see a cast on his arm, a dazed expression.

"What happened?" he asked.

I told him the facts. "We will find him. We will *not* lose him. I'm sorry I just listened to Mimi's message — I didn't recognize her number so I didn't answer and I went to the house and found it empty . . . I've been waiting there."

I stepped back to gaze at him. This was what I'd wanted — my brother at my side — but not this way, not for this reason. Not because another one of us had disappeared in Watersend.

"We will find him," Owen repeated.

Sometime during the night Bonny crawled into bed with Owen; when I awoke and saw them curled together, I felt safer. Mom came in and kissed us each on the forehead with a soft murmur of love. We were all one family now and Mom was home, stoned and half-asleep, already murmuring her apologies and probably set to sleep through the next day.

But at dawn, when the softer light of morning hadn't yet given way to the slicing light that hurt my eyes, Bonny's dad stood in the living room to inform us that Mom had left a note saying she was leaving for good and, although they were sure she was okay, she had packed her things and gone. It had all been a terrible mistake. She hadn't meant to leave. She would come back or we would find her. But children know when their parents are lying and we kept quiet because we needed to believe what we were told.

I glanced around the living room, where the parents were assuring us of a good outcome, and panic bloomed. All night, I'd slept shallowly and fitfully, seeing Mom floating in the water and being eaten by small fish as they nibbled at her toes and fingers. So I knew my mom was gone, and Bonny's handsome dad was a liar and my brother, Owen, a fool for believing him.

"You made her leave," I screamed at my dad and lurched toward him, my hands out in claws. "You made her leave."

"I made her leave?" he asked and gently wound my hands together while I kicked at him uselessly.

"Yes, you."

Search crews spent days all around Watersend, and on the water. Dead or alive, they were determined to find her. But I believed she walked into the sea. "There's more ocean in the world than land," Bonny said. But it was Bonny's mom who told us, "Everyone knows she didn't want to die; she's just scared. She'll come back. We will find her."

CHAPTER 30
BONNY BLANKENSHIP

The town mobilized so quickly that I found myself wondering if they'd been waiting for a moment such as this. I made photocopies of George's face from a photo in Lainey's cell phone. We dialed frantically to gather more people and hung a map of the town and the beach to show what areas needed to be covered and where others were already searching.

If I'd believed the worst pain I could feel was for my mistake in the emergency room, I was wrong. I was hollowed out with fear for George, for Lainey and for Piper, who scoured the beach searching for a child she was meant to protect.

Lainey and Daisy sat on a chair in the far corner of the bookshop. Lainey refused to let her daughter loose, and she held a tiny Matchbox truck in her hand. She rocked Daisy back and forth and read to her from books scattered around the chair. She refused food. They were sealed together — mother and daughter.

During the last weeks of waiting for my own verdict, I'd often thought that unknowing was the most intolerable of all the emotions, and I was right. Not knowing where George was, or if he *was* at all, felt like a hole in the universe had opened and we couldn't see an inch inside. Every few seconds people checked their phones, wanting the one text or call that we all waited for: *We have him.*

I knew Piper would be unable to bear this loss, if it turned out to be such a terrible thing as that. Fear clenched at my belly, turned my limbs wobbly. It was a nightmare repeating itself, an echo from the past, a body gone and not found. I wound my way to the back of the store and to Lainey. "What can I get you?" I asked.

"My son," she said.

"We will. We will. He's . . ."

Lainey's swollen eyes spilled with tears; her mouth contorted with the pain and the wondering. "This is the worst thing that could ever happen. I should have never come here. I . . ." She pulled her sleeping daughter to her chest and mumbled into her hair. "I can't live without him."

"You won't have to," I said.

Lainey lifted her face again to mine. "I should have left last night when I wanted to. This place is cursed. I shouldn't have come back."

Maybe she was right. God, maybe she was right, but I didn't want that to be true. I wanted the opposite. "Lainey, I wanted it to be different."

"What you want and what you get don't seem to be the same thing."

"I know." I sank to the floor and knelt at the side of her chair. "We will find him."

"Don't say things you can't make come true, Bonny. You don't have the power to do that. Just stop."

A sob ripped from the insides of my chest and let loose, waking Daisy with a startle.

"Mommy?" she asked in a cracked voice.

"I'm here," Lainey said and pulled her daughter closer, if closer was even possible.

I stood and placed my hand over my mouth to stifle my cry and made my way back to the front of the bookshop. Mimi stood within a circle of people handing out maps with small markings of where others had already searched. The worst part was the boat crews that had been sent out, teenagers in their johnboats, men in their fishing boats, to jog up and down the beach, looking . . . God, looking for a floating child.

My phone buzzed and a small little hope burst inside my chest. But instead of good news I saw the number to MUSC, the hospital, *my* hospital. This would be the verdict I'd waited for, the verdict that would determine my life in so many ways hereafter. The call that meant tests had been run; papers had been reviewed; an autopsy had been performed; meetings had been held.

But I didn't answer the phone, and I didn't check the message. Right at that moment it didn't matter whether I'd been right or wrong, that I might be accused or recused. Only finding George mattered.

The clock on the far wall told us that four hours had passed. A hundred years had passed. I found Mimi behind the desk, her face weary, and told her, "I'm going to go out and search, too. I can't just stay here doing nothing."

"You aren't doing nothing. We aren't doing nothing." She pointed to the map I'd set up in the middle of the room on an easel. "You did that — and whatever that group-messaging text is — GroupMe? — that lets everyone know everything at the same time. I didn't even know something like that existed. You did that."

"Well, now I'm going out to look."

"Where?"

"The beach. Backyards along our house. This little boy is obsessed with fishing and netting shrimp."

"It's been covered," Mimi said.

"Then I'll cover it again." I stood and grabbed a bottle of water from a pile of them, which the Market had donated along with fruit and snacks.

The street was hushed in reverence. The few people outside whispered quietly and moved slowly. A small group of teenagers were knit into a circle with a man in a clerical collar. They held hands and took turns praying one by one. I didn't want to listen, but I heard — the man began praying that this group, about to head out to the marshes, would find George, find a tired but fine little boy. My prayer, over and over, didn't need to be spoken out loud because if it was, only sobs would be heard, with a mantra of *Find him Find him Find him Find him,* as a never-ending prayer twisting around and around.

I reached for my phone and texted Piper. Where are you now?

But it came back as undelivered, which meant she was either in a no-service zone or she'd run out of battery. I didn't have Fletch's number and wave upon wave of panic consumed me, obliterating my thoughts. I stood in the middle of the street, not knowing where to turn or how to move, when Owen came from the inside of the store and ran to me. I hadn't seen him go in.

"Oh, God, say they found him," I said.

He shook his head. "No."

"How did you know? I thought you were gone . . ."

"No. I told you I wasn't leaving." He pulled at me. "Let's go find him. Let's go."

"You saw it. There's a whole system in there." I pointed at the bookshop. "Areas that have been covered and areas that haven't. There are police and groups and . . ."

"I don't care. Let's just start somewhere. Anywhere. We have to do something." His voice broke.

"Piper lost him," I said.

He stopped in his forward movement, abruptly, and almost tripped over his own feet. "Oh, God."

"Yes," I said.

"We are going to find George."

"Okay." I followed him and then climbed into the passenger seat of his truck. "I keep thinking I can't stand this, that I can't move another step, that I can't take another breath unless we find him," I said. "And then I do."

Owen started the car and backed up.

"Let's start in the backyards," I said. "That's where he always goes, although it's already been checked. Or we can go to the docks. He's always going to the dock to throw in a line or crawl into the mud or dig out an oyster shell."

"He's probably sound asleep in the hull of some boat with a shrimp net for a pillow," Owen said.

"I hope you're right. Let's go back to Sea La Vie and start there . . . . Maybe he's made his way back by now."

Owen drove too fast, but who would stop us? We arrived at the house and ran out to the backyard, where we again called George's name. We wandered from backyard to backyard along the river. Whatever brokenness there was between us fell away in a single motive: find George.

Time elongated and pulled back, stretched and shrank. My mind spun out and out, trying to think where George would go or what he'd do.

Our conversation took place in fragments. "The hospital called," I told him as I peered into another johnboat at the edge of a dock.

"What did they say?" Owen came next to me and we both sighed with disappointment that the boat was empty.

"I haven't listened to the message."

Then silence and another conversation just as quick. "It's like the night we lost Mom. Where could she be? That's all we asked," Owen said.

"I know."

"How could she have left her children?"

"She was scared, Owen. So scared."

We never finished a full conversation and the words always morphed into George's name.

We wound our way to the backyard of another anonymous cedar shake river house empty with possibility. Owen stopped in front of an upside-down canoe and lifted it, peered under and then placed it back. "Shit." He spun around to me. "I came here because I love you, not to make things worse. I didn't mean to . . ."

"You love me?" I spat out the question with such vehemence I didn't recognize my own voice. Somehow in losing all I'd lost the past weeks, and now George, I wanted to know what it was that kept him coming back again and again and again. "Is it because I love you so desperately? Is it so you can come here and see me and make sure I still love you before you head out into the world again? Like you need me as a ballast to make it *out there*? Why?" My voice climbed higher and higher, my arms flying around me as if I were in a tribal dance that only I could know.

"A ballast?" He froze where he stood, one leg in front of the other like the freeze tag we played so long ago. "Are you kidding? I don't know why I love you. It's not something I can define like one of your medical diagnoses. It's not a sickness or a disease. I just love you. I always have." He then set himself in motion, taking two large steps to me and grabbing each shoulder. "I do love you. I hate that I haven't been able to be the man we both need me to be. But I don't need reasons to love. I don't need a list. It just is." He kissed me and pulled me hard and close.

I took both my hands and rested them on his chest and, with great sheer will, I shoved him away. "I lost the job at Emory."

"I know you blame me for that. I will take the blame for everything: for the job loss, for George, for your broken heart. I will carry it, but it doesn't change that I love you."

"I don't blame you. I blame me. And my obsession with you. But none of that matters now. Only George matters."

I twisted away from him so quickly that

my ankle caught in the thick grass. I stumbled and yelped as my ankle torqued. Owen grabbed and steadied me. "I love you because you care as much about others as you do about yourself. I love when you get angry and then trip over your own feet. I love how you stare at the sky and get lost in it. I love how you drop your voice when you're saying something that matters. I love . . ."

Tears sprung high into my throat and I rested my hand on my chest. "Stop. I only want to find George. I only . . ." My phone buzzed in my back pocket and I lifted it to see a text from Piper: We found him. He's okay.

I grabbed Owen's arm and lifted my phone to show him. "Thank God," he said. "Now you can check the message from the hospital." He ran his hand through my hair.

Part of me knew that he needed to absolve himself for what he saw as his own part in it — as misguided as that was — as I did, for myself, and that was why he wanted me to check.

"No. Not now. This is too much already. I do not want this to be the place I find out."

"I just know that all this unknowing has made you crazy, and here, right here, you can find out."

"Not now."

CHAPTER 31
LAINEY MCKAY

I'd already died inside, wondering how I would live with two great disappearances. How I would ever take another breath. My head rested on top of Daisy's and my eyes were closed when Piper called to say she'd found him.

The broken weep that came from me must have scared her on the other end. "Where?"

Piper was crying in the same jagged sobs. "A friend's house. I'd taken him here before to play. We're on our way back."

Sirens squealed in the background and I knew they were in a police car. "George has always wanted to ride in a police car," I said so foolishly, with such abandon.

"Loretta had already called them before we got there," Piper said.

"Loretta?"

"The house he wandered to . . ." Piper's voice trailed off with a sob.

"Let me talk to him," I said and then I

heard his voice, his precious voice.

"Mommy?" George's cracked voice came over the line and I collapsed inside with relief.

"My big boy," I said. "I'm waiting for you. Hurry . . ."

"I'm going as fast as I can," he said. "The policeman even put on the lights and siren."

"That's still not fast enough," I told him and I heard his laughter. God, his beautiful laughter.

I shook Daisy awake. "He's okay," I told her.

"What?" She lifted her face to mine and wiped at my tears with her hands. "I dreamed he was okay." She closed her eyes again. "Piper found him."

"Yes," I said. "Yes, she did."

I lifted my phone to call Tim, but it went straight to voice mail — he was probably halfway here on a plane.

Piper and my son were on the way, and did it matter where they'd found George? We would learn all the facts; we would find out how and where in time. What mattered — the only thing — was that my son was safe.

Out in the bookshop the crowd must have been told because I heard a cheer. I lifted Daisy onto my hip and walked into the main area. People hugged and high-fived and we watched the jubilation without yet being seen. Mimi, in one great act of triumph, tore down the map and posters. My dazed expression must have made me appear as though I'd come from a dream, or a long trip. I smiled out at everyone, but my eyes weren't focused on anything but the front door.

Bonny and Owen came through the door first and her steps toward me were slow and unsure, but then I covered the ground with a run, threw my arm around her.

"Oh, God. I was so awful to you. I was scared out of my mind. Of course it wasn't Piper's fault. I've lost him so many times — in clothing stores, in the mall, at the park. He does that. He wanders off. Forgive me."

"Oh, Lainey. There's nothing to forgive." She took Daisy from my arms and set her on the floor.

"Uncle Owen," Daisy cried out.

He leaned down to her. "Hey there, bunny."

Daisy yanked at Bonny's T-shirt. "Look! It's my uncle."

"I know, Daisy. Isn't it great?" Bonny said.

Owen picked her up and she wrapped her little arms around his neck. "Are they almost here?" he asked.

I stared at the front door. "They can't get here fast enough." I wiped at my face, at the leftover tears. "I want to kill him and smother him with kisses. I'm going to tether him to me with a rope forever. He'll have to take me to college with him."

Then we heard the police car. I ran out to it, opening the back passenger door to see George's face burrowed in Piper's shoulder. She held her hand over his head, protecting him. I grabbed my son from Piper and took him in my arms. He squealed in fright and twisted away from me, reaching for Piper, calling her name.

Piper leaned toward him and kissed his face. "Look, George. It's your mommy."

George's hair was tangled, a white mass of curls. His cheeks red with sunburn and heat, his chubby hands and round feet crusted with sand. His sweet face swiveled around to see me and he cried out, "Mommy!"

Fresh tears started. He wept in that hiccuping way of a small child, without reservation, so full of relief and pent-up fear. I sank, slowly and with care, to a bistro chair outside the bookshop on the sidewalk, held my son against my chest and rocked back and forth, uttering his name over and over.

An older woman stepped out of the back

of the police car, blinking in the sunlight and walking toward the bookshop. Slowly, one by one, the crowd moved outside. This was the exact moment they had worked toward for hours and hours. This was what they had whispered about and prayed for. There were tears and hugs and I absorbed it all. Bonny sat next to me. The older woman who had stepped out of the car stood there staring at us, her eyes filled with tears. I took stock of her: I felt like I knew her — but how? Piper stood next to her, holding Fletch's hand, collapsed against him.

The old woman was tiny, a hummingbird. Her eyes were blue; her hair both platinum and curly and pulled back into a knot at the base of her neck. She wore a sundress, flowered and old-fashioned, a fifties throwback. Flat ballet shoes on her feet. I wondered why she stared at us with such a fixed gaze, unwavering even with the tears.

My breath hitched and stayed right there in that space under my heart with stubborn resolve.

The old woman took a few steps toward us and I saw Piper glance from her to me and then back again. "Ms. Loretta?" Piper asked. "Are you okay?"

Loretta, the woman, didn't answer but

stood before me.

"Lainey?" she asked.

"Yes?" I stared at her with a shuddering sense of familiarity. *A dance at the square. A card game at the river house. A birthday party with other girls.* What was it? My mind, already jumbled and scattered by the day's events, couldn't find a name.

"I'm Loretta Rogers," she said.

I grasped onto the name like a life preserver, something to keep me afloat in the confusion. "Mom's friend," I said. "You were . . . Mom's friend that last summer."

"Yes, I was."

I grabbed on to her arm with my free hand, still not releasing my son. Deep in my weary bones, I knew this woman knew where my mother was. "Where is she? Where is my mom?" I asked. "Tell me."

She lowered her gaze. "Lainey Greer, not now," she said. "Not now."

"What?" I wrapped both arms around my son, pulled him closer. No one called me by my full name, not since Mom left.

"Go home with your son. We can talk another time."

This wasn't right. Mom was in Texas. Had I made a fool of myself? A crazy old lady and a horrible day. The fight with Owen; my lost son. I was going insane.

But I wasn't. This woman knew my mom.

"I don't understand," I said. My hands shook. I came undone inside, traveling through time. "Who are you?"

Bonny's voice joined the confusion. "You know Clara?" she asked Loretta.

Then Owen repeated me. "Our mom? You know her? What's happening?" he asked.

The woman turned to Bonny. "Oh, look at you, Bee Moreland, a mom now yourself. It's your daughter I've come to love so much." Her gaze wandered to each of us one by one in slow motion. "Yes, I was Clara's friend all those summers ago."

Bonny reached for Piper behind her, took her hand.

"Mom?" It was Piper's voice. "What's happening?"

No one answered Piper and I asked again, "Where is she?"

"I can't tell you everything now, Lainey. Get some rest and be with your son. Let's meet tomorrow," Loretta said quietly.

I clung to George even tighter. "Tomorrow. Where?"

"Right here."

"Mommy, that's Ms. Loretta," George said in my ear. "She has a million crayons in her house. And juice boxes with dancing apples on them. And she plays pretty music.

She gave me the big yellow flower . . ."

Loretta placed her hand on George's chapped cheek and then withdrew it before speaking. "I wanted to find the right time to tell you about your mom, Lainey. But the longer I waited, the harder it became. When I met Piper I knew the time had come. I knew that it was finally the right time to tell you everything."

"The time?" My voice wasn't holding steady; I wasn't holding steady. I fought two urges — one to shake this woman and make her tell me everything, force her to set the world aright, and the other to run. "Is she in Texas?"

"Texas?"

Just by her question I knew it was wrong. "Is she here?" My gaze shifted left and right, scanning the crowd.

"No. I have a lot to answer for, but there is time for that. Please just take care of your son right now."

"Mommy." George snuggled into my shoulder.

Bonny came to my side. "Let's get you home. Okay?"

"Let me drive you." Owen stepped up. "Please."

But I still had more questions. "How did this happen?" I asked Piper. "How did

George find this woman?" My mind moved and twisted, trying to find a landing spot.

"He walked for miles. He must have gone up to the road or behind houses for no one to see him. When he saw Ms. Loretta's house he went there because we'd taken him there when we were delivering groceries, and before we went to the beach."

"What were you looking for?" I asked George, running my hand over his body just to make sure he was really there.

"Treasure." His little voice so scratched with fatigue.

"We've been hunting treasure all summer," Piper said, and her voice broke again. "It's my fault. It's all . . ."

"I told you he runs away. It could have been any of us."

"What if he hadn't gone to Loretta's?" Piper shook her head, imagining the worst, as I knew she'd do for a long, long time. As I'd done before.

"You know," I said, empty and exhausted, turning back to the woman named Loretta, "yesterday, I would have given anything to find my mom. I've looked and looked for her all of my life. But to almost lose my son to find her, it was *not* worth the price. Wherever she is, you tell her that."

The meanest part of me hoped I'd hurt

her with my words. But she stood there prepared to take it. "All I ask," Loretta said, "is that you let me try to tell you the story, to explain it all to you. Please."

I nodded. Piper then sank to the curb and Fletch with her. She dropped her head on his shoulder and they sat there in the heat.

"I'm so tired," Piper said. "I could die."

"Let's just all get home," Bonny interrupted. "This has been a . . . day."

Loretta touched my arm. "I will meet you here tomorrow at noon."

I nodded and then glanced at my brother. "Please take us home." We all moved toward the car, except Piper, who stayed seated on the curb.

"You all go on," she said. "I'm going to stay with Fletch for a little while."

Bonny spoke up. "You need to come back to the house with us. Get something to eat and drink. Some rest."

"I will make sure she's okay, Mrs. Blankenship," Fletch said. "I promise."

"This day does not seem real. Nothing about it seems real at all," I said before I walked away.

"It is," Loretta said. "It's all very real."

CHAPTER 32
PIPER BLANKENSHIP

Fletch's hand on my head was a weight of comfort. I was emptied out. I'd spent all day imagining the worst and praying the worst hadn't happened. And now, with George in his mom's arms, I collapsed onto Fletch, his body solid. The day had been wrung out with all it could hold. We sat on the curb outside Mimi's bookshop and I rested my head on his shoulder. "That was the most horrible thing that has ever happened to me."

"I know. But please don't blame yourself or go crazy thinking of all the terrible things that could have happened, because they didn't."

"You never left me." I lifted my face to him. "You could have left, embarrassed at my stupidity, and . . ."

"It was a mistake, Piper. One his mom has made before. One people make every day — to look away, to get preoccupied, to

377

get lost . . . this is not new in the world."

"But this . . . this could have been the end of everything. My dad once told me that I was just like Mom. And maybe he's right — she screwed up because she was distracted, and so did I."

"They call it an accident because it's an accident. They don't call it an on-purpose." He pulled me closer and my body shaped into his, molded around him. I laughed just a little bit and started to feel the residual effects: the sunburn, the aching on the bottom of my bare feet, the blisters and scrapes.

"I hurt," I said and closed my eyes. "Everywhere."

"Let's get you some water and then we can go back to my place if you want. Or do you want me to take you to your mom's place?"

"Are you kidding? What could possibly be going on there? Lainey reassuring me that it really wasn't my fault? My own mom looking at me with pitiful eyes because she feels so sorry for me? Owen showing up again while I try to figure out the weirdness between all of them? Um. No, thanks. I think I'll go with you."

He laughed and stood, helping me to my feet. We went into the bookshop, where Mimi was cleaning. Soft flute music, something Celtic and mysterious, played in the background. When she saw me, she dropped the pile of paper plates she was carrying into the trash and came to me with a hug.

"Are you okay?" she asked.

"I don't know."

She took my hand and we sank to the little white couch. Fletch followed us, but stayed a few feet away pretending to be enamored by a pile of books on the front table.

"Do not beat yourself up about this," Mimi said. "Not one little bit, dear. It was scary and yet it turned out all right. Everyone is safe."

"I lost a child, Mimi. I didn't get drunk and make a fool of myself." I choked on my fear. "I didn't fail a class. I didn't . . . steal someone's boyfriend. I lost a child."

Mimi reached across the couch. "We all make mistakes."

"Not like this we don't."

"Piper, life holds all the terrible and all the good in one place. And you can't expect to never make a mistake."

"I think I just need to sleep or . . . I don't know, just get out of here for a while. But I don't want to go back to the house. I can't face everyone yet. I'm still shaking inside with the way it could have gone. And Ms. Loretta? I mean, what is that all about? I'm so confused."

Mimi squeezed my shoulder. "Go get some rest, Piper."

Fletch came then. "Let's get something to drink and eat," he said. "I promised your mom."

"Yes." I rested against him as he took my hand.

I hugged Mimi, stood and stretched, tired all the way inside to my heart.

The Jeep and the wind and the smoky smell of a bonfire somewhere on the beach lulled me to sleep in the few short minutes it took to get to Fletch's house.

He kissed me awake and I opened my eyes to see we'd pulled into his driveway and parked around the back of his carriage house. He hadn't brought me here before, yet he'd told me he lived behind his mom's house in a separate place. My head lolled back in fear, a quick half beat because I thought George was still gone and I'd fallen asleep before finding him. I let out a small cry.

"It's okay," Fletch said and unhooked the seat belt, took me in his arms and gently placed me on the ground. I fell into his chest and then together we shuffled into his little home. He took the weight of my fear and I let him absorb it and negate it.

I had tunnel vision for only what was right in front of me — a narrow vision of bleached hardwood floors and a blue barn-style door that slid aside to a small bedroom with a huge rumpled and unmade bed. White and blue pillows, blankets and sheets were scrunched in the form of a human as if someone hid beneath them. Fletch laid me down, and I sank into the comforter and looked to the ceiling where a fan whirred with the soft noise of wind in leaves.

He brought me a glass of water and I sat to swallow the whole thing at once. He climbed into the bed and stretched out long next to me, drawing me close until his legs wound around mine and his arms encircled me from shoulders to waist. My faced rested on the notch between his warm clavicle and chest. His fingers ran through my hair and untangled the knots, gently like Mom would have done when I was a child.

"It's all okay now," he murmured. "He's safe."

Languid and dreamy, a comfortable safety fell over me. His lips swept across my forehead.

"You feel like you have a fever," he said. And then he kissed my nose and cheeks, my neck and ears until I was eager for him to kiss me. I took his face in both my hands and kissed him as if he could take away the fever and the fear.

My tongue lingered, not wanting to miss anything of him. Together we explored each other, not gently as I'd imagined but desperate.

Our clothes came off so smoothly, like it was a dance we'd practiced for years, choreographed for this moment. My skin no longer felt burned and hot. I wanted every part of me to touch every part of him — he was the cure. His hands and his fingers and his mouth found every tender part of me, and by the time we made love, I was fully awake. I drew him closer. Fletch offered all of himself to me at that moment and yet I still wanted more, and then more.

When I was little, I'd believed that the sun slept in the waters off Charleston, and then it rose to shake off the water and hang above us until it had to go back to sleep again. But of course that wasn't true — the sun was merely lighting another part of the world.

So many things weren't what they seemed, and I'd learned that slowly — when the sky looked on fire with sunset it wasn't; when the horizon appeared like the edge of the world it wasn't; when a star fell, it wasn't falling to earth. I thought of all the other things, the adult beliefs, that weren't what they looked like either.

Mom and Lainey and Owen. Mom and Dad. Ms. Loretta. Was anything as it seemed? My mind wasn't making sense, my thoughts mixing up words and language, useless.

It was night dark in Fletch's room, his shades closed and the fan whirring overhead. Fletch lay on his side, facing me on the pillow, his face soft with sleep. I did have a fever; I burned with it. My mouth felt scorched and my eyelids like sandpaper against my eyes. I moved slowly from the bed; I needed water. I stumbled in the dark, crashed into the side of a dresser and let out a yelp.

A light flashed on and Fletch stood quickly, naked in the dusky room. "Baby, you okay?"

"I think I'm really sick," I said.

He bent over and yanked on his boxers and shorts, still crusted with sand from the previous day. He took my hand and led me, still naked, to the kitchen and on the way grabbed a blanket from the couch, threw it over my shoulders. I tossed it off. "I'm so hot."

He opened a kitchen drawer, pawing

through it with the sound of clattering knives and forks and whatever else was in there. He drew out a plastic digital thermometer.

"Here," he said.

I sat on the hardwood floor, not bothering to find a chair, the coldness of it on my bottom a relief. I lay flat then, my cheek resting on the cool surface, my lips pursed around the thermometer as it settled under my tongue. Running water from somewhere sounded like a waterfall, and Fletch sat next to me, spread a cold washcloth on my neck and I moaned. "Feels good," I said, or something that vaguely sounded like it around the thermometer, which then beeped.

Fletch took it from my mouth and looked at it. "Oh, God, Piper, you have a 103.2 fever. We have to get you to a doctor."

"My mom's a doctor." This was a statement I'd said my entire life. Now it mattered.

"Come on, let's get you dressed and to your mom."

I mumbled something affirmative. The rest was blurry — Fletch helped me get dressed and buckled me into the Jeep. We were at Sea La Vie in minutes and banging on the front door. It was Mom who answered and Mom who took me into her arms and into the kitchen. Fletch told her of my fever.

"Oh, Piper," she said and placed her hand on my forehead. "You need IV fluids. You're dehydrated. Come on; let's get to an emergency clinic. Fletch?" she asked. "Where is the closest one?"

"We don't have one."

"Closest hospital?" she asked, but she was already grabbing at her phone to look it up.

"Derry, about twenty minutes away," he said.

"Okay, let's go."

Mom and I were in the car and I fell asleep again. I drifted off to vivid dreams of bonfires and lit matches tossed into the air to land on my skin, sparks settling onto my forearms and thighs.

CHAPTER 33
BONNY BLANKENSHIP

I sat in a hardback chair and monitored the IV pump that dripped fluids into my daughter's veins. She had been dehydrated enough to spike a fever, and she needed fluids badly. I should have brought her home and made sure she drank water. I should have insisted. I should have done a lot of things I hadn't done.

It was an hour after I walked Piper through the door of the ER, after I'd told everyone what to do, that I realized I hadn't been hit with an anxiety attack at the first sight of the hospital or the stretcher. My daughter's own sickness had been the cure for my own, I thought.

How had I believed that I could give up this profession? I sat quietly listening to the thrumming operations of a place I knew, although I'd never been to that particular one. I wanted to get up, instruct them on why the patient in the next cubicle had stomach pains or how to keep the IV pump from beeping with air bubbles. I wanted to . . . well, I wanted to be a doctor again. All it might take was listening to the voice mail sitting in my phone — a condemnation or a redemption — a voice mail I hadn't yet listened to.

I watched Piper sleep and had the most desperate feeling that I wanted to do it all again: a home; a family; a nice little life. I felt homesick, but I didn't know for where. Where was *home*? Maybe that was what I'd been trying to do all along — make the home that I wanted to return to, make the home that I longed for. But instead it was all now a mess, a broken toy, a replacement house that didn't feel real. Sea La Vie now held all the secrets and trash of the past like debris that had floated in on the tide, flotsam.

Maybe everyone ached for something that didn't exist, and that was what we searched for in each other, and everywhere we went. I'd believed that I could gather everything that mattered the most and build a new life, but the old one returned again and again. I felt sick with the kind of abandonment I hadn't felt since I was a child at summer camp where Mom and Dad had sent me off for an experience "all children should have."

Maybe it was too much to hope that I could find a new way of being when I'd already lived another way for so very long.

I needed to call Lucas and tell him about Piper. He would be livid, and I needed to prepare myself.

"Mom." Piper's voice broke my reverie.

I opened my eyes to see her looking at me, her blue eyes washed of color and hollow in her face. Her little nose peeled already.

"Hey, sweetie, how do you feel?"

"Are you mad at me?" She winced with the words.

"What? No. What for?" I covered her forehead with kisses. "Why would you ask that?"

"You told me to come straight home and I didn't. I just couldn't face everyone. I just couldn't . . ."

"Baby, no. I should have made you come with us. I should have taken you home. I didn't know you were so dehydrated, so sick."

"I didn't either, Mom."

"I'm not mad. Not one bit. I've been worried sick, but not mad."

"Mom, I'm so, so sorry. I'm so . . ." Her face crumbled and tears slid down the left side of her face onto the pillow.

"Stop, sweetie. You can stop saying it."

"I can't face everyone. Everything bad that has happened is my fault. Everything. I texted Owen. I lost George. I made you take me to the hospital."

"You didn't cause everything to go wrong. It was all well on its way to wrong before you came along." I tried to make her laugh, but it didn't work.

"Mom, you can try to make me feel better, but no one lost George but me."

"And no one found him but you."

"I was the one who texted Owen, Mom. I made him come here. I pretended I was you. I'm such an asshole."

"Piper!" I took her face in my hands and kissed the tears on her cheeks. "What does Lainey always remind us? Words have power. Do not call yourself such a horrid thing. You are no such thing. You made a mistake. You were angry and you reacted."

"It was such a bad move. I just felt so badly for Lainey and I thought you were hiding him from her."

"I wasn't."

"I know that now." She closed her eyes and heartbreaking tears leaked out from under her weary and purple eyelids. "I want to go home. To the river house. *That* home."

"The nurse went to get your discharge

papers, sweetie. We will go home in a minute."

Home.

It didn't take long for them to pull her IV, have me sign the papers and offer instructions on how to care for her, what to watch for. The nurse was going through her list, and had gotten to "check her temperature every two hours," when Piper interrupted.

"She knows what to do. She's an ER doc."

The nurse laughed. "Well, you should have said something." Then she pointed to the line where to sign. "Right here, Dr. Blankenship."

Now Lucas. I needed to call Lucas.

After a silent twenty-minute drive, I parked at Sea La Vie and called him; he answered on the first ring.

"Finally," he said.

"Hi, Lucas."

"Is everything okay?" he asked, able to hear my weariness, my hesitancy. He'd always been able to read me so well.

"Yes, it is now, but I just wanted to let you know that Piper got sunburned and dehydrated . . . she needed some fluids and we're just returning from the hospital now."

"What hospital?"

"The one in Derry. They don't have one in Watersend. But really, she's okay. Here, you can talk to her."

Piper and I climbed out of the car, and I handed the cell phone to her. She started a conversation with her dad, beginning with the morning, when she took the kids to the beach. I would let her tell Lucas in private, the way she wanted to tell it. I kissed her on the cheek and motioned that I was going into the house. She followed me in, telling the story without taking a breath, not waiting for his response. Her voice cracked and she wiped at a tear even as the torrent of words continued.

Once inside, she went back to her room, still talking. I couldn't hear her any longer and I was relieved. I was as tired as I'd ever been. No all-nighter in the ER had ever taken out of me what the past twenty-four hours had. I went to my own bedroom and closed my eyes. It was nine in the morning by then, and yet the house was still quiet with sleep. I couldn't check the message from the hospital, as Piper had my phone. I closed my eyes to let the sunshine, sneaking through the slatted blinds in stripes of lemon yellow, fall over my face.

A couple hours later, I awoke confused, and then remembered where I was. I rolled over and saw my cell on the bedside table. Piper must have slipped in earlier with it. I picked it up and hit the button to hear my messages, whatever those messages might be.

"Dr. Blankenship, this is Frank Preston. Can you please call me as soon as possible?"

Now I knew how patients felt when we had their diagnosis, a paper with their results on our desk, and yet asked them to come in or call us back. The doctors, the privileged ones who knew it all. I hit "call back" and the phone rang far off into my other life, the one I'd thought I could just leave to start again. How very wrong I'd been. My past was still there, waiting, lurking in the background the same way Owen had been, the same way Loretta had been, the same way an ignored lump in the breast grows large enough to take a life.

"Hello," his deep voice said.

"Hi, Dr. Preston. It's Bonny."

"Hello, Bonny," he said, as if he agreed with me before he let loose the worst of it. "I'm calling to let you know that the committee has met and the diagnostic tests were confirmed. It has been determined that your mistake — a wrong dosage of Dilaudid — was a contributing factor in Nicholas Rohr's death."

"A contributing factor?" I asked. Bile, fear and shame, now tasting like death, rose in me. "Or *the* factor?"

"He had multiple injuries, Bonny. At least two of which probably would have taken his life. That's why this committee took so long. You are a respected doctor here. One of our very best, and we don't want to lose you over one mistake on a night when many mistakes could have been made in the chaos."

"I appreciate your vote of confidence in my abilities," I said slowly, carefully, seeing a way out of this, seeing that I could skim over this thin ice and not fall in if I granted myself the chance. But I needed to take the truth to its end, past the unadorned "we love you" truth.

"But what I need to know is, *this time* did I cause a death? I'm not asking you to weigh it against the other lives I've saved."

He was silent for too long, which predicated the answer that eventually came. "Yes. Technically, yes. But he wouldn't have made it, Bonny. Even without the dosage error, he would *not* have made it."

"Okay," I said. "Now what?" I could wait to fall apart when we hung up. I could face the worst of the worst, but I would wait.

"Bonny, he had a grade-four liver laceration. He'd lost a lot of blood and was already in hemorrhagic shock. The surgeon doesn't believe he could have been saved even if he had made it to the OR."

"But he didn't make it to the OR," I said.

"No one is pressing charges. There is no malpractice. You will be able to have your license back immediately, and start work when you please."

"Thank you, Dr. Preston," I said. "Can I get back to you? Let me absorb this information?"

"Of course." He paused and I imagined him as I'd always seen him — behind his mahogany desk with diplomas framed and hung on his walls, a white lab coat with his name stitched in blue ink and a furrowed forehead that never relaxed. "Take all the time you need. We are here for you when you're ready."

"Thanks, Dr. Preston. I'll be in touch soon."

I didn't know if I'd be in touch soon. I didn't know anything other than that the outcome I'd been staving off was finally here in its ugly truth: I'd killed someone.

I ran to the bathroom and vomited so violently into the new porcelain toilet that Lainey came running, banging on the door. "Are you okay?"

"Yes," I said from the tile floor, my face flat to the coolness of the marble I'd chosen in a store in Charleston when I imagined a new life, a new start and a better way to live.

All this time I'd been thinking of that night in the ER like a hinge on a door, one that swung open to allow me to reassess my life, to start over and try again. To take stock of all that was important and focus on finding that "one thing." I'd been acting like I was going to camp to learn how to darn pot holders, or attending a retreat to learn to paint with watercolors. But it was nothing like that: I was running away from the cold hard fact that I'd killed someone because I was obsessed with someone else.

I could live here at the river house or in a shack or back at home with Lucas, and the facts of who I was and the damage I'd done wouldn't vary. Nothing would ever be the same.

I don't know how much time passed before Lainey banged again on the door.

"Bonny, please. What's wrong in there?"

The marble felt too good against my cheek, a stony and cold reminder of the truth, and I didn't want to get up. But out there in my house, the home I'd thought would save us all with some kind of magical thinking, was my best friend, my daughter, and now I heard his voice — Owen was out there, also. The man I'd loved for far too long. I couldn't stay in here. I needed to face them. All of them.

I knew the hospital would not make the full truth public, and I would never have to speak the truth if I didn't want to. I could carry this around for all of my life and let it eat away at me, and destroy only me. Yes, that was the best way.

"I'm fine," I called out to Lainey. "I just got really sick to my stomach. I'll be out in a minute."

"Okay," she said and her footsteps faded.

Far off, in the bedroom, my phone rang over and over. It was like a train whistle in the middle of the night, something you knew was going by but had no idea to where, or why. And I didn't care.

Until Piper banged on the bathroom door. "Mom? Are you okay in there?"

The standing took time: one foot and then to one knee, and then another foot and another knee. I pulled myself up and balanced my hands on the sink. The air-conditioning vent blew cold air between the V of my legs. My face stared straight back at me from the mirror, eyes ringed and dark hair sweaty and stuck to my right cheek: crazed. I took in a long breath and pulled my hair back and stroked it into a smooth ponytail at the base of my neck. I splashed some cold water on my face and then I opened the door to find Piper standing there waiting, her face a mask of confusion. "What is going on?"

"I just don't feel good," I said.

"No. Something happened," she said.

"A lot has happened, Piper."

"I know, but still . . ."

I walked past her with a pat on her shoulder as if she'd done something good at preschool. The living room was buzzing, with talk from Owen, and also from the kids and Lainey. The words were like bees, and my thoughts like a net catching only snippets of conversation.

How did you learn to capture an emotion in your art so well? Owen.

I hate peanut butter. Daisy.

Can I please have more lemonade? Daisy again.

What time should we meet for dinner? Lainey.

Mom, are you okay? Piper.

"I'm fine," I said.

"Mom" — Piper handed me my phone as her face wavered in front of me — "Dad has called, like, six hundred times."

I felt but didn't see Owen's gaze between my shoulder blades. I took the phone from her and tried to smile, but smiling wasn't anything I could do right then. "I'll be right back," I said in a voice I didn't recognize.

Alone in the back bedroom, I pushed Lucas's number and waited for him to answer. His voice came on the line and he didn't greet me but only told me what he had called to say. "The hospital has been trying to call the home phone. Have you talked to them?"

"Yes," I said. "I'm coming home today. I will talk to you then."

And I hung up on him. I returned to the living room and glanced around at the improbable room. Who would have thought all these people would end up in my river house? Only months ago it would have seemed impossible. "Listen, I have to go back to Charleston. Just for a day or so. Please, all of you, stay here. I know there is so much going on, and I don't want to leave. But the hospital called." I paused and in that space of time, the confession rose to my lips, a sacrament to all the truths set free here in the last days. "It was my fault. I killed a man."

Silence, heavy and thick, fell into that room. I didn't want anyone to say anything; I wouldn't have been able to bear a platitude, depleted in its ability to save me.

"I have to go, but I'll be back. In a day. Or so."

"Mom." Piper stepped forward. "Can I come with you?"

"No." I shook my head. "I promise to come right back."

"We'll be here," Lainey said.

"Where's Tim?" I asked. I'd known he was coming to Watersend and had heard his voice while I was in and out of sleep, but I hadn't yet seen him.

"I sent him on a run to the grocery store." She smiled. "He needed to stop hovering over George."

I took a step toward Owen and his pained expression so clearly etched on his face and in his eyes. "It's not your fault," I told him.

He took my hand and led me outside, to the back porch and then to the dock where I'd called George's name so many times that my throat was still sore.

"Please let me come with you," he said. "Let me be there for you."

"You don't owe me anything, Owen. You do not have to follow me to fix anything or save anything. This is mine alone, and I don't want you with me. I don't."

"I want to be with you. I want to go with you. Please."

"For the first time in my life, Owen, I do

399

not want you. I'm not being cruel, or maybe I am, but I need to go home."

"I'm not leaving. I'm going to be right here when you return."

"Here's the problem, Owen. Now you're tangled with all that is dreadful. Right now when I look at you I think of the night we lost your mom. I think of killing a man. I think of losing my job. You've become entangled with all that breaks my heart. With all that hurts."

"Let me untangle myself," he said.

The river moved by the dock, and there Lainey and I were, thirteen years old and jumping into these waters at high tide, baptizing ourselves and believing that we could wish ourselves a perfect life. We knew our future was charmed, that whatever we did, from that underwater moment on, would be as magical as the full moon and the dolphin that had nosed by us, touching us with its silken skin. Lainey and I, naked and making wishes, diving our heads underwater with each wish, wanting life to unspool itself at our command.

"Lainey and I skinny-dipped here one night, made wishes."

"I know," he said. "I saw you."

"You saw us then? You never told me."

"It was so beautiful and private. And I

loved you even then."

"Owen." It felt as if everything I'd ever wanted or needed to say had already been spoken. "I have to go." I touched his cheek and walked away. I'd driven halfway to Charleston before I realized I'd grabbed my purse, my phone and my wallet, but not my shoes. I was barefoot, humbled and returning to what I'd left behind.

CHAPTER 34
LAINEY MCKAY

The sun beat with viscid weight as I walked to the bookstore alone. Fear joined with expectation as I walked along the Watersend sidewalks. Would Mom be there with Loretta? Would they show me pictures? Would the old woman tell me something awful or wonderful?

Loretta had been right to make me wait, to send me home with my son and family to sleep and reconcile both the losing and the finding. Whatever there was for me to know about my mom, or even see, couldn't have been done with any consideration the day before. Tim had arrived hours after George was found, and it was *my* family, the one I'd chosen and made, that had mattered last night.

I hadn't told Tim *why* I was walking into town, and this was a betrayal. Yet for me to explain to him that I was leaving for a few hours, when he'd only just arrived, and that

I was sneaking off on one more possible wild-goose chase, would have seemed to be another kind of betrayal. Which was worse? Sin by omission or by acting yet again on my obsession?

I hadn't told anyone, actually. Not even Owen, who must not have heard her say "tomorrow at noon." I felt that this moment was all mine, right or wrong. I'd left the house with some mumbled excuse about going to the store, needing fresh air.

Yet again I had walked away from my family to discover if someone else knew about Mom, if someone else had found her. I would ask a woman who lived in a cottage by the edge of the ocean, a woman my son had wandered to for crayons and apple juice.

The bookshop door was propped open, and Mimi stood at the front table rearranging the display. I glanced at my watch: noon exactly. I could become preoccupied and lose a son, lose track of time, and yet arrive on the dot to discover what these women knew about my lost mother. Mimi glanced up as if she felt me outside on the sidewalk staring at her, as if I'd whispered in her ear, *I'm here.* She smiled and waved.

I entered the store, and the cold blast of

air hit me like a splash of water. I shivered. The other woman, Loretta, came from somewhere in the back of the store. She wore a long muumuu, flowered and as bright as her smile. Her hair was plaited into two braids like a child's, one falling over each shoulder. "Good morning," she said.

I nodded, not trusting my voice just yet.

She came to me and placed her hand on my forearm, and then took my hand. "Follow me," she said.

Mimi called out Harrington's name and he appeared from behind a bookshelf. "I've got the store covered," he said.

The three of us exited the shop. I dropped Loretta's hand and found my voice. "Where are we going?"

The two women glanced at each other and then both at me, but neither answered. A block later we turned left at the corner where the barbershop light twirled in a hypnotic swirl. We walked two more blocks until we reached Thomas Street, and then walked past the hardware store and the real estate office with photos of houses and lots pasted on its windows. Onward for another minute or two until, still in silence, we reached the town's small African Methodist Episcopal — AME — church. It was a simple wooden structure on the river, painted white with a spire reaching toward the clear sky. The river, the same waters that coursed behind Bonny's house, ran alongside the church as a companion.

Had Mom been hiding inside a church? I moved toward the front, a curved double door with an iron handle. I placed my hand upon it and glanced at the cross, which was carved into the door. Mimi placed her hand on mine. "No, dear."

I spun around. "What?"

"This way," she said, and she led me around to the side of the church where the graveyard, simple and surrounded by a rusty iron fence, filled the yard and ended abruptly at the river.

We stopped beneath a wild and exuberant live oak tree, its branches gnarled and spread into many arms of green and canopied protection. "Can you please tell me what is going on?" My heart beat in the bottom of my throat, slow and sluggish.

"Hold on, dear," Loretta said. "Hold on." She took in a long breath and lifted her face to the sky, closed her eyes. A small tear ran down her cheek and she allowed it to settle in the wrinkles that webbed from the corner of her mouth.

I glanced around. Was Mom on a bench?

Living homeless on the river's edge in a tent or, worse, out in the elements? Crazy? Roaming Watersend like a haunted and wasted ghost? Tim was right — some things are best left to mystery. Some knowings are best left to their secret places, crouched in the dark to stay.

"Enough," I said.

"Yes," Mimi said. "Enough is right." She then stepped out from the shade of the tree and I followed. Only steps later we reached the ornate gate of the graveyard. A week before, I'd come here with the kids to let them walk out onto the church's long dock. They'd giggled at the fact that "dead people" were only a few yards away. "Were there ghosts here?" they'd asked with horrified laughter. "Why would they *plant* them here?" Daisy had wondered out loud.

"I'm sure they were here long before the rest of the town," I'd told her.

Dead people. The phrase caught in the back of my mind, in the sticky places where I'd feared this answer.

Loretta and Mimi entered; I followed. Headstones were scattered in a random pattern. No planning here. I already knew but didn't want to know. Maybe Mom was standing behind a tree or waiting at the river. Maybe . . . always a maybe.

Mimi stopped at a worn headstone, then brushed off a magnolia leaf and a web of fallen moss. One large sunflower lay on the ground before the stone. I squatted to read the etchings. *Rosie O'Hare: May 24, 1941– January 28, 2016.* Then, below that: *Announcing her place in the family of things.*

"Who is Rosie O'Hare?" I asked, even as I knew. "And *announcing her place*?" I ran my hands over the etchings, slowly tracing each letter.

"She changed her name," Loretta said in a voice full of tears, flooded in sorrow. "And that is the last line to a poem she discovered during her final days. A poem by Mary Oliver that begins . . ."

" 'You do not have to be good. You do not have to walk on your knees . . .' " I quoted the beginning of a poem I knew well. "I know it. I've used it in my art."

"Yes." That was Mimi's voice.

"You know this?" I glanced up.

"Yes, she followed your career. She bought that piece. I have it now," Loretta said. "It hangs in my bedroom."

"What?" I stood then, a great surge of anger and fear and confusion in a hurricane of conflict. "I don't understand."

"Your mother died less than a year ago, after a horrid battle with the flu. Pneumonia took grip of her fragile body and she couldn't fight it." Mimi's voice cracked with emotion.

"She's gone?" I cried out. "And no one thought to tell me? To call me? To call Owen? Her children?" One emotion won out: anger. It flooded and overflowed; my voice echoed across the yard, bouncing against headstones.

"We promised," Loretta said and glanced at Mimi.

"You promised what?"

"That we would not betray her by telling you what she did not want you to know until you were ready," Mimi explained. "We vowed."

"Until I was ready? I've been ready for over thirty-five years. I was ready when I waited all night for her to come home. I was ready when I went to live with my distracted aunt. I was ready when I went to boarding school and then college. I was ready when I married and wanted her there. I was ready when I gave birth to two of her grandchildren and searched for her, hiring detectives, combing morgues and searching homeless shelters." I ran out of breath and sank to the ground, next to her grave. The warm and damp earth soaked through my shorts.

"Oh, darling," Mimi said.

"Why would she let me wonder? Why would she . . . ?" A sob of great pain broke free. "What did I do so wrong that she couldn't come back to me?"

Mimi lowered herself to the ground, slowly, until she sat next to me. She rested her hand on the earth of the grave. "There's much to tell you. But whatever you may believe now, know this: any choice she made was out of love. Every single choice. We didn't always agree with her. But those were her choices, not ours. And as I said, they were made in love."

"Tell me everything."

We stood and made our way to a bench under a live oak. A plaque stated: *Dedicated to all those who mourn yet have hope.*

Hope.

Right.

"Everything," I repeated.

Loretta began. "She made us vow that we would not tell you or Owen of her life unless you returned here. She believed that if you came back to this place, to the river house, then you'd be ready."

I closed my eyes. My God, they were right. Maybe they were right. "I thought the worst thing that could happen was knowing my mother was dead. But the worst thing might be finding out that she was here all along but didn't want to tell me, to be with me."

Loretta spread her hands toward me, a supplication. "That's not it at all, Lainey. Not at all. This, my child," Loretta said, "was not a case of not wanting. She ached. She wept. She felt unworthy to return to you. No matter how much we told her that she was worthy, she didn't feel ready. She'd only been clean a few months. She knew you were happy and safe and she didn't want to disrupt your lives."

"Happy and safe?" I said this in a voice that wasn't mine, one I'd never heard, and I almost turned to see where it had come from, a scratchy yelp. "How could she have *possibly* known that?"

"She kept up with both of you — on the Internet and even using us to ask questions and seek answers."

"And you think the Internet is the best source to tell you that I'm okay?"

Loretta cringed, her face tight, and then relaxed. "It was more than that. Do you remember the time someone bought your large piece of Marilyn Monroe, the one with newspaper articles about her life, covering her body?"

I paused. "Of course."

"That was all of us . . . for your mom."

"Oh." The world as I knew it slowly shifted. "You are going to have to start earlier. When did she come back here or was she always here?"

Mimi took over now. "No. She wasn't always here."

"I've been looking for her all these years. I even hired a detective. For a little bit I even thought of leaving this vacation to fly to Texas, where a woman named Kara came out of a facility without ID, and I was going to *go* there. That's how desperate I've been through the years. That's how . . ."

"She *never* wanted you to hurt." Mimi's voice broke and I took terrible satisfaction in it. "She wanted the opposite. In some ways she did die the day she disappeared," Mimi said. "And every day afterward for years. To herself and to the world. There's no way to tell you how she crawled out of that grave. It took years and years."

"I would have helped her," I said. "I would have helped her dig her way out. No matter what."

Loretta looked me in the eyes. "You were a child. She would have dragged you in with her." She shook her head. "And your dad was going to have her locked up by the time she crossed the Georgia border. First jail time, and then make sure she never saw you again while you were children. When your dad told her that everyone would be better off without her, she believed it to be true. She killed the dog, and it could have been you."

"She didn't kill the dog," I said. "We adopted him and had him for another twelve years. He was the best part of my life after she left."

"What?" Loretta lifted her eyebrows as if they'd been pulled from above.

"Yes," I said. "We named him Ned."

"After Nancy Drew's boyfriend," Mimi said, and she closed her eyes. "Right?"

"Yes," I said. "Ned Nickerson."

"She didn't kill the dog." Loretta stated the fact one more time.

"Does that matter?" I asked. "If she'd known that, would she have come back?"

Loretta opened her eyes and tears sat in them unspilled. "No. She didn't leave because she thought she'd killed a dog. She left because she'd endangered the only things in her life she loved: both of you. Because she could have killed you. If she'd stayed, she would have lost you anyway. That was the living hell of it all. She could lose you *her* way or your dad's way. She chose her own. After she was locked up for a while, he was going to make sure she

412

didn't have custody. He threatened to cut her off from the family. It was his way, or hers. And with her way, she could find a way back to you. At least she thought so."

"But she didn't." My mind raced, wanting all the information to download without having to wait for explanations.

"You're right." Mimi shifted in her seat to allow shade to fall across her face.

"What happened? . . . Everything," I said. "Every little thing."

"Well, here is what she told us. After she left that night, she wandered from city to city. She tried to get clean." Mimi took a breath. "But for all her life, she had nightmares of that car wreck, but in her dreams you were both gone . . . dead. And she would descend into the drink or the sedating pills again."

"Dear God," I said. "But it didn't happen! We didn't die. Where did she go at . . . first?" I asked so quietly that Loretta strained forward to hear me.

"That first night, she walked as far as she could and slept in an empty house, and then another and another, until she found a shelter in Columbia. She told them that her name was Rosie O'Hare, and from there she moved from shelter to shelter. She lost the names of cities and towns. Or she didn't tell us. Either way, she stayed mostly with the Salvation Army, where she could work and help others. She put her sewing skills to use, and although she never lived on the street, she never again had a home. She never told us the exact reason for returning here, other than one day, while sewing a wedding gown for a woman in South Carolina, she decided to come back. We can't know all her reasons, as she never told us, except to say that she just knew the only place she might find hope for finally becoming clean was in the place it had all started . . . or ended."

"That sounds like something Bonny would say," I said. "What is it with *this* place?"

"There's a little bit of magic in our river," Loretta said with a small smile. "When she arrived, the first thing she did was go to Mimi, who'd always been her ally, even during those summers when everyone else shunned her. Mimi called me and we gathered. She asked us to keep her secret and we did. She'd only been sober for a few months and she wanted it to last before she called you or your brother."

"How long ago was this?"

"A little more than a year."

"She's been here? Right here? Didn't she wonder about us?" I asked. "I mean, all the time? Didn't she think we might need a mother in the world?"

Loretta's face crumpled with the threat of tears, and she took off her glasses to look directly at me. "I will not ever" — her voice shook — "be able to tell you of the hurt and pain your mother experienced being away from the two of you. You were the only reason she even tried again. Every day she was sober she thought it brought her closer to the day she would see you again. She stayed away because she thought it was best for you and because she was ashamed of not only the life she'd lived since leaving you but also the way she looked, how she'd done damage to her body and mind. She felt she looked . . . ravaged. She wanted to get right and *then* see you."

"That's not how it works!" I cried out. "I didn't love her only when she 'got right' but because she was my mom."

"She believed that one day it would be the right time. Don't you for one second believe it was because she didn't hurt or that she didn't care. She loved you both deeply." Loretta waved her hand toward the direction of the river. "I understand you must hurt, but she loved you without wavering."

"Love is showing up. It's being there. It's

not *just* a feeling."

"True," Mimi said. "But she believed, rightly or wrongly, that showing up for you was the opposite of love. While she was still using and falling into addiction over and over, she believed that she would cause more harm than good if she entered your life. Her act of love was inaction. Maybe it was wrong, but it was hers, and she suffered with it every single day."

"How could she just change her name and pretend her old life never happened? That *we* never happened?"

"She had to change her name. It was easy back then — find a guy on the corner, get a fake birth certificate and that was that. She chose 'Rosie' because she believed the rose represented new beginnings. Starting over. And she kept trying and trying." Loretta took in a long breath. "And that is the hell of the disease of addiction. It is the hell of trying and failing."

For all the times and years I'd wept over the loss of my mother, I didn't cry as Loretta told me that story. Inside, my body lurched as if it needed and wanted to sob, but nothing happened. I was parched and exhausted. Losing George. Finding George. Mom in a graveyard. None of it integrated into anything that made sense.

Mimi spoke then, quietly. "I helped her set up in a little home at the edge of town. Loretta moved into her house only a few months ago."

"My son went to my mother's house?" The realization fell over me like fog, shrouding the landscape. A shiver ran through me and a soft buzz rang in my ears like a bee or mosquito.

"Yes."

"Oh, my God," I said. "This doesn't make sense and yet it makes perfect sense. My son wandered to my mother's house."

"After she returned here," Mimi continued, "she slowly started a new life. She sewed for the town — dresses and little dance recital outfits, alterations. She helped me in the bookstore after hours, shelving and such when no one was around. I took her to AA meetings a few times a week, and she was beginning to find her way, her mind clearing."

"You know, for years I have been writing letters to her with nowhere to send them."

"Letters?" Loretta asked.

"Yes, letters. I brought them here to finally toss into the sea in some bizarre ritual."

"Where are they now?"

"In a box back at the river house. I will keep them now. They're all I have . . ."

"Oh, Lainey." Loretta wiped again at her eyes, at the tears that betrayed her calm voice. "Your mom's body was frail and she was fragile. Everyone here believed she was a hermit or recluse, but she was protecting herself and everyone else."

"I cannot imagine the hell that must have been." Like a flash of light out of the corner of my eye, I saw a glimpse of her secret soul, of the addiction that ruled her life. In the graveyard, headstones etched with names and dates and epigraphs, I caught a whisper of her story, one so different from the one I'd made for her or for us.

"Yes," Loretta said. "I know how hard this is for you. After a betrayal, I know forgiveness doesn't come easy, if at all. But I'm here whenever you want to ask questions. I will tell you what I can."

I stood, started to pace around the bench. "I missed her by months? She left it all up to me. To me? *If* I came back, she'd tell me? That's not fair."

"It's not fair at all," Mimi said. "But she did the best she could. We all do the very best we can. If she'd known she was dying and you'd be here a few months later, don't you think she might have decided differently? We do what we can with what we know at the time, and with what we believe."

A gray heron lighted on the marsh at the edge of the river, its wings settling and gathering around its body, smooth and slow. His long, arched neck curved into a C, and his eyes, two small beads of darkness, settled on the water, still and utterly focused. His twiglike legs didn't appear strong enough to hold him so very still. I wanted to be like that heron. "Can you leave me be for a while? Leave me alone with her?" I asked.

"Yes," both women answered simultaneously.

As they walked away on the soft earth, not leaving even a mark, as if they'd never been there, I returned to the gravesite and dropped to my knees. There my mother rested. If I'd returned just months earlier, I would have met her. One year. One night. One hour. Did it make any difference? She was gone, and along with her so many answers.

This was what I'd dreaded, what I'd hoped wasn't true: her death. But did knowing the truth ease that despair at all? Yes.

There came a loosening of the knot inside me, a shift of the horrid unknowing that had lived with me for so very long, leaving space for something new. But what swept into the momentary emptiness was not more wondering or longing, but grief. It was anguish I'd held at bay for far, far too long. When there had been hope of seeing her again, I hadn't needed to grieve her loss. But now there was no doubt: she was gone.

A many-armed magnolia tree spread its branches over the gravesite of Rosie O'Hare. I lay flat on the leaf-strewn ground alongside the dirt over her grave. I picked up a handful of the soft, fuzzed husks of magnolia flowers and held them tight in my fist. I'd been looking, all my life I'd been looking, and now I'd found her. "Mom," I said. "I came back. Too late, but I did come back."

A flurry of wings and wind blew across my face as the heron, which had sat so still and waiting moments before, flew across the sky. Its thin legs dangled, its wings splayed wide and majestic directly above me, feathers gray and white and black separating sky from earth. Swooping lower and lower still, it finally rested only three feet away, standing as still as the tree, its dark eyes staring at me with intensity.

She did the best she could.

CHAPTER 35
PIPER BLANKENSHIP

It had been a day and a half since I'd lost George. Mom had left for Charleston and I reclined in bed, my eyes now fully open, and I looked at my phone to see the time: 2:10 p.m. The first thought on waking had been, *I lost George.* And then I remembered with profound relief that I'd also found him. I wondered how long it would be before I would awake with the finding-him memory and not the losing-him memory.

Outside, the little ones' voices were rising and falling in crescendo with their mom's voice. If losing George was a nightmare for me, what must it have been for her? I needed to find a way to apologize, to make amends for something that was horrid for me but everything to her.

But then there'd been the beauty of finding him, and then my night with Fletch. Our night together had erased the "first time" with Ryan. The way he'd held me obliterated all that had come before, so that it almost didn't count, as if Fletch was my first, as if I'd waited for him.

I sat and Owen's voice joined the chorus outside. Already I recognized his voice. Cowardice rose, the part of me that couldn't imagine what I'd done, and I wanted to lie back down, to find the cold spot in the pillow and again disappear into the heavy sleep. Instead, I stood and went to the bathroom, looked myself in the face, right into my own ineptness, right into the sorrow I'd brought to all of us.

"You can do this," I said to me. "Go face your own sins."

I slipped into a pair of shorts and a T-shirt, scrubbed my face clean and rubbed lotion on the sunburn. My nose was already an exposed pink mess. My cheeks flaking now where the sun had sat harsh and brutal for hours as I screamed George's name. My hair was tangled. I tore a brush through it and set it on top of my head in a knot before leaving the room.

Remnants of lunch were scattered across the screened porch: sandwich crusts and Goldfish crunched underfoot. The dented, empty juice boxes had straws sticking out of them like antennae. Damp towels and coloring books were in a pile on the wicker coffee table. I lifted the towels because Daisy got upset when her pictures were ruined, and I walked outside, my hands clasped in front of me. I watched them — Lainey, Tim, Owen and the kids — wrestling a baby shark from the river on the fishing pole. They laughed and Lainey stepped back to try to capture it on video with her iPhone.

"It will eat us," Daisy screamed.

"Baby sharks don't bite. You're dumb." George sounded no worse for the wear at all.

"Don't call your sister names," Lainey said in a voice tired but firm.

I should have let them know I was there, but instead I just stood and watched them, all of them, light falling on an ordinary scene of parenthood and siblings on a summer day by the river. Unless you knew. And maybe that was the case with anything — it seemed like something other than what it was: *unless you knew the story inside the story.* Mimi had once said that, hadn't she?

Every photo or Facebook post or Instagram with Ryan and Hannah told a truth — *unless you knew the story inside the story.*

George saw me first and ran to me, his arms spread wide and waving like I couldn't see him and he had to flag me down.

"Piper!" he hollered. He'd dropped the

fishing pole.

"Hey, George." I squatted to let his arms wrap around my neck. "I'm so sorry." A small sob, when I thought I didn't have any more, escaped into his tiny shoulder.

"Why?" he asked so simply.

"Because I lost you," I said.

"No, you found me." He poked his little finger into my cheek.

I picked him up, balanced him on my hip and faced the adults.

"Piper." Lainey said my name first and came to me so quickly and without any hesitation or reluctance. "I've lost him, too," she said as she reached me and hugged me, with George in between us like forgiveness was contained in his tiny body. "Please don't carry this regret around with you." George jumped to the ground because Daisy was thoroughly enjoying the fishing pole he'd let go of.

"It was the most awful day of my life," I said to Lainey. "And I've had some awful ones. I would have died a million times over if anything terrible had happened to him."

Lainey smiled sadly. "Me, too. But it didn't happen. And he runs off all the time, and this is just the first time he had a goal of where he wanted to go and he did."

"What do you mean?"

"He wanted to go to Loretta's house," she said, but she peered at Owen and Tim, who were mediating between a stubborn George and a pouting Daisy. "I need to tell you something."

"What?" Fear fluttered in my chest.

"Because Loretta was friends with my mom, she was able to tell me a lot about what happened to her." Her eyes filled with tears. "Because of you, and how you took George there, I was able to find out that Mom had come back here."

"What? Is she . . . here?"

"Yes, but she's passed away, Piper. She's gone. But now I know. It was Loretta who told me."

"I'm so sorry. I know you wanted to find her another way. I know . . ."

"No more regrets, Piper." She took my hands. "George and Daisy love you so much. And so do I. So much. You are such a special and beautiful girl, Piper. A true gem in the world. Don't let anyone or anything convince you otherwise."

"Thank you," I said but couldn't meet her gaze. "You sound like my mom."

Lainey smiled. "Your mom is much stronger than I am. And so are you." She let go of my hands and kissed my cheek before calling for her kids. I approached the dock and shyly said hello to Tim.

"I'm sorry for what you went through," he said to me as if I hadn't done anything at all.

"I love George and I didn't mean to . . ."

Tim held up his hand. "Stop. We are all here and well. I've lost him, too. So has Lainey."

"But not like that."

Tim gave me a weary smile and returned his attention to his kids. Owen stood a few steps back and untangled the shrimp net.

"I need to run into town and see Mimi," I said. "I was supposed to have the book club over this afternoon to pick a new book and I don't want to let anyone else down."

Owen glanced up then, and I'm not sure which one of us felt more uncomfortable. We exchanged one of those looks that can't have words. I didn't know enough to know why we were at odds. I didn't know enough to even say what was wrong. What I did know: he loved Mom. That much was as obvious as my peeling nose. But what did that mean for me? For us? For whatever life held in front of us, or had held behind us, I had no idea.

I nodded at him and turned to leave.

"Piper," he called after me.

"Yes?" I turned.

"You did a good thing yesterday, not giving up, finding him like that."

"Thank you," I said.

I couldn't look away from him. We stood there, twenty paces apart, staring and unable to speak. It was Lainey who broke the hard ground.

"Go on, Piper," she said. "We'll be here when you get back. We aren't going anywhere."

I nodded, but a choked feeling rose inside my chest, that feeling right before the panic hits: the knowing that I will never do anything right, that I would never *be* anything right. I closed my eyes to it. I wanted to be done with the crying and the needing and the wanting and the disasters. But something told me that I would never be done with those things. They were right there mixed up with the good and the laughter and the beauty and the magic.

The walk into town was quiet, and I carried a large Thermos of water, felt my skin tender under the sun. I'd left my cell phone at home because I didn't want to check it every five seconds. I didn't want to know what was going on anywhere but where I was at that minute. I whispered out loud the details of the world: a yellow dandelion growing between the cracks of the sidewalk;

a hummingbird swirling around an empty feeder; sunlight falling in leaf-shaped patterns all around me; a picket fence that needed painting but looked better without it; a bicycle with training wheels leaning against a porch; a vegetable garden burdened under its own weight as it bowed to the earth.

By the time I reached the bookshop, the panic had ebbed and I strode inside to find Mimi behind the counter.

"My dear. How are you feeling?"

"Well, I've slept for almost two days, so I'm feeling a little better; but I needed to go to the hospital to get IV fluids."

We talked in low whispers although the store was empty, recounting the day and the night and the horrors.

"And now Mom is gone, too. I don't know what's going to happen to her." I swallowed the fear. "The very worst thing that could ever happen to her might have happened. All she has ever wanted was to save people. That's what she does."

"Piper." Mimi took both my hands like she did sometimes. "Inside the very worst things you can find the power for change. Nothing needs to be the end of it all; anything and everything can have new meaning." She grimaced with a smile. "I know it sounds like I'm just trying to make it all better with a little Band-Aid of words, but I've lived it. I'm telling you the truth. It is awful. It is painful, and your mom will suffer because it hurts. That's true also."

I shook my head. "I can't stand to see her hurt. I mean, I'm supposed to be the one. I can't stand it for her."

"That is what we call love," Mimi said and hugged me.

"How is *your* love?" I asked her.

"Thanks to your mom, he's just fine. They gave him that medicine she told the hospital to have ready and it's like it never happened really. It could have been completely different. It could have been . . . the end."

"I know that feeling," I said.

"But it wasn't, Piper. George is at home right now playing with his mom and dad and uncle."

"I just need something really good to happen. To all of us," I said.

"Then let's not sit around waiting for something good. Let's do good."

"Like what?"

"You tell me," she said. "Give me some ideas."

We batted things around from the preposterous to the boring until we landed right where we were probably meant to land all along: an art show for Lainey. And right there, the world took on a new shape and we had something to move toward.

"We better tell her," I said. "What if she decides to go home?"

"I'll let you do the honors," Mimi said.

The book club meeting didn't last long, but talking about books shifted something inside of me. The group sat in a circle and although we'd only met once it was as if we'd known each other for longer. Already there were inside jokes and bantering about the scenes in the book, as if sharing one book had allowed us to understand a bit about each other and form friendships.

It was Fletch's ex who suggested the next book and everyone agreed. It was Sam, a high school girl with long dark hair, who broached the subject of George at the end of the meeting.

"It must have been so scary for you," she said. "I helped look for him. It was . . ."

"It was scary," I said. "But the worst thing ended up with some good in it." I could feel Mimi's words coming out of my mouth and it made me laugh. "It's not funny," I said. "Not funny at all. I just . . ."

"I know. I know," Rachel, another local high school girl, said. "It's so bad when a laugh comes out at the wrong time. I totally lost it at my grandma's funeral. I couldn't stop. My mom made me leave and I thought my dad was gonna kill me."

"Well, he's safe now," Sam said. "Right?"

I nodded, a prickle of embarrassment crawling on the back of my neck. "He's great." I tried to smile.

"I get scared about that every time I babysit," Rachel said. "Every single time. Now I'm probably gonna tie the kids to me with bungee cords."

The group laughed in unison and I thought again of Mimi's words about being who you are meant to be and finding your real friends. I glanced around the circle and I didn't know if they were real friends or ever would be, but it was some kind of start.

When I was leaving the store, Ms. Loretta walked in, and for a minute I forgot who she *really* was — the woman who had known where Lainey and Owen's disappeared mom had gone. Then it hit me and I raised my eyebrows and stared at Mimi. Suddenly Mimi wasn't *just* the adorable woman who owned a bookshop and liked movies on opening night and ate pound cake at four p.m.

"You knew," I said. And then I looked at Ms. Loretta. "How could you have played with George that day and not said anything? Did you know he was your friend's grandson?"

"I did, Piper. I did know who he was. It was one of the best days of my life." She smoothed her hands along her flower-print dress, a faded yellow pattern that looked as though it had been left in the sun too long.

"Were you going to tell Lainey and Owen or just stay hidden?" I knew these weren't my questions to ask, but I loved Lainey. I'd seen her be sad about her mom, heard her talk about the heartbreak. And what would *I* do without my mom? How could I live without her?

Mimi rested her hand on my arm as if to quiet me, but Ms. Loretta answered anyway. "Yes, I was going to tell them. I just wanted to find the right words and the right time. But I guess that was decided for me."

"And why didn't you tell us?" I asked Mimi. "I thought you loved us and that . . ."

"It wasn't my story to tell," Mimi said slowly.

"Well, like you said, sometimes your stories tell on you." I meant to sound funny and witty, but it came out cruel and sharp.

Ms. Loretta set her little purse on the counter. "I understand why you'd be angry, Piper. I really do."

"It's not me. It's Lainey. She was obsessed with finding her mom. It tore her apart."

Ms. Loretta's eyes filled with tears and she set her hands, one over the other, on her chest, over her heart.

Mimi stepped in then. "Okay, darling. I think you need to get on home and tell everyone about our grand idea."

"Okay," I said and glanced between them. "That really was none of my business. Ryan always used to tell me that I put my nose into . . ."

Mimi placed her hand on my arm and rubbed it as if she were applying sunblock — or enough love to keep me from my terrible thoughts. "Darling, who really cares what Ryan thinks? And honestly, you can ask us anything you want."

I tried to smile at them both before I walked away, but my mouth didn't seem to be working toward smiles quite yet.

CHAPTER 36
BONNY BLANKENSHIP

The For Sale sign swung in the wind from its perch in my yard. Lucas had put the house on the market just as he'd said. It was *You left? Then I'll make the decisions.* In my haste his way of saying, to escape the pain I'd relinquished everything.

I drove past the house and around to the alley behind to park the car. If Lucas was waiting for me, he would be able to see me out the kitchen window, a place he'd stood all our married life to watch for my return from work late at night or early in the morning. It had always been a comfort knowing someone waited.

The car felt like a shield as I took a few deep breaths before entering the house. I'd thought that going to Watersend would be the answer, the way to peace, but just because I'd left, it hadn't meant Lucas or my mistakes had gone anywhere else.

The pebbled walkway to the back door

shifted under my feet with that familiar crunch of walking toward home, a sound of the past when I'd returned from a long day at work. I entered the kitchen and Lucas stood at the sink, a coffee mug cradled in both hands. I was startled by his good looks, just as handsome even in middle age as he'd been the day I met him. Polished and successful. But he'd become a stranger to me.

He didn't speak as I dropped my purse onto the counter. Gus came bounding in, all energy, all loping gaiety. He plowed into me and I crouched to hug him, bury my face into his fur. "Hello, old buddy." He didn't know my sins; he didn't know anything but love.

I stood at the table where we'd eaten our meals for twenty-two years, where we'd helped Piper with homework and sifted through mail and bills, where we'd drunk coffee in the morning and wine at night, where we'd entertained guests and family.

"Do you want to tell me what happened with the little boy Piper lost?" he asked and didn't move to sit.

"That's where you want to start?" I asked. "I can tell you about that. But first let me go upstairs and take a shower . . . get on some clean clothes." I pointed to my feet. "And shoes would be nice, too. I just walked out in a daze."

"It seems like you've done a lot of that lately." He ran his hands across his weary face and then he gazed directly at me. "We'll talk now. You can take a shower later." He placed his hand on my arm to stay me.

A battle took place in my chest, one that had warred before, between the two needs: to please and appease him, be the good wife who would make it all okay, and, on the contrary, to do what I felt was needed, do what felt *right* to me. I took his hand from my arm and took three steps around him. "No, Lucas. I'll be back in a few minutes."

He grabbed me again. "I said you can shower after we talk."

I again took his hand from my arm and moved forward toward the stairwell. His body passed mine in the hallway, a rough shoulder to shoulder, and then he stood in front of me before I reached the stairs.

"What are you doing?" I asked. "I need to take a shower. I'm a mess." My voice broke like a brittle twig he'd stepped upon.

"You *need*? What you *need*?" he asked, his voice so deep and full of resentment that his words felt like a physical punch.

"Yes," I said. "Please move out of my way. This is crazy, Lucas. Don't . . ."

"Don't what? Don't be your husband? I've

already got that part figured out. Don't stand in your way? I can't see much that has. Don't tell you what to do? What is it you *don't* want, Bonny?"

"Don't make this worse than it needs to be. Please move."

He did. He stepped aside just enough that I could pass while brushing against his body, immovable and firm. I took the steps one by one, shifting to the left as I always had because the right side creaked. The family photos framed and in chronological order marched up the wall against damask wallpaper, a montage of our lives from our wedding photographs to Piper's high school graduation.

I walked through our bedroom straight for the bathroom, although what I really wanted was to curl into the bed, keep the shades drawn and sleep until it all went away — the guilt, the death, the divorce and the hole in my stomach that seemed to open to the magnet of all my misdeeds.

Once showered and changed, I found Lucas exactly where I'd left him — glaring up the stairwell. Without discussing it, we found ourselves again in the kitchen, our positions resumed, facing each other over the table.

"Right now can we deal with your medical license? Your suspension? And then our divorce and our daughter, Piper, with whom you absconded to another town."

I laughed, and it felt really good. "Absconded. For God's sake, Lucas. She's almost twenty years old."

His face tightened and his eyes narrowed. His face became a blueprint for all his anger and frustration.

"Right now I need to go to the hospital and meet with Frank Preston."

"First you are going to tell me what's going on."

"It was my fault. I made a mistake and a man died. Is that what you want to hear?" I wasn't in the room anymore. I was floating above it, watching us having this conversation that seemed unimaginable.

"You're so cold," he said, shaking his head. "I don't even know you. You just said you killed a man, and you're like ice."

"Ice?" Tremors ran across my face; the twitching of my mouth and eyes were a dead giveaway that I would start to sob. "I'm dying inside, Lucas. This is the worst thing I could imagine. I don't know how to be or what to be. This loss, this death, does not go away. My imagined future is gone. It changed me. It changed my life. Now I have to find new possibilities, a new beginning that wakes up the forgotten parts of me, the pieces of me I'd set aside."

This was our chance. I saw it from my detached position. He could step in right now in my pain and be the man he said he wanted to be. The man he'd promised all those years ago when he'd said, *I will be there for you. For us.*

"It's bad. You're right," he said, his face still hollowed out with anger. "I don't know how you could have done this. What were you thinking that night?"

The bottom of everything there could be between us dropped out right there, and I closed my eyes without an answer.

He tented his hands to prop his chin on two forefingers: the lawyer ready to make an argument. "You don't know what you were thinking? What you were doing? You have no idea *why* you were so preoccupied that you made a mistake?"

When Lucas asked a question this way he already had the answer. I'd been here before. His clients had been here before. His defendants and the prosecutors.

I stood and pressed my hands to the back of the chair, then leaned forward so our faces were close enough to kiss. "Stop." I turned and headed for the hallway.

"Don't walk out on this."

I spun around. "Out on what? You berating me? There's no need for you to tell me how badly I've messed up. I've berated myself for as long and as deep as I can."

I moved toward the front of the house and ran up the stairwell. He called after me. "What are you doing?"

"Looking for something in the attic."

"Hopefully your mind. Because obviously you've lost it."

I opened the hallway door where stairs led to the attic. I flicked on the lights and stepped up. It didn't take long, but I dug through the boxes in the very back, the ones with my childhood paraphernalia. My Girl Scout uniform. My corsage from the debutante ball. Photo albums from high school. Yearbooks. And there it was under the junior high class pictures, still in its crinkled plastic envelope: the Girl Detective notebook. I sat on the dusty hardwood floor and opened it. The single lightbulb hanging above delivered a circle of jaundiced light on the page. I opened the notebook and a sheaf of dried and golden sea oats fell out. Lainey and I had used it as a bookmark all those years ago. My eyes scanned the words we'd written, the doodles we'd drawn.

But it wasn't time for this, for reading and delving into the notebook. I also grabbed a box of childhood photos and tucked it under my arm. Before I took this back to the river house, I needed to face Frank. I returned to the main floor and dropped the notebook and box into my bag. I hugged Gus one more time and told him, as I had before, that I would return for him. And I would. But not Lucas. Never again. These were silent promises made to my soul and no one else.

As I left the house, Lucas's words pelted me like gunshot that followed me out the door and to the car. And even when I could no longer hear his voice, his words repeated over and over in my head. *You killed a man. What were you thinking? You've ruined everything.*

Robotic, I drove into the hospital parking lot and parked in my old spot, which was vacant. Approaching the sliding glass doors of the emergency room, I felt fear swimming inside my belly, gathering strength. *One step and then another. Don't meet anyone's gaze. Don't look toward the waiting room where you spoke with the widow.* Then I was at the door of Frank's office.

He greeted me with such undeserved kindness that my knees bent and almost buckled beneath me. I sank into a chair across from him, where he explained all that he had already told me on the phone. *I could come back to work. It was a grade-four liver laceration. The widow did not blame me. Errors are made. In fact, up to four hundred thousand errors a year. We are all human. Mr. Rohr had life-threatening injuries already. He wouldn't have made it through surgery. I was one of their finest doctors. Surely all the good I'd done needed to be balanced against this one mistake, couldn't I see that?*

All the words Frank meant to be a panacea could not change how I felt.

"Do you know the last thing he said to me?" I leaned forward and asked Frank. "While he looked right at me, before that last breath, before he exhaled, before his eyes went from bright and scared to empty?"

"No. You didn't tell me."

"He said, 'I haven't done the one thing I meant to do.' "

Frank closed his eyes and his hands went to the lapels of his lab coat, grabbed their corners and rested there.

He opened his eyes. "It's so hard to lose a life, Bonny. We all feel the pain. You let me know when you think you might want to return to the ER. We are ready when you are."

"I don't know if I can, Frank. I just don't know."

"You can. But if you need more time, I understand."

"What would *you* do?" I asked and placed my palms flat on the desk, spread them wide and leaned into them.

"I've thought about it every day since you left," he said. "What would *I* do? How would I handle it? Where would I go? And honestly, Bonny, I have a new answer every day. I feel your devastation. We are all here to save lives. We are all here to make a difference in the world. We are all here because we've never wanted to be anything other than what we are: doctors. And I know that no matter what my answers are to all of those other questions, I would return to being a doctor. It is who I am. It is *my* one thing."

"Thank you, Frank." I stood and shook his hand. I glanced around the room on my way out, the diplomas and awards and accouterments of a well-lived doctor. I thought of my own diplomas and awards on the walls in my study at home, and thought of their worthlessness compared to a life, another breath taken, another day lived.

CHAPTER 37
BONNY BLANKENSHIP

Tory Rohr's house rested under the twilight of late evening at the dead end of a marsh-lined road. A front porch swing hung empty with a book open and facedown on the seat. She lived in Mount Pleasant, over the bridge from my own home on the way to the islands. I hadn't called, although maybe I should have, but I didn't want to take the chance that she would refuse to see me. But as I parked in a curve of the road it occurred to me that she might not be home or, worse, I would be unwelcome.

The pebbled pathway crunched under my feet as I approached the front door, an announcement of an arriving guest proclaimed by a barking dog somewhere inside. The door opened before I reached the porch and a woman's voice said, "Stop, Lincoln. Stop. It's just a guest." Then she looked up, this small woman with silver hair, and waved at me like she'd been expecting me.

"Hello, there," she called out.

I didn't answer because my voice was stuck in the depth of my chest, caught on my ribs, trying to make it up. I reached the bottom of her porch stairs and met her gaze.

"Oh, my." She placed her palm on her chest, her fingers on her throat fluttering like she was reaching for a necklace that was no longer there — something essential missing from her life. "Dr. Blankenship," she said.

"Yes." I took two steps back. "I should have called. I see that now."

Tory released the dog, a black poodle that plodded down the stairs to immediately stick his nose into my crotch. Tory busted out laughing. "Lincoln," she shouted. "No!" She came down the stairs to grab him by the collar and shoo him off to the yard.

"He has no manners and Nicholas was his only disciplinarian . . ." Her voice trailed off and I knew where it went — along the lost path where Nicholas had gone before her.

I clasped my hands in front of my stomach, a knotted ball to keep myself from wringing them or waving them frantically in the air like I did when I was nervous. "I'm here to tell you how deeply sorry I am about your husband. I was the doctor that night.

It was my job to save him."

"Come, dear," she said as if I were a child who needed calming. "Come sit with me on the porch."

I followed her up the stairs and we sat on two rocking chairs facing each other across an iron coffee table. "Would you like something to drink?" she asked.

"No, thank you. I don't want you to go to any trouble. I'm just here to ask what I can do. How I can help you. To make sure you're . . . okay." I stopped and exhaled. "I don't know why I'm here except to apologize as deeply as possible. That night was the worst of my life. And yet, as awful as it was, it was much, much worse for you."

"They told me everything," she said. "How chaotic the ER was with the wreck and then another injury in surgery. Nicholas wouldn't have made it; I know that. Even if he had rolled into the surgery room, he wouldn't have made it. There were too many injuries inside his beautiful body. I don't blame you, Dr. Blankenship. I blame the drunk driver who was texting while he tried to get to the next party. I blame the construction on Church Street. I blame his work partner for making him go out on the night he wanted to stay home. I blame the world and all its misery. I blame myself for marrying an extraordinary man who ran hard and fast and whom I always knew took chances. I blame love and hate and drunks." She smiled and leaned across the table, held both hands out for mine. "But I don't blame you."

"I do." I took her offered hands.

"Please don't. There are enough burdens in this world. Don't make this one of yours. And I beg of you not to let it keep you from being a doctor. I've learned of your reputation and it's one of the best out there."

"I need to tell you what he said when he died."

She released my hands and placed hers in a knot on her lap. "You told me that night."

"Yes, but there was something else."

"Tell me," she said.

"He said to tell you how much he loved you, that you and the children were all that mattered to him. Then he said he hadn't done the *one* thing he meant to do." I paused before I said the truth, the sentence that had traveled with me for days and weeks since then. "Because of me, he didn't get to do his one thing."

"His one thing," she said so quietly I wouldn't have known what she said but for repeating me.

"What was it?" I asked. "Please tell me.

Maybe I can . . . do it for him."

"I don't know," she said. "I have no idea."

"What?" I'd expected so many answers, but not this one, not this.

"I really don't know."

"I *need* to know." My voice overflowed with that need. I'd waited and waited to find out. I wanted to know. "Would anyone — your kids — anyone — know?" My words tumbled over each other.

"I have no idea. He did so much good in the world, I don't know what was left for him, what he kept hidden inside." She closed her eyes and then opened them again. "He kept things to himself until he was ready. He wasn't secretive and he wasn't dishonest, but sometimes I wouldn't know how much something meant to him until later, until it was done."

"I want to be able to do it for him. To have that one thing done. I *need* to do it."

Tory held up her hand. "He wouldn't want that at all. He would want you to do whatever *your* one thing is."

She looked off into the yard and called for Lincoln, and then her gaze returned to me. "And I don't think there is one thing — but maybe there is one thing at a time. He was about being present, aware. He lived that way. One thing at a time. He believed that one should be completely present for anything they were doing."

"There wasn't one thing that arched over his life?"

"If there was, it was his to know. He would want *your life* to be your one thing. I think if he said that to you, maybe he meant the one thing that meant the most to him at *that* moment. Right then. Something, the next thing, that was important to him."

The hope I'd held on to — that redemption might come with doing Nicholas's one thing — crumbled. "I wanted . . ."

"To fix this."

"Yes," I said. "And if not to fix it, to make it better. To do something. Just *do* something that might help, that might fulfill a wish, that might . . ." All these months, I'd believed that I could redeem myself, in some small way, by doing Mr. Rohr's one thing. How could I save myself when not even his wife knew what this was? What it might be?

"There's nothing like that here, Dr. Blankenship," she said as Lincoln bounded onto the porch and sat next to her. She dug her fingers into the fur of his neck and absently petted the dog. "I miss him every minute of the day. And you doing something he left undone won't fix that. It's not your fault he

449

died. It's not your job to fix this for me."

Tears fell then, down her face and into the corners of her mouth. "I wish it was your job, or anyone's job. I wish you could fix this pain, end this grief, do whatever it is he left undone, but you can't. The best way you can honor him is to live your life to the fullest the same way he lived his."

To see the raw pain of this woman displayed on the porch of the home she'd shared with a man she loved so deeply was almost too much to bear. I would not break in front of her; I would not allow my grief to damage her further or ask her to carry my own guilt.

"Okay," I said. "I promise. I will."

I stood to leave and our good-byes were awkward and quick. She sat still with one hand on her lap and the other in the dog's fur. I almost stumbled down the stairs, determined not to look back.

When I reached my car to return to Watersend, I turned. Tory remained on the porch with her faithful dog beside her. She waved at me and I did the same, pausing to say out loud, "I promise."

CHAPTER 38
PIPER BLANKENSHIP

His name — Ryan — popped over and over on my cell screen. I could only stare at it, frozen in the middle of the bookshop. From the speakers, Chris Stapleton sang about Tennessee whiskey, and Mimi's voice startled me.

"Piper, love, get your eyes off that screen and join us here in the real world."

It had been four days since we'd found George, or since I'd lost George, depending on how you looked at the whole situation. Mom had returned sans Gus but with a promise to get him when things settled down. Lainey's friend had sent a big crate full of her art, and there I was setting up for an art show in two days.

"It's weird. The guy I wanted to hear from all summer long is trying to get ahold of me."

Mimi shuffled over with that sly smile on her face, one I'd come to rely on, and she took the phone from my hand. "Doesn't matter right now."

I stood there with my hand out, my palm empty like I was taking communion or waiting for someone to give me something. I closed my hand into a ball and dropped it by my side.

"But I want to know what he said. I've been so sad about him. You know that."

Mimi held my phone back out to me. "Here you go, but you must not forget who you have become this summer."

"Meaning?"

Fletch passed me then, his arms full of canvases. "You, love," he said, imitating Mimi, "you gonna just stand there or help us drag all this stuff in?"

"I'm gonna stand here and look pretty, because that's my job," I said with a smile, and I placed my cell back on the counter.

Fletch laughed and kissed my cheek. I felt the sweat of his hard day's work, of his commitment to this art show, and I felt the littlest bit guilty for my intense need to glance at the phone. As he disappeared around the corner, Mimi's gaze followed him and then returned to me. She didn't need to say a word.

"I know," I said. "I'm just curious. I mean" — I took a step closer to her and whispered — "I have no idea what happened. I just want to know what happened between us. It was so awful. He literally just . . . poof." I raised both hands in fists and quickly undid them as if blowing smoke from them.

"And you want to know *why*?"

"I want to know what I did wrong." Tears sprang into my eyes.

Mimi grabbed my hand. "Stop. Now."

"I know."

"You didn't do anything *wrong.*"

"You've said it before — don't take things personally. But you know, it's way easier to say than do. I just want to find the right . . . guy."

"Piper, my dear, I think it is much more important to be the right girl than find the right guy."

I didn't exactly believe Mimi carried the secret of life, but sometimes I wondered. Just then Harrington ambled through the doorway as if he'd never had an emergency. He walked straight to Mimi as if she was the only one who existed in the store and kissed her. Love had no age limit, that was for sure.

She waved her hand at me. "Now help Fletch set up. We have a big party in two days. I'm going to run to the print shop and pick up the posters and you can go hang them in storefronts this afternoon."

"You know," I said, "you've made it so I can't live without you. That's not good."

"That's my evil plan," she said and left, waving over her shoulder, Harrington at her side.

I grabbed the phone from the counter and glanced at the screen. I would like to think I was the kind of girl who could hear something so wise, from a woman I loved so deeply, and adjust my actions. But I didn't. I needed to look. I needed to know what he wanted.

Pip. That was the first text. And I hated that nickname. Hated. It.

You there? The next text.

??????? The next.

I miss you. The final text.

I stared at this and swiped my forefinger over the screen. Delete. Delete. Delete. Delete.

And yet, my heart picked up its pace as it raced to the old feeling where I *needed* him to approve of me because I couldn't approve of myself. To that old moldy corner of my heart where I needed the drama to make sure I felt *something,* anything. I inhaled deeply and from far back in the store came Fletch's laugh.

I wanted to tuck all of this — the book-shop, Mimi, the quiet friendships, Fletch, the river behind the house — into a safe place inside. I wanted to always *know,* the way dusk arrived just when you thought the day would last forever; how the moon hung so low over the ocean that it touched the waves with its night light. How the hydrangea bushes burst forth with glorious blue bundles, and the earth was soft and wet with morning dew. I wanted to be in a world where only that kind of beauty existed. I wanted simple forgiveness when I messed up. I wanted it all forever to keep me from feeling empty again.

But already I knew that emptiness would come again, and it would be my job to fill it with new things, and not with Ryan things.

The art show posters Mimi had made flapped in the wind as Fletch and I held them in our hands. We ambled from storefront to storefront asking if we could pin up the posters to let people know about the show. Yes was the only answer. My favorite image of Lainey's was stamped on the front of the poster — a photo of June Cleaver in her pearls with Lainey's brilliant take on it all. The announcement — ART SHOW — was curved around the image with Lainey's name and the other details listed underneath.

When I first went into the garage to see her work, which had arrived overnight, I'd been hit by a kind of stunning beauty. Maybe what someone makes shouldn't change how you think of them or see them, but her art changed her for me. What is closer to who someone is than what they make? And I hadn't seen all of what she'd made.

I'd come to love Lainey, to wake to her voice in the kitchen humming a song while she made coffee. She was always the first one to wake, and now I knew she was out in the garage at all hours of the morning.

"You know," I said to Fletch as we exited the Bloom Boutique, where we'd hung posters in the window and dressing rooms, "I wonder if it's weird to see Lainey differently now that I love her art. Can you love someone more because of something they made?"

"Probably." He pointed at the poster. "Especially if it's that good."

He grabbed me around the waist and kissed me. I kissed him back, right there on the sidewalk. "You're crushing the posters," I said with a laugh and a kiss on his neck.

"If you kiss me like that again, I'm throwing these old things away and taking you home."

"Then I won't kiss you like that again," I said.

"Right." He took a couple steps back. "As if you can resist."

Fletch and I laughed, a team now, and by the time we'd finished with the posters, dusk had done its sneaky thing and worked its way into our day, another day I didn't want to end, when before there'd been so many days I wanted to end as quickly as possible. We made our way back to the store, where the party paraphernalia was now hung. A banner made of triangular-shaped felt hung across the bookshelves and said ART SHOW AND LAINEY MCKAY.

Mimi pointed at my phone. "There. That phone of yours. It's going crazy. You might want to answer it."

I rolled my eyes just as the shop door opened with that jingle. To see his name on my screen and his face in the doorway at the same time felt a little crazy, like I'd just downed a shot of tequila and double vision confused me. This wasn't exactly double vision because one was a name and one was a face, but they were both Ryan. I didn't know where to look — to Mimi for help or to Fletch to explain. But no one was helping me. We all just stood there. This was mine.

"Ryan," I said as he strolled so confidently toward me.

"I've been texting and calling and texting . . ."

"I know," I said. "How did you find me?"

"I asked around. This is a super-small town. It wasn't hard. Some girl told me you spend all your time here. I said, Yep, that's my girl — in a bookstore."

"My girl?" Fletch echoed his words and yet didn't move, stood a few feet away.

Ryan turned around. "Yes."

"No," I said. "No."

Ryan turned back to me and reached for me. I took two steps back and held up my hands. "Stop, you."

He grinned. "I love when you call me 'you.' "

I shook my head. "You can't just come here like this."

"What do you mean? I'm here for you. To make it up to you. To make it all right again. I'm an idiot. An asshole."

"Language," Mimi said.

We both turned to her and I smiled at an echo of only weeks before when she'd said that to me.

"Pardon, ma'am," Ryan said. He lowered

his voice. "Who is she?"

"Follow me," I said and motioned out the front door. He did follow me and I thought of the old adage, the one we know and don't know when we need to know: *you always want what you can't have.*

Fletch grabbed my hand as we moved past. "Piper?"

I kissed his cheek. "Give me a minute. No worries."

He smiled at me just as Ryan glanced over his shoulder to see the kiss. "What the hell?"

We exited the store and stood on the sidewalk outside. A day, not so long past, I'd walked straight into this shop as steel to magnet. If I was the scrapbooking type at all and had a photo of the blue awning, of the window display with the piles of books and the little desk with the antique type-writer, I'd write underneath it, *And then everything changed.*

I sidled out of view from Mimi, Harrington and Fletch so I stood between the market and the café. I gathered my strength to say what I'd always imagined saying when he came crawling back.

"You can't just come here in the middle of my summer, in the middle of my life. I don't want you here." But these were words I only partially meant. They were words I wanted to mean, but wasn't sure I did . . . yet.

He grinned, the smile that drew me in, the one that I'd seen on his Instagram feed all summer. The one I saw with Hannah. And then, right then, I *did* mean the words I'd already said.

It wasn't any *one* piece of Mimi wisdom, or the books I'd read, or the terror of losing George, or Mom's bravery in changing our life when hers was falling apart, or Fletch's strong humor and gentleness, that had transformed me. It wasn't *just* Mom drawing me close and trusting me as she always had no matter my misbehavior. It was everything and all things. These people, these books and the losses had done their job inside me: an alchemy of stories and wisdom and experience.

I didn't want Ryan. *At all.*

His face shifted. He wasn't so sure of himself anymore or his place in the world.

"I thought you broke my heart, Ryan, but it wasn't my heart at all. It was some part of me that thought I deserved to be treated terribly."

"Baby," he said and took my hand and placed it next to his cheek like some ridiculous gesture from a movie he'd seen.

I yanked my hand away. "Don't," I said.

"Will you just at least listen to me? Let me tell you how I feel and what happened."

I nodded and we sat on the iron bench facing each other. I scooted so far from him that the armrest dug into my back.

"I made a huge mistake," he said.

"You already said that part."

"God, can you just cut a guy a break? I drove all the way here to see you. To talk."

"And you went all the way to Europe with Hannah." The anger in my voice shocked me. I took a deep, calming breath. "Go ahead."

"It was a mistake with Hannah. I don't know why it even happened. I'm in love with you. And it scared me because I started thinking about things like what we'd do when we graduated. Where would we live? How long until I could propose to you? Could we live together next semester?"

He took in a long inhale, the kind George and Daisy took when they were afraid the grown-ups were going to stop listening and they'd have to rush all their words out on one puff of air.

"You were thinking those things? Really? Or are you just telling me this in hindsight now?"

"No, I was thinking those things." He moved closer, an inch or two but enough that our knees touched. "It just scared me. I didn't want to be so . . . tied down. Then Hannah came along." He cringed, his eyebrows dropping into a V. "And she had this trip to Europe . . ."

"And all that money," I said.

"And all that money," he repeated. "Yes."

The town was quiet, and I thought of it as *my* town. I was stronger there. The oak trees that bent and gnarled like the hands of an old crone showed me how I could withstand whatever came my way. That afternoon the Spanish moss looked lit from the inside, a nimbus around a saint.

I could have told Ryan about each storeowner or the movie theater and how it had come back to town. I could tell him why cars never parked in between the white lines. I could tell him all of this and so much more, but I didn't want to. I wanted to go back inside Mimi's store and set up for the party. I wanted to pick wildflowers from the meadow beside Loretta's house and arrange them in blue enamel water pitchers. I wanted to color with George, or fish with Daisy.

What I didn't want? To sit here and have Ryan explain to me why he'd run off with Hannah to Europe, to hear how he loved me so much that it scared him.

"You shouldn't have come all this way," I said slowly, carefully.

His face wrinkled in confusion. "You didn't hear me, did you? I mean, if you did, you'd understand. I love you and only you." He reached for my hands, and I shook my head.

"No."

"You're breaking my heart here, baby."

"Please, please stop calling me baby. It's making me a little sick."

"What happened to you here? It's like I don't even know you." He stood and pointed at the bookshop. "Are you sleeping with that guy in there? Is that what's happening here? Because if it is, I can get over it."

"*You* can get over it?"

"I can. I promise I can. I can forgive . . ." His voice trailed off because even he must have heard the complete absurdity of his pleas.

"Ryan." I stood to face him. "This" — I waved my hands between us — "is never happening again. We don't always get a second chance."

As Mimi would say, for gravy's sake, I thought he was going to cry. His eyes filled and he turned away. But it was his ego that was dented, not his heart. A woman shuffled

463

by, dragging her big-wheeled cart, just as I'd done the first day in town. Two little girls were in the back playing with yarn and trying to make Jacob's ladder. I greeted them and they waved at me. It was the simplest expression, but it was also so grand — community.

"Second chances," Ryan said, repeating me. "We all deserve one."

"That's true," I said. "I've needed second chances and I've had them. But not us. This won't work, Ryan. I don't want it anymore and it wasn't all that great to begin with."

"I don't get it." He sank back onto the bench.

I glanced at him. "Neither do I, really. Because honestly, if you'd shown up even two weeks ago I would have fallen into your arms." I sat next to him and this time I took his hands. "Don't be sad. You have at least a million girls running after you."

"But none of them are you."

"No, they aren't." I leaned forward to kiss his cheek just as Fletch opened the door of the bookshop to check on me. It looked bad. I knew that.

Ryan wound his hands around the back of my neck and pulled me in for a real kiss. I strained backward and shook my head.

He dropped his hands and sank into

himself. "Okay. Got it."

Together we stood and I hugged him. "I'm sorry you drove all the way here," I said.

"Me, too." He yanked his keys from his front pocket as if they had been screaming for his attention.

Fletch reached my side and Ryan stared at us as Fletch dropped his arm over my shoulder.

"Really? *This* is your guy?" Ryan rolled his eyes.

"He is," I said.

"Rebound," he said with disdain and a curled lip.

I moved closer to Fletch. "No, it was you who went after a rebound."

A train whistle sounded far off and a motorcycle gunned around the corner — the perfect soundtrack to announce Ryan's departure. He exhaled in defeat and walked off.

"You okay?" Fletch asked.

"Yep." I kissed him, lingered there for a moment and felt the thrill of his touch. "I'm *more* than okay."

"Did you make him leave because of me?" Fletch glanced at the empty corner. Maybe he thought Ryan wasn't gone, that he would come back.

"No." I kissed Fletch again, pressing my

lips against his. "I did it for me."

"Even better," Fletch said. "Even better."

CHAPTER 39
BONNY BLANKENSHIP

If a month back, someone had told me of the crowd I would have at my river house, I wouldn't have believed them. Mimi and her beau, Harrington. Ms. Loretta, who had been Clara's best friend. My daughter, happy and laughing. Lainey and Tim with their children. And Owen, who had stayed in town. So far.

The days after Mr. Rohr's death, there'd seemed to be a secret I didn't know, a habit I'd never formed, a friend I'd forgotten to call, a repair I hadn't known needed doing: I'd been adrift. Yet all those previous weeks at the river house I'd been able to keep the reality of my part in his death at bay, hold back the possibility with the flimsiest of walls. Because there'd been the chance it wasn't true, I'd been able to live on that little chance, nurture myself with its optimism. No more. I lived in the truth now.

It was the dinner party that night that kept

me moving forward — a goal. I shaped my day with the to-do list and, like my leather binder, it became a structure for me, a kind of holding cell to keep the questions out and keep the focus in. Lainey had me do yoga with her that morning, and I only fell over twice. She taught me a ten-minute meditation, which felt like four and a half hours, honestly. Sitting still had never been my thing. My thing was going to change. It must.

The dining table in the main room was set for ten. I'd arranged seashells and candles in the center, and a basket full of pictures from not only the past weeks, but also our childhood summers I'd found in the attic. Our Girl Detective notebook sat on the coffee table.

The menu: Shrimp and grits. Biscuits. Pound cake and bourbon for Mimi. A salad with every fresh vegetable I could find at the farmers' market that morning. The guests would all arrive soon and I was ready, which felt like a small miracle because when I'd woken that morning the panic had spilled out from inside me.

"I can't do this today," I'd said out loud to my empty bedroom.

But I was wrong, because you don't know who you can be, or what you can do, until you have to be and do.

The screened porch fans whirred their whispers and I went out to sit on the wicker couch, to stare at the river. The house would fill up any minute — one by one they would arrive and voices would fill the rooms as I'd bustle around the kitchen and life would continue.

"Mom?" Piper's voice called.

Piper and the kids burst onto the screen porch from the house. Piper held up her hands. "Promise you won't be mad."

"What?"

And then I saw what she meant: in Daisy's arms was the tiniest little bundle of brown fur, and at first I thought it was a bunny. Then she set it down and it emitted a tiny little bark and scurried between Daisy's feet.

"A dog?"

She flinched. "I took the kids to the animal shelter because Lainey asked me to keep them busy for a couple hours and . . . and we couldn't help it. Daisy went crazy when we left without it. And the poor dog cried and cried and cried."

"Daisy? George?" Lainey's voice called, and we turned to see her and Tim walk onto the porch. When Lainey saw the puppy, she dropped to the ground and picked it up, rubbed her fingers behind its ears and nuzzled its face. "Where did you find this little bundle?"

"Mom." Daisy's voice rose with such pleading. "You have to let us keep it. You have to. I found him with Piper and it imprinted on me."

"Imprinted?" Lainey looked at her daughter. "What?"

"That's what the lady at the shelter said. That when he started following me around, he'd imprinted on me."

"Oh," Tim said. "I bet she says that to all the girls." But he, too, petted the now quiet puppy. "He's awful cute."

"His mommy died when she had the puppies and there were six of them and he was the last one left without a mommy. And could you imagine not having a mommy? We have to keep him." Daisy pulled at the edges of Lainey's sundress and buried her face in it. "Say we can."

"We can," Lainey said. "Right, Tim?"

"Who am I to disagree with imprinting?" Tim held his hands out in surrender.

"One rule," Lainey said.

"Anything," George piped up.

"I get to name him." Lainey pulled the puppy closer.

"What is it?" Daisy asked.

"Ned."

■ ■ ■ ■

All the people I loved most in the world were in one room.

Piper and Mimi were huddled together in a corner of the couch, scrolling through photos on Piper's phone. Tim, who'd been there for three days by then, and Lainey stood with Loretta, Owen and Harrington at the table where the jigsaw puzzle had been all summer without anyone fitting another piece in. They sorted the edge pieces from the center ones and made two piles before they began. Beach music played from Piper's iPod and candles cast shadows against the walls.

I could even feel my parents' presence. I felt them in the river house so strongly, the scent of lilacs pervading the room, that I almost turned to call for my mom. If they could see us all here, gathered around in the house they'd bought for just this reason, they would have been so proud. They'd given it up because of a tragedy and I'd come here because of a tragedy. But now it was shelter. It was home. But it was because of the people here, not just the structure that surrounded us. If I'd been homesick, it had been for these people.

One by one we'd all leafed through the Girl Detective notebook, and laughed, or shook our heads. Although it was true that we'd unwittingly gone where we shouldn't have gone, seen what we shouldn't have seen, written what wasn't ours to know, we hadn't caused Clara to leave. It wasn't the notebook that had changed our lives; it was Clara who'd changed our lives.

By the time we sat for dinner, twilight had folded into darkness. Owen sat next to me, and Piper on the other side. The conversation ebbed and flowed.

"Isn't it strange," Loretta said from the far end of the table, "how Piper arrived at my door with Fletch? How y'all returned here so you could find each other again?"

"Destined?" Piper asked.

"Oh, it's just that river out there," Mimi said and waved her hand toward the backyard.

Harrington shook his head. "All of you and your magic. I'm just happy for Bonny's logical, scientific mind."

When the plates were emptied, it was Lainey who brought out the homemade pound cake for Mimi. We retired to the porch to eat it on small flowered plates while the river flowed behind us.

Mimi rested her empty plate on the coffee

table. "I just can't believe this is real. That I'm sitting here with all of you. It feels like a begin-again."

"Begin-again sounds so wonderful," I said as I peered around the room. "And we all have to do it at different times. But what no one ever tells you is that there is this horrible, gooey, mud-sucking, scary-as-hell middle place that you have to slog through before the begin-again gets to start."

"Exactly," Mimi agreed.

"Can I ask you something?" Lainey said to Loretta.

"Of course, darling."

"Why is Mom buried at the AME church? How did she come to have a place in that sacred spot?"

"With every question you ask, you will learn more and more of her," Loretta said. "Your mother was very dear friends with a woman named Opal Harrison, another seamstress in town. It was Opal who would go to the house and pick up your mom to take her to church on Sundays. She became part of that African American church. She knew more gospel music than I did, and I grew up in the Baptist church. They became family to her, and she to them. When she passed, Opal placed your mother in the Harrison family plot, making room for a woman she'd met a year before, sharing revered ground with a woman who'd never told her the full truth of who she was. They knew she had secrets; they knew her name wasn't Rosie; and they loved her all the same."

Lainey let out a small sound of sorrow, a whisper almost. "Oh, Mom, why wouldn't you let *me* be your family?"

Lainey had told all of us the story that Mimi and Loretta had told her. She'd taken Owen to the gravesite and told him the same way she'd been informed. Together they'd been trying to piece together their mother's story, small inch by very small inch.

I reached across the table and took Lainey's hand, and she smiled at me, but only with sadness.

"And why are you now living in her house?" Lainey asked.

Loretta glanced at Mimi and Mimi nodded as if giving permission for this part of the story. "Mimi and I bought it for her, and she was paying us back in small but consistent increments with her sewing money and by working in the bookstore to chip away at the payments. I'd been living in town and was frankly quite tired of it so I sold my house and moved into hers." Loretta leaned back in her chair. "But every flower, every vegetable, every small and lovely thing there belonged to her."

Lainey nodded and repeated Loretta's words. "Every small and lovely thing. Maybe that should always be enough. If that is how she made her life, out of those things . . ."

Where once there were overlapping conversations and interruptions, there was only silence. Piper made a little noise in her throat that sounded like she might start to cry.

Owen glanced at me, as he'd been doing all night. Our gazes grounded us in the middle of a new world that had been created out of chaos and hurt and uncertainty. But what universe had ever been created out of anything but chaos? That was how everything began.

Mimi lifted her glass, now with only a thin line of bourbon on the bottom of it, and said, "To begin-agains." Harrington lifted his glass and then it began again, the symphony of mixed voices that had come from every corner of my world to this one place. A porch full of people I loved, and had hurt, and who had hurt me. No one knew what would happen next or how. There were personal narratives so convoluted and yet there we were filling a house with talk and food and drink, with stories and laughter — and love, most of all. Maybe that was all that mattered, not the untangling, not the fixing, not the "figuring it out," but the love itself. And the forgiving — that, too.

A smile spread across Mimi's face. It occurred to me that if I did believe in such things, I would believe that she'd conjured this dinner party. That a month before, when Piper strode through the bookshop door, she'd begun to gather her books and her witticisms into a transformational magic that brought us together.

CHAPTER 40
THE ART SHOW

Lainey

The Sea La Vie living room thrummed with music and Bonny and I bustled around, trying to grab everything we needed before we left for the art show. Bonny gently placed a few vases of wildflowers into a box. "I think we're ready," she said.

"I'm never ready for something like this," I told her. "Never. It's very nerve-wracking to stand in a room full of people with the art you created. Sort of like being naked with a spotlight on your worst flaws. You know I don't do very many of these, but having it here, in this town, feels right."

Things were still tenuous between us, but we weren't going to let it destroy our friendship. The loss of George had made clear what Bonny had been talking about all along: draw close to you what really matters. And Bonny really mattered. "Bonny," I said.

477

"Yes?"

"I think when you came here you unleashed the past."

She laughed. "Not exactly what I meant to do. In fact, I meant to do the opposite. Start a new future."

"My brother. Your daughter. Tim here now. My art . . ."

Bonny came close to me, her voice soft. "Lainey, in the busyness of getting ready for this art show, I haven't been able to say what needs to be said."

"You don't have to say anything," I told her. "I know."

"I'm going to say it anyway. I must." She sat on the sofa and patted the seat next to her. "I should never have kept it from you that Owen and I talked so often, that he was so important to me. I could hardly admit it to myself, let alone another person. I know now how much I've hurt you, and others, while trying to survive in a lonely marriage. Deep inside I knew that it wasn't going to work, but I rationalized."

"Do you still love him, Bonny?"

"Yes." She looked away and pressed her forefingers into the corners of her eyes. "But not everyone or everything we love is good for us."

"What will you do? Will you go back to

your job? Back to Charleston?" I asked.

"I don't know. I love that city and the hospital wants me back. That job was the only place where I knew who I was, but in the other places of my life I'd become someone I didn't like or admire: I was living with a husband who didn't really love me but wanted the safety of family. I was keeping secrets from my best friend and loving a man I couldn't have and couldn't change. I set a terrible example for my daughter. I don't want to go back to that way of living. Now that I have exactly what I couldn't live without — my career — I still don't know what I'll do."

"Isn't it funny when we get what we want?" I asked and then stood to look at her.

"What do you mean?" She also stood.

"So often, our wishes are fulfilled and then we see things altogether differently. You have your job and Owen is here for you, and yet you're confused about what to do. But you've always seemed *so* sure of everything you decide."

"Right now I'm completely unsure. But also right now we are late for the party and it's all about you tonight." She squeezed my hand. "Let's go!"

■ ■ ■ ■

It was an odd thing to stand in a room full of people with the art created in solitude and then shared in community. I held on to Tim's hand as we moved through the party.

Ever since his disappearance, George had been my shadow. He stood right behind me, his little hand in mine or else holding the tail end of my shirt. Daisy was attached to Piper with fierce loyalty. They took turns carrying Ned around the room, or running after him under patrons' feet.

When a quiet moment offered me some space, I turned to Tim, who stood next to me. There were things I needed to say, and that was as good a time as ever. "Sweetie, you're the one who has suffered because I've felt incomplete without a mom. I've believed that I couldn't be fully me without her. But I now know that's not true. I'm all of me. And all of me loves you. I was waiting for something that I already had: a full sense of myself. I wish I could take back every minute you didn't believe I was committed to you, or you thought I didn't want our family just as it is. I wish I could take back every minute I searched for her while neglecting you or our kids."

"Love, I understood every single time." He laughed. "Doesn't mean I liked it, but I understood."

"Well, it's over. No more wondering . . ."

"Is knowing she's gone better than wondering?" he asked and squeezed my hand, letting me know he was asking with compassion.

I gazed around the room at my art hanging on walls and stacked on easels, hidden messages in photos and scraps of words and images. "I don't know which is better. I don't know if there is a better," I said. "Like my art sometimes reveals my internal life, this was her *other* life, the one she decided to live. It wouldn't have been the one I chose for her, or for us, but it was hers."

"And yours?" he asked.

"Is with you." I squeezed his hand. "Take me home," I said. "Please take me home."

"I think you need to finish your party and then I'm taking you home, and loving you for as long as forever. Sound good?"

"Sounds perfect."

Piper

There was so much energy in that one party that it felt like electricity had been let loose in the bookshop. Lainey was so cool and collected, as though people weren't strolling

481

around talking about something she'd made in private. I'd be a wreck, hiding behind bookshelves and listening to what they were saying about me. But she's like Audrey Hepburn or something, just tall and beautiful and emitting this I-dare-you attitude, which I wanted so badly.

Mimi and her beau were sequestered in a little corner like they were trying to avoid talking to anyone else, which, come to think of it, they probably were. Owen wasn't there yet, but how could he possibly miss his sister's show? Fletch was with Loretta and they seemed to be having more fun than anyone there. I was kind of in love with him, but I hadn't said a word out loud. I'd been wrong before, completely wrong, so I would tread lightly. As if I knew how to tread lightly.

Honestly, I felt like part of a family I hadn't even known existed. I wasn't going back to school yet. Mimi said I could work at the store, and Fletch's mom said I could pick up shifts at the Market, also. I knew it wasn't permanent, but if there was anything I might have known by then it was this: nothing was permanent.

It was in this calm place that I didn't even think about a joint or a beer, about Jack Daniel's or sneaking off into the night. Living this way, I liked being me.

I'd been destroying myself. And I decided that I would do my very, very best not to do *that* anymore. Feelings came at me so hard and so fast that I needed to remember that the goal was not getting rid of the feelings, but letting them flow through me.

Fletch caught me staring at him and he winked from across the room. I waved with one little finger and he sauntered toward me, one slow step at a time, and it was like I was watching a movie about someone I wanted to be. There I was, standing in a bookshop with a boy who loved me, surrounded by stories and by friends.

Bonny

Lights flickered everywhere — candles and string lights, the moon, the stars and tiny flashlights given to the kids to play with. I needed solitude and had stepped outside for a few minutes when an empty storefront caught my eye. The All Things Seashell gift store had closed only the week before, and through a grimy window, I stared into its cavernous space. Crumpled paper and empty coffee cups littered the floor. A seashell wind chime hung from the ceiling: the remaining vestige of someone's dream.

Footsteps echoed behind me and I turned

to see Piper. Her cotton dress caught in the wind and for a moment she seemed like a sailboat the way she glided.

"You okay, Mom?"

"Yes, I am, sweetie. Why aren't you at the party?"

"I saw you leave and just wanted to make sure . . ." She stood next to me and linked her arm through mine. "What're you looking at?"

"This empty store."

"Okay . . . are you going a little nuts?"

Laughter bubbled and I squeezed her arm close to my ribs.

"No. But I was thinking about that night you had a fever and we needed IV fluids. I was thinking about how scared I was and how . . ."

"Mom. Don't. This is such a beautiful night and we're celebrating. Don't think about that because it makes me think about George."

"No, something else about that night — this town needs an emergency clinic. When we desperately needed one, there wasn't one."

"Oh." Piper's voice raised an octave and she, too, stared into the empty space. "Maybe it's your *one* thing," she said in a reverential whisper.

"Maybe."

Piper unwound her arm from mine and faced me. "Do you really think we all have a *one* thing? Like we have to find that one thing or nothing is right? Because that kind of makes me crazy. I can't figure out what mine is . . ."

"Slow down, sweetie. I think that Mrs. Rohr had it right — maybe there's one thing at a time. When we came here, my one and only goal was to save us from whatever downward spiral we were in. I didn't know *how*. I just believed that coming here and gathering only what mattered most would save us. But now there might be *another* one thing."

"It feels like my one thing is just figuring out what my one thing is."

"I think that is exactly perfect."

"Mom, do you remember in third grade when the teacher told you that I wasn't fit to be in a regular classroom because all I did was wiggle and talk and draw and fall out of my chair?"

"How could I forget?"

"I was in the hallway during that conference. I never told you. I heard everything."

"My God, Piper. You remember this? You were eight years old."

"Yes. And I heard you."

"What did you hear?"

"You told the teacher that she was confused as to who wasn't fit to be in a classroom. You told her that she was the one who wasn't fit if she really believed that a creative, inventive, beautiful child like me didn't belong there. And then you walked out and took my hand and we stopped at the art store and bought more colored pencils. You never told me what you'd done or what you were doing. But you were protecting me. Saving me."

"I remember that," I told her. A crow cried out, and a breeze lifted my hair off my neck as a siren squealed far off. I shivered in the heat and then it passed, like the breeze, like a quick wave that slammed us when we'd bodysurfed as kids. There. Gone. I focused on my daughter.

"Well, that's what you did when you brought me here. You saved me without me even knowing it."

I pulled my daughter close. "I don't do the saving, Piper. I just do what I think is right at that moment, and I've been wrong many times. Sometimes I don't save at all."

"Maybe one day I'll finally get my act together and surprise the world. Surprise those teachers who didn't understand what I'm made of."

"I know what you're made of, Piper. Brilliance and light and dark and surprise . . ."

"And a dash of you," Piper said.

"Yes, a dash or two of me."

She smiled at me. "Let's go back to the party."

"I will in a minute. You go on and have fun."

Piper left me there on the sidewalk and I gazed into the empty seashell store for a long while, forming an idea that seemed far off and close at the same time.

"Bonny." Owen's voice.

I turned to him. How long had he been standing there? How long had he watched me gaze into an empty storefront with a smile on my face? When he hadn't shown up for Lainey's party, I knew it had happened again: he'd left.

I wanted to wind myself around him, but I stood firm. "I thought that you'd left by now. Gone back to Colorado or . . ."

"No." He came closer, took me in his arms. "I know everything that's happened has been terrible. But now you're free, Bonny. You can go anywhere or do anything. I want you to come to Colorado. Start over with me."

I fell against his chest, listened to the rap of his heart, a one-two beat of waiting. "I can do anything. I know that. But *that's* not what I want. I don't belong there. Maybe you do, though."

"I belong wherever you are," he said.

It was the perfect thing to say, and the magnetic draw to him consumed me. He pulled me closer and his hands were in my hair, his body arched against mine. I wanted to let him pull me closer and closer, until closer couldn't be had. I could do this — be with him again and find myself exactly where I always dreamed of resting. Except in that moment, it wasn't where I wanted to be. What I'd once needed for love, warmth and connection had become, in the death of another, something else altogether. Mr. Rohr's death was alchemy that had changed the safe to the dangerous, if Owen had ever been safe at all.

I held my hand on his chest and pushed back an inch or two. "I can't." I finally understood the truth of it and I needed him to understand also. "The minute you touch me, I feel the old pain of your leaving. I want to believe you. I want to trust you, but I can't, and my heart won't stand one more loss when you decide you must leave again."

"I can't talk you into trusting me. But I can show you. And I will." He kissed me, but even as the desire for him awoke, I tasted heartbreak. Our endings had seeped into the beginnings, suffusing hope with dread.

I already missed him and he hadn't yet left. I already hurt and he hadn't yet abandoned me.

I let him go, stepped back. He took me in with his gaze, a slow reckoning. "I can walk away right now because you want me to," he said. "Or because you need me to. But I'm not leaving Watersend until you believe me."

"I love you, Owen. I do. But I've been accommodating to one life while waiting for another for far, far too long, and I won't do it again. For all those years, I'd hoped for you and I'd wished for you and I'd lived in the *maybe-this-time,* and yet I never once changed my own life. I'd only hoped that you would come change it *for* me. This time is different."

My sight shifted, and instead of fixing upon his dark eyes, I gazed into the storefront and imagined a check-in counter with a large white clock above it; comfortable red-and-blue-striped chairs in a waiting area; a corner with bright plastic toys to keep children occupied. Then, behind the counter with the sign-in sheet, there was a bright blue door swishing open to a medical clinic for minor emergencies: locals and vacationers, children and adults. There were crisp white curtains separating the exam rooms; stainless steel equipment against the walls and locked cabinets with labeled supplies. There were patients with sunburns and lacerations, with broken bones and rashes. It was a clinic for the community. A clinic for Watersend.

I gently kissed Owen. "Not now, Owen."

"Ever?" he asked, his hand in my hair, his mouth so close to mine.

"I don't know. I can't know. But right now, I know my *one* thing."

"What's that, Bonny?"

I pressed my hand to the window of the empty storefront. "This," I said, and then for the first time in our long, complicated history, I was the one who walked away.

Mimi

Logic tells me that the river isn't magic, unless you consider nature magical, which I do. I believe that the rich estuary brought these people of the past here at the same time, just as divine timing brings the tide in and then draws it out, just as the osprey knows when to return to the nest it made years ago. Just as these things happen in and on my tidal river, so had the gathering.

I'd hidden Clara's secret and yet when I'd seen Piper walk into my bookshop, I'd understood that something had been set in motion — the gathering of the past to unfold the future. Bonny might have believed she was coming here to forget everything, but she'd come here to remember. So had Lainey.

I watched the party in my bookshop, lights strung from the ceiling like stars winking their secret messages, voices a symphony of such a myriad of relationships they couldn't be counted. Lainey's mixed-media artwork hung from hooks and leaned on easels. I stood in front of my favorite: a photo of Nancy Drew and the hidden staircase. There she was, the girl detective who'd once inspired the Summer Sisters to shine light into places where light wasn't welcome. Nancy Drew stood at the bottom of a dark stairwell, her flashlight spilling a cone of light into the darker corners, just as they had once done.

Lainey had pasted on words like "illuminate" and "shadow." Streaks of bright yellow paint and scraps of golden paper flew across the artwork.

I tapped the microphone; it crackled and reeked of spoiled beer. I spoke softly, but the crowd hushed immediately.

I welcomed everyone and thanked the appropriate helpers. I called out Piper's name and each of the Summer Sisters' like an invocation, an uttering of gratitude.

"Art and stories," I said, "offer meaning to our lives in a way nothing else can. Science can't. Logic won't. The soul needs story and meaning to help us endure this life. This is what Lainey's art does for us — it offers us meaning. You know I believe stories do the same. Books can be medicine for the heart just as Lainey's art is medicine for the soul. There is magic here."

I nodded my head as my words resonated through every empty space. Fletch clapped first, and the sound rippled through the crowd as everyone joined in, adding a few whoops and hollers. I handed the microphone over to Fletch, who would strum his guitar and cause the girls to swoon with his love songs about losing and loving.

When the night was over and the crowd had dispersed, the women gathered. We walked to the white AME church, its steeple glowing under soft moonlight. No one had suggested it, but by some quiet acquiescence we moved that way. Lainey and Bonny. Loretta, Piper and me. Loretta carried a bundle of sunflowers, which she often did to leave on Clara's grave.

I'd kept my promise to Clara. She'd never wanted her children to suffer, or to know of her suffering. She believed they'd finally found a way to thrive in their lives, and she didn't want to cause more pain. Although I'd encouraged her so very many times to at least let them know she was alive, she wanted to wait until she'd completely cleaned herself up. It had been Opal who'd told her, "God doesn't ask us to come to him clean, and I'd bet your kids don't either."

But Clara had wanted to call them when she felt whole again. She was almost there . . . almost. Her dream had been to reunite in this very place. Meanwhile, I'd promised her, a promise between best friends who support and keep each other safe, that I would not betray her whereabouts. Now with Lainey by my side, for the first time I wondered if I'd done the proper thing. By Clara's request I'd done the right thing, but by this wounded child, had I? A promise kept to one, causing heartbreak in another.

We all walked to the river's edge, and one after the other we each tossed a sunflower from Clara's garden into the moving water. No one spoke but Lainey as she repeated what I'd said to her only days before: "We all do the very best we can."

There was forgiveness in this admission. We were all doing the very best we could: as women, as mothers and as daughters. We hurt each other; we heal each other; we mend and we break and we try again, until we can't and the headstone has its final say. And yet still our hearts reach out for both love and forgiveness, granted and accepted.

Lainey walked to the exquisite river and knelt at the marsh's edge, her knees sinking into the dark, rich mud of low tide. She didn't toss her flower but placed it gently upon the current, holding on to it for long moments before speaking broken lines from the poem on her mother's grave. " 'You do not have to walk on your knees . . . repenting.' " She then released the yellow sunburst of a flower and stood.

I closed my eyes and listened to that flowing river, for what it would bring to us next.

ACKNOWLEDGMENTS

Stories, we know, bind us together and enrich our lives. But it isn't *just* the stories that accomplish this; it is also the writing of them. And there were so many souls who were part of the community in this book's journey, many I want to thank although mere thanks is never enough.

First I must express my deeply felt gratitude to Berkley for truly seeing and understanding this story. To Claire Zion, it is a delight to work with you again — your deep understanding of story and your keen eye and wit are irreplaceable in this world. Oh, Danielle Perez, what a wonder to have met you and worked with you! You have helped create a story and world that would have been less than what it is without you. Any mistakes are mine alone. And to my Berkley team — you are what teams should always be: smart, funny and inventive. Jeanne-Marie Hudson, Danielle Dill, Craig Burke (who is a title genius as well as a PR guru), Liza Sweeney, Roxanne Jones, Fareeda Bullert and Sarah Blumenstock. And to our leader, Ivan Held, much gratitude is sent your way! I am so honored and proud to be part of the Berkley family.

And then after we do our work — it is the sales staff at Berkley that carries my book into the wider world. You all rock my world and I am grateful.

It is said that when we do the work we are called to do, we find our "tribe." I believe this to be true. I am sending great gratitude to my author tribe, every single one of you who listened to pages read out loud, who brainstormed and prodded and brought out the very best in this novel by asking me to go deeper, search for more, who believed, who laughed and lamented all the same. And I send special gratitude to Signe Pike for being a first reader with profound insights.

With great thankfulness to my agent, Marly Rusoff, who saw with generous eyes and heart the soul of this and other stories I long to tell.

And to my readers and my bookstores and reviewers and bloggers and all those who take my book to the eyes of others — I bow to you with admiration. Hats off! Stories would languish on shelves and in computers without you.

Then there are the angels who swoop in and assist me in the things that would otherwise keep me from writing: PR and marketing and book tour. Thank you, Kathie Bennett from Magic Time Literary, and Meghan Walker at Tandem Literary. Your energy and vision are an inspiration.

Oh, and how would I create anything without my friends and family? Those who must tolerate the long silences and absences while I live in a world they can't see or understand, and yet they love me all the same. I love you!

■ ■ ■ ■

READERS GUIDE:
THE BOOKSHOP AT
WATER'S END

PATTI CALLAHAN HENRY

■ ■ ■ ■

QUESTIONS FOR DISCUSSION

1. The river is a prominent presence in *The Bookshop at Water's End.* What does it mean to you and what does it represent? To the characters?

2. Bonny has wanted to be a doctor all her life. Is there a job or purpose you've been called to in your life? A profession you wish you'd started? (And if so, why not now?) Are we "called" to certain vocations? Is there anything you were "meant to do"?

3. When Bonny's career is on the line, her identity collapses and she must find a new way to move through life. Is this a hazard of identifying so strongly with one's career? Has this happened to you or someone you love?

4. Lainey is an artist and she expresses herself in the world this way. Does art help

us express our internal world or is it just another career? Does Lainey's art help her find her way to a better way of living with her husband and children? To reconciling the loss of her mother?

5. Both Lainey and Owen have lived without their mother since childhood, not knowing if she is dead or alive. Lainey has been obsessed with finding her, sometimes to the detriment of her husband and children. Would you continue to look for her or accept this loss? How far do we go to find those we love or bring them back into the fold of the family? How did living without a mother affect Lainey and her relationships and choices? How did living without a mother affect Owen and his relationships and choices?

6. Female relationships populate this novel — mother/daughter; best friends; mentor/teen. How do these relationships shape and change each character? Do you have a Bonny or a Mimi in your life? How has that affected you?

7. Bonny has been in love with Owen for as long as she can remember. Is this "real" love or a pining for the past? Can she ever have a lasting relationship with him?

8. Lainey and Bonny have been best friends since they were eleven years old and yet Bonny kept her deepest thoughts about Owen to herself. Is this a betrayal of their friendship? Should she have told Lainey how she *really* felt all along? Have you had a friendship so long-lasting and grounded in childhood?

9. When Piper loses George, each character blames herself in a different way: Piper for looking away; Lainey for being obsessed with finding her mother; and Bonny for distracting everyone when Owen appeared. When you read that scene, did you blame anyone? Did you find yourself blaming one of the women more than another? Why?

10. Mimi the bookseller visits this novel from *The Idea of Love*. She has affected these women's lives for generations with her bookstore and with her book suggestions. Do books and bookstores have the capability to change us and/or our lives? Is there a book that has changed you? Your life? A bookstore that feels like "home" to you?

11. *Home.* All of these characters are trying to identify and find "home." Is this a place? A house? A group of people? A feeling? A town?

12. One of the very last lines is about Lainey's mother — "We all do the very best we can." Do you think she did the best she could? Is this true in your life or with those you love?

13. Mimi believes that the river brings "what it will" and as the novel ends, she waits for what it will bring next. Is nature an omen? Does it hint at what comes next?

ABOUT THE AUTHOR

Patti Callahan Henry is a *New York Times* bestselling author whose novels include *The Idea of Love, The Stories We Tell, And Then I Found You, Coming Up for Air, The Perfect Love Song, Driftwood Summer, The Art of Keeping Secrets, Between the Tides, When Light Breaks, Where the River Runs* and *Losing the Moon.* Short-listed for the Townsend Prize for Fiction, and nominated multiple times for the Southern Independent Booksellers Alliance (SIBA) Book Award for Fiction, Patti is a frequent speaker at luncheons, book clubs and women's groups.

The employees of Thorndike Press hope you have enjoyed this Large Print book. All our Thorndike, Wheeler, and Kennebec Large Print titles are designed for easy reading, and all our books are made to last. Other Thorndike Press Large Print books are available at your library, through selected bookstores, or directly from us.

For information about titles, please call:
  (800) 223-1244

or visit our website at:
  gale.com/thorndike

To share your comments, please write:
Publisher
Thorndike Press
10 Water St., Suite 310
Waterville, ME 04901